Bound by Ties of Marriage,
Blood, and Passion . . .

ISABELLA—A proud aristocrat humbled by fate, she seized marriage as salvation . . . until she discovered love.

JAMES—Once she'd been far above him; now she was his: a penniless girl to place in his setting and mold to his tastes.

ANGUS—He returned from the dead to reclaim his beloved daughter, using his last energies to tear her from a loveless marriage and cast her into the flames of passion.

LIAM—In Chile they'd called him *El Médico Borracho*, the drunken doctor. A lost soul, he'd saved himself and Angus, but what would his life be worth without Isabella?

No Price
Too High

"THOROUGHLY ENJOYABLE . . . ABSORBING, FAST-PACED . . . DELIGHTFULLY WITTY."
—*Richmond Times-Dispatch*

No Price
Too High

Madeleine A. Polland

A DELL BOOK

Published by
Dell Publishing Co., Inc.
1 Dag Hammarskjold Plaza
New York, New York 10017

Dell ® TM 681510, Dell Publishing Co., Inc.

ISBN: 0-440-16433-8

Reprinted by arrangement with Delacorte Press

Printed in the United States of America
First Dell printing—November 1985

acknowledgments

I have to say thank you to Mr. Ken Woodroffe for all his detailed information about Chile, and to Dr. Columb MacNichol for helping me to be correct about my crippled baby.

No Price
Too High

chapter
1

Brighton in the spring. All the squares and elegant crescents awash with bright windy light: sun glittering from their long windows and in their careful and well-tended gardens, perfume blowing from the opening lilacs. Tiled pathways were bright along the edges with the small flowers of the season; arabis and the royal purple of aubretia; the bright mixed splatter of the polyanthus.

Glimpses of gray water between the white houses had turned to deep blue, racing with the same exciting light, and the wind itself was warm and frivolous, teasing the sea, and whipping at any forbidden piece of rubbish in the tidy streets. Snatching mischievously at the skirts of a small group of girls coming as decorously as the wind would let them, down Egremont Place toward the sea.

Five of them. All eighteen or thereabouts, lively as the spring itself in their own smooth youth, and all exceptionally well groomed and cared for: self-confident young faces under close-fitting cloche hats, with long legs and thin strappy shoes. There was not one of them who had not tried, by pulling in her belt, to hitch her skirt up to the new shorter length that their headmistress still thought to be an impropriety. She did not realize, they told each other bitterly, that this was nineteen twenty-five. Longer skirts were *out*.

There was mischief and alertness in all their faces, a sort of splendid amiable corporate mischief, despite the demureness they showed for the two mistresses escorting them. The mistresses were not deceived, and wore a settled look of resignation, even apprehension, as to the subtle and hilarious embarrassments they would undoubtedly be subject to, before they got their charges home again. They did their best, but knew they were little more than half aware of all the delicious improprieties that these charming and beautifully behaved girls managed to snatch from a simple shopping expedition, and the coffee and cakes afterward at the carefully chosen establishment patronized only by the most genteel of Brighton's ladies.

On the edge of their adult lives a group of girls from Miss Elizabeth Catchpole's Select Finishing School for Young Ladies were on their privileged outing for Saturday morning shopping. For bits of ribbon and lace and sewing materials and a carefully supervised library book: any small thing they could think of, rather than have Catchpole say they did not need to go. Thereby missing unbridled hilarities like having to ask the embattled young man behind the haberdashery at Cubbington's for a yard of narrow elastic, knowing he would certainly realize it was for their bloomers.

Becoming Familiar with the World, Miss Catchpole called these outings, together with carefully dressed evening expeditions to chosen concerts and soirées. Rarely was her mantelpiece without some gold-edged card of invitation for cultural societies who knew how it enhanced their standing to have Miss Catchpole's exquisitely groomed and dressed young ladies in the front row. Exotic young birds of paradise resting for a moment among the staid cultural chickens of Brighton.

Every time they went out, she would remind them of the purpose of their expeditions.

"It is necessary," she would say solemnly, fixing them with sharp gray eyes over the pince-nez they were sure she wore only for effect: her firm bosom uplifted, her neck an upright column of decorum above the lace modesty vest discreetly filling the V-neck of her black dress. "It is necessary, since you are to go out into the World, that you become familiar with how to conduct yourself there."

She prided herself on her sophistication on behalf of her girls, and they listened to her with polite and decorous patience, never pointing out that since they all came from very well-heeled families —many of them abroad, since Miss Catchpole specialized in young ladies in her total care—they saw more of the World in their holidays with their families than the good well-meaning Catchpole had ever known existed.

Nor did they remind her that the world they were straining to get out into was becoming known already as the Roaring Twenties.

The wild reactionary aftermath of war and death for those who had survived the holocaust, or grown up to fill the gaps. Skirts were rising and standards and conventions falling, and most of them, within weeks of leaving school, would have turned themselves as fast as possible into Bright Young Things. Several had already written home to ask permission to cut their hair, although the shingle was still something that people turned and stared at in the streets. They hitched their skirts as high as they dared and looked in envy at free, smart girls who flashed their long legs in flesh-colored stockings even in the streets. For them it was still black, and in the evenings gray; perhaps rose or lilac if it matched their dress.

While a world of youth that was still astonished to be alive ran wild about them, creating whole new rules of life, they continued in their sheltered backwater. Studying English and history and art and needlework, with endless classes on conduct and decorum, and on cookery and housecraft, Mrs. Beeton their Bible on all the mores of living for a top-class household. Because, of course, they would all have top-class households, destined every one of them for a top-class marriage. What else could lie before them? They learned to wash a clean sponge in vinegar, and boil a spotless dishcloth, and heaven help the maids if both were not clean before they started. They made heavy disastrous pastry, and put on gleaming white aprons to troop upstairs and dust their bedrooms where no dust dared lie. They learned the intricacies of Calling, and leaving cards, and how to make polite but not frivolous conversation with a gentleman at a ball.

Isabella Frost was bored with it all, going through much of it for the second time round. She should have left at Christmas when she was eighteen, but it had been quite impossible for her father to make the time to leave the mines for the long journey and the holiday in England, until the winter came.

The winter in Chile. Summer here. They were coming in July.

Heavens above, almost nineteen and still at school. She felt ashamed of her black stockings and discreet dress of dark-blue lawn with white scarf collar, and the little cloche hat of blue straw pulled down over her thick brown hair. It was only quite recently, with pressure from home, that Catchy had let her put it up. That was another thing. These plaits coiled over her ears made all her hats too small. This one was perched on the top of her head. Now, if she could have her hair cut. Have a shingle. But probably even her father would have an apoplexy at that one.

As they turned into the Old Steine and met the full bursting wind from the sea, she gave her hat an irritable bang with a white-gloved hand.

The World, she was thinking. Poor old Catchy. Catch as Catch Can, they called her, for her enormous talent for pouncing on any smallest breach of discipline or decorum. Poor old Catchy, whose World would go on forever being her old-fashioned school in Brighton, apart from her much discussed annual visit, as imponder-able as a journey to the mountains of the moon, to her older sister who lived in some remote village called Iron Acton in the depths of Gloucestershire. And when she grew too old to teach, that village would become the circumference of all she knew.

Isabella knew with a certain adult compassion that her fears for them in the streets of Brighton were born of her own terrors on her annual journey to Swindon and then down into the West Coun-try, never relinquishing her portmanteau to anyone, her ticket in a specially sewn pocket in the bodice of her dress.

Isabella shook her head and nearly dislodged the unstable hat. She gave it another thump. She supposed that now her hair was up, she should have a hatpin. That's what was wrong. Hatpins were rather deliciously grown up, too. In the only decent paper-covered novels they managed to smuggle in, ladies used them to repel gen-tlemen when they made advances. She had only the haziest notion what advances were, but it would be rather a jazz to find out.

Catchy's World.

She herself would be going home to Chile.

Even to think of it made the sun brighter and the wind more cheerful. Her future lay like a fair land viewed in happiness from a tall mountain. Waiting for her, full of splendid promise and sun that cast no shadows. Almost she did a small dance along the pave-ment. Smith and Rumbold, vigilant at the back, would probably have had a seizure.

Already she was marking off the days until July on the calendar on her bedroom wall. Still, it might be worse. Before Catchy she had been in a convent, and it was certainly better than all the bells and prayers and holiness.

Her father was a mine owner and engineer in Chile. Copper and nitrates, although goodness knew, she knew little enough about it. When they came in July, they would spend two months at Enderby, a lovely spacious house of creamy stone, looking down on a sedgy lake in the lush green countryside of Suffolk. When her father came to England he always took Enderby. A big house; beautiful. Wealth and big houses had always been part of her life, and the unquestioning assumption that her father was rich. And that pretty well everything she wanted was hers.

After Enderby, Chile. Where she would at last be allowed to grow up. Fall into all the patterns. Marry, no doubt, some nice young man discreetly chosen and encouraged by her mother. She had been familiar with the notion all her life and found no fault with it.

Live all her life, probably, in Chile. And nothing wrong with that. Bare ochre-colored desert lying out beyond the flower-filled towns: vast tortured mountains as a barrier against the outside world. Among the Indians in the villages and the edges of the towns, terrible disease and poverty that never touched her.

For her a big white house some distance from the mines, but not so far that they could not see the belching smoke from the chimneys of the smelters. All the furniture was English, brought out painfully and slowly around the storms of the Horn by her father's grandfather: assembling England again nostalgically in the spacious rooms and the wide cool terrace, where they would sit in the flower-scented evenings. Dimly, even as a child, Isabella was aware of the physical splendor of both her parents, and of the feeling lying between them, tangible as the last rich pools of golden light on the verandah tiles before the sun went down.

Her mother was darker than she was, almost black-haired—a little touch of the Inca crept in somewhere, she liked to say with a smile: her dark-blue eyes like Isabella's resting always with tenderness and tolerance on the fine ebullient vitality of her husband. He had met her as a child, himself the son of a rich mineowner, and had never rested until he had married her. In due course, as she was an only child, he had inherited her father's mines.

Angus Frost could tell himself he had done well. But he was far from over yet. Piling up his wealth with almost no end in sight other than the loving care, and luxury of his beautiful wife and daughter.

At this moment Isabella knew they would be as excited and impatient as she was, marking the passage of the weeks until that silly fool Smith would chaperone her to meet them at Southampton. Thank God for the Panama Canal. It had taken absolutely weeks before that round that ghastly Horn where everybody was so sick.

To her their happiness was the pattern of marriage, her father the rock of it, a wonderful excitement and vitality in his character that made everyone around him safe. Grace of living in a settled life. Marvelous. Absolutely marvelous. Her eyes, the astonishing pure sapphire of so many Chileans, were bright, and a small smile of anticipation curved her lips.

She knew now, too, that she was beautiful. A proud, growing excitement before her mirror told her that no one could possibly think her otherwise. Beautiful and young, and eager to be gone into the splendid exciting world. Sick of the imprisonment of old Catchy's careful training. Sick of being held up as a model to the younger girls.

Once again she grabbed her hat against the wind, and the plump pretty girl beside her gave her a glance.

"Cat got your tongue this morning, Isabella?"

Never were they allowed to shorten each other's names. Bella would have been for a servant. Neither were they allowed the kind of slang that Daphne had just rejoiced happily in using.

Isabella smiled. Easy curving smile like her father's.

"Sorry, Daphne. I was only thinking of going home. I'd like to go to sleep and not wake up until July."

"Hm," said Daphne. "Aren't you lucky. I have to go until next Easter. But it's Delhi then. Think of that, Isabella. Delhi. All those gorgeous young officers." Her voice fell with something close to reverence. "My sister only took a month to get engaged. Spiffing. Are there many eligibles in your part of the world?"

"Eligibles?" How would she know, who had not been there for five years? That would be her mother's business.

They passed the fretted walls and onion domes of the Pavilion and the wind gusted up at them over the open space from the sea. Warm. Heavy with salt. Like some exciting messenger from these years ahead.

Into North Street in all the roaring bustle of Saturday morning, horse-drawn drays and carts clanging over the cobbles with iron wheels; the still exciting motor buses filling the warm air with a rich smell of oil and petrol, the mildly apprehensive faces of their passengers peering from the windows. Somewhere they were mending the roads and she could get the hot rich smell of tar. Motorcars were so common now that no one stared anymore unless they were something special. Pedestrians jostled on the pavements and the paper boy yelled incomprehensibly at the corner of the street beside the peanut seller. The milkman followed his patient horse, big shining churn with its tap dripping on the back of his flat cart. From the tenements above the shops and the dark courts in between them, children and women ran with jugs to buy their milk, their money warm in their hands, and the drips fell and soured in the sun. From the poor streets farther over, a few grimy children held out their hands to beg and fashionable women in the new shorter dresses moved carefully among them as if they were not there.

Isabella watched all the women carefully to see if she could find one with her hair shingled. Not that old Catchy would ever allow such a thing, and her father would kill her anyway. Her mother would smile her lovely languid smile and buy her a new dress to go with it!

In North Street they were allowed to visit the bookshop, and the big draper's emporium, peering farther along with frustrated curiosity toward the forbidden area of the Lanes, to which Catchy always awarded vague overtones of danger and unmentionable disaster. Enough, thought Isabella, to make any right-minded girl want to go along at once and have a look.

"Nothing there," one of the girls had said once. "My parents went there once and they said it's only a lot of old curiosity shops. Or so they said," she added darkly, with the innate suspicion of all of them that they were always being fobbed off.

Cubbington's Emporium was dark after the bright sun outside. A deep, old-fashioned shop of gleaming mahogany and gilded glass: smell of cloth and dust in the shadows, and the faint lingering sweetness of the customers' perfumes. The dimness was alive with the whirs and clicks of the little gleaming brass boxes that held change, running from the counters along overhead wires to the back of the shop, where a fierce lady in rimless eyeglasses sat in a sort of pen of mahogany and glass. She unscrewed the little boxes as they came with all the care and solemnity of dispatches from some distant war-torn land. Her thin lips moved in fearful concentration before she counted out the change and reached up to place it in the little box for the journey back.

Bolts of cloth stacked the open shelves and behind the haberdashery counter the wall glowed with the knobs of a hundred little glass drawers, filled with buttons and needles and all the things vaguely known as notions. Headless, discreetly shaped bodies on three wooden legs displayed the ladies' modes, and Isabella looked at once toward the hems. A little shorter, but only a little. But Cubbington's was nothing. Always behind the times. That was why Catchy let them come there. She had seen shorter in the streets outside. She turned with distaste from a bold black velvet bosom on the counter with a shower of lace and a choker of green beads. Would have done Catchy herself, thought Isabella.

Seeing them come in, the young man behind the haberdashery had already begun to sweat, leaving damp palm prints on the gleaming counter: trying desperately to rub them out with his sleeve before the manager saw them.

But Mr. Crump was too busy bowing and smiling inside the door, ushering in these important customers, and Beech moved anxiously and despairingly and with a certain sort of fury toward his weekly ordeal at the hands of Miss Catchpole's young ladies.

He was one of the few real men they were ever allowed to speak to. Even if it was only to ask for a spool of thread or a yard of white lace, they managed, however carefully they were watched, to overwhelm him every Saturday morning, with bright mischievous eyes and innocent faces, like some delicious disaster which filled him with terror and which yet he would have been desolate to avoid.

Shamelessly and deliberately they flung him into confusion; giving him their orders all at once, eager young hands in spotless white gloves reaching to point out his mistakes and muddle his stock: every invoice scribbled and rescribbled until the lady in the glass pen had to descend grimly from her high stool and make her way to the front of the shop to ask him the meaning of his confusions. The girls giggled softly at his discomfiture and crowded close, muddling their requests when he tried to make his explanations to the furious cashier.

"But, Mr. Beech," they would say sweetly, "you are in a muddle." Shaking with laughter while poor Beech, miserably conscious of his thinness and paleness and his pimpled face, would watch in anguish for Mr. Crump, in his plastered hair and frock coat, to bear down majestically on the scene of the disaster.

"Girls," Rumbold would say. "Girls!" Poor Smith twittering ineffectually at her elbow, nearly as good for a ribbing as Beech himself. Poor Beech. Aware in every inch of his ineffectual body of young faces and bright clear eyes and shining hair. And every one of them, as all Brighton knew, young ladies rich beyond his wildest dreams. Trained by life into subservience, he would frenziedly wrap up their small purchases, leaving the damp marks of his sweat on the thin brown paper.

As she picked up her little parcel, Isabella turned on the poor fellow the full power of her sapphire eyes, holding him with a small smile until she saw the tide of helpless scarlet rising up his face from under the stiff collar. She had to turn away then before she laughed.

"Thank you, Mr. Beech," she said with faultless manners, and dared not look at her friends lest they all collapse before they managed to leave the shop.

The corner of one red eye glaring at the unfortunate Beech, the manager bowed them ceremoniously out the gilded doors, all of them full of decorum again, turning eyes of amazed innocence on the two mistresses who fell on them outside the door.

"We only try to help him, Miss Rumbold."

"He gets in such a muddle if we don't help him."

With small satisfied smiles and sidelong glances among themselves, they would set off then for the bookshop, where there was rarely any fun, and the chocolate shop, where there was always the hope of devastating some young man escorting a mother or an aunt.

"And it is *not*," the manager would be saying by then to the cowering Beech, "it is not, Beech, the amount of money that they spend, for everybody knows their clothes come from London and Paris and such places. It is the *cachet*, Beech. The cachet of having the business of Miss Catchpole's young ladies. It means a great deal."

Every week he said this furiously to Beech, and every week Beech would listen and rub his hands on his handkerchief and think to himself that if he could get hold of that tall one with the blue eyes, he'd give her cachet. He would turn back to his work leaving enough furious frustrations and impossible dreams in his cold attic bedroom in the small house out beyond Kemp Town, to fill the week until next Saturday would come again.

These things she would miss, Isabella thought, her mind still on the promise of July. Baiting poor Beech, and giggling about it afterward in the white and gold chocolate shop with the mirrored walls and spindle chairs. Saturday mornings were *fun*.

Odd, though, she thought irrelevantly, that she hadn't had a letter for so long. Not long enough to worry about. But long. Her father was marvelous about writing, her mother not so good. But it was a long way, and ships seemed to take their own time. Maybe there'd be a letter when she got back.

"We will go back," boomed Rumbold. Fat, tedious Rumbold with her glasses round her neck on a piece of black string because she could never find them if she put them down. "We will go home by way of the Aquarium and the Marine Parade." She spoke as if permitting some unheard-of license, and the girls all smiled a little wearily, for was it not the way they went home every week? Their World was not permitted to be very wide, and they went home along the sea so that they might officially breathe some of the beneficial sea air that Catchy made so much of in her discreet advertisements, and in her fulsome letters to their parents.

"Breathe deeply," she would cry to them were she here. "Breathe deeply. In. Out. In. Out."

Her own ample bosom heaving so strongly that they could see the small gold safety pins at the edges of her modesty vest.

They began to cross the open space at the foot of the Old Steine toward Marine Drive, the Aquarium crouched in the middle of the road, itself like some vast stranded monster of the deep. Across the road the gilded tops of the Pier railing glittered in the sun, the open wrought-iron gates beckoning to pleasures they would never be allowed to know. There was not one of them who had not heard from some servant that you could see Everything, simply everything, and they were a little vague as to what that might be, in the magic-lantern pictures for a penny in the slot in a row of red machines along the windy, slatted walk. They never passed the Pier without thinking of Everything, one of the wistful things of the future, but they also knew, too, that a tweaked blind on a summer Sunday saw more than Catchy had ever dreamed of. Among the cheerful trippers who on all holidays swarmed the green park across the road from the school, taking what opportunities they could for a bit of privacy among the crowd.

Isabella would smile as she put back the blind, envying them some broad freedom she would never know, even when she had left school. And Catchy would never know it. Nor want to.

But for her there would be so much else, her bright future all part of the wind and the sun and the shining day.

A sudden frolic of wind from the tumbling sea, and Isabella's neat blue hat was gone, bowling off happily, as if it enjoyed itself, into the middle of the crowded road.

Instinctively she began to run after it herself, stopped by a shrill protective screech from Rumbold. Someone else was quicker. From the far corner by the front of the Aquarium, a young man in brown shot into the road, dodging expertly between the carriages and carts and cars and laden drays, to where the blue hat was dancing between the wheels and the horses' legs. Snatching it up, he took time to brush it carefully on his sleeve, and then moved back more slowly to the other corner. Isabella could hear Rumbold breathing heavily beside her, close to panic.

It was not a normal part of Experiencing the World, to have a good-looking young man with a wide smile bearing down on her cherished charges, who were all waiting for him with unconcealed pleasure and excitement. Already anxious words of explanation were forming in her mind, her hands damp. There was no hope of

Miss Catchpole not hearing of it. Miss Catchpole heard of everything.

"Miss Isabella's hat blew off in the street."

She could see clearly the expression on Miss Catchpole's face, indicating that it could have been nothing but her fault. As though she herself had failed to put in the missing hatpin.

Isabella stood quite still, the sun in her brown hair, and her blue eyes bright, waiting for the hat and the young man.

"Thank you. Thank you indeed," she said as he gave it to her. A quick impression of hazel eyes and a thick moustache. Fair.

No more. No time for more, as Rumbold raced them on across to the Marine Parade as though a case of plague had been discovered in Old Steine.

Isabella shrugged and smiled and pulled the errant hat down over her eyebrows, a little dusty, but undamaged. A little bit of excitement, complement to the bright day and that it was Saturday, the day of their small freedom.

Still, she thought, with some faint surprised pleasure that went deeper than all the laughter at the little episode, still—he was nice. There had been some brief immediate contact that had made a pleased disturbance in her, to whom as yet all men were carefully kept as shadowy creatures of her future, poor creatures like Beech not counting. Belonging to some other world, glimpsed a little under the lifted blind on summer Sundays. Nice. With warm eyes and a merry sort of face. And he had looked at her as though he saw her, Isabella, and not merely some nameless schoolgirl in a group, mindless and sexless under the vigilance of their teachers.

A sort of astonished expression on his face.

Nice, she thought again, and smiled a small smile, and knew that for a while at least she would think about him.

His moustache was thick. A good shape. Although of course, moustaches were going out of fashion now.

Fortunately neither Rumbold nor Smith was as mad as Catchy on deep breathing, and the girls walked and breathed at their own pace along beside the iron railings above the sparkling sea. Isabella looked at it regretfully as they turned away up the Rock Gardens past the discreet boardinghouses that were already beginning to assume a small air of bustle: a warming toward the season to come. A bucket and spade stood here and there already at the top of scrubbed steps, and the swimming towels and striped bathing suits of hardy gentlemen hung from the fretted balconies.

The school was a row of three tall houses joined together on West Drive, facing the lake and the green spaces of Queen's Park, which, like the beaches, swarmed with trippers in the summer. Miss Catchpole was apt to say with severe disapproval and self-pity that when she had started her select school some twenty years before, such people had known their place and had not dreamt of invading the peaceful provinces of their betters. And on summer Saturdays and Sundays the Holland blinds were drawn down along the fronts of all the houses, lest the cherished minds of her charges be influenced and outraged by the cheerful habits of the masses. It never occurred to her that her lively pupils regarded the drawn blinds merely as a challenge and an added excitement to their sedate days.

She was waiting in the polished hall when the girls returned from the World, her eyes alert behind her rimless glasses for any appearance of irregularity.

"Isabella, your hair is untidy. Have Effie brush it for you before lunch."

"Yes, Miss Catchpole."

There was something there. Isabella looking ruffled and having a small air of being the center of attention. Never mind, she would get it out of Rumbold later. No irregularities were to be allowed, above all with Isabella, probably her richest and most important pupil.

All the girls had rooms of their own, and the services of a maid, but all was not equal between them. Those like Isabella, with parents rich enough, had their rooms decorated to their own taste, and only last year Isabella had cajoled her father into letting her do hers. Miss Catchpole did not like it. Young gels like Isabella should not be given a completely free hand, and she looked down her nose at the banishment of old Victorian furniture that had been good enough for her since she was a child, and so should be good enough for Isabella Frost. But she could not argue. One did not argue with a parent who paid as highly as Isabella's father.

Now the room, that had been all red turkey carpet and red buttoned velvet held pale and, to her eyes, flimsy furniture; the brass rails of the new bed as thin and tall as reeds. Languid lilies, wreathed on the dull yellow William Morris wallpaper, and in thin black frames girls as frail and languid as the lilies with clouds of hair and flowing dresses looked out at the changed room with enormous dark-fringed eyes. The carpet was a pattern of dull green and yellow and the curtains and spread of what Miss Catchpole thought of as the same unappetizing color. She did not like Isabella's room and went into it as little as possible, saying she did not care for the colors: crushing the small ugly snake of feeling that knew it angered her, who must work for her living, that one young girl should have so much. And startling beauty, too, and all that would go with it. Catchy suppressed such thoughts. She was nothing, she told herself, if not fair to all her pupils.

Isabella herself adored her room. All her own. The one place she could be herself in this world of boring protracted childhood. Not merely one of Miss Catchpole's products; stamped out like gingerbread men.

She took off the offending hat, unwilling to come in out of the bright day, longing to throw open the shrouding net curtains that had been insisted on, even though for Isabella they ruined her room. And threw open the window beyond them. She peered into the shadowed mirror. Never enough light for vanity. Never enough light for anything. In the house in Chile all the rooms opened through wide archways onto the big verandah. The sun became an enemy to be withheld by drawn blinds through the long hot afternoons.

She sighed. These English years had been long. Thank God they were coming to an end. Catchy was right about something, anyway. Her hair was like a bird's nest.

There was a small knock at the door and a girl younger than Isabella herself came in, neat in the black dress of a maid, with ruffled cap and apron of spotless muslin. A small girl, pear shaped, with narrow shoulders and protuberant pale blue eyes. There was a look of amiable steadiness on her sallow face, but Isabella had often noticed that she rarely smiled.

"Miss Catchpole said you wanted your hair brushed, Miss Isabella."

"Thanks, Effie. My hat blew off."

"Oh, Miss." At once Effie reached for the hat, flicking at imaginary pieces of dust. "I'll brush it. Sit down now, Miss Isabella, and let me do your hair or it'll be lunch."

Obediently Isabella sat down, and watched Effie in the dark mirror quickly and skillfully unpinning the coils of plait above her ears and brushing the thick brown hair to shining smoothness. She looked at the pale girl, always so docile, and wondered if she ever felt captured, as she did, by the light of a spring day like today. By a restlessness to have done with all the Catchpoles and the Rumbolds and the girlish chatter. Did Effie ever long for change?

"Effie," she said impulsively. "Do you *like* being a maid?"

Effie liked Miss Isabella. Always please and thank you, and pleasant, with none of the silly airs and superiorities of some of the others. She was a real lady, Miss Isabella, and they were always different. She thought a while before she answered, not much given, as she would say herself, to thinking, nor ever having had much chance in life to ask herself what she might like or not like.

"Well, Miss," she said, with a deft twist of a plait. "I find it better in the summer when I don't have to do they fires."

They fires. All the difference in the drab sameness of a life, but Isabella persisted, although touched by shame.

"Don't you ever want to do anything different, Effie?"

Effie lifted her narrow shoulders in a shrug.

"Bain't nothing different for me to do, Miss Isabella. Never did go beyond seven, to school. Bain't nothing for a girl with no learning, and there's six little 'uns to keep. Have to do what work you can when there's no money, Miss Isabella."

Carefully, methodically, she combed the brown hair from Isabella's brush, rolled it into a small ball around her fingers, and put it neatly into the hair tidy of embroidered satin that hung beside the mirror.

Isabella could not let her go, as though on this restless day she craved some contact with a world outside the school.

"What about your father?" she asked.

As she asked it, she knew it, with a little shame, to be ridiculous to think about her own father, who gave her everything she had. Tall, a little fairer than herself but with the same Chilean blue eyes: arrestingly handsome; always immaculate in his white suit and Panama hat. Witty, lively, and endlessly amusing and affectionate to her and to her mother. Proud, he always said, of his beautiful women. His habit, when saying something specially outrageous, of stroking his heavy moustache with great solemnity, the blue eyes glittering with mischief above it. With it all, unshakable dignity and authority and intelligence.

Papa. For a moment as she waited for Effie's answer, she felt physically sick with the longing to see him. To hear him laugh. To have him make her laugh.

"Dead," Effie said then, flatly, about her own father, and Isabella looked at her in the mirror, appalled. Had she adored him, in whatever terrible little place they lived, as she adored her own fine handsome father? How sad. How sad. How terrible. "Two year ago," Effie went on. "He were a carter, see, and load slipped on a dray. Crushed to death, he were."

The blinding reality of Effie's loss, the dumb look on her face even after two years, struck Isabella so deeply that she sat there for a few moments in mortal terror for her own father. Touched with panic that she could not reach him to reassure herself of his very existence.

She felt shattered with pity, and with it helplessness.

"Oh, Effie, I am so sorry. How awful for you."

"So Mum and me have to keep the little ones."

No self-pity. The soft Sussex accent held only long resignation. Isabella fell silent at the gulf that divided them. Should her father die, she knew without telling that everything would be provided for. She and her mother would never know hardship, like Effie.

"What about a shopgirl, Effie?" she said then.

"Bain't able to sum or write," Effie said briefly, as she hung up Isabella's jacket, straightening it on the hanger as carefully as if it were her own. Neither rancor nor jealousy touched her, her place in life long accepted, and it was good when there was pleasant ones to look after, like Miss Isabella.

Down below them a gong rang hollow through the school.

"There's lunch, Miss Isabella. Be you eating downstairs today."

Unlike evening dinner, when all the girls were expected to dress and dine in the oak-paneled dining room downstairs, they were allowed if they wished to have lunch in their own rooms.

"Thank you, Effie, I shall go downstairs."

She felt suddenly too restless to have her lunch alone, touched after their small conversation with some senseless guilt that she should add anything more to Effie's endless day. Although she knew her friends would think her taking leave of both her wits and her position, to be giving such thought to the circumstances of a servant.

The train heaved and clanked and drew great breaths, and slowly inched away from the small station to gather speed into the limitless tawny spaces of the Atacama desert, southward on the long blazing haul to Valparaiso.

Isabella's father grinned and gave a wave as he passed, to the guard, who for a small handful of gold had stopped the train for him, his hand on the bridle of one of two mules he and his friend had led down the ramp of a horse car.

Almost he shouted, Don't forget, four days from now. But José was dependable. He would not forget. He would stop the train again on the way back up.

Angus Frost had much to look forward to and no time for mistakes, his thoughts concentrated as totally as his daughter's were on next month's voyage to England, and the longed-for meeting with Isabella at Southampton. Good to be a rich man, he thought with an almost mischievous smile. As his friend had said, only a rich man could stop trains where he wanted them, and bringing the mules like this had made a couple of days' job of it, instead of a long, exhausting haul through the broiling yellow desert.

His friend was also an engineer, in the company, but now with a light of almost nervous eagerness in his light-gray eyes. Long years a friend, so that Angus Frost had been willing to give him all the help he could when he arrived, these gray eyes burning with excitement, to lay before him his hopes for branching out and sinking his own mine.

"Would you come, Angus?" he said, sitting eagerly on the edge of the deep cane chair on the wide verandah so often in Isabella's thoughts. He took a deep anxious gulp of his whiskey. "Would you come and have a look at it with me, before I even put the geologists in or anything? I'm wanting to be as secret as possible in case some bastard gets there before me by getting wind of it. But I'm my own grandmother if the place isn't rotten with copper."

He was from Glasgow, in Chile since he was a child, but the traces of his home city still hung about his tongue.

"I'm gey sure of it, Angus," he said.

He often would tease Angus about being a forgotten Scot, only in the name, to which Angus would reply soberly, without his customary smile, that three generations had made him a Chilean. His great-grandfather had been the Scot.

"Where is it?" Angus asked. His life was bedeviled with people certain they had found the biggest mine unopened in Chile. But Gordon was different. Gordon had seen the hard times and sweated toward the better, and Angus had watched him with both admiration and affection and almost a little shame. It was his great-grandfather who had had the sweat, although all that he controlled now, over and above the mines, was enough to give him sweat and sleepless nights of another kind.

He often thought with a wry twist of the mouth that he was like the farmer's boy in the song, when the good old couple died, and left the farm unto the lad and the daughter for his bride. He had been doing well enough with his own inherited money and his mines, but the legacy of all that had been owned by Clara's father had put him at once into the world of great wealth. Not in the bracket of the mining kings like John Thomas North. But enough for the dreams of any man. And all his dreams were centered on his wife and his adored Isabella. That they should lack for nothing that the world and he, Angus Frost, could give them. He had already transferred a great deal of money to England, lest she should wish to marry an Englishman. Or merely to spend time there now she had got used to it.

Give her Enderby for a wedding present. The old girl who owned it would surely part for a big enough offer.

Enderby.

Not long now. Suddenly he was hungry for green fields and the great spreading trees: the sheen on the reedy lake. And Isabella.

Gordon looked back at him in the few moments of silence. Although he was composed and quiet, waiting to hear more, the wide room was alive with his vitality. The cracks of the shutters at the side threw bars of light across his handsome face, and his amiable but noncommittal half smile showed the even edges of his teeth. Something my friend wants, the half smile said, but not even for my friend will I move blind or easily.

There would be no hesitation, Gordon knew. The answer would be yes or no at once, doubt and prevarication lying nowhere in his character. Frost always knew immediately what he wanted, and almost invariably got it, leaving bemused opponents in a deal buoyed up by his personality into thinking they had done at least as well as he. Until the small print proved them wrong.

Gordon envied him the sublime self-confidence and strength of character that had so built on everything he had inherited. But he also knew him over the years as a good man and a good friend. Simple, old-fashioned words, but they were right for Angus. Which was why he had come to him now for help with what could be the biggest decision to make or break his own life.

"Where is it, then, Gordon?" Angus said. "Out with it, man."

Gordon told him and he whistled.

"What my father would have called the arsehole of nowhere," he said. "Supplies, Gordon. Immediately you have accessibility problems. The road there is no more than a mule track by the maps."

Gordon leaned forward eagerly.

"As the crow flies, it's no more than twenty miles from the railway. And there's a defile that would take a railway. We could build a branch line. The terrain is not impassable. There's a track leading up to an Indian village about a dozen miles before it. There's water there, and labor. We'd get the men, no doubt of that."

"Not so much of the 'we.'" Angus grinned. "Come into the office," he said, getting up, and together they walked through the quiet evening house, the white walls soft with sunset, the tiled floors dark, and the big fans still moving on the ceilings against the heat.

The office windows were still shuttered and the room half dark. Angus sank into the chair behind his desk and switched on the green-shaded lamp. He reached to a rack of rolled maps and spread one in the pool of light. From above, the fan swirled it with slow shadows, and already against the green shade a huge moth searched and battered for its death. Angus weighed down the corners of the map with rough samples of rock.

"Show me," he said, and his friend's eager finger found at once the spot where the ochre color of the desert began to go brown on the map with the onset of the mountains.

Angus grunted.

"It's a terrible risk, my friend, sinking your own mine. Are you not well enough as you are?"

The other man's long Scottish face set in a look of obstinacy, and his chin came out. Angus looked up and then reached over and clapped him on the shoulder. He laughed his deep infectious laugh.

"You're set on it. And you're right. The only boss worth having is yourself. So I might as well help you. If I like the look of the reports, I could take a share or two."

It was obvious that for Gordon Adams all this came later. Nor was it the moment for even the most affectionate laughter. Carefully his blunt, short-nailed finger ran across the shadowed map, tracing the distance from his mine to the railway that roared and clattered through the coastal desert.

Angus listened to him in silence and no longer smiled, studying the map intently.

"Tell you what we'll do," he said then. "We'll put a horsebox and a couple of mules on a train. There's a small town there, look, and I'll bribe the guard to stop the train and let us down. We can do the same to come back. Then we can ride easily to your mine. Sleep out the night or go to your village."

It was then that Gordon Adams said without rancor what a thing it was to be rich. Stopping trains wherever you fancied.

Angus smiled, but his eyes were still on the map.

"We must do it in the next few days," he said, "and not take too long. We're off to England to collect Isabella. For good this time," he added, and now smiled with open pleasure.

Gordon Adams remembered clearly the lovely tall child with the staggering dark-blue eyes, and thought she had probably grown into a raving beauty. He had a son a little older. Could be interesting. In even holding such a thought, he knew little of Angus Frost's mind. The King of England himself would not be good enough for Isabella. But he would settle for aristocracy. Chilean or European. Old and genuine. Money would not be of any importance. Position and quality everything. Already he was briefing Clara on whom she must invite to Enderby, and she annoyed him by the look of loving tolerance in her great languid eyes.

"Angoose," she would say, and could never manage the name better. "Angoose. You are wasting your time. Isabella is too like yourself. We may choose whom we will, but I know that when the time comes she will never marry as she is told, unless she is happy with the man. Isabella, my husband, unless I am much mistaken, will do all the right things, for she is a gentle daughter, but she will get round it all in the end and marry for love. As I did, *cariño*," she added softly, but although he smiled, a spasm of real sick fear shot through him at the idea of his precious Isabella married to someone totally unsuitable.

It was almost a giddiness, so great the shock of the idea. Finally he bent to kiss his wife.

"As I did, too," he said. "And surely she will have the same good sense as ourselves."

He gave her the wide confident smile that never allowed problems, since he knew he could always solve them, clapped his fine broad-brimmed Panama on his head, and was gone.

Clara, who was wiser in such things, smiled and shrugged and hoped for his happiness. And Isabella's.

"No difficulty about Clara," Angus said now to his friend. "She's staying with friends on a hacienda some way out of Valparaiso, so that she can slide in and out and spend a fortune on clothes for England. I'm collecting her there to catch the boat. I can give you a few days."

"Capital, Angus. Capital. There's no judgment I'd trust like yours."

Angus gave him the quick, warm, generous glance that so bound people to him, and put his finger again on the map.

"Here," he said. "Here. Papadillo. We'll have the train stopped here. But, Gordon. Not a word about where we are going. If it is good, then the longer we keep it to ourselves the better. I'll just tell them I shall be away for a few days."

"And I," said Gordon.

It was still dark when the long train ground and hissed to a halt, clatter of the bogies echoing in the starlit night. In the poor houses, and the tin and cardboard hovels, families huddled together against the night cold: too uncomfortable for deep sleep: lifting their heads and here and there peering from their door curtains to wonder what had halted the express. In the bigger houses the rich stirred in their comfortable beds, only half alerted by the noise: the occasional one reaching for a gold repeater and listening sleepily to the soft chimes in the cool darkness. Wondering, like the restless poor, what had stopped the train.

Within minutes the mules were off it down a ramp, and it was heaving its way on into the night.

Angus waved to the guard, who in turn hung from his cab and waved to the two men, no more than shadows in the first dull gray glimmer of light before the dawn.

By the time they were settled on their way, the first glow of the scarlet sun was above the mountains to the east, and soon the cold desert night would melt into searing heat. Gordon led unhesitatingly away toward the east and the strengthening sun, at right angles to the railway, which appeared, now the last lights of the train had gone, to run unknown to man from nowhere into nowhere in the gray dawn.

"I have a feeling you have been here before, Gordon," Angus said dourly, and Gordon, gripped with all the unbelievable reality of a thousand hopes, grinned at him and kicked his mule.

"Today through these hills," he said, "and then we turn north." He added then, unable to try and stop persuading Angus. "But a railway could be more direct."

It was the high heat of the middle of the next day when they rode out of a defile through the mountains into a broad ochre-colored valley, rising on its other side to far higher mountains, touched with pink and yellow by the sun, shadows dark as night in their deep clefts. Bitter land where it was not possible to envisage man taking hold. But on the lower flanks of the far mountains was the strung-out straggle of an Indian village. Like a cutout toy pasted to the rocks in the searing light.

No neat white houses of a town. One here and there, probably belonging to the priest or the Mayor, the rest a raggle-taggle of dirty huts made from whatever could be found. No more was needed than protection against the sun, and the cold at night; and if in the rare heavy rains they should be washed away, then it was no more than the will of God, and a search must be made for more old pieces of cloth or cardboard or broken carts or corrugated iron, to start again.

Gordon was right about the water, Angus thought immediately. Below the village the bare mountain bloomed with irregular patches of green or ripening crops. Probably, he thought, some cold clear spring running dark below the ground all the way from the high Andes, and in the place where it surfaced, men would have lived and tilled since the beginnings of time.

Somewhat lower down, on the steep track from the village, was a convent or monastery, white-walled, three bells idle in the high open sections of the bell tower.

"Water there," Gordon said, confirming his thought. "A good spring. Labor, too. They're all half starving."

He led the way a little downhill from the defile toward the sandy, rocky wastes of the wide valley.

"North here," he said. "About seven kilometers." Before them was a looming overhang of rock above the thin trail, all of it unstable in the high glaring light. As they turned along under it, clinging to the thin strip of shadow at its inner edge, all the dogs in the village began suddenly to bark at once, infecting the mules, who sidled senselessly and jibbed at nothing.

There was no warning. Not even one second. Only the animals had known, and the last thing Gordon heard in life was the jingle of harness from the restless mules, and Angus cursing his with his usual cheerful gusto, for the barren no-good offspring of a misplaced union.

He grinned, and the warning rumble did not last long enough

even to wipe the grin from his face. He barely heard the roar before the earthquake had enveloped them, smashing across the timeless line of the overhang, making of it in seconds a brand-new world awhirl with blinding dust and the grinding roar of sliding rock, the earth still trembling at its own fearful shock.

Half the mountain above them had slid down its own flank, bringing with it the overhang under which they had been riding, and in the final dust-blind silence when the roaring and the shaking had stopped, the three bells of the convent jangled over the ravaged valley like a demented requiem, ringing mindlessly in their cracked and shaking tower.

Gordon and his mule had disappeared as completely as the old shape of the mountain, and at the foot of the long new slope of raw yellow earth and sand and torn rock, the other mule was trapped, and fearfully screaming against the dying clangor of the bells. Over all the rest of the wide valley lay some dreadful, special silence, as though the very earth must pause and breathe before life could start again, exhausted by its own cataclysm.

Slowly the whirling dust began to settle and steady, and there were no more tremors. As if at a sudden signal all the little birds in the green crops began to chirp and sing, and the first dog barked and then another and another. Announcing the end as they had announced the coming. In the convent tower the bells fell silent.

With dark fearful eyes the people in the village, who had raced out into the Plaza or onto the open mountain, looked at each other and crossed themselves and breathed a prayer of thanks to the Holy Mother who had once more brought them safely through a tremble. They prayed automatically to her as the priests and nuns had taught them, but deep in their primeval hearts was still the dark terror of the old gods, who shook the world when their people had angered them.

They had been watching the two gringos across the valley, turning out of the track to the coast and making northward. Already, with the barking dogs, and the silence of the bells, the bravest of them had started to run down the hill.

Not with any thought of help, from their thin veneer of Christian teaching.

As the two men had ridden out of the opposite mountains,

they had seen sun glittering on silver harness: seen with their keen mountain eyes the rifles at the saddlebows.

Rich men. Dead or alive. Who knew what could be found around them in the fallen stones?

No one man spoke to another, nor needed to, but they fluttered in silence down the steep ochre face of the mountain like blown scraps of torn paper. In the middle of them, the small black figure of their priest, who knew that after the earthquake there might be little left for man, but scrambled and ran with terrible urgency, lest there be something he could salvage for God.

The dogs still barked behind them, and in the green crops the little birds sang madly, as though they thanked some personal god that they were still alive. But down in the changed and shattered valley even the mule had stopped screaming.

At the edge of the red earth, below what had been the track, lay the body of a white man, stripped down to his skin, his paleness burning already in the fierce heat of the sun. As they arrived panting round him, the ones who knew there had been two men before the mountain fell grew silent and did not look at each other, their flat Indian faces impassive. Priests had strange ideas, and in the heat of the day he might think that they should dig the other out.

The priest thrust through them, small and thin in his greening cassock, sweat pouring down his narrow face.

"Cover him," he said tersely, aware of the women pounding down not far behind, and reluctantly two of them took off their cotton serapes and put them over his scorching nakedness. As the women arrived, they milled around, their broad faces blank with disappointment.

Nada. Absolutamente nada. Nothing to steal. Not so much as a shirt that could replace the worn rags of their *niños,* and indeed he was even covered with the clothes of the men, who could ill spare them. They slipped and slithered in their bare feet in the raw broken earth, and tried to get near enough to see into his mouth, round which the men were already jostling, lest in the manner of his kind, he might have gold hidden in his teeth. Whole teeth of gold, it was whispered, some of them had, in the cities.

The wisp of a man that was the priest lifted his face from where he knelt by the man's legs, his face blazing with fury.

"In the name of God," he shouted at them, "have I taught you nothing? May He forgive you that you would rob the very dead! It could easily have been you. You!"

He took his furious eyes from them and bent his head to compose himself to pray, and they drew back abashed. Shamed, here and there some of them crossed themselves, knowing it true that the smashing hand of the earthquake made no choice, and it could as easily have been one of them as this poor battered, earth-stained body under the serapes.

Suddenly, in the middle of the hasty prayers for the dead, begging God not yet to have taken the soul while it was still in sin, the old priest stopped. He stayed silent a moment and then laid his head down on the man's chest. Blood was already crusting in the sun at the top of his head, and the bones showed clear and white through the torn skin of his twisted legs. Flies were already gathering, and in the brazen sky the dark dots of vultures had appeared and circled lazily.

"This man is not dead," the priest whispered, and then looked up sharply, glancing round the now silent people. "Where is the *médico?*"

They all shuffled and looked at each other from the corners of their great liquid eyes, and moved uneasily as if they shared some collective guilt.

"Where is he?"

"Señor Padre." One of them shrugged as if he spoke of something as incalculable as the earthquake. "Señor Padre, for the *médico,* it is not a good day."

The priest grunted and quietly swore. For the *médico* a bad day meant impossible. El Borracho, they called him. The Drunken One. A bad day meant sprawled almost lifeless on his bed, with the stone bottle of *agua ardiente* on the earth floor beside him. Or just as likely in the squalid hut of La Conchita at the back of the church among the prickly pears: where men could go in secret without the sniggers of their friends, and where El Borracho seemed to find the only solace that the raw spirit could not bring him.

A bad day.

Quickly he scrambled to his feet, the front of his darned cassock stained now like the body on the ground, with the raw red and yellow earth of the landslide.

"This one," he said, "is not dead. Go up to the Sisters and get a door."

They looked at him as if the sun had taken his wits, as it could do to men in the high heat of the summer.

"A door," he shouted at them. "To carry him on. Tell the Sisters we are bringing him. And the rest of you go up," he said, fixing them with fierce dark eyes. "The rest of you go up and get the *médico*. Bad day or no bad day. Get him wherever he is."

"Padre," they cried aghast. They would rather have been in the heart of the *terremoto* itself. "Padre. He will kill us."

"It would be small loss," the little priest said tersely. "Go and get him."

chapter
2

Miss Catchpole had actually seen it in her carefully folded copy of the *Times*, one morning in the middle of May, in the half hour after her solitary breakfast, when she permitted herself the relaxation of becoming acquainted with the day's news: prior to her majestic entry into morning prayers.

Only a small paragraph, obviously not ranking as of much importance.

Earthquake, said the unobtrusive headline, in Chile.

Small words, to take Isabella's life and crumble it, as the earthquake had crumbled the dry earth of Chile. Never to resume its same course again.

The small article went on to report that the tremor had struck in the northern edges of Valparaiso, and in the open country north of that. Fortunately the lack of population in the desert area prevented casualties. In the city itself, however, there were a number of dead, and considerable damage.

Miss Catchpole stared at it and caught her breath and read it again. She always prided herself on being an unimaginative woman. "Common sense," she would say, "is what girls need." Pursing her lips firmly and dismissing all the half worlds of imagination and intuition. But as she looked at the neat print of her newspaper, with the calm sun of early summer flooding through the window, and the voices of her girls coming up from the garden below, she felt an unaccustomed chill and certainty of far-off tragedy. Looking up at the sunlit window, she tried to tell herself that her thoughts were only of Isabella and possible loss. But she was unable to keep them away from herself, who would undoubtedly be faced with many difficult problems, some of which had already arrived with the bank statement that did not yet show Isabella's fees. She had told herself that they were merely delayed in the post, or indeed—and her mouth tightened—had not yet been sent.

Never one to hurry with his fees, Mr. Angus Frost had once said to her genially that the money was better off earning interest for him than for her, to which she had somewhat tartly replied that Isabella's school fees were to keep Isabella at school, and that she started eating the moment she arrived. He had laughed amiably and given her a check with a charming smile, but also with an irritating air of understanding that Miss Catchpole was not keeping Isabella and her friends for the love of them, and that the Select Finishing School was far from an unprofitable business.

She offered him her most repressive gaze, and let it go, but even for Mr. Angus Frost too much time had elapsed this term.

"Not both of them, please God," she said now, with an unnatural humility, more apt to address God with the same firm authoritative manner with which she addressed her pupils. Nor again did she know on whose behalf she was being so humble. Isabella's or on account of the Responsibilities.

Abruptly she pulled herself together. What nonsense. There had been earthquakes, far bigger, in Chile in the time she had had Isabella. They were as common as the dandelions here in the long grass around the edges of the Park. For the moment she would put it firmly from her mind and wait for some normal delay to be resolved.

Firmly she picked up her paper and composed herself to read on until Rumbold's timorous knock on the door.

"Prayers, Headmistress, please. The girls are waiting."

"Thank you, Miss Rumbold."

Miss Catchpole smoothed down her dress and picked up her Bible and her *Hymns Ancient and Modern*, already marked at the correct places for the day, and sailed past Rumbold: on down the corridor where the sun laid window shapes of gold on the spotless brown linoleum.

In her place as Head Girl Isabella held the door for her, neat and happy-looking in her school dress of blue cotton, with small white ruffles at the neck and sleeves.

No matter how she tried, throughout prayers, Miss Catchpole was aware of her: and of her own fear that if anything had really happened, her most lucrative pupil may have been swept from her by one stupid convulsion of the earth. She could not do without Isabella's fees for this term, not to mention the donations apt to be made to the school by rich and grateful fathers as their daughters left it.

Isabella caught her rigid glance, and through prayers and announcements sat on her hard chair and wondered what she had done wrong. Running over her activities of the early morning, she found nothing on her conscience, but did remember that she had forgotten to cross yesterday off her calendar.

Contentedly she smiled down at her hymnbook. Whatever Catchy was mad about, it couldn't any of it last much longer.

But she had got no letter by the end of May. With the way the ships ran, she usually got one about the middle and about the end of the month. Nothing now since she had come back in the middle of April.

Her father never failed her.

"Nothing for you, Isabella, I'm afraid."

Miss Smith looked down her long pink nose, an ineffectual woman who looked colorless and cold even on this bright day. She still had some letters in her hand. She was quite stupid enough to have made a mistake.

"It's the right time for the boat," Isabella said, not quite daring to ask her to look again.

Smith gave a weak and ineffectual smile that could not hide a hint of malicious pleasure.

"Perhaps the boat broke down or something. Or sank."

For Isabella the sun went from the day. Stupid Smith. Stupid pallid Smith with her horrid smelly breath. What a thing to say. Worried by the lack of a letter, her mind filled at once with the thought that boats did sink, and her parents would be on one at any moment, starting the long voyage up to Panama and then across the Atlantic. Anything could happen. She stared at Smith with something close to panic.

"Isabella, should you not be in class?"

Catchy had come in while she was still loitering depressedly in the Common Room, and there was nothing in her face to show that she had received no letter either, and no check, and for her the sun also had gone from the day.

"Please God," thought Miss Catchpole uncertainly and meant it, an unaccustomed expression of doubt taking over her large handsome face. Although as a matter of Good Example to her girls, she asked the help of the Almighty formally and regularly at morning prayers, it was normal for her to feel that she could cope perfectly well without any divine assistance in the management of her small successful world. The sudden loss of large fees, coupled with her genuine fear for the girl herself, and her anxiety about what to do with her with the end of term only weeks away, and her holiday looming near, made her turn with more realism to the Almighty, for, from whom else could she ask help at the moment? Isabella might laugh at Catchy's world, but it had for long been ordered and secure, and totally within the good woman's own control.

By the middle of June she felt it time to get help from more than the Almighty. The first immediate contact would be the London bank that sent her money on Mr. Frost's instructions from his bank in Chile. She reached for her writing pad and dipped her fine steel nib into the souvenir inkwell of Vesuvius; relic of a daring long-gone visit to Italy with her sister. They had not cared for Abroad, and had never gone again.

Then she made her majestic way down to the Post Office, and sent a cable to Isabella's father. She knew from the child a certain amount of their lives. The father traveled quite a bit about his various interests, but surely the mother should be at home. If there was a home. This also was gnawing at her. At what point should she tell Isabella what she had read about the earthquake? But nothing surely could have happened to both of them. The other must take the Responsibility. Unless, and she found it impossible to believe, in the steady unchanging Brighton streets, something had happened to both of them. She felt appalled and almost querulous. Earthquakes. A world far too difficult and distant and unordered for her to have to deal with. She felt caught by the nervousness that assailed her every year on her long journey into Gloucestershire.

With difficulty she made herself wait a week for an answer to both these communications. Her knowledge of the earthquake loomed with ever more terrible certainty in her mind, and she was now as nervous of the answers as of not receiving one at all.

"I will write," she said firmly, "to the Chilean Embassy in London."

Isabella looked at her, the dark-blue eyes heavy with tears. Touched now with hope.

"And what will they know?"

They will know, thought Miss Catchpole grimly, about the earthquake.

"They will know all about important people in Chile. Your father is important, isn't he?"

"Oh, yes," breathed Isabella. The big low spreading house of whitewashed adobe. The cars. The carriages with canopies. The fringes swinging in the sun. The special carriages on the trains. The air always of privilege and success. Oh, yes, he was important. Nothing seemed real now that she did not hear from him. Nor would again, until she saw his name and all the messages of love scrawled at the foot of his hasty letters. Strong upright writing. It was always he who wrote, her mother just adding a small piece at the end. Your loving father. Never Papa or anything like that. Your loving father. Her loving father.

The answer from the bank came first. They regretted that they, too, had heard nothing in the last weeks from Mr. Angus Frost, and equally regretted that even though it was a regular payment, they could do nothing about sending her a check until they got routine instructions from the bank in Valparaiso.

They much regretted being unable to help her.

They will know, thought Miss Catchpole, about the earthquake. They will know, but it is not their job to tell me. The cold certainty of disaster was like the chill of winter.

There was no answer at all to the cable she had sent direct to Angus Frost.

In another week came the letter from the Chilean Embassy, and Miss Catchpole knew she could prevaricate no longer. It told her, as if she did not know, about the earthquake, and that as was always the case, some people remained untraced for quite long periods. It was careful, saying nothing definite, but that through immediate inquiries they were unable to locate any information about Mr. and Mrs. Frost, who did not appear to be at their home address, but who, in effect, did not seem to be anywhere else, either.

Miss Catchpole sat and stared at it. The only thing in its favor was that she could allow Isabella to read it, and so conceal the fact that she had known about the earthquake only a day or two after it happened.

Not, she told herself firmly, that there was anything more she could have done. If they were missing now, they would have been missing then.

Taking a deep breath, she rang the little tinkling handbell on her desk. Smith answered it, doubling as secretary in the limited amount of information with which Catchy would trust her.

"Send me Miss Isabella," she said.

Isabella afterward went slowly up the polished stairs to her room, ignoring the sound of the classes being released for their morning break. Against all the rules she pulled aside the lace curtains to look out unseeing, her face against the glass, at the green spaces of the Park. Deserted at this hour of the morning except for a couple of elderly nursemaids with their charges in high perambulators, and a man with no jacket over his blue shirt, racing with a collie dog.

There were no tears yet, for she did not yet believe, still rigid with the shock of what Catchy had told her, taking refuge from impossible grief in thinking of the lesser thing. What would she do? she wondered. What would happen to her if something had happened to them? Her very being lurched at the thought. But if it had, what then? It was easier to think of. She was so very precious to them, she had always said, because they were singularly alone in the world. No parents left and both of them only children, just as she was. Her father had always said he had nobody. There was some far outlying family of her mother's down in Santiago where her father had met her, but there was no knowing where.

They had friends down in Valparaiso, handsome glittering people like themselves, but it was five years since Isabella had been there and she had no notion who they were. Smiling faces to which she curtsied and chattered nicely, allowed into the salon for half an hour before supper. Listening from her bed afterward with a small smile of security and content to the laughter and music.

People at the mine. Five years, too, and she had known nothing really about them. They certainly would not know where to find her.

In any case, why should they concern themselves with her? Nothing was definite yet. The letter from the Embassy had said so. Grief was only possible. Panic about being alone not yet necessary. Yet they hovered over her black as the clouds of a coming storm, while the sun is still uncertain gold over the threatened countryside.

The bell for the next class underlined her thoughts and she let the curtain drop.

"Try not to think about it, Isabella," Catchy had said. Poor Catchy. She was doing her best to be kind. Try not to think about it. Do all your daily tasks as carefully as usual, and that will get you through the days until we have some news.

Her daily tasks. Her lessons. She had only ever done them so conscientiously to please these two who were her world. So that even at that distance she would not disappoint them.

Before she went down, she crossed the room with a sort of agonized obstinacy, and put her pencil through yesterday's date, and as she left the room, Effie came in with her morning burden of brushes and dusters and the covered china slop pail. She knew all about Isabella's parents' seeming to have vanished. For all Miss Catchpole's efforts at discretion, Isabella was now the object of pity and curiosity through the school. And a certain mean satisfaction on the part of people like Smith, who had always thought she had too much.

Her wan face touched Effie's heart, and she so forgot her place as to speak first.

"Don't take on so, Miss Isabella," she said. "You'll hear one of these days."

Although, she thought sadly, what she might hear was another matter. Like the day with her Mum bathing the baby out in the scullery sink, and the hammering on the door when the man came to tell her about Dad.

Isabella stopped, touched by the apologetic kindness in the pale blue eyes.

"Thank you, Effie," she said politely, and then remembered what Effie had told her of herself. Her eyes filled with hot, hopeless tears, and she looked down at the dumpy little servant.

"Oh, Effie," she said. "You would know—"

"Yes," said Effie, "I would know. But don't take on, Miss, because it don't help any."

In the rustling silence of the girls, who were not allowed to speak on the stairs or in the passages, Isabella went slowly down to her drawing class, isolated in the crowd by her terrors of a life grown barren. But strangely comforted by the matter-of-fact words of little Effie. And a little shamed. At least, if anything had happened—her mind would not encompass the word *dead*. If anything had happened, she would not have to go out and be a servant, like Effie. Her father would have provided for her.

There was another letter from the Chilean Embassy. No attempts to trace either Mr. or Mrs. Angus Frost since the earthquake had been successful. But Miss Catchpole must understand there were always in such circumstances some bodies that remained unidentified, unless complete details of their whereabouts at the time of the earthquake could be established by their relatives. Did the young lady know exactly where her parents were when it occurred? More information might be gained by writing to her parents' friends than by official inquiry.

Miss Catchpole snorted. Handing on the responsibility was all they were doing. Of course they were not British, so little could be expected of them. She had a poor opinion of all foreigners, and barely excused Isabella.

There was another letter from the bank. They had been in further contact with Valparaiso and regretted that no trace had emerged as to the whereabouts of Mr. Frost. It would appear that there was by now a certain risk that he had perished in the earthquake. But this was only presumption, and Miss Catchpole would realize that until he was officially presumed dead, there could be no access to his money. And this could take years.

They could not know that a similar anxiety and confusion raged at the mines out in the Atacama desert, where week after week they continued to implement the instructions Mr. Frost had left to cover his absence of a few days. Communicating themselves with the bank, to be told also that nothing could be done unless he was found, or officially presumed dead. And no one thought of Isabella, except vaguely that there was a child somewhere.

Thus was simplified into a few formal words the five seconds of devastation that had shattered Isabella's life into the same irreversible fragments that had shattered the mountain. And Isabella, if asked, would have said her father was as solid as any mountain.

As the term wore on, Miss Catchpole began to be possessed of a panic not far removed from Isabella's. What would she do if the time came for her holiday, and Isabella remained still here, unclaimed, and a charge upon the school? In her austere study she sat with the unhelpful letters before her and watched the hazy sun of high summer fading into warm purple dusk behind the trees of the Park.

It was necessary to make a Decision.

Gradually her mouth took on the severe lines familiar to delinquent girls. Sentiment must by now be dismissed. Her life held no room for it. Already she had supported Isabella through almost a term in all the luxury of her parlor boarding, and she could afford no more of it. Forever before her loomed the specter of her old age, and the stone cottage down in Iron Acton, where the old sister barely had enough to keep herself in winter fires.

Compassion, or even charity, were luxuries she could not afford. Arrangements must be made for Isabella. And for some measure of recovery of her fees.

The next day was the School Picnic, given apparently by the beneficence of Miss Catchpole at the end of every summer term. In actual fact it was covered by cheeseparing in other directions, and involved no folly like diminishing Miss Catchpole's personal assets.

To the girls it was the high, splendid point of their year. Better even than Christmas, when all the parents sent them presents, or the September garden party, when Miss Catchpole laid herself out to impress all parents within reach, and especially those who had come maybe half across the world to entrust new girls hesitantly into her care.

The Summer Outing was undertaken in two old-fashioned horse-drawn brakes, frothing with soft-colored dresses and flowered straw hats; with two big picnic hampers in the well, and an amnesty for almost every indecorum. Like waving and calling to the passersby in the summer lanes, and singing, traditionally, on their tired way home through the lambent dusk. For all of them the blissful knowledge that schooldays were at an end for the year. For some of them, like Isabella, forever.

Isabella said she would not go. Could not bear the frivolous excitement of the journey between the summer hedges adrift with wild roses and the pale haze of traveler's joy. She had loved too much, and even loving, had longed to leave, the bare green slope of the Downs with the little harebells and pink rock roses in the chalky turf. Perfect curve of the green hills against the pale blue sky adrift with cotton clouds. The races and the games of rounders and French cricket, and throwing themselves in the end on the dry grass where Catchy's usual magnificent lunch was laid out in a style befitting her young ladies.

The sea away below them when they had time to look at it. Pale blue of high summer and wrinkled like unironed silk.

She couldn't bear it.

"You must go, Isabella," Miss Catchpole said. "It will be good for you to take your mind off everything."

She forbore to point out that Isabella's excellent classwork had fallen away to nothing in the last weeks. What did it matter now? There was no one to receive a report. "It is no good to sit alone brooding here. It will not help. If there is news, there is news."

"And I not here to get it," thought Isabella. Yet she did realize that her endless vigils for the postman and the telegraph boy did nothing to help anything. She had thrust completely out of her frightened head all thought of what she would do in three days' time when so many of the others would be collected by delighted parents, or drive off, escorted, to meet them in London.

Tomorrow she should have gone to Southampton, and she did not know if they had ever even left Chile. If they were alive to leave Chile. If she thought of anything at all in her mindless anxiety, it was that she would simply stay here with Catchy or somebody until her parents turned up. They were bound to, earthquake or no earthquake. Bound to. It was just all some ghastly muddle. Her mind closed against it all and wanted to close against the happy nostalgia of the Summer Picnic. Always especially poignant for those about to leave.

Miss Catchpole was adamant.

"I insist, Isabella," she said firmly. "Weeping here alone will help nothing. I am not going myself tomorrow, as I have some urgent business, so you will be needed to help. For the moment you are still our Head Girl, Isabella," she said, and for a moment the fog of Isabella's grief was penetrated by some unusual note in her modulated voice. She looked at her, but could see nothing in her face, thrusting aside the conviction that every single change of tone meant that Catchy had heard that her father and mother were dead.

Catchy saw the two laden wagonettes off the following morning from the school steps, a degree of decorum still holding among the excited girls as long as they were under her chilly eye, which she adjusted carefully to a degree of benevolence suitable to the occasion.

When they had disappeared round the corner at the end of the Park, her manner changed abruptly, and she turned briskly aside in through the open door, closing it firmly behind her. As she went up the stairs, Effie stood aside from her endless polishing to let her pass, and looking at her face she felt a pang of pity for someone. Catchpole was on the warpath. Pity, thought Effie that the nice Miss Isabella didn't have someone other than that gorgon to see her through her troubles, poor thing, what was going to become of her, but then she was rich, and the rich never came to much harm no matter what happened to them.

"Effie, stop daydreaming and get on with your work."

Effie went back to polishing the stairs and Miss Elizabeth Catchpole went into her bedroom to get her hat.

Effie was wrong. It was not the warpath she was treading today, but an infinitely more devious path that led her through the small streets of Brighton; disdaining the Front and the sea breezes she so urged upon her girls; and the sight of the crowded beaches where barelegged children in shady hats dug for crabs down at the water's edge, and their parents and grandparents sprawled and snoozed in canvas deck-chairs. Ukuleles and strolling singing coons with badly blacked faces; and loud-voiced men selling Brighton

Rock. All the things she despised and slightly feared, as they did not belong inside her World. Things for the crowds with whom she would never mix now.

The devious path she was treading firmly in her two strapped shoes with modest heels and polished toe caps brought her in the end in out of the bright day, surely made for picnics and happiness, through the glass and mahogany portals of Cubbington's. She stood a moment and blinked at the change of light, and from the gloom at the back of the shop the owner registered her as he registered every customer who came through his doors, and for Miss Catchpole he pulled himself a little more erect and smoothed unnecessarily the top of his oiled black hair. Trying to estimate immediately what she might want on so unusual a visit, and living in eternal hope that it might be to tell him that she had decided to change her suppliers and get all the girls' clothes from him. Even the sheets. Or the table linen.

Mentally running over his suitable stock, he folded his hands across the gold watch-guard on his ample waistcoat and advanced on her with neat steps through the forest of the ladies' dresses.

"Miss Catchpole. Madam. An honor. May I ask what I can do for you?"

May the God of all shopkeepers grant it was not a complaint.

Miss Catchpole looked at him as though she barely saw him. She was not nervous. That was something that afflicted her only on her annual journey that she would soon have to undertake. When all this difficulty was cleared away. But what she was doing was something to test even her steady character and lack of imagination.

But it was necessary. Some arrangements had to be made about the girl.

"Ah, Mr. Crump. May I have a word with you in your office, please?"

Pleasure flooded the heavy frame of Mr. Crump, and he rose onto his toes. What else could need such privacy, other than a long discussion of increased orders?

"But of course, Miss Catchpole. Of course. This way, if you please."

Nimbly he preceded her down the dark passageway to his

office at the rear of the shop, his small feet twinkling with astonishing speed under his vast bulk. He fussed to get Miss Catchpole seated on a horsehair chair that must have been there since the shop was new, and made a few unnecessary and self-important adjustments to the ledgers and order books and limitless papers on spikes that covered his vast old hardwood desk. As though to emphasize to her the prosperity and importance of this emporium to which she was about to entrust her business.

All round the walls the room was stacked with half-opened packets of merchandise, bursting through cream-colored paper wrappings: socks and sheets and warm fleece-lined knickers; a few odd shoes stood upon the desk itself. The whole place smelled faintly of mice and camphor, and little light came through the high barred window looking out onto an alley at the back. On Miss Catchpole's right a large window opened onto the shop, and down through the length of its crowded shadows she could see the brilliant square of sunlight that was North Street.

She made no preamble, firmly grasping her embroidered purse, too intent on what she wanted to be bothered with the niceties.

"Mr. Crump, I want you to employ one of my girls."

Mr. Crump had taken up his position in his own chair on the other side of the desk, removing the odd shoes, and folding his hands in front of him in a proper position to receive the good news without being too subservient about it. After all, he was trying to tell himself, to quell his excitement, Miss Catchpole was no more than another customer.

Now he stared at her, his soft mouth fallen slightly open under his moustache, unable to adjust so quickly to the loss of his dreams.

"One of your girls? Employ? I do not understand, Miss Catchpole."

Nor did he. No one employed Miss Catchpole's girls. Everyone knew that. At the end of their schooling they vanished back to the rich exclusive worlds from which they had come, from all corners of the earth. The next year there would be another batch coming into Cubbington's, exuding even in their school clothes the wealth and polish that gave his shop that treasured cachet on Saturday mornings.

He lifted his plump hands and dropped them on the desk in a gesture of incomprehension.

Briefly Miss Catchpole explained Isabella's circumstances.

"You will understand, Mr. Crump, that much as I would like to keep the young lady, I am not in a financial position to do so. I will, of course, continue to make all inquiries on her behalf. And I hope to reunite her as soon as possible with her parents."

There was a long silence. Voices came faintly from the shop, and the whirr and clack of the cash railway. Mr. Crump stared at Miss Catchpole with eyes that no longer needed to be subservient; shrewd and bright and wondering what she was up to. The girl could surely have been kept in the school as a pupil teacher or some such. No need to turn her out into the world.

Miss Catchpole stared back at him with the fierce eyes that so easily cowed poor Rumbold or Smith, and the lace on her modesty vest trembled only slightly.

"I would hope, Mr. Crump," she said then, "that we could continue our pleasant arrangement for the girls to come here and do their shopping on Saturday mornings. I do not see that the young lady's presence need alter that."

Ah, thought Crump. So that's it. Either I take the girl on, or she stops the others coming on Saturdays. A lady to be reckoned with, Miss Catchpole. Knew what she wanted and knew how to get it. Mr. Crump was not a hard man. He had his own masters to satisfy, but on the other hand he had daughters of his own, and made a mental note to keep the girl, for take her he clearly must, in the stock room on Saturday mornings so as not to subject her to the ridicule of her friends, who he realized would immediately become as remote as the Eskimos at the North Pole. Miss Catchpole would see to that.

He felt a pang of pity for the girl, whoever she was. He knew he would have to take her, and even as he stared at Miss Catchpole with all these thoughts running through his head, he began to brighten. There was no doubt that one of Miss Catchpole's Young Ladies behind the counter would lend a first-class resident cachet. He would put her on haberdashery to help that fool Beech, where she would make an immediate impression on people as they came through the door.

"Do I know the young lady?" he asked, trying to show a little doubt. Miss Catchpole must not have her victory, whatever it was, too easily.

"Isabella Frost. The tallest of them all." She added then, as though it excused her somewhat: "And the oldest."

Crump's eyes popped. The pick of the bunch. She would lend an air to the front shop that it would take him years to cultivate. Fiercely he subdued the delighted smile that was twitching to spread under his moustache.

"Ah, yes. Quite suitable, I imagine. A quiet girl."

Whether she would be so quiet when she found what her headmistress had arranged for might be another matter.

"Does she know, Miss Catchpole?" he asked, and still could not fathom the woman's motives.

Miss Catchpole made a small, slightly uncertain adjustment to the black Leghorn hat with the yellow rose that she wore uncompromisingly square across her head.

"Not yet," she said then. "So that is settled, Mr. Crump? She may begin on Monday."

"You will tell her to approach through the staff entrance there at the back. Monday? Is that not a little soon?"

"The school is closing, Mr. Crump, and I shall be going on my annual holiday to the West Country."

She did not add that the sheer panic caused by the gap in her bank statement would not permit her to have Isabella another day living like a princess at her expense.

"Very beautiful, Miss Catchpole," Crump was saying. "The West Country. I have myself with my wife and family, enjoyed the pleasures of Weston-super-Mare."

Miss Catchpole was not interested in Mr. Crump's vacations. She had completed one step and must now complete the other. Majestically she rose from the horsehair chair. She did not offer her hand. One of her girls may have become an employee, but the rest of them were still her young ladies. It would not be suitable to shake hands with Crump.

Mr. Crump escorted her back along the dark passage and through the shop, bowing her out into the bright afternoon. She careened off along North Street like a ship in full sail, some expression of satisfaction and relief clear even in her departing back.

Crump was an astute man, and he stood watching her for a few moments before he went back into the shop. Speculating as to what was in it for Miss Catchpole. Some lingering doubts as to his side of the bargain, and indeed Miss Isabella Frost's, made him bark sharply at Beech, who was fumbling himself into a hopeless tangle with a length of yellow ribbon behind the haberdashery.

Unaware that she had been anything but totally convincing with Crump as to having Isabella's good at heart, Miss Catchpole went serenely on, skirting round the doubtful area of the Lanes until she reached a collection of small streets, little different, on the other side of them—a world far from the white paint of the Pier and the gleam of gold on the onion domes of the Pavilion. Another Brighton, and she had had to make careful and discreet inquiries from her housekeeper before she knew where to find it at all. Necessary, she had said, to see Mrs. Quickly herself before Monday, to make laundry arrangements for the holiday.

The housekeeper had looked at her as doubtfully as Crump, and debated whether she should bridle at this invasion on her territory. Miss Catchpole had never arranged the holiday laundry in her life. But the woman's own mind was on her holidays also, and she let it go, telling Miss Catchpole where to find the laundress, and giving little more than a passing frown as to what she was about.

Consulting a piece of paper from the embroidered purse, Miss Catchpole stopped outside a small house that could once have been white with a bright-green door. At once small dirty children gathered as if they had come from the cracks of the broken plaster, holding out their hands and sniveling for pennies. Miss Catchpole looked down at them with cold distaste, almost terrified that they would touch her with their filthy hands, brush against her with their rags of clothes. No one had told her it would be like this.

She looked up at the house, the once-white plaster gray and chipped, stained black and yellow by the rains of years. The paint cracked and peeled on a door that she dared not bang too hard lest it should fall apart. Even from outside she got the crisp, hot smell of iron on linen: even a hint of scorching that made her purse her lips and determine to tell the housekeeper to examine the school linen with especial care.

She stood with her back determinedly to the begging children, who had begun to shout remarks she found difficult to ignore, relieved that her peremptory rap brought a tiny woman, who opened the door very rapidly. Her thin face was set in the servile anxiety of someone who had known a lifetime of peremptory raps, all of them meaning demands, and many of them trouble.

This time she stood with her mouth open, unbroken by any line of teeth in the dark gap. They were kept carefully in an old jam jar on the kitchen mantel, transferred to her apron pocket when she went out, the agony of wearing them only bearable for the few moments she must confront her customers or her customers' servants. She had picked them up for a few pence in a pawnshop, and they held little relation to the shape of her own mouth.

But they were the first thing she thought of when she opened the door. Her badge of respectability that took her just above the level of the toothless old crones in the streets around her. Never before in all the years she had laundered for the school had Miss Catchpole come in person to her house. Indeed it was only by chance she ever saw her, if she should happen to be inspecting the kitchen when she came with her cart of laundry. Had it been the King of England or the Pope of Rome himself in his high gold hat, she could not have been more surprised. And she without her teeth, thinking it only someone from the street. Her thin red hand went instinctively to her mouth.

Her second shattering thought was of disaster. The washing from the school stood between her and the poorhouse, all the rest that she got not enough to feed a cat, let alone pay the rent, and the cost of the yellow soap, and the coal for the fire that she had to keep going all the time to heat the flatirons.

All these things raced through her mind and she was too frightened to speak, her eyes on Miss Catchpole like a rabbit on a snake, waiting for the inevitable end.

But Miss Catchpole was urbane.

"Good afternoon, Mrs. Quickly," she said. "Can you spare me a moment? I would like to speak to you about something."

Spare her a moment. Mrs. Quickly felt the threat recede.

"Why, yes, Miss Catchpole. Certainly, Ma'am. Please step in, Ma'am."

Inside the door she fell into another panic. The tiny parlor, unused since she and Cedric used to sit there of an evening, was draped with all the fresh ironing, hung about the furniture. The kichen was full with the overflow of damp sheets from the yard, hanging from lines, between which Mrs. Quickly dodged and slapped her way backward and forward to get the flatirons from before the glowing range. The room was red-hot and rank with steam, and had her fear not been so great, she would have felt a certain resentment at being caught like this and without her teeth in, too. It was her place to go and call on her customers, not the other way round.

Miss Catchpole made up her mind for her, waving a regal hand toward what was obviously the kitchen.

"Don't disturb yourself, Mrs. Quickly. You can continue ironing while I talk to you."

Mrs. Quickly still had to disturb herself to the degree of moving a couple of sheets so that Miss Catchpole could settle herself into the lumpy old carpet chair beside the range. Then she took her at her word, for was not every minute money, and in the heavy padded holder she picked up one of the irons from before the fire. Expertly she spat on it and watched the spit sizzle into nothing down the flat face of the iron. A little hot, thanks to the interruption. She must be careful. Scorching a chemise under Madam's eyes could do nothing but hurry on disaster.

"What can I do for you, Ma'am?"

Go on. Get it over. Tell me if this is the end of all the struggling and the sweating and the dragging of that handcart up and down the hills of Brighton. The poorhouse would almost be a rest.

Miss Catchpole wasted no more words than she had done with Mr. Crump.

"Mrs. Quickly, I wish you to do me a favor."

Mrs. Quickly collected herself sufficiently to put the iron on the stand before staring across between the hanging sheets at Miss Catchpole, sitting upright on the edge of the old red chair, her hands folded over the purse in her lap, and an expression of careful benevolence on her severe face.

"A favor, Ma'am?"

What in God's world, she thought, could I do for her?

Miss Catchpole came at once to the point.

"One of my young ladies," she said, "has—ah—suffered a financial disaster. She has lost her parents in sad circumstances."

"Poor young thing," said Mrs. Quickly at once, her toothless mouth pinched into compassion. She had thought to make a dive for her teeth when they came into the kitchen, but did not know how long her visitor would stay, and whether she could endure them for that length of time.

"Yes, but you see," Miss Catchpole went on, "she has now no means of support, and I am doing my best to rearrange her life for her. Mr. Crump of Cubbington's has most agreeably promised to give her a position there, and I am here now to ask you to rent her your spare room. I understand you have one."

This time Mrs. Quickly did not remember to put the iron down until the smell of the burning iron blanket rose between them, hot and pungent.

"Why can't she live at the school?" she demanded truculently.

Miss Catchpole's face was cold.

"It would not be suitable."

Mrs. Quickly sensed a trap.

"But, Miss Catchpole." Her voice held all the horror of speaking to one who had violated a shrine. As Miss Catchpole had. "Miss Catchpole, Ma'am. That's Cedric's room."

Miss Catchpole nodded. She had heard from the housekeeper all about the death of Mrs. Quickly's seventeen-year-old son two years ago, and how everything in his little dark, ill-furnished room had remained untouched ever since.

Mr. Quickly, it appeared, had disappeared from the family scene with no reasons given when the boy was seven, and Mrs. Quickly had supported the two of them by taking in washing ever since. Miss Catchpole prided herself on not being a hard woman, and surely this little creature must see that she was doing her a favor by providing a respectable lodger for her. This damp steam-filled atmosphere was enough to give anyone tuberculosis. She forgot this when she pressed on in her determination to put Isabella into it.

"I think, Mrs. Quickly," she said, and from the tone of her voice Mrs. Quickly knew she was being given an order.

Cedric's room. She laid down her iron the better to face what was coming.

"I think, Mrs. Quickly," Miss Catchpole said, "it would be a great pity to disturb the excellent relationship which we have had for so many years."

Mrs. Quickly's mouth tightened until there was no mouth at all, her nose almost resting on her chin. One of the irons on the range smelled red hot, but she didn't look at it, her tired, faded eyes on Miss Catchpole. She was no more stupid than Mr. Crump.

"Take this girl," Miss Catchpole was saying, for some reason of her own. "Take this girl, or I will take away the school washing." As simple as that.

What choice had she?

Cedric's room. She hated Isabella before she had ever set eyes on her.

"Wouldn't it," pressed Miss Catchpole. "Be a pity."

"Yes, Ma'am," said Mrs. Quickly, and with careful benevolence Miss Catchpole ignored her tone of voice.

"There, then. That is settled. Splendid. It will give you a little more money. I will bring Isabella on Sunday evening. You can arrange the money with her when she finds out how much Mr. Crump will pay her."

Isabella. There couldn't be two Isabellas in the school. She knew all their names: carefully stitched with embroidered labels to their clothes. The finest and the most beautiful of all belonged to the one called Isabella.

For a moment Mrs. Quickly knew a pang of pity. The Isabellas of this world did not belong in these mean streets. Then she thought of Cedric's room.

"Yes, Miss Catchpole" was all she said.

Miss Catchpole rose with satisfaction and groped her way distastefully through the damp sheets to the door.

"Good day to you, Mrs. Quickly."

Mrs. Quickly followed her to the door but did not answer her good-bye. Nor did she do anything to protect her against the abusive children who swarmed around her. She watched her down the narrow dirty street exactly as Crump had done, wondering what she was up to.

But she wouldn't have Cedric's room, that girl. She could have her room and she'd go into Ceddie's, with all the treasures. The faded eyes brightened nostalgically. Might be nice. Like having him there, nights.

Miss Catchpole gained assurance as she emerged from the mean streets and came out into the sun and bustle of North Street. She turned up the long hill toward the glass-roofed station, managing to forget those terrible children in the prospect of buying her ticket for her holiday. Going up the crowded street, she had all the spirit and contentment of one who has Brighton at her command.

Mr. Crump and Mrs. Quickly had no cause to wonder what she was up to. She was up to nothing. Merely solving an immediate problem with the sort of ruthless innocence that Isabella had long suspected in her.

chapter
3

They succeeded against all odds in getting the *médico* to come and see the foreigner, who had been hauled with small mercy up the hill to the convent on one of its doors.

The priest fluttered round them, furious and despairing, as with haphazard brown hands they bundled the man onto the door. He could see the chances of life diminishing with every ungentle gesture, the poor legs no more than sticks of twisted, bloodied bone, and blood still soaking from the great wound in his head. It was clear that, not for the first time, they thought their padre touched by God: troubled in his own head that he should urge them so frantically to take care with a man already dead.

He shouted at them in anguish. They were giving the man as little thought as if he were a bundle of maize stalks, to be hoisted from the fields for the roofs of their appalling homes. As little thought, God pity them, as they would give to themselves or each other, for where in their precarious lives did they learn to have respect for human life, hanging onto it by little more than a thread, through poverty and disease?

They dragged him finally up the steep, stony track and, banging the door on the peeling gateposts, into the courtyard of the convent. Here the nuns, although they had little more to spare than the people themselves, of their charity set aside a few bare rooms for the care of the sick of the village who were past any other help.

Sister Jesús María came in only when all the men were gone, leaving the priest staring down at the crumpled, bloodstained figure stretched out on the low cot in the small, peeling white room, where the ferocious heat of the early afternoon struck through a high unshuttered window. She inclined her head in respect for the priest, and moved over at once to close the shutters, and in the white filtered bars of light, turned to look at what they had brought her.

In silence, with dark careful fingers, she felt gently up and down the shattered legs and bent to examine the torn wound on the top of the head. The man groaned, and with sunken anxious eyes the old priest watched her and had no idea again whether he should be saying the prayers for the living or the dying. The man's face was ashen, sunken. The thick brown hair matted with blood and sweat. It was difficult to tell how old he was. Not old. These city people were not worn into old age like the poor souls of his village. Not old. The undamaged parts of his body looked firm and strong.

"God have mercy on him," was all he whispered, knowing that, living or dying, he was going to need it.

Sister Jesús María sighed and laid back the coarse cotton sheet. She turned to the priest, and although her hands folded automatically to acceptance of the will of God, she would not accept it without a struggle.

"Father, it is beyond me. Have you sent for the *médico?* Even with God's help it is beyond me."

She regarded him with her calm, controlled face, her white cotton habit that had been darned upon darn and patched upon patch, barred with light from the broken slats of the window. God help her, he thought, she was little more than a child, but there was about her a serene and firm authority that made him rush to assure her he had done all he could, once he realized the man was alive.

"I have sent them up for him," he said, and rubbed his hand unhappily over the gray stubble of yesterday's beard. "I do not know if he will come. It is a bad day," he added, lamely and apologetically. Even she would understand that, who had so often waited for him, watching the dying.

Sister Jesús María's soft young lips tightened into a firm disapproving line. She was prepared to accept the will of God, but not the wayward will of the *médico*.

"He must be got."

Before entering the convent she had been a nurse in a big hospital in Santiago, and had asked when she entered that she might be sent where her experience would be of use to those who

most desperately needed it. For three years now she had been looking after the ones in the village who would otherwise have been left
to die, threading her way through all their wretched illnesses of
ignorance and malnutrition. Sending them back, astonished at their
recovery, to the heat and poor food and blistering toil that would
soon bring them back to her. Or comforting them in a death that
could only be a relief, fully believing it when she told their weeping
relatives that they were better off with God.

Sadly, she thought the *médico* himself one of the sickest of
them all, although no medicine would help him. His was some deep
and dreadful sickness of the heart, closed away beyond reach. But
she had saved more of her people since he had come two years
back. Curiously they had learned to trust him, and many fewer
were brought down to her with the look of death lying already on
their faces.

Now they had learned to thread their way up the narrow rocky
path to his bleached and peeling door, between the prickly pears
and tangled pink and yellow glory of the hibiscus: beginning slowly
to understand that help lay in the dreadful one-roomed hovel with
the floor of beaten earth and the merciless sun searing in jags and
splashes through the broken shutters. What food he consented to
eat was given to him by the priest's housekeeper, and there was
nothing in the room save a cot with rumpled cotton cover and a
table and a chair. And some strangely tidy shelves on one wall, at
variance with all the squalor, holding bottles and instruments they
did not understand.

At first he had refused to have anything to do with any of
them, appearing from nowhere like an exhausted ghost. Every day
was a bad day, and only the charity and concern of Father Ignacio
kept him alive.

Then he had looked at them as if for the first time, and slowly
after that they had come to realize that he could cure them and
cure their children.

That the baby with the swollen belly need not die, as it would
once have done; the dying wife could be brought back to her children and her usefulness. The old ones given a few more years.

Unless it was a bad day.

Then there was nothing to do but go away from the sun-peeled door, weeping, knowing the baby would probably be dead before he was fit to see it. Or the mother. Or the old one.

They had known him weep himself when this occurred.

But the bad days were his masters when they came.

He was not Chilean. Not English. A little country beside England, the priest said, and this meant little, since they had never heard of England. Everyone in Ireland, the priest told them, had this fierce red hair and pale faces that would never take the sun. A cold land, he told them, of endless rain and mists and much green country. And the people, who had never even seen the fertile plains of their own land along the coast, looked at their brown skins and the barren, ochre-colored land as far as they could see, and smiled at the priest, not believing.

But not even Father Ignacio could tell them, for he had never been told himself, what shattering sorrow had made such a man leave the city and wander to a remote mountain village to drink himself to death.

He prayed for him, and hoped for him, for when he was fit to he worked among the people: and every three months when the wagon from the convent made the long grueling journey to the town for supplies, he gave an incomprehensible list to Groucho, who must thread his way with the mules through the busy streets, to a given address, where a well-dressed man would give him a parcel in exchange for the list. The unknown things that mended wounds and healed the *niños* and the old.

"A Chilean gentleman," Groucho would tell them every time, as though they had never heard it before, and they listened avidly, desperate for any word from the far world beyond their isolated village. "A Chilean gentleman, very fine. And they took me into the special room they have for cooking food, *aiee*, a room for nothing else but to prepare the food. They gave me a meal of meat. Real beef, as God saw me eat it, and beans." His whiskers drooped in depression that there was even one thing he could not enjoy. "The potatoes, I did not like."

Always this man, who sometimes wore a white coat, would ask after his friend, the *médico*.

"And I tell him," Groucho would say, making balancing movements with his two hands. "Always it is the same, I tell him.

Some days good and some days bad, and always he asks me where he is, and I swear before God I cannot tell him."

For the *médico* had assured him, also before God, who witnessed all things, that if he should disclose where he was, he would take one of the small sharp knives he used to cut wounds and let out the evil, and carve him, Groucho, into a heap of little pieces.

And looking into those fierce green eyes, with that strange red hair hanging above them, Groucho believed him, and crossed himself fearfully as he left.

Liam Power, if the day was good, would grin as he put away his precious stores. God bless his friend Guillermo. But they were like children, these people, God help them. Like children.

The one person who was no child, and who was not afraid of him, was Sister Jesús María, well aware that he had no supernatural powers or potions, but was merely a very good doctor. But like Father Ignacio, she wondered what had washed him up like driftwood in the lost dirty shambles of the village.

Liam himself regarded her with a degree of caution, all his instincts telling him that if he gave her half a chance, she would be after that destroyed thing she would refer to as his immortal soul. Father Ignacio knew better.

But unlike Father Ignacio, Sister Jesús María was young, and a woman, and in spite of all the disciplines of the convent, she could not fail to be aware of the fine neglected good looks that were falling into ruin, and it may be she eased her conscience by telling herself that it was his soul she was concerned with. There was nothing of his soul in his height; a splendid man almost twice the height of any of the villagers. Those strange, compelling green eyes and the thick dark red hair falling over them. The fine strong bones that no ravaged gauntness could disguise.

It was often necessary, before the risk of sin, for Sister Jesús María to turn her thoughts firmly away from the doctor.

"He must be got," she said again now to the priest, and the old man raised helpless hands, brown and gnarled as the mountains of his own village.

"It is a bad day," he repeated, as if he could say nothing else. "You know what that means."

"Padre." The respect she owed the priest was fraying under

irritation and his inertia. "This man will die. Is dying. The *médico* will never forgive himself if this should happen. To one of his own. A gringo. There might never be any more good days. For any of us."

In the uneven slatted light the nervous old man looked at her and knew that what she said was true. And would God ever forgive him, if he allowed that to happen? Determination stiffened him, and real fear for his own immortal soul.

"You are right, Sister," he said, and did not know whether he was apologizing to her or to God. "You are right. I will go myself."

The nun glanced at the motionless figure on the primitive bed, blood already soaking through the sheet.

"Be quick, Father," she said.

It was almost two hours before Liam Power came down the hill, ashen, walking stiff-legged like a man who had no surety where the next foot would go down. Like a man in a trance. Looking on the edge of death himself. The priest almost scampered to keep up, his anxious face showing clearly all that it had taken to get him there.

"Only because it was a gringo," he whispered afterward to Sister Jesús María, shaking still with the monstrous undertaking of tackling the *médico* on a bad day. "Only that it was a gringo. That seemed to reach him."

He dragged a grimy handkerchief from the pocket of his soutane and mopped his face, glancing sideways at the *médico* as if still not certain he had got him. Liam Power was over six feet tall, gaunt and gray and haggard from his destructive life; he would have been the first to tell anyone, himself that raw alcohol was no substitute for food.

By now the high sun had passed, and the small white room was shadowy, filtered through the shutters with the rich gold light of a declining afternoon. The air was like a furnace.

He stood a long moment in the middle of the room, rocking slightly, and seemingly unaware of his patient, holding the black bag the priest had thrust into his hand with the pious prayer that it might hold what was needed. Now Father Ignacio looked up at him in desperate anxiety and uncertainty, fully expecting him at any moment to buckle unconscious to the floor, leaving them both helpless while the other man died beside him on the bed.

He had a frightening look of not knowing where he was, never mind why he was there.

Then with agonizing slowness he put down the bag on the rickety table and spent a long moment staring at his hands as though their condition surprised him, but yet will alone could still them.

Then he turned to the bed.

"Open the shutters," he said abruptly, and the nun flung them back on the last flood of sunset light before the sudden dusk.

"Lamps," he said then, and did not look at either of them. As though it took every ounce of his strength and concentration to focus his wandering brain. Father Ignacio, who knew how he had found him, was still flinging his prayers urgently at heaven. For nothing more spiritual now than that the man would not collapse finally on top of his patient.

Liam sighed then and turned to the nun and told her what he wanted. Much of it she did not have but would not have dared to say so lest the fragile concentration break, and the man go vaguely off again back up the hill.

"Put the lamps close," he said then. "Close. In the name of God, have you no more?"

Five hours he worked, with those blind eyes, and all the little priest could tell himself was that the gringo was as good as dead anyway and they had done their best, and yet torn with hope as he watched the hands grow steady in the small light of the guttering oil lamps in their earthen pots. He was about to stitch the torn scalp of the battered head, when he seemed to understand for the first time what he saw.

"Jesus, Mary, and Joseph," he said, and both priest and nun recognized it as a prayer for help as desperate as anything more conventional they might be offering up to God. Before this the doctor had been almost as oblivious as his unconscious patient.

"Who is he?"

"We do not know," said the priest.

"What happened to him?"

"He was caught down in the valley by the earthquake."

Now Liam turned to him, slowly, as though his head hurt and he had trouble in seeing him. The flickering light of the little lamps ran along the gaunt planes of his face.

"What earthquake?" he said, and although the nun's eyes flickered to meet the priest's, they did not try to answer him.

He was too desperately busy struggling to dredge the doctor in him to the top and he waited for no answer, and did not speak again other than with a list of instructions and demands that brought a hopeless look to the nun's face. His Spanish was as good as theirs, but when he grumbled and muttered and cursed to himself, he spoke in English.

They whispered together and the priest threw out hopeless hands. Where in God's name in a convent was he to find straight flat pieces of board to stretch the man's legs on? Finally he finished up with Groucho splitting the tailboard of the wagon with a machete; cursing and grumbling, but from all the habits of a lifetime, unable to refuse the priest.

"Have no fear, Groucho. The men will come from the village tomorrow and mend it. I have no time to go up there now."

Carefully. Shakily. Hour after hour, the sweat pouring down his hollow face. The torn head. The splintered bones and the skin to be sewn back over them on the shattered legs. The splints, rough as their making, bound on with torn sheets from the convent's meager stock. And echoes in his head coming from some other world he had once known.

The little lights flickered against the hot darkness and moths as big as bats whirled in to singe their wings above the tiny flames. In his deep unconsciousness the man occasionally moaned, causing Liam for a moment to lose his blind look and glance at him sharply, lifting an eyelid. For there was no anesthetic.

At the end of the long hours he straightened slowly, his hands to his tired back.

"Madre de Dios," he said. "Well. He'll either live or die."

He looked down at the bed.

"He's a good strong-looking man," he said. "Well fed and cared for. He could have a chance, more chance than most, though it's in God's hands if he'll ever walk again."

"Who could he be?" the priest ventured. "Alone on the road like that. He had a mule with silver harness."

He drew in his breath. What, in all his anxiety about the man, had happened to the silver harness? Hidden by now probably in small pieces round the huts of the village. He must deal with that. They could kill each other for it.

"Not a poor man," Liam said. "Chilean. Brown hair and blue eyes. But his skin is very fair. Chilean of European stock."

"Indeed, a gringo," said the priest, but Liam had already turned away from him. Carefully he gave Sister Jesús María instructions for the care of her patient.

"But I'll not go," he said. "You'll call me if there's any change at all. I suppose," he added with a grin at the nun, "there's no chance you'd have a drink in this place. Even a drop of the altar wine would do."

Through the flickering shadows Sister Jesús María looked at him with grave sadness and disapproval.

"I can give you a drink of water, Doctor."

"For God's sake. Do you want to damage me? Well, it will do to wash my hands."

He grunted his thanks when she brought him the chipped tin bowl of water, and then without another word flung himself full length on the earthen floor. Within minutes he was asleep. Quietly and carefully the nun repacked his bag and cleared up the room: then she composed herself beside the bed in her stained habit, on the one rickety chair, excused for that night of all the bells that would otherwise have called her from short sleep to prayer. At every vigil she recited the prayers by heart and did not know if they were for the poor creature on the bed, or for the long man sleeping on the floor, who seemed to her to be equally deep in some different kind of trouble.

The little Father had already slid exhausted down the wall to lean against it from the dirt floor, and there they spent all the rest of the long hot night, waiting for the hand of God to fall one way or the other.

The priest dozed and muttered, and the nun prayed on her long rosary made from the beads of the Judas tree, and got up regularly to look at her unmoving patient. In the quiet moments she had to fight and beg for help to keep herself in these timeless hours from looking with carnal thoughts at the tall doctor in his bloodstained serape and rope sandals like any peasant from the village: sprawled there at her feet in the restless and uneasy sleep of the unsatisfied drunk.

Yet he was awake and up with the first touch of scarlet dawn, bending over his patient.

"There has been no change all night," said the nun beside him, as she blew out the small lamps frugally.

"He's alive, the good man. And that's all I ask of him at the moment. Will you wake up Father there, and give him another mutter of prayers, and then we'll be off up the hill for a bit of Christian consolation. 'Tis poor hospitality when they won't even give you a drop of the altar wine."

"We could give you breakfast, doctor."

"Ah, Sister dear, my stomach wouldn't know what to do with it."

The old priest levered himself painfully to his feet.

"I'll say Mass for them before I go," he said. "And were you a different man, Doctor Liam, you could at least have the Communion."

"Indeed, Father, but I'm the kind of man I am."

The priest had long ago decided that the wild *médico* must be a Catholic, as he dropped the name of God so often and so easily in his conversation, not knowing that this was the manner of all the Irish.

He had asked him once, and the green eyes had fixed him satirically.

"I'm able to look after myself, Father," he had said. "What God do you think would have any use for the likes of me?"

"There is but One," Father Ignacio had said hopelessly, but Liam wasn't listening.

He glanced once more at his patient before he left, his face little more gaunt and sunken than his own.

"Call me at once," he said, "if there is any change. Send Groucho."

"You will understand, Isabella, that things cannot continue as they have been before."

Isabella sat before Miss Catchpole in her study. Numbly, sick with disbelief, she had watched the school empty, except for a few girls who could not join their parents and would be staying there under the uncertain care of Rumbold and Smith, while Miss Catchpole took her Journey to her sister.

Trunks and portmanteaux and holdalls cramming the passages, excitement and anticipation and a few emotional tears: promises of lifelong friendship from girls who would have forgotten each other by the following month. The wagonette drawing up to take them all to the station. The group of respectable chaperones in the hall employed by Miss Catchpole for any girls who had to go beyond London, where parents were expected to meet the group.

Victoria. The crowds, the wrought iron of the curved glass roof, the belching steam from the great black-and-green locomotives. The big clock hanging at the end of the platform under which her father had once told her you could meet anyone in the world, and always the wind whistling down the two long passages to the street. Red London buses glimpsed at the end of them, and she had wanted to see them because they would all be motorbuses now. No more horses.

What a little thing to shatter one. But all these things made Victoria Station. The gateway to freedom and the end of school life.

All these things should have been waiting for her. Dumb with misery and a sick terror of anxiety she dared not admit even to herself, she kept to her room through all the going away, knowing herself, with a terrible unfamiliar bewilderment, to be only an embarrassment to the happiness of others.

Her real friends came to find her and to say good-bye, and that could cause nothing but tears, sitting on the edge of her bed, sobbing her heart out as she had not wept before. While school went on, it was just possible to pretend that everything was normal.

Effie came to her as she would rush to one of her small sisters, presuming beyond everything Miss Catchpole would call her Position, to take her in her arms.

Isabella was speechless, choking with grief held back.

"Eff—Effie," she managed to say in the end. She did not care whose arms were round her as long as they held comfort. "It should have been today. I should have met them today."

Effie looked at her, her pale protuberant eyes filled with compassion. So had her mother wept when she had heard about her father. Hopeless, abandoned, as though the very end of the world had come.

But it had not come. It was all there the next day, and the next and the little ones to feed, and Effie knew with shrewd sad certainty that her mother would be more capable of coping with sorrow and hardship than Miss Isabella.

She sighed and got up, going to the chest of drawers for two of the fine lace-edged cambric handkerchiefs that lay there in a neat pile. Laundered by Mrs. Quickly. What could Effie say other than There, now, Miss Isabella, blow your nose and try not to take on so. Something is bound to turn up.

"Earthquakes is funny things," she added, as though familiar with them in the streets of Brighton all her life.

So had Isabella thought, when Miss Catchpole had earlier mentioned to her the occurrence of the earthquake. Until the passing days had proved some other dreadful possibility, they had always been for someone else. To the north or to the south, or a brief gentle tinkling of the glasses on the chiffonier, that no one really noticed.

Obediently she blew her nose, responding to the voice of authority recognized by all Effie's younger brothers and sisters, and then she lifted her head and looked at Effie for a long moment and did not speak, the huge dark-blue eyes awash with tears and full of fear.

"Effie," she said slowly, "I am sure they are dead."

Privately Effie thought so, too, and so did most of the kitchen, who discussed all they knew of the matter avidly over their meals. But what puzzled them was that in the absence of the parents, no one else had come forward for Isabella. It was the considered view of Mrs. Bloom the housekeeper, who had seen Good Service, and knew much of the ways of the upper classes, that when rich people died, lawyers came up out of the ground like weeds.

A lawyer had indeed surfaced for Isabella, prompted by the

bank, but with only the same information. That he was helpless until her father was presumed officially dead, and that, he said, as had the bank, could take years. Matters were not helped by the fact that the lawyer's head office in Valparaiso had been on the edges of the earthquake path, and they were still struggling to find everything in the burnt-out ruins.

The words had not yet come for Effie to mention failure of communications, but she knew what she meant, although at the mines the bewildered but loyal and efficient management continued to function, and no one even remembered a child who had been gone for seven years. Neither of them knew that Mr. Frost could not be reported either dead or missing, since no one knew where he had gone. And Mr. Adams missing, too, without a word. Nor had the day come when, in tardy Chilean fashion, the ruins of the hacienda north of Valparaiso would be cleared, yielding, among her friends, the body of Isabella's mother.

"Now, now, Miss Isabella," Effie said, with more certainty than she herself believed in. She could not bear to look at the poor ravaged young face, nothing in her heart but pity, unlike the kitchen maid who was a follower of those new socialists, and found nothing but pleasure in seeing any of the toffee-nosed young misses come to grief. "It will be all right, Miss Isabella," she said. "Something just slipped up somewhere. Here, let me brush your hair. I come to tell you really that Miss Catchpole wants to see you. Maybe she's got something settled for you."

Isabella was buoyed up by that, the first hope for a long time touching her as she went along the empty, echoing corridors, but as soon as she went into the room, one look at Miss Catchpole's careful, watchful face disillusioned her.

"You have not heard anything," she said flatly, forgetting all respect and protocol.

Miss Catchpole looked at her and the light in her pince-nez gave her a look of blind implacability. In her silence Isabella became aware for the first time of a gray summer rain pouring down onto the garden outside.

"Sit down, Isabella, please. No, I am afraid I have heard nothing new, and now I feel the time has come to say to you that I have done all I can on your behalf. You must understand that my responsibility for you in any way comes to an end today." Bleakly, and without any attempt to be gentle, she reviewed all that had happened. No more than a distasteful task that must be cleared up before she went on her holiday, and her world could be brought back to normal.

She reviewed it as a judge might make his summing up. Told her again of how long ago she had seen the news of the earthquake in the *Times*. Of how she had written to the bank and to the Chilean Embassy in London. Got no help from either, no help from the lawyer.

If her mother knew of anything that had happened to her father, then she surely would have written.

"So you will see, Isabella, that I cannot come to anything but the sad conclusion that your parents have perished in the earthquake. Both of them."

"Why don't you write to the mines?" she cried. "Someone there might know someone."

"To whom?"

Isabella stared at her helplessly. To whom. She knew nothing of the people at the mines, except vaguely to remember the ones that were close friends. A man called Adams.

"Mr. Adams," she cried. "He was a friend of my father."

Miss Catchpole inclined her head.

"You can do all this now for yourself, Isabella. I have tried to tell you that it is no longer my responsibility."

All her life Isabella would carry the overwhelming impression of Catchpole's big tight-skinned face as she tried to believe in what she was saying, her eyes riveted on the pince-nez bobbing on the end of her long nose as she talked. All Miss Catchpole could think of on her part was that the girl was unnaturally, almost irritatingly calm, sitting there staring blindly with those great big eyes. With the shining hair all drawn back she looked, she thought with a twist of distaste, like one of those objectionable statues that Catholics stuck up in their churches. Although several of her pupils were Catholics, they were sent to Mass segregated in the charge of Smith, who was herself of that unhappy persuasion. Miss Catchpole looked the other way.

Across the tidings of disaster and death they stared at each other, preoccupied by foolish details that their minds dredged up in the long gap before Isabella could face through them to reality. The bleak misery of the young face, the terrible dignity with which the child held herself, would have touched the heart of anyone less ironclad than Miss Catchpole.

Dead. She tried to understand it. Dead. Yet the curtains stirred as always in the wind that had brought the rain, and the drenched roses clung about the window. Children shouted in the park across the road, excited by the cool rain.

Dead. She could grasp it more easily for her mother, never very strong in her grip on life. Beautiful and languid and always faintly far away.

But death was not for her father. Made for living, with his fierce vitality and his good looks. So funny. So clever. He *was* life. To Isabella, he was life itself.

But he might not have wanted life without her mother. She might not have been enough, for he adored her mother: as if her gentleness tempered a spirit that might otherwise have run wild. Would either of them have wanted life without the other? Was it not better that they were gone together?

Earthquake. She knew them as common in Chile as the summer heat. She had seen the ruins. The huts of the poor like piles of rags and matchwood. Bigger buildings still standing, but with great threatening cracks searing their white walls. Had they known terror? Her father desperately trying to protect her mother? Where were they when it happened? Had they been mutilated, all their fine looks smashed? Their loved faces.

All the questions that were going to haunt her nights surged over her at once. Anguished and unanswered. Loss as cold as winter and as desolate, and all the worse for not being understood.

"If I could only *know*," she was to cry a thousand times. "If I could only *know*."

She realized Miss Catchpole was speaking again.

"I have made all the inquiries I can. Now tell me, Isabella, have you any relatives I can approach? Or rather," she corrected herself, "whom you can approach?"

She knew the answer already. One of the reasons Mr. Frost had wanted Isabella at school was because of the solitariness of her homelife as an only child. But there might be someone the girl could think of.

"No, Miss Catchpole. My father often used to say that we were very important to each other, since there was no one else. My father's parents died when he was a child. My mother's parents died within a short while of each other just before I came here."

She had been home at the time, between the convent and Brighton, and had a vivid sudden memory of being taken to Santiago, all the long dusty journey on the train. The black clothes, even her own, with black silk stockings that made her feel grown up. The horses with silver harness and great black plumes, motionless in the heat. The silver hearse, hung with ribboned wreaths all along the side. A black wreath with gold and purple ribbons on the day it was her grandfather: pink roses and silver ribbons for her grandmother.

Her mother weeping desolately behind her black veil, her father's arm around her, his other hand holding her own. The sun and the sharp black shadows of the cypress trees in the cemetery and all the people who had come to watch.

"My mother," she said inconsequently, "had a sister, but she died when she was a little girl."

Death. A little girl. Her splendid father. It was for old people, but not for her father and little girls.

In her final anguished comprehension, hot terrible tears stole slowly down her cheeks, and she would not lift a hand to wipe them away: if she acknowledged them, then she acknowledged the truth of it all.

"We must take special care of each other," her father had once said, "since there are only the three of us. No one else."

"No friends?" persisted Miss Catchpole.

Desolately Isabella shook her head.

"I have been here seven years, Miss Catchpole. I would not know their friends, nor they me. When my parents came to Enderby every second summer, we were not concerned for friends. We were so happy together, we had no need for friends."

At the memory of all the happy summers spent in the big house set in the green fields under the wide skies of Suffolk, she began to weep in earnest. Here lay all her happy memories. Chile all seemed long ago and half forgotten: real only because her parents were there. Enderby was close and real. They should have been arriving there this evening. The trees growing dark and heavy and the light still lying in the lake. Evening at Enderby.

Miss Catchpole sighed. Such a distasteful task, and going no better than she had expected.

"Isabella," she said to the sobbing girl, "you must be strong. You are not without friends here, and I have been doing all I can to arrange a future for you."

Isabella looked at her with drowned eyes.

Future? What future was there? She hadn't even thought about it, dimly supposing that she would stay where she was until some word came about her parents. As it must do. Grief and sorrow made a strange road she had never before traveled, facing out on a dark highway to a different world.

Future? Now she looked at Miss Catchpole with apprehension rising on top of grief.

"I can't stay here?"

Miss Catchpole was grateful. It was just the opening she wanted, for the difficulty of what she had to say. Had to say, she told herself firmly. What else could she do? In her rights. Completely. Her Academy was not a charitable institution. She was very wise to have it all arranged and ready so the girl would be into her new life without any interval of waiting and wondering.

"You will realize, Isabella, that I have had no money from your father since April. Nor do I see, I am afraid, much hope of any in the future. If everything turns out for the good, then no one will be more pleased than I am." In which she did herself more than justice, as the only thing that held her back was a small snake of fear as to what might happen to her if Isabella's father should indeed be still alive. And reappear. He wasn't, she told herself. He couldn't be. And in any case she was in the right. "For the present," she went on, "you must live and I must live, and neither of us can do that without money."

She shuffled the papers on her desk. Ridiculous to be made uncomfortable by the stare the girl was now fixing on her, as if already she was accusing her of something.

Money? Isabella was thinking. Money? Something that was always there, like the fine houses and the horses and carriages and cars, and all her lovely clothes and the jewels her mother thought suitable for a young girl. And being the most privileged parlor boarder, with first call on Effie.

She had a sudden vision of Effie, who liked her job better in the summer, because she didn't have to do them fires.

Money? What was Catchy up to? She didn't trust her. Had never trusted her, even as quite a young child, and since she had mentioned money, she looked twitchy and guilty and uncomfortable. The tears on Isabella's cheeks dried under new apprehensions.

Miss Catchpole gathered herself together.

"You are very fortunate, Isabella. I have succeeded in finding you both a position and somewhere to live."

Isabella barely understood her.

"Not here?"

Miss Catchpole told herself she must not get exasperated. The girl had been very spoiled, and could not be dealt with as easily as Crump and Mrs. Quickly.

Patiently she said, "Isabella. Now there is no money coming from your father, I am afraid you will have to work to live. I have been very fortunate in placing you in a position in Cubbington's. In the Haberdashery, I think Mr. Crump said."

Isabella had an immediate vision of Beech, with his damp hands and slimy manners. Beech. She and Beech did not belong on the same side of the counter. She felt as if someone had taken one of those ice cream scoops they used in the café and with it removed the whole of her inside.

Leaving a great space into which rushed fear and disbelief.

She couldn't. It was impossible. To work with Beech. And would the place to live be as bad?

She was Isabella Frost. These things were not possible. Isabella Frost. Her name seemed like a talisman to protect her, but in Catchy's still, emotionless face, she saw that these things *were* possible. And fell quiet.

"I couldn't" was all she said, and whispered it. "I couldn't."

It took Miss Catchpole the best part of an hour to make her understand that not only could she, but she must, or be homeless on the streets. Also, for the same reason, she must be prepared to live with Mrs. Quickly.

Isabella could only stare at this, having no idea what it would entail. Submission was creeping in now, numbly, and the bewildered understanding that she was helpless. And there was no one, no one, her bereft mind was beginning to understand, to whom she could turn for help.

The sting, as Miss Catchpole herself would have said, was in the tail.

"You will take with you only the plainest and simplest of your clothes, suitable for Cubbington's. Nothing more. No jewelry. Nothing. All the rest must go, I am afraid, to be sold to pay for these last months as a parlor boarder."

She was even forgetting to assume her expression of professional compassion, unnerved by the way the girl had begun to look at her, no longer distressed, leaving the tears to dry on her face. As though, thought Miss Catchpole indignantly, she found her even more impossible to believe in than her father's death.

Isabella looked down a long moment at the sodden handkerchief in her lap, and then up again at the woman across the desk.

She voiced her own secret fears.

"I think, Miss Catchpole," she said, coldly and clearly, "that it will be very unfortunate for you if my father *does* come back. I will be ready to go tomorrow."

She got up at once and left the room, and Miss Catchpole, trembling a little, fussed unnecessarily with the papers in front of her.

Of course, she told herself. Of course she had a right to do it. Now she must think about her holiday.

chapter
4

In the convent below the ragged village the winter crept toward the rains and the high summer, as in Brighton the late summer in its muting colors began to show the first hints of the coming autumn.

The unknown stranger was still alive, and Liam Power was beginning, when he examined him, to grunt with a certain hope and satisfaction. He was drinking a little less, as though, for the first time since he had rambled into the village, he had found some greater preoccupation. But there were, nevertheless, still days when if the man were going to die, then he would have died with no more than the prayers of the old priest and Sister Jesús María to help him.

Bad days still. And no words that would bring the *médico* to anyone, all his knowledge and his responsibility blasted from his mind by the fire of the *agua ardiente*. Like the sorrow for which he drank.

As the stranger began to swim back in the end to periods of half-consciousness, he became aware in a vague way of the same face often above him. Of hands firmer and less tentative than those of the woman he sensed to be a nun.

The face was pale; colorless as the peeling walls against which he tried to bring it into focus, gaunt, with red hair hanging over the forehead. Hands that moved gently over his head and sometimes did agonizing things to his legs. He wanted to cry out: yell at him to stop, to go away. And that he had a fearful headache. But he never reached the protest, sliding away again helplessly on the tide of unconsciousness: away from pain and effort into welcome darkness.

Liam stood and looked down at him for a long time one day, when he felt he had had him close to consciousness, but he had eluded him once again.

His thin face was taut with concern and concentration.

"Talk to him, Sister," he said then suddenly. "Talk to him. We have to pull him back before he likes it all there too much and becomes an idiot."

Sister Jesús María did not understand him. She so forgot all her rules as to lift big gray-green eyes and fix them on him, wide with surprise. Very lovely girl when she did that, Liam thought. Very lovely. He must surprise her more often. Very lovely. A bit of the Indian about the cheekbones that only added something. He grinned and Sister Jesús María dropped her eyes and blushed as scarlet as the scapular of the Sacred Heart that hung about her neck.

"Talk to him, Doctor?"

"Yes, talk to him. Try and pull him back into this world before he slips into the next one because it's easier. And never mind about a soul for God. We can keep this one for ourselves if we try. Say your prayers to him, if you can't think of anything else to say—as long as you say them with conviction."

From the corner of his half-malicious eye he saw the soft mouth tighten with disapproval. "Tell him all you believe in," said Liam. "Talk to him of the Kingdom of God, Sister. That's enough to get him exercising his mind. Though, by the same God, if he wakes up and proves to be a pagan, you have trouble."

She was composed again, wide telltale eyes masked by drooped lids. But surprised and interested, she understood what the *médico* wanted. A thread. A thread to hold this man to the world. Even though she might herself believe he would be better off in the next. Usually it was love that held such people. The love of their families bulwarking them against death. Holding them.

She looked down at the man on the bed, seemingly no nearer life than on the day he'd come. Ghastly, hollow cheeked, and with the gray look of death hovering around his face. Who but the strange mad *médico* would think to pull him back to life by words?

Liam went off up the long stony hill, covering the ground quickly with his long legs, aware with wry self-knowledge of the sharp shapes of the mountains across the valley against the lemon sky of sunset: aware of them as he could never recall them touching his senses before.

Behind him in the darkening room the young nun pulled up the straight palm-seated chair and began to talk to the white face on the bed. Not, as the *médico* had said, of the Kingdom of God, but against all the rules of her Order, of her own banished childhood in a street of clean white houses in Santiago. After a while she took and held his limp hand, instinctively trying to increase the current of life.

Isabella had in fact been little more than a month in Cubbington's, although to her swollen feet and her bewildered mind it seemed more like a thousand years.

In the surface of her mind that was able to think what she was doing, she tried to remain her neat competent self. One day after another, she told herself. One day after another no matter what it brings: until the day that is different. The day that I get news.

In the long, sleepless night after her interview with Catchpole, she had even managed to come to some sort of terms with the situation, knowing that there was absolutely nothing to do about it at the moment. In order to live, she must do what had so shatteringly come to hand.

That was the calm and thinking side.

On the other side was Beech.

And the facts of what had happened.

And the loss and sorrow that assaulted her when she least expected it with pain so blinding and stupefying that behind her calm beautiful face, she would cry up to God in despair as old as when men sacrificed for their puny wishes to the ancient gods of her native land. Only the huge blue eyes gave any clue to the almost blind madness of her grief and loneliness.

All she had against it was Beech, and the implacable hostility of Mrs. Quickly.

Crump was as watchfully kind as he dared be without showing favoritism, wondering shrewdly all the time what Catchpole was getting from the situation. He was surprised to find the girl accurate and quick to learn all the fiddling notions of Haberdashery, and Beech wore a look of settled astonishment, as a man who has walked down his familiar home street and found a different world at the end of it.

It took him two days to recover and to begin with his mean little mind to savor the pleasures of his new situation. For twenty-four hours he could not adjust to having the tall one with the dark-blue eyes there as his actual inferior. The worst one. The one that got most under his skin. Crump hadn't actually said she was his inferior, but of course she was, wasn't she? Didn't know nothing about anything.

Automatically, from years of habit, he deferred to her for the first few hours almost as obsequiously as before, unable to understand why she was there. Then the whispers from the cold, dark little Staff Room where they ate their dinners began to reach him. All his old resentments and hostilities came back up to the boil, and by the second day he could hardly get fast enough to the shop; resenting every step of the long walk from beyond Kemp Town; too poor to afford a tram and the pavements, even in the mornings, a torture to his tired feet through his paper-thin boots.

Cachet indeed, he had begun to think with revengeful pleasure. Not much cachet now about Miss Frost, as he understood her name was. He sniggered as he dodged between the traffic across the Old Steine. Thaw a bit of the Frost he would, before he was finished with her.

He began on her just before the dinner hour, when the morning's rush was dying down. Isabella was shifting unhappily from foot to aching foot, longing to bend down and open the straps of her shoes, but knowing that if she did, she would never do them up again. Longing for a chair. But this was in the time when even if a shop was empty, the assistants must look always alert and sharp, ready immediately behind the counter for anyone who might come. Or even pass, looking in.

Crump would have liked also a bright and ready smile, but even he knew when he was beaten, driven as far as a grunt of dry amusement at the idea of Beech particularly, with a bright and ready smile. He noted with approval that even in her present state Miss Frost's training had been such that she greeted every customer with a polite, if not bright and ready, smile. Catchpole's loss was his gain, he thought, and then thought again that this was wrong. In some way Catchpole would have gained by this.

Isabella's feet had begun to dominate her over all her other troubles, swollen and aching through the straps of her shoes at the end of the first day. They were no better on the second, and the only respite would be the friendless dinner hour, when they ate in the cheerless Staff Room; indifferent meager food cooked by Mrs. Crump in the rooms above the shop. She could hardly wait for it, furious to be dominated by something as stupid as her feet, who had never before known physical discomfort.

Beech reeled in a spool of black tape, watching her, savoring his moment. He put it in one of the mahogany drawers. Nothing to do for the moment, though no doubt old Crump would be saying he should be showing Miss Frost the stock. Let her find it for herself.

"Feet hurt?" he said, and Isabella thought he was being sympathetic, but even so was still too close to Miss Catchpole's to yield to sympathy from such as Beech.

"No, thank you," she said, trying to ignore the burning ache of them, which seemed even worse for having been mentioned. A rectangle of golden sun lay on the worn floor inside the open doors, and she longed desperately to walk out into it and away; away from this dark shop and from Beech and everything that they implied. To where? She busied herself tidying a basket full of little cards of pearl buttons. Who would sew on her buttons now? she thought, picking on the small problem to defend herself against the large ones. She had never sewn a button in her life. Involuntarily a small sigh escaped her. She would have to learn more than how to sew a button, even to survive for a while until they came back.

Beech pounced on the obvious moment of weakness.

"Same as me now, aren't you, Miss?"

No Miss Frost anymore. Equals now.

She turned and looked at him, from the top of his oiled colorless hair: the shifty eyes filled with mean triumph: pale spotty face and celluloid collar not altogether clean. Right down to the cheap cloth-topped boots already distorted by the bunions of his years of service. The shop was dark. As long as the sun shone outside no bulb must be switched on, but there was light enough for Beech to see her face, and although she said nothing, a flush of pure fury purpled his face.

He was not to know that it was his character she looked at,

even after twenty-four hours: the pettiness inherent in every action: the meanness of the light eyes: his determination in some way, despite his subservience, to try and get the better of every customer he served.

"I don't understand you, Beech," she said then.

However poor, she would never be like Beech and he read the thought in her face.

"No money now," he said venomously. "No more grand Miss Frost."

So it had got about, thought Isabella. Would the faces at the dinner table ever be anything but hostile? Like Beech? Would she finish up ostracized from both worlds, unless she made friends with people like Beech? (She had not been there long enough to know that all the staff disliked Beech just as much as she did.) But how, she wondered, would she ever make values at all? Find people? Make friends? If everybody hated her simply because she had been rich. Spoke differently. Still looked different.

Dear God, she thought, would she herself in the end have that indefinable drab look of these people, struggling to live on what pittance they earned? Every halfpenny, every farthing important. Lose her beauty in exhaustion.

No, no, no, her desperate mind cried. They will come back. It is only for a while. They will come back.

Even one day had brought her to these thoughts. She had understood nothing, she already realized: sheltered beyond belief; incurious of all the worlds that ran beside her own. Now she had shifted. Not forward, but sideways, into one of these other worlds.

Beech saw with mean pleasure that he had disturbed her.

"Two yards of white satin ribbon, please, Mr. Beech." He viciously mimicked her accent. "Saturday mornings are such jolly fun." He had overheard that one, too. "And muddle me change after," he said bitterly in his own voice. All the resentments of the years boiled up until he thought that he would burst.

Cachet. He'd give her cachet. As he had hopelessly promised himself so often.

Isabella was appalled. Ashamed. He had been aware all the time of what they were doing; what they thought their harmless fun on Saturday mornings. Aware, and hating them for it. How he hated them.

Like hardship, she had never met hate before and her voice trembled a little in the face of it. But it was no time to go apologizing to Beech. She may have come crashing, but never to the point of apologizing to Beech, who would only treat her with contempt.

"I think, Beech," she said in her best Catchpole voice, although her hands were shaking, "I think you had better polish the counter before Mr. Crump sees it. Your hands have left sweat marks all over it."

"Mr. Beech to you, Miss," he said venomously, but nevertheless gave the counter an alarmed and furtive rub with his cuff. "You're my junior. Mr. Beech to you."

As time passed, he grew braver and more vindictive, as the understanding slowly seeped into his mind that he really had got Isabella for most of the day in his small and petty power.

"How about Sunday?" he said to her one day at the end of August. It was a gray day of thin rain as if the summer were rushing to autumn, and there were few customers in the gloomy shop. They were tidying out the ranks of tiny drawers behind the counter. Isabella was knowing a moment of small content, her orderly mind enjoying setting back into order the contents of the drawers, jumbled by hasty fingers. Pins; safety pins; packets of needles; a thousand cards of buttons; packing needles; crochet hooks; hooks and eyes, and all the glowing colors of the reels of Sylko.

She tried to ignore him, but there was a sense of pressure in his voice, warning her that he was trying something new.

What now? she thought. She did every smallest job as perfectly as possible, not because of Mr. Crump, but to evade the snide and condescending reproaches of Beech. If she did not answer him, he would come closer, and that she could not bear. The smell of sweat and his own permanent anxiety; clothes worn too long and never cleaned; the cheap macassar oil that smarmed his hair.

She moved away a little, but she answered him.

"What do you mean, Sunday?"

The one brief day of respite when she sat in her miserable little room and put her feet into her shoes only to go downstairs for the ill-cooked meal that Mrs. Quickly graced by the name of Sunday dinner. Isabella was always hungry on Sunday, and it had taken a couple of Sundays to understand that if she wanted more to eat, she must go to the steamy crowded pie shop on the corner of the street. Sunday was holiday for Mrs. Quickly also, and she made that very plain.

"I mean Sunday," said Beech, as though she were a bit simple, and there was a light of excitement and something more in his pale eyes. "Will you walk out with me Sunday? Up the cliffs or somewhere like that. Somewhere quietlike."

He almost leered.

"Walk out?"

He was impatient.

"Go for a walk. Don't you know anything? Be my girl. We could have a right time up on the cliffs or somewhere."

Vividly into her mind came the views through the lifted blind on Sunday afternoons. The park. Littered with couples who in the new freedoms kissed and fondled each other while the music thumped from the bandstand. Another world they giggled and pushed to watch. Quite certain they were watching something that would never be like that for them. Without privacy or dignity. Long, pale legs of the braver girls and boaters discarded on the grass, and in the end they would get up and go away, their arms around each other.

Was that what Beech wanted? A right time, up on the cliffs? It appalled her almost more than anything else that had happened to her.

"No," she said vehemently. "No."

Up Beech's face crept an ugly dark flush: accumulation of an adult life full of similar rejections.

"Too good for me still, eh? Still Miss Isabella Frost. Well, you ain't, see?" Beech's carefully refined accent fell apart under the torrent of his resentment and anger. "Yer nobody. And who else but the likes of me is going to look at a shopgirl? That's all you are. A shopgirl. You might as well settle for me, Miss Hoity Toity, for you'll get no better."

Numbly Isabella looked down at the little skeins of beads she was disentangling. Lovely rich colors for the embroidery of the kind of dresses she had always worn herself. Deep ruby red and black and amethyst and blue. Pure white and green and gold and silver. So pretty. She had a sudden piercing memory of going with her mother to her modiste, and being given just such small skeins of beads to play with. Clearly she could remember the pleasure of the lovely colors, exactly as she saw them now. A white dress, she was wearing, and soft kid shoes with two straps for the buttons. Red.

Lost happiness ripped her with pain, but she would die before she allowed Beech to see it. She hoped he had not noticed that the little skeins of beads were trembling in her fingers. It would give him such pleasure.

Why had she never thought about what he had just said? It was true. No man would ever look at her now, except the kind who would be interested in a shopgirl. For Beech was right. That was all she was.

She had been so desperately building hour upon hour and day upon day, and trying to accept her situation, that she had never thought about a future. If they did not come back—and the very thought filled her with sick fear—would she spend all her days behind a shop counter, growing old and sharp and sour like Miss Fellowes round in Modes? Unless she took someone like Beech. And to do that, even for a Sunday afternoon, would be to capitulate; to accept. Instead of fighting her situation with every corner of her mind. Holding fiercely to the certainty that it was only temporary. That her father would come back.

Why only her father? Already for some reason she had almost reached the drear acceptance of her mother's death.

But Beech!

Not that anyone else seemed likely to approach her. The rest of the staff were civil but carefully distant. Beech!

Fiercely she turned to him, the lovely colors of the beads dripping from her fingers; reflected in the deep polish of the counter; glowing in the dim light. The blue eyes blazed with disgust and almost panic fear.

"I wouldn't go out with you," she said, "if you were the only man in the world."

As at that moment he almost was.

In her world.

She was close to tears. Miserably she knew that she was only making life harder for herself. She didn't have to go out with him, but she should at least have tried to get on with Beech. At least to get him to accept her. But she was not yet able, mistaken though she knew it was. She was still too much Isabella Frost, in spite of her tired face and unpressed dress and swollen, aching feet. It had never occurred to her what would happen to her feet.

Beech never forgave her. His thin mouth tight with all the inferiorities and resentments she had so deeply increased, he lay awake at night in his hard narrow bed, planning a campaign of harassment that was almost instinctive. What he could not get, he would take, insofar as he could take it.

There was not much room behind the counter in Haberdashery, and Beech began to find it too little altogether. Should he need to pass Isabella, he would manage always to brush his arm across her breasts, or seem to lose his balance and lean on her, going back to his customer with bright eyes and a small pleased smirk, leaving Isabella sick with disgust and fury.

Should she be serving, he would manage to give her bottom a quick fondle as he passed behind her, assiduously busy then with some triviality. It was Isabella that Crump always noticed, frowning that his showpiece girl inside the front door seemed already to have lost much of her poise. Downright confused she seemed to be at times.

Isabella dared not complain. Beech had been there years. She might lose her job, and what then? Hardly could she bring herself to go to work, where Beech's thin smile told her he knew he was being successful in making her life a misery. And loved it.

She felt degraded beyond any imagining. Every lecherous brush of Beech's body seemed to do her some deep and dreadful damage. To mark her in some way, so that if her parents did come back, she would be a stranger to them. Sullied.

It seemed like a hundred years, but was in reality only just a month after she had started, when she came one evening out of the peeling back door that was so grandly described as the Staff Entrance of the shop. It led into a small grimy alley, untouched in its gray drabness by the gold of the evening sun. Chill, as though it had never been warmed. Nothing but the backs of other shops and the blank windows above them, or the drab curtains of poor rooms for rent.

She hated it, and even feared it, and always hurried to get out of it, thinking sometimes of how it would look in the winter with its few feeble gaslights. It seemed to her to reflect everything her life had so suddenly become.

This evening a small figure stepped out in front of her.

"Miss Isabella."

"Effie!"

It had been a bad and horrible day with Beech and there was nothing to go home to but Mrs. Quickly. Isabella stood and looked a long moment at the plain, friendly little face in the shadows of the alley. Even with no words spoken the expression of kindness and concern was too much for her.

"Effie," she said again, and the helpless miserable tears began to roll down her cheeks.

"Oh, Miss," cried Effie, horrified. "Oh, Miss Isabella, is it as bad as that!"

Isabella struggled to smile at her, already ashamed of her weakness.

"No, Effie. It's just—just that I knew you'd be kind to me."

"And no one else is," said Effie grimly.

Even to Effie, all Isabella's training and dignity forbade her to complain.

"It's not too bad, Effie. It's just me."

Effie's lips tightened.

"I'll walk home with you, Miss Isabella."

They walked in silence the shadowed length of the alley between the dark walls and opaque windows. Employees of Cubbington's were not supposed to come out into North Street until they were well clear of the shop. Effie was silent for distress; seeing Miss Isabella white and tired and looking downright defeated. She wasn't managing, poor Miss Isabella, and what in the world would happen to her if she lost that job? Something worse, for left to herself she could find no better. Rage rose in her again against Catchpole, who could in the first place have found her something better.

Isabella was silent because she felt totally spent. It was so

NO PRICE TOO HIGH   79

unfair. She had been doing her job well until Beech began his tricks, and now she knew that Mr. Crump thought her all kinds of a fool. Effie's kind concerned face was all that was needed to let loose her carefully damned-up sense of total dereliction. Even Effie, poor as she was, had a place in life. A home to go to. Where she would find a mother. However hard, it was a home. If she spoke at all, she knew that she would weep, and that if she started she might never stop.

"Wot's it reely like, Miss Isabella?"

She herself would have thought it a grand step up in life to get a position on the haberdashery in Cubbington's, but she realized that Isabella would not see it in the same way.

Isabella choked back the tears.

"My feet," she said, choosing the smaller of her persecutions.

Effie looked down at where Isabella's once neat ankles bulged miserably over her black shoes. She found it hard to believe that once she had polished those shoes until they shone, and laid out the stockings to go with them. She clucked with pity and annoyance.

"Hasn't that Quickly helped you with your feet? My goodness, she should know, on hers all the hours God gave."

"I don't think she likes me very much."

Once again she choked back the tears. Beech hated her and Mrs. Quickly didn't like her. Or want her. She seemed to resent doing anything for her that she did not feel compelled to do for fear of Miss Catchpole. She could not know, and might have liked her better if she did, that Isabella would have suffered anything on earth before she would go back to Catchpole with complaints. Or anything. The only way she saw herself, in the last moments before she fell asleep in her lumpy bed, was in lonely dreams of going back to confront the woman with her father at her side. The mean fat pig would go into a jelly with sheer fright.

Still so young. Battling with miseries she had never dreamt of.

"I'm so lonely, Effie," she burst out, and was at once ashamed and apologized. All her life she had been taught that you did not embarrass other people with your miseries. They usually, she had been taught, had enough of their own. Hers should have been the other side of the coin: learning with her mother the charitable works that diverted some of their great wealth to the poor.

Now she was the poor, and involuntarily she sighed, finding it at the moment more than she could handle.

Effie shot a shrewd glance at the pale unhappy face: tears spiking the long lashes. Trembling, she estimated furiously, on the edge of giving in completely. And what then?

She did a quick and slightly desperate calculation.

"Tell you what you need, Miss Isabella," she said.

They were crossing at a corner rounded by a gray stone public house, frosted windows glowing in the dull evening with warm lamplight, its outer doors of polished mahogany standing invitingly open. Looked respectable enough, thought Effie. Clean and cared for and neither drunks nor sniveling children round the door of the Public Bar. Set to catch the end of the North Street trade before the district went down into the small streets.

Effie hesitated a moment and then put her rounded chin into the air and marched firmly for the door of the Saloon Bar.

"Come on, Miss Isabella."

Isabella did not even know enough to look doubtful and appalled. At the moment she would have done anything, gone anywhere, that Effie told her, so pitifully grateful was she for a kind word and face. Obediently she followed her in through the open doors and the swing ones inside it.

She looked round without shock or real curiosity, accepting that she found herself in a snug, clean place of frosted glass and great big gilded mirrors; shining mahogany and red-buttoned velvet. There were little places sort of like pews in church, with tables in between them. Effie shepherded her protectively to one of these, glaring down the few men who stopped with their drinks even halfway to their lips to stare.

It was like, thought Effie tartly, bringing the Virgin Mary in person into a church. None of 'em would believe it.

"Sit there, Miss Isabella."

Isabella sat, offering her same mild curiosity to the open gaping admiration of the men. Lost in these last weeks to her own beauty, seeing herself only worn and tired in the dim old mirrors of the shop, obsessed with her feet and her unhappiness, it no longer even occurred to her that men might find her beautiful. Beech and his filthy habits was something quite different.

Effie, with tight-pursed mouth, and looking as if she knew exactly what she was doing, marched up staunchly to the bar. Behind it a well-found lady with a golden shingle patted her hair and toyed with the cascade of long glittering beads down the front of her purple satin dress. But there was something so indomitable about Effie's small figure, little more than head high above the polished bar, that she gave no more than a flicker of black, curious eyelashes. Odd couple. But then she saw more odd couples than she'd ever even remember.

"Two ports, please, Miss."

"With lemon?"

Effie didn't know. She knew her mother liked to go down to the Public on their corner on Saturday nights and have a small port with her friends. Small reward for a week of endless work. But Effie did not know if she drank lemon with it. That was the Public, anyway. Things would be different in the Saloon, but she couldn't take Miss Isabella into the Public. Lemon, she reckoned, would cost more. Better not have lemon.

"Neat," she said.

Have to make do with her shoes for another couple of weeks for this. As long as Catchpole didn't see them. She barely paid a living wage, but expected her servants always to look neat and tidy. Uniform provided, and heaven help you if you tore it or anything, but not shoes. She took out her thin worn purse and fumbled in the frayed lining for a coin, taking the two small glasses of warm ruby liquid back to their table.

"Thanks, Miss." When she got there she carefully placed one in front of Isabella.

"There, Miss Isabella, drink that. Make you feel better."

Tentatively, still passive with obedience, Isabella sipped.

"It's nice, Effie," she said, surprised, as if, like medicine, anything good for her could not be nice. Catchpole had said Cubbington's and Mrs. Quickly would be good for her.

"Do you good," said Effie again.

After a few sips some color began to seep back into Isabella's cheeks, and she sat up a little straighter and looked round her curiously.

"What is this place, Effie?"

God pity yer innocence, thought Effie. The sooner you lose it the better.

"It's a public house, Miss."

"A what?"

"A public house. Place where people can come an' buy themselves a drink. Like you an' me."

"How nice," said Isabella.

Effie sighed. What if she saw the Public by closing time, and even the Saloon was often little better, with all the men reeling out onto the street and the women shrieking with laughter at their own coarse jokes, an' all the kids waiting there for hours for them to come home.

"I've never been in anywhere like this in my life," said Isabella with interest. The port was warming her and her eyes had grown a little bright.

"Nor me, Miss," said Effie tersely, with bitter truth.

That was how she knew all about it. Sent down by her mother to get her father home, when she was no higher than the doorstep. Hanging round outside the Public with all the other kids, waiting for him to come out, genial and unsteady with brown ale, the money spent that he should have brought home for food and clothes for the children. That she remembered all the time he lived, and the row then when he got home with next to nothing. She would hide down in the bed beside her sisters and pull the thin blanket over her head not to hear them yelling at each other. But her mother had still loved him. She had wept like Miss Isabella when he died.

Isabella did not understand the lovely creeping warmth that was beginning to take over her stomach. She only knew that for some reason she felt much happier, suffused by affection and gratitude for the small stolid figure in the black dress across from her on the crimson velvet.

Effie. Her only friend.

She was exhausted, and it was the first drink of her life. She looked at Effie and felt she wavered a little, and hoped she wasn't feeling faint. For she knew suddenly that she could tell her about Beech. All about Beech. She even began, as she spoke, to find Beech funny, giggling as she mimicked for Effie his awful smarmy ways with the customers. She took another sip of the lovely red drink, noticing regretfully that it was almost finished. Effie looked very bright and clear to her now, looking across the polished table with soft kind eyes that invited confidence. She told her all of it. Had to tell someone. And Effie would understand. Effie seemed to understand everything. Her friend. Told her about Beech brushing against her breasts and fondling her bottom. Told her she couldn't work like that and she was sure Mr. Crump thought she wasn't doing so well, and she was awake all night in fear that she would lose her job. She began to giggle again as she told her about his awful hair oil and always having to polish the counter after his sweaty hands, and looked down with surprise at her empty glass.

Suddenly in the middle of the giggles she was weeping again, tears pouring helplessly down her cheeks, and Effie's face was black with fury.

"Come along, Miss Isabella," she said. "We better go. People's looking at us."

She got her out onto the street and steered her as fast as she could toward Mrs. Quickly's. Isabella was talking like a machine gun from the War, babbling away suddenly with all the fears and terrors she had crushed since she left Catchpole's. Effie listened, holding her arm and steadying her steps, and she was grim with pain for her. Feeling herself old and wise and sad in the matter of trouble. Listening patiently, with no idea of what she should do.

"Effie. Supposing they don't come back and I have to marry someone like Beech. He asked me to walk out with him, you know. He did."

Bloomin' cheek, thought Effie. Beech indeed.

"They'll come back, Miss Isabella," she said indomitably, for she could not bear to think of what might happen to the girl if they didn't. She was like a babe unborn against the world.

Isabella grew more calm, believing her because she wanted to. Believing the only reassurance she had had in weeks.

The port was not quite yet done with her.

As they came up to the house, she burst again into helpless giggles.

"Mrs. Slowly," she said, and thought it wildly funny. "Mrs. Slowly."

"I hate her," she added then.

In the hierarchy of the school service it was hard to know who came highest, the laundry woman or the upstairs maid, but it was the small, determined figure of Effie that had all the authority.

"Quickly," she said at once accusingly. "Why didn't you tell Miss Isabella how to look after her feet?"

Mrs. Quickly, toothless, and not finding her company worthy of her teeth, looked up from the ironing she would surely be doing in whatever Paradise waited for her. She plonked the iron down on its brass stand.

"Not my business," she said sourly. "Bed and board's my business, no more."

Effie snorted, and without asking cleared the ironed sheets off the seat of the carpet chair, ignoring Mrs. Quickly's glare.

"Sit down, Miss Isabella," she said, and with a last murmur of "Mrs. Slowly," Isabella subsided into the chair. Why, she wondered vaguely, did they not seem to get as tired as she did, unaware of Effie's aching back and legs and raw chapped hands at the end of every day. Or that the bag of Epsom salts that Mrs. Quickly reluctantly produced was for her own exhausted feet and swollen ankles, which she soaked as the one pleasure of her day, each night when Isabella was gone up to her room.

"Take off your shoes and stockings, Miss Isabella."

She settled her in blissful agony, her miserable feet in a bowl of hot water and Epsom salts. Isabella could have wept again with the pain and pleasure of it.

Mrs. Quickly looked at her shrewdly over the iron, her toothless jaws clamped together.

"Girl looks funny to me," she said. "Like she'd had a drink. Don't want none of that in my house. Respectable, I am. None of that."

Effie ignored her.

"Now," she said with satisfaction. "We'll deal with that Beech. Got any protectors, Quickly?"

Isabella did not understand her. She wiggled her toes and felt the exquisite relaxation.

"Course I have," said Mrs. Quickly. She spat on an iron as though it were all her personal troubles. "Think I can afford a fortune in shoe leather, out on them streets morning, noon and night with the cart?"

"Gimme four," said Effie, indifferent to her complaints. "I'll give 'em back to you. And the hammer?"

Mrs. Quickly jerked her head.

"Shelf in the yard." Take the price of them from the girl, she would, if they didn' come back.

Effie took Isabella's shoes and thrust her way through the forest of damp sheets. She could be heard hammering vigorously out in the yard. Mrs. Quickly continued ironing as if she were alone, but a blessed ease was stealing through Isabella's feet, and with it some ease of the fearful, hopeless loneliness that was beginning to destroy her.

Effie came back in, mischievous satisfaction in her pale eyes.

"This'll do fer Beech, Miss Isabella."

On the heel and toe of each beautiful shoe was a small crescent of heavy metal.

"What are those?" asked Isabella, and Mrs. Quickly gave a derisive snort.

Effie wheeled on her.

"She bain't used to it like you and I are, Quickly," she snapped. "Wouldn't do you no harm to remember that a bit."

She turned back to Isabella.

"They're so you don't wear out your shoes so quickly. Protectors," she said. "But I'll tell you how to use them on Beech. Put him in his place."

She told her, and a slow smile spread over Isabella's face.

"I have to go now, Miss Isabella. Get back to school."

"Thank you, Effie. Thank you for everything. Thank you."

"Bye, Quickly," she said, and was gone, leaving Isabella with the first faint, exhilarating thought of fighting back.

Beech had by now assumed a sneery, triumphant expression. Got the girl on the run, he had, and with a bit of persistence he'd run her out of the job. Crump was already getting tetchy.

Isabella clacked and skidded to Cubbington's the morning after Effie's visit. Cheered by one small evidence of companionship and care, she was even smiling a little at the idea of dealing with

Beech, livened by the bright late August morning that laid even the shabby alley with a mellow gold light, telling of the autumn that was near.

Experimentally she stopped occasionally and stamped heavily with her heel. Grinning irresistibly.

It worked. Beech, so sure of himself, was defenseless. The first time he came up behind her with his confident, groping hands, she did as Effie had told her, and stamped down with all her strength and her metalled heel, onto the cloth instep of Beech's buttoned boots.

His choked bellow of agony brought Crump at once, red in the face as Beech himself.

"What is the matter, Beech? How dare you make a noise like that?"

Beech stared at him, scarlet with the sudden pain, involuntary furious tears in his pale eyes. Bitch. Young bitch. Beside him Isabella went on demurely sorting needles.

"Musta choked on something, sir," he said.

"Don't do it again," he roared. "I won't have it." Even as he crushed Beech he noticed from the corner of his eye that his showpiece young lady on the front counter looked more like herself today. He was pleased, both for the shop and, being a kind man at heart, for the child herself, whom he pitied. Had Beech but known it, she was never in any danger of losing her job, while his own hung by a thread.

He gave Beech one further quelling look that put the fear of God in him, and moved on in his own soft unprotected boots.

Beech did not trouble her again, nor did he ever as long as she was in Cubbington's speak to her one word more than was necessary. She looked almost with reverence at the small bright crescents on her shoes. Protectors. True, she thought, absolutely true.

The small victory did much to cheer her.

It was a matter of living from day to day, and even if the bigger news did not come, some one thing made one day better than another. Putting them one upon another carefully, precarious as a card castle, to pass the time until her world came right again.

"Come again, Effie," she had said to the little maid. "Please come again."

But Effie had little time. Little time from the school, and after that even less time from the demands and responsibilities of the brood at home.

It was almost a fortnight before she came again, two weeks in which Isabella had begun perversely almost to miss the persecutions of Beech. Without them there was nothing; the day's work and the careful distant greetings of her workmates; the lonely walk home along the darkening alleys, and after her meager meal, the evening alone in the sad peeling room above Mrs. Quickly's front door. She would have even welcomed an hour in the steaming atmosphere of the kitchen; indeed offered to help. But Mrs. Quickly had made it clear at once that her duties did not include having Isabella under her feet. Bed and board. Friendship of any kind was not included.

She had tried to go walking on the Sundays, even venturing onto the sinful territory of the Pier, passing the gold-spiked gates with a sense of excitement and adventure. Only to be driven out again by the persistent advances of the footloose young men who haunted the Pier on Sundays, marching the slatted boards to pick up girls more willing than Isabella; walking with their arms round one another in giggling groups, flashing inviting eyes and ready and willing to "get off."

Isabella found it all almost frightening, and she began to be depressed again, feeling she was different from all the world, where these young people seemed to enjoy themselves in ways she had never known. Everyone seemed to know where they belonged, except for Isabella Frost, who was beginning to feel that she belonged to nowhere, and to no one.

She felt quite sick with pleasure to see Effie waiting for her outside the back door, and was so full of her own relief that it took her a little while to realize that Effie's round pale face was alive with excitement. She could hardly wait for greetings, while Isabella in her isolation could not make enough of them.

"Miss Isabella. I've something for you. No," she added, seeing her face. "Not news. But summat good."

She snapped open the frayed leather purse and pulled out a cutting from a local paper.

"Bain't able to read, as I told you," she said, "but Cook was reading this out in the kitchen. Makin' a joke of it, see. Telling the housekeeper she should go for it. Just the thing for you, Miss Isabella. Right as rain for you."

In the shadowed alley Isabella stood on the cobbles and read the little piece of paper.

> Young, well-educated girl of good appearance required
> as companion to titled lady in well-found house in Rot-
> tingdean. Live in. Call evenings 6:00–7:00 P.M.

Isabella stared at it, oblivious of the fact that it was being pulped by rain in which Effie had been patiently waiting half an hour. Naked fear lay on her face. Better, to be sure, than Cubbington's and Mrs. Quickly, but it had a terrifying air of permanence. As she was she could tell herself that she was only in a position where Catchpole had put her. Only waiting. Passing the time.

This, if she got it, would be a whole new life chosen by herself. A rejection of hope. As though she had given them up.

Briefly she looked down at Effie, who read her like the books she could not understand.

"Better place to wait, Miss Isabella," she said practically. "And a better place, I'd reckon, for getting letters. Don't trust that Quickly, I don't."

Isabella folded the piece of paper.

"I'll go now," she said.

chapter
5

It would have been about the time that Isabella left Miss Catchpole's that Liam came loping one day down the mountain from the village to the convent. There had been heavy rain for days and the steep track was still a running stream of treacherous yellow mud: the sky was sunless and opaque, and cloud hung low along the mountains, ripped to drifting tattered shreds by a bitter wind driving from the high snows.

Liam huddled his poncho closer round him, hating the cold: in truth no poncho but a threadbare blanket with a hole cut for his head, given to him in his first shivering winter by someone little better provided than himself. Close around his ears was pulled a blue-and-white-striped woollen cap with a pompom on the top of it, in which the somber Indians found him so bizarre they did not know whether to laugh behind their hands or revere him as one of the chosen of the gods.

It was one of the few things he had rammed haphazard into a haversack the day he had fled Valparaiso, never pausing to think where he would go, or what he might need. What came had come by chance, and with the bag in his hand he had walked blindly to the edges of the city and then begged a lift from a man with a team of mules, driving north. It could equally well have been south. All he asked was to put space between him and the place he had once loved so much, and to do that he might well have walked unknowing into the dark tropical sea.

He had no idea if it was days later, or weeks, when he saw the lonely village on the high side of the mountain, and as randomly as he had asked to be picked up, he asked to be set down.

The driver, a garrulous man who had thought to enjoy some talking on his lonely journey, was not sorry to see him go. Not one

word had he spoken in the actual eight days they had been traveling, other than to say thank you for food and offer to pay his share
of it. Staring straight in front of him, as if he saw as little as he
spoke. And for all the man could see, it was the same all through
the nights. Unnatural. Possessed. As he drove away, the man
blessed himself against the possible evil, and looked back once at
the tall figure in crumpled city clothes, staring up at the mountain
as if it were perhaps beyond him to tackle the long climb.

No business of his. He whipped up his mules, and as if it were
a signal, Liam Power started up the track to the village.

He had never taken to the *agua ardiente* to make a refuge from
his memory. Rather to protect himself against the terror of its
onset. Anesthetizing himself to the degree where even his few possessions from the past meant nothing. Negative objects that chance
had brought to his possession.

But this morning, as he pulled on the woolly cap against the
cold, memory had caught him like the thrust of a dagger. Mortal.
Treacherous. Surprising him with pain so dreadful that he gasped:
standing immobile, waiting appalled for it to ebb away.

It would not go. It brought to him another wind, sharp and
unbidden in his mind. Cool and fresh and splendid, cracking like
pistol shots in the sails of his yacht as he whipped over Dublin Bay:
sun in the green-blue sea and an edge of white along his wake: the
mail boat beginning its swing into the arms of the harbor at Dun
Laoghaire. The grass green and running with the wind on Howth.

And dear merciful God, Bridget with him, no cap for her,
black hair streaming in the wind. When they were both young. No
more than children. Long from marriage and his wanderlust that
brought them in the end to Valparaiso.

They were young enough even then, God knew.

He leaned against the dirty wall and breathed deeply, no less
shattered than if it were a physical injury, astonished and terrified
that he could still feel who thought he had stilled pain and memory
forever. Into nothingness.

Very slowly he moved away from the wall, still moving as if
injured, and made his way out through the door and along the path
between the draggled winter plants. In the small plaza he came to a
halt again and looked numbly at the patient villagers still scrabbling

in the liquid mud for their possessions and beginning to rebuild the pathetic homes that had been washed away. God help them, some part of his mind still managed to think, they had desperate need of a few days' sun to dry it all out. There would be the usual crop of sickness and fevers after the lot of them being sodden for so long.

Still shaken, he picked his way through the yellow puddles, and it never occurred to him that he had not reached for the bottle. As though he knew it hopeless to look for protection. Memory had struck and he could not staunch it.

And Groucho had brought a message an hour ago. Sister Jesús María wanted to see him urgently about the man down the hill. El Perdido, they had begun to call him. The Lost One.

It was three days since he had been down there, too much occupied up to his knees in muddy water with old Father Ignacio at his side; trying to help salvage the floating sheets of tin and linoleum; the sodden cardboard and the old carpets and the bedspreads that these poor miserable souls called homes.

Curiosity was overriding the terrible pain of memory. The patient had lain so long with no more than useless flashes of half-consciousness that Liam, inexperienced in head wounds, had begun to wonder if he would ever do any better.

He was allowed to come and go now as he wished, through the front door of the convent, reserved for visitors, before the locked doors of the convent itself; given all these permissions by a nebulous Reverend Mother he had never seen. Nor would, her words coming to him like the word of God, down through Sister Jesús María. He pushed the door and heard it grating over the wet flags of the outer patio. Groucho had been going to hang it ever since the earthquake, when it had been shaken on its hinges. But like so many other things it had come to rest in the gentle world of *mañana*.

Sister Jesús María was waiting for him at the inner door, beyond which she was not allowed to pass, and once more excitement had opened and lifted the gray-green eyes.

"Doctor! He is conscious!"

Liam stopped.

"D'you say so! Really conscious? Speaking?"

They had been praying for him up in the village, lighting

candles in the shabby church. It may be that their God, who had forsaken him, had worked a miracle for El Perdido.

"Speaking, yes," said the nun, "but—"

Liam had not waited for her, and her long skirts rustled unsuitably as she tried to keep up with him along the passage, her big wooden rosary beads clacking together at her waist.

The yellow light of the winter day filled the little room, and as he leaned over the bed, he found himself looking into a pair of the darkest blue eyes he had ever seen. By damn, like sapphires.

Wide open. But incurious, devoid of any of the anxiety and confusion common to people recovering consciousness after an accident in a strange place. Plagued at once by all the circumstances their unconsciousness had cut short.

Perhaps, thought Liam hopefully, it had just been a long time. And it would come.

The blue eyes ranged over him, accepting him without question. Poncho and sailing cap and all. Exactly as they had probably accepted Sister Jesús María.

"Hallo," said Liam clearly and carefully. "Glad to have you back with us."

"Hallo," said the man weakly.

"I'm a doctor," Liam said. "I am afraid you have had an accident. Do you remember?"

If he remembered, he would think it had happened yesterday. Time eclipsed. But there was no answer at all. No reaction. The eyes were empty.

"Do you know," asked Liam, "who you are?"

A long silence, the first faint glimmer of anxiety in the blue eyes, which quickly faded.

No. No identity. No panic yet. Only for a fraction of a second had he even realized he should know who he was. Maybe they all had longer to wait. Or maybe they would wait for nothing, the man a vegetable until some mindless death.

"You have no idea what your name is?"

"Thirsty," was all he said, his dry lips mumbling, unaware of all the long weeks of Sister Jesús María pouring gruel into him through a tube.

She brought him water and lifted his head a little, and thirstily he drank. It seemed to revive him a little. She left the room and came back with another straw pillow, covered in patched cotton. As his head was raised, the blue eyes roamed round the room, a little more life and curiosity touching them.

"Where am I?"

The standard question, but without fear or anxiety, or any knowledge that he should be anywhere else. When Liam had told him, he looked at him blankly.

"Means nothing?" Liam asked.

He shook his head and winced.

"That hurt," he said. "And I have a headache."

"I would imagine," Liam said drily. "When you take half a mountain on top of you, it's apt to leave you with a headache."

He told him then all that they knew of him, and what had happened to bring him where he was.

"A *temblor*," he said, amazed, and Liam noted that he used the Spanish word for earthquake, although all else he said was in English.

An educated voice. And a cared-for body, although God knew, it would never be the same again.

"And how much am I hurt—now," the man asked then.

"You took a terrible clobber on the head, but it's healing nicely."

He did not tell him that although the surface wound was healing, every moment at the present was filling him with alarm as to what had happened inside the head. Still, it was early days yet, and he had been unconscious for a long time. He might be no more than confused. Moithered, as Liam's mother used to say. Moithered was about the right word. The inside of his head, poor creature, was probably clean close to scrambled egg.

"I'm afraid both your legs were smashed up below the knee, but they've done well, too, thank God. We'll have the timber off them within a week or so."

The very immobility of the patient had helped to heal them, although they had yet to know if he would ever walk again. Depended on himself, largely, once they had healed. If he had the guts. Probably he would. But badly. Never without sticks or crutches. He could do without knowing that for the time being.

Liam tried one more question.

"You have no idea where you were going, or coming from, when the *temblor* struck?"

The tired voice showed a flash of spirit.

"If I remembered that, for heaven's sake, wouldn't I remember a *temblor?*"

But there was weariness now, and bafflement, and anxiety, showing in his eyes. Liam patted him on the shoulder and gave him a warm encouraging grin.

"Yer doing fine," he said, and his accent was broad and rich. "We'll have you galloping around again in no time."

The tired emaciated face on the patched pillow lit for a moment with a faint answering smile, touched even in his extremity by the irresistible charm; the warm conviction that bred belief.

Then the translucent lids dropped and he was asleep.

"Well, that's better for him than coma," Liam said, but across the bed his eyes met those of the nun, and there was little in either of them but a doubtful question. Had they merely dragged him with such long difficulty from one darkness, to find him immersed in another almost more terrible? Please God no, whispered Sister Jesús María.

"Keep talking to him, Sister. Keep talking to him every minute he's awake. Keep his mind struggling a little, but not too much. I'll be down meself, too. And ease him upwards. No reason now he can't sit. But he'll be a jelly. We must get his strength back with all the good food at our disposal."

Sister Jesús María thought of all the poor winter fields washed down the mountain by the days of rain.

"You are making a joke, doctor," she said.

"Yes," said Liam, but he looked at her gently, and she had to look away, crushing the thoughts she was driven often to confess. God bless the little creature, Liam was thinking. She'd know all the difficulties without telling, stealing pillows from the stores, no doubt, or from the other nuns. She managed to conjure up from somewhere everything her patients needed. Especially this one. He would never have a better chance.

He went with her along the tiled hall to the big whitewashed room where his few other patients lay on beds that were no more than wooden frames strung precariously with canvas: the men divided from the women by a haphazard curtain hung down the middle, leaving pain and suffering almost without distinction. An ancient nun crept between them, fretful and protesting as the patients themselves, and the air was sour with the smell of sickness, the high windows shuttered against the wind.

"And when, Doctor," she said, complaining, as he went, "when will Sister Jesús María be back to help me here? She has only one patient, and I all these. What is so special about him?"

"Soon," Liam soothed her, hiding his revulsion to the old tortoise face that had long forgotten all the sorrows and the joys and the sufferings of the world; that still lay unguarded at certain times, in the eyes of Sister Jesús María. "Soon. He is conscious now. Getting better."

Back in the small room the young nun looked down at her sleeping charge and prayed almost desperately to God to help her avoid the sin of singularization. A good nun loved all the world without discrimination, and it was her duty to try to love even more the ones she hated.

She was guilty, please God forgive her and help her, of becoming totally involved, and absorbed, in two people. The enigma of the gray-faced man, deep in exhausted sleep from his first effort back into the world, which all her young curiosity reached out to solve. The bond was already formed with him through all the long hours of talking, holding his limp dry hand: holding to his very life: dredging up for him all the forgotten simple happinesses of her world that the convent had bidden her forget. Years of discipline she had thrust aside. And would God ever give her the grace to get it back?

To get it back through endless hours of prayer and silence, with no more than her turn of duty with old Sister Concepción in the big ward, which had always before been enough of fulfillment and satisfaction. But now there was sick guilty fear that she might not even be there when the *médico* came, always unannounced, appearing suddenly, bending his red head to the small door. Bringing to her a sick shock of pleasure that she knew to be an occasion of sin.

And today he had come in that ridiculous hat that made him

look like the little foreign children she had seen in the winters in Valparaiso.

Once more she looked at the sleeping man, her hands folded in her sleeves in the correct gesture of submission. How long, she wondered with an unbearable sorrow. How long before he was better, and she would be freed of the loved occasions of sin?

Outside Liam faced up the mountain, leaning against the screaming wind that tore the clouds in ribbons across its face. The day of memory, he thought sardonically. The day of memory. His was plaguing him as it had never done before, pain as though the wind itself were tearing and probing at a rotten tooth.

And the other one seemed to have lost his. Well, let him find it and good luck to him. He hoped it brought him happiness. For him it was to be held at bay. With almost blind terror. A beast crouched ready and waiting to leap out and ravage him: as it had done this morning over the woolly cap. Only the knowledge of the bitter wind in his ears prevented him from tearing it from his head. Memory. A beast he had thought already safely dead.

As he walked blindly across the small plaza of the village, those who saw his face kept well away, and crossed themselves and sighed. God keep their families in health for the next few days, for it was clear even to their ignorance that for the *médico*, these days would be bad ones.

From the steps of the church Father Ignacio watched him and sighed that man could so destroy himself. He turned back to helping the people scavenge for little more than rubbish to rebuild their flattened houses. Even the very dogs cringed and hid from the wind, and Liam's door when he reached it was plastered with the dead fragments of the summer flowers along his path.

He kicked it open and the wind and the dust and dead leaves and rubbish raced into the room ahead of him, and in his desperate haste for solitude he cursed and almost wept with the time it took him to get it closed again.

Closing out the intrusive world into half-darkness: the broken slats of the shutters pulled down on the gray day.

Solitude. Forgetfulness. Obliteration.

He did not even trouble to take off the poncho or the woolly cap before crashing onto the unmade bed, reaching for the bottle that would defeat the enemy. Memory. Memory was for the other one down the hill, and good luck to him.

When Isabella came up the hill toward the address given in the advertisement, she realized that it had not lied. The whole district was indeed well found.

Shaking with hope and almost on the point of trying to remember her childhood prayers, she had taken the public omnibus out along the coast, the adventure of it dimmed by an anxiety as great as any of Effie's, as to the pennies it had cost her.

Several times after she got off in the center of the village, she had had to ask the way, embarrassed by her drabness and tiredness before people who looked as she had once looked herself in an almost forgotten world. Utterly different from the ones she had begun to get accustomed to in the dreary streets between Cubbington's and Mrs. Quickly's.

It was a pretty village, only seen like a remembered dream from the top of the wagonette on the way to the Summer Picnic from Catchpole's, when they had laughed and waved and thrown flowers to the people on the winding leafy road. And they had smiled and waved back indulgently, knowing even out here in the country of Miss Catchpole's exclusive Young Ladies.

They looked with doubt now at the black dress that was as tired as the girl herself.

"Next time I come, Miss Isabella," Effie had said, "I'll press your dress. Goodness knows there's enough irons."

And Mrs. Quickly had snorted and spat on one, as if to mark it as her undisputed possession.

She stood without grace on her exhausted feet, but there was something of dignity still in her tired face: some indomitable poise, and a directness of the dark-blue eyes, that made the people she spoke to answer her. Thinking she did not look quite the usual servant type, but that that was clearly what she was.

So she found herself when it was almost dusk going up a long lane outside the village, rising steadily toward the downs between tangled hedges touched already with the dull golds and browns of autumn. The dry ghosts of the summer flowers were pale in the ditches along the roadside, and every so often she passed through the deep shadows of a towering elm, the first yellow leaves adrift around her feet.

She passed wide gates into the occasional house, lamplight warm as Christmas in the dusk, and the evening sky was the clear perfect dark blue of autumn: the air soft with the cool touch of the turning year, and in the hedgerow one thrush sang as though he could not bear to relinquish the last of the day.

She could hardly bear it. Beauty had left her life with kindness, and as she walked she prayed now desperately and involuntarily to a God to whom she had paid scant attention through the happy years. Said her prayers and gone to church as she was bidden. But her father had provided everything her world could want. There had been no need to beleaguer God.

Now she beleaguered Him.

Please, please, please, she begged Him. Breathing the cool air fresh with the smell of the fields and trees, and the damp moss of the ditches. Please let me get this position. I'll do anything. Scrub floors, anything, to get up here out of the alleys.

It was the last house at the top of the lane, looking down across the others to the sea. Long and low, with windows to the ground, and all the red walls blanketed with the turning leaves of a Virginia creeper. There were wide carriage gates, with a small wicket at the side, opening onto a graveled drive curving round a green lawn to the house. Over on her right she saw a tennis court, with a paved terrace along its side, and garden seats: and at the left-hand end of the house a curious extra room, obviously added; blank walled but with a sloping roof of glass through which light streamed. There were lights in a couple of the rooms upstairs, and an old-fashioned iron lantern hung from a chain in the bricked porch.

For a long time she stood beneath it, smoothing down her dress and tucking in the edges of her hair. Although she had thought about it a great deal, she had no idea exactly what a companion might be. Or what she would have to do. But anything in God's world would be better than Beech and Mrs. Quickly. Now that she had escaped them even for an hour, and seen this place, she did not think she could drive herself back if she failed to get the position. Whatever it was.

She licked her dry lips and pulled the iron bellpull at the side of the heavy door.

It was opened with an air of resignation by a tall, thin, and bored-looking housemaid with a white apron and a frilled afternoon cap that gave her the appearance of being about seven feet high. With one glance she summed up Isabella. They'd been flocking up here all day and yesterday, and the mistress wouldn't even look at one of them. All pink legs and face paint, not that the mistress had any right to object to that, since her daughters were the same, and she wasn't far off it herself some times. But she knew the old lady would have none of it: wouldn't interview even one of them herself, but created regular old Harry if they didn't pick exactly what she wanted.

Brick, for that was her unlikely name, sighed. She didn't even wait for Isabella to speak.

"Come about the position?"

Isabella nodded, and Brick noted with a faint gleam of hope the dark dress still below her knees, and the uncut hair under the close-fitting hat.

"Come in and I'll ask. Though if Madam has gone up to change for dinner, you'll have to wait until tomorrow and come again."

Isabella began again her frantic litany of prayers as the maid went off through a door on her left.

The hall was square, paneled in dark wood with colored plates on a shelf all round the top of the paneling. The polished floor held a scatter of rich-colored rugs. The stairs went up to her right, and in the wall opposite her was a fireplace, the fire unlit, but a sofa of pale, faded chintz was drawn across it, piled with colored cushions. There was a hatstand, with hats on it that certainly did not belong to an old lady, and a cram of walking sticks and shooting sticks in the two racks at the side. A couple of tennis racquets in their presses leaned against the wall: signs of life and youth, but the house was deadly silent, and Isabella stared round and tried to make some sense of it while she waited for the maid to come back and take her to the old lady.

The door opened suddenly, and a light switch clicked on two

Tiffany lamps, glowing with color like a stained-glass window, their fringes trembling gently in some air from an upstairs window.

"Ah—you're the gel."

The voice was rich and self-assured: a little husky: overtones of affectation, and Isabella failed to answer for a few moments while she tried to take in the vast sweeping figure in the paint-stained cotton djibbah reaching to her ankles, bare feet below it thrust into a pair of sandals. A colored scarf was bound around a cloud of thick fair hair as though without it it would be uncontrollable, and she wiped her hands on a painty rag and surveyed Isabella from bright dark eyes in a fleshy face that still held the memory of beauty.

Not Beech or Quickly, but still beyond the limits of all Isabella's new experience. What sort of world did this one belong to? She looked quite well able to look after herself and find her own companions.

"Yes, ma'am," she managed to say in the end. "I've come about the position."

Careful to try and impress this indefinable person, who might be the one to remove her from Beech and Quickly, she spoke as beautifully as her parents and Miss Catchpole had ever taught her.

"Gracious me," said the woman and looked at her with frank curiosity, "she speaks the King's English. You're very beautiful," she added then bluntly, but as though it was a matter of doubt and misgiving, and not a compliment.

To Isabella it was a surprise, lost as she was to any memory of beauty she had possessed, obsessed with her feet and her hungry young stomach. Miserably she wondered in what way her looks had given offense, but there seemed no answer. Impossible to say thank you over something that seemed to be a drawback.

But the woman seemed to overcome it, surveying her for a few moments longer and then turning away through the door with a sweep of the yellow folds of djibbah.

"Come along, then," she said, "and let's hear all about you."

Isabella followed her, painfully aware of the clicking of her metal-shod shoes on the polished floors.

The woman turned in front of her.

"Gracious me, whatever have you got on your feet? If you

think to come here you'll have to get those off, won't you? Ruin all my parquet."

Isabella's heart gave a double jump. One because there was the possible suggestion that she might come, and the other because surely if she did, in such a household there would be no one who would need to be either kicked or stamped on.

The room was long, two rooms thrown into one by folding doors, with views to the gardens back and front. Out the long back window she had a quick glimpse in the last lambent light of more lawns and a blaze of scarlet dahlias: lilacs tangled along a path and at the end a cloud of silver birches drooping above a small rocky pool.

Please God. Whatever a companion was, please God. It looked like the first haven she had seen since she was set adrift.

"Sit down, please," said the woman, and before she sat herself, took a long amber cigarette holder from the mantelpiece and a cigarette from a black-and-white box on a little inlaid table.

While she fitted it and lit it, Isabella glanced quickly around the room, where the same Tiffany lamps as in the hall cast their same warm-colored glow. There was a grand piano flung with a fringed Indian shawl, and covered with photographs in which at a glance everybody seemed to be laughing. The walls in the warm light seemed to be a faint green, and all the doors and paintwork the same color, many pictures that it was too dim to see, hanging from the picture rail on gilt chains. In the corner behind the piano was a fashionable arrangement of spread peacock feathers and pampas, but she realized the chair she was sitting on was old. Green buttoned velvet, low and comfortable, framed in the heavy gleam of old mahogany. Books everywhere there was space left to put a bookcase.

Isabella longed to yield to the comfort and sink back into the chair and stretch out her poor tired feet, but she sat carefully upright and alert; painfully aware that she was shaky and unstable, close almost to tears for the simple delight of being once again in a beautiful and comfortable room. It made her miss her parents with a bitter sadness that she had learned almost to control.

She fixed her eyes on the lady of the house opposite her, and waited, mesmerized by the way she drew in a deep lungful of smoke from her cigarette and blew it out in a great cloud. She had never seen a woman smoke before.

"I am," said the lady at last, "the Honorable Mrs. Peregrine Armstead-Britten."

Another long drag at the cigarette, the long holder delicately between her paint-stained fingers; poised. A small wind of evening came through the open window of the dining room and whirled the cloud of smoke: setting the fringes dancing on the lamps so that the whole room shimmered.

"My mother-in-law, Lady Angela Britten, is eighty. She is in no way sick." A pause that Isabella could not read. "Indeed, quite the contrary. But you see, I have my Art." Another pause in which the bright dark eyes fixed themselves on Isabella in order to make sure she was suitably impressed. "I am all day in my studio, and indeed"—the rich voice sighed with the burden of the genius—"at times of inspiration, half the night." She bent her head under the great unavoidable stress of the gifted, and Isabella murmured sympathetically, noticing at the same moment that, as well as she could see, the bare feet sticking out below the djibbah were not entirely clean.

"So you see," Mrs. Britten went on, with the deprecating smile of one who must be excused everything, but what could not be avoided. "I do not have time to give my dear mother-in-law the companionship she requires."

"Ah," said Isabella, a great light dawning as to the position of companion. But Mrs. Britten interpreted it as an expression of doubt.

"No nursing," she was quick to say, as though it had been a stumbling block before. "Absolutely no nursing. She goes to bed at ten, and once you have seen her settled with her milk and book, from which you will read to her for ten minutes—her eyesight is poor, poor darling—then you are not needed until ten the next morning, when you go in with her breakfast and to do her letters. You would do all her reading and writing for her, and take her walking in her bath chair—she does not walk beyond the house."

Isabella was staring at her. Ten to ten at night. That was even longer than Cubbington's. At least she would be able to sit down while she did all this reading.

Mrs. Britten seemed to read her mind.

"She has a nap in the afternoon," she said, and she added with another long drag at the cigarette, and an air of conforming distastefully with a nuisance, "You will of course have one day off a week."

Then, as Isabella had just about mentally settled herself with the old lady, long hours and all, Mrs. Britten said briskly, "Now please tell me something about yourself."

And Isabella realized there were two sides to it. She must make Mrs. What-was-it Britten want her.

"Well, Mrs. Britten," she said. Always, said the class in etiquette, use a person's name, and make them feel you are speaking direct to them. She didn't know where the Honorable came in, so she would just have to forget that.

"Well, Mrs. Britten—" And she told her the whole story about being at Catchpole's, and at that Mrs. Britten's eyebrows lifted and she never took her eyes off Isabella as she stubbed out her cigarette in the majolica ashtray at her side. One of Miss Catchpole's Young Ladies, indeed. It would be a feather in her cap to have caught her to look after Gran. Her mind raced. This girl would know how to organize parties when the children were here, and make a good presence on the rather irritating occasions when Gran insisted on coming down in the evenings. Such a trial, waving that ear trumpet. She looked again at Isabella. Her own gels of course had gone to the rival establishment out along the bare Downs, from where indeed some of them went on to be finished by Miss Catchpole.

This girl would be a catch, and she thought, the dark eyes hardening shrewdly, if she was homeless as she said, she wouldn't be so apt to go giving notice for some nonsensical complaint.

She concealed her pleasure and took another cigarette from the black-and-white box.

By now Isabella was telling her very briefly of Mrs. Quickly and Cubbington's.

"But I am not happy there," she said, giving no detail. "I saw your advertisement and thought it would suit me much better."

She looked around the rosy lamplit room and out into the

shadowed garden and could have begged Mrs. Britten to take her. She could cope with one old lady.

"And your name?"

"Isabella Frost."

Mrs. Britten almost purred. All the other girls who had come here had been Annie or Grace or something like that.

"Well, Miss Frost. That does all appear to have been very sad for you."

"You will understand," said Isabella quickly, "that if—when my parents come back, then I shall have to leave at once."

At once. She felt herself grow pale at the idea of her father's anger. Nothing, though, to what it would have been in Cubbington's and Quickly's.

"Indeed," said Mrs. Britten, thinking privately that it was obvious they were long gone in this earthquake or whatever it was. "Of course."

There had been no compassion in Mrs. Britten's voice, her mind concerned only with the hope that at last they had solved for once and for all this one thorny problem of her household, which kept intruding on the peace and privacy of her long blissful hours with paint and canvas, indulging her mediocre talent. At least this one could not get up and walk out, if she had no home to go to. She sighed happily and laid down the amber cigarette holder.

Isabella watched her, swathed in her folds of yellow cotton, the paint stains on her hands and the untidy hair wrapped in the colored cloth. She would have certainly thought, well schooled by Miss Catchpole in what to look for, that despite all this she was a lady. It may be that the depths of her inspiration did not leave time to wash her feet.

"Please," she said silently again, to what she hoped was a listening God. "Let me have it. Get me away from Quickly."

She minded Quickly much more than Cubbington's. Even than Beech. She could put up with anything with a decent place to live.

"I won't take you up to see my mother-in-law this evening," Mrs. Britten was saying, so preoccupied with the solving of her own problems that she forgot to tell Isabella she had accepted her. "She gets a little tired in the evenings, as you will see."

Isabella's heart leaped, but Mrs. Britten was not even looking at her or thinking of her, completely absorbed in the new hopes for her more peaceful household. Isabella was to find that this total self-absorption wrapped the entire family; like a cocoon that no liabilities to the outside world could ever touch.

Mrs. Britten's mind dwelt only fleetingly on the question of a reference. If the girl had been at Catchpole's, then that was reference enough. It would be such a divine relief to get Gran off their hands. And the children were so impatient with her, but the darlings had their own lives to lead, and so much always to do at weekends, down from that miserable city. They couldn't, the poor loves, be expected to wait on Gran. In which thought, Mrs. Britten betrayed that she had reared four children of such monumental selfishness that it was now beyond control.

Isabella could not know what was going through her mind. She trembled with pleasure and excitement.

"Then, I may have the position?"

Mrs. Britten looked faintly surprised, having been in her mind reorganizing a household containing Isabella.

She tried to sound even faintly doubtful.

"I think," she said, "you will probably be very suitable."

Since Isabella knew nothing of the need for a reference, she didn't gather the sense of urgency that prevented Mrs. Britten from asking for one.

"When could you start?" her new employer was saying. "My mother-in-law needs someone."

By which she meant that the incessant demands of Lady Angela were driving them all stark staring mad, and Brick refused to push the bath chair, and who was she to do it, heaving and sweating round the lanes while her paints lay unused and her talent stifled. As for the children:

"Mother *darling*," they said. "Don't be so ridiculous. Get some other gel."

People simply did not understand.

At the very thought of it all she reached for the long amber holder and puffed furiously at another cigarette.

"It's Friday today," said Isabella, and tried to hide her almost sick delight. All the massive sorrows and problems were for the moment forgotten. The loss of everything she held dear for the moment obscured by the simple fact that she had taken a step up in the world into which her troubles had thrust her. "If I gave a week's notice tomorrow, then I could come next Sunday."

From the conversation round the grubby dinner table in Cubbington's back room, she had at least learned that you could not walk out without giving notice. Although she was not quite clear what notice was.

"Divine," said Mrs. Britten, and blew a long, relieved cloud of smoke. "Divine. In the morning?"

Then they would have her for lunch. Such a relief, and the gel looked ideal. It had been so difficult at weekends with all the children there and their friends, and Gran so determined to be in the middle of it all. That ghastly ear trumpet.

There were many questions Isabella wanted to ask, like would her clothes do? Not that she had the money to buy any more, but she wondered in her ignorance if companions wore a uniform, like a nurse, and if so, how did she get it? If it was just ordinary clothes, then Effie had been very smart and always delighted to outwit Catchpole, and had packed a few nice dresses carefully folded inside the plain ones, so that when the ghastly woman had inspected the suitcases, they were not to be seen.

"Ten shillings a week and all found," said Mrs. Britten, and Isabella gaped at her. What was found?

"Ten shillings a week, and you live here and get all your food," she said a little irritably. She hoped despite the good impression that the girl was not stupid.

Same as Mrs. Quickly, thought Isabella, but from the smell drifting in from the kitchen here, the all found might be very different. If only she could stay here now, and not have to go back even once to the damp sheets and the smell of ironing and the clamped mouth of toothless disapproval.

And ten shillings. She got seven and six and her dinner at Cubbington's. All sense of her old values had gone. Riches were now for other people. She had bettered herself and warm excitement filled her. On the bleak nights of lonely Sundays she had seen herself in Cubbington's forever. Now, in little over a month, she had escaped. The world seemed a different place, full of unimaginable hopes that were nothing to do with her father, and she gazed, hazy with relief, at her new employer.

And children, she had said. Several times. Probably at school like she had been. That would be good, she liked children.

"I'll do my best," she said earnestly.

"I'm sure you will." Brightly Mrs. Britten flashed her a quick rabbit smile, as relieved, if Isabella only knew it, as she was herself. She glanced at the polished wooden clock on the polished wooden mantelpiece, and stood up briskly.

"The gardener drives in every evening to meet my husband from the train from London," she said, almost absently, and Isabella felt her mind must already be back with her Art. She must be brilliant, she thought, humbly. "This evening he is late. If you go now, he can take you back into Brighton."

Isabella's exhausted feet creaked with gratitude, and Mrs. Britten rang for Brick to tell the gardener to wait. She came with Isabella to the front door in a haze of mutual satisfaction. Outside in the darkness with the smell of some bonfire hanging on the chill air, a man was just climbing into the dark-brown Austin Seven.

"Bendle," called Mrs. Britten in her rich husky voice: "Will you drop Miss—er—Miss Frost somewhere in the middle of Brighton?"

As she was about to close the door on the comfort and the warm light, she turned back.

"And, dear gel," she said. "Do get rid of those things on your shoes."

They belong, thought Isabella in great content, to my past.

Bendle was taciturn. He had seen too many of these girls come and go, fed up in no time with the capricious old woman and the goings-on of all the rest. No doubt this one wouldn't last long, either. In the shadows of the car he barely glanced at her, grinding through the gears and lurching out from the drive into the dark lane.

Isabella did not mind; sitting bolt upright in the hard little seat, the thin tires bumping in the darkness over the country road picked out by the candle strength of the headlamps. At first she was amazed to be in so small a car. In Chile there had been two shining black Mercedes, and in England her father stored a Humber tourer that would have taken the Austin Seven in the back seat. Fleetingly it crossed her mind to wonder where it was, but there was small time for such thoughts. The whole business of living from day to day had come to be enough.

Effie. She longed to tell Effie. She had said she would come in and find out what happened.

"But you'll get it, Miss Isabella," she had said. "Lady like you, they should pay to have you."

And the blissful pleasure of telling Beech and Mrs. Quickly. But she felt almost sorry to leave Mr. Crump. Crump was kind. Kind.

She clutched her purse close to her in a haze of pleasure, her fingers tight with excitement.

"Where d'you want, Miss? I'm going to the station."

She had even forgotten Bendle, as though the small noisy car were progressing on its own, and she realized with surprise that they were going along the Marine Parade.

Memories of deep breathing with Catchpole.

"Oh—the end of North Street, please," she said. That would not take him out of his way.

She said good-bye and thank-you to him, and he did not even look at her, only grunting and slamming shut the small tinny door.

Never before had she been out alone at night, and at first in her mood of pleasure, she thought it was exciting. Lights on all the moving traffic in the Steine, and the flaring gas lamps and old naphtha flares outside the small shops that were still open and would stay open as long as anyone could be persuaded to spend a farthing. Cubbington's was closed, and she walked past it brazenly. Cubbington's was carriage trade, and such people did not go shopping after dark. Light and noise flowed from the public houses on the corners and the occasional scrape of a fiddle or the rich swell of an accordion, and along the narrow streets children weaved carefully from the Jug and Bottles, with the family's evening ale. She thought warmly of Effie's kindness in taking her into one of these bright cheerful places, and still did not realize that she should never have been there.

After that the lights grew fewer, and in the little dark streets before Quickly, the alleyways and closes yawned like dark mouths on either side of her, whispering with secret menace. She dared not look, but she knew that for the last hundred yards or so a man had been following her, keeping pace with her on the other side of the narrow street. A little behind her, as though awaiting his moment.

"I will never have to come here again" was all she could say to herself. Never have to come here again.

For the first time ever she was glad to reach Quickly, hammering on the door and standing in the small dim hall too sick with fright even to hear the shrill reproaches about the spoiled dinner and staying out without a word to no one until all the hours of the evening, and Mrs. Quickly would have her know she kept a respectable house and wanted none of that. And so on in a high grumbling voice.

"Yes, Mrs. Quickly," she said automatically. "Yes, I'm sorry," but a small part of her mind said mutinously that it must be all of half past eight, but she could not be in the street without being terrified outside, and railed at inside.

She thought of the high lane and the hedgerows and the last thrush singing. Of the gentle lights of Newstead. That's what the house was called. Newstead. There would be darkness up there, too, but none of this sense of evil. And no one surely to rail at her like this.

"I'm leaving, Mrs. Quickly," she said.

Mrs. Quickly was contemptuous and disparaging. No good would come of it. All this moving about, and wasn't Cubbington's good enough for her, many would be glad to have her position. But her little eyes were bright with pleasure, and she champed happily on her toothless gums. That Catchpole hadn't managed to bother her for long.

Mr. Crump, when she told him the next morning, was benignly pleased, and wished her well, reassured that the name she mentioned was at the head of one of his more substantial accounts. Better place for the girl than with that young Beech, who he suspected had been bothering her. Get rid of him soon, useless young weed. He just hoped the old lady concerned wouldn't be too much of a tartar. Miss her, he would, he reflected with a small feeling of real surprise. She always had that lovely smile for him. Like spring it was, or something, having her there behind the counter. He sighed, and left her, to have one of endless sour arguments with old Miss Fellowes round in Modes.

Beech himself said absolutely nothing. He did not care one way or the other. Baiting Isabella had somehow lost its savor.

She said good-bye to Mrs. Quickly, and Mrs. Quickly did not even raise her head where she bent over the goffering of some fine blouse. Work to be done, even Sunday. The door closed behind Isabella.

It was then that Mrs. Quickly set down her iron and sat down in the carpet chair and decided to clear her Ceddie's room. Had anyone tried to say to her that the girl she had so unwillingly accepted had helped to clear her grief, she would have snorted in derision.

Nothing but a nuisance. Highfalutin' ways. Nothing but a nuisance.

chapter
6

Isabella saw Newstead on the Sunday morning with a wave of relief
and gratitude. Her arms trembled from the long haul with her
suitcase: to the omnibus in Brighton and then up the long slow hill
from the village. There was no time or thought this morning for
birds and hedgerows and elm trees, desperately shifting her load
from one aching arm to the other and wondering what on earth she
would have done if Catchy had allowed her to keep more. Gone
were the days when the chauffeur shifted luggage into the tonneau
of the car and the family knew nothing whatever about it.

To allow herself to arrive with a little breath and decorum, she
set it down for the last time outside the gates of the house. Iron
gates, wide open between brick pillars, and beyond the lawn she
could see the brown Austin Seven in which the man Bendle had
taken her to Brighton: behind it a bright-yellow small car with a
dickey seat, and a blue tourer with its hood folded back to the
bright day. She was not very good at knowing one kind of car from
another.

Company, she thought nervously, and hoped it would not all
be too daunting for her first day. Cubbington's had removed the
gloss of bright confidence with which she would once have sailed
into any situation. There would also be the children, of course, so
often mentioned by Mrs. Britten, but there was neither sight nor
sound of them. The house lay quiet in the soft October day, and
she noticed that even in a few days the creeper on the walls had
turned red.

Inexplicably she suddenly feared winter. As though cold and
darkness would inevitably increase her loneliness. Be insupportable.
Firmly she crushed the thought and picked up her suitcase for the
last struggle to the door. In this house there would be neither cold

nor darkness, and surely, insecurity neither. She was very lucky, she told herself. Very lucky.

As she passed the tennis court, she saw Bendle sweating up and down it with a heavy iron roller screeching on its axles. All the white lines looked bright and newly painted.

"Ah," said Brick flatly, when she opened the door. "You've come." As though Isabella might well have had second thoughts. "Madam said to show you to your room, and tell you to get ready for lunch."

Through the closed door of the drawing room she could hear voices and took them to belong to the company that was obviously here for Sunday lunch. Coats and scarves were thrown across the sofa in the hall and a shooting stick was laid across a chair. A bright fire burned, and from a landing window the autumn sun flooded down the stairs, glowing in the pattern of the carpet. Bright, and lived in, and welcoming, touching the lonely girl with hope and pleasure, and at the door that Brick opened for her she stopped and smiled with pleasure. Not like Chile, or Enderby, but those days, it seemed, were gone for ever. Not even like her room at Catchpole's —but after Quickly's! A small room, looking out on the side of the house, soft with the colors of well-washed chintz on chairs and bedspread: old-fashioned flowers, big roses and peonies and faded spikes of blue delphinium: a rose-red velvet cushion in the armchair: trees beyond the small-paned window.

"Bathroom at the end of the passage, Miss. I'll come in half an hour and take you to Madam. You're expected down to lunch."

"Oh—"

Quickly she turned before the maid left the room.

"Oh, Miss Brick. What should I wear for lunch?"

"Call me Brick, Miss, same as everybody else. An' I've been Mrs. Brick in my time. Never born with a name like that."

The long laconic Brick was not without kindness. With an experienced eye she looked Isabella up and down, and found her different from anything else they had had come rambling up the drive: even though she looked half down and out and as though a good meal would do her little harm. Something about her, though.

"What've you got?" she asked, more to encourage the girl

than anything else. If it was all the same as what she had on, it would be a pity. Madam wouldn't be pleased.

Eagerly Isabella snapped the locks on the cheap cardboard suitcase that Catchpole had given her, her own beautiful leather ones gone with everything else.

Brick fell silent, fingering the heavy silk Isabella held out to her.

"They're a bit crumpled, I'm afraid," she said apologetically. Hidden for all these last weeks in her suitcase lest Quickly go and tell Catchpole she had got them. She did not realize that Brick was wondering if she had stolen them from her last position, but something in the honest apology in Isabella's eyes reassured her.

Some story here, she thought to herself and looked forward to speculating over it in the kitchen with Cook.

"I've got ten minutes," she said. "Cook's well on. I'll iron it for you."

She went off down to Cook, who inhabited her kitchen like a large old spider in its web, gathering to her all the gossip of the house and passing her judgments.

"Been rich, that one," she said, wiping her fingers on her apron before she touched the heavy blue silk. "Rich, that's what that is. Less she stole it."

Brick frowned.

"Don't think so," she said, but a certain spice was added to life by the thought of finding out.

Before she came for Isabella, Mrs. Britten knocked on the bedroom door.

"Ready, my dear," she said brightly, hoping desperately as always that if she was nice to her, this one would stay. She stood and stared when Isabella opened the door, even as Brick had stared although the dress was crumpled, and wondered for one minute if she had made a mistake. Lance, dear boy, was always so susceptible. It never occurred to her to think as Brick had done that Isabella had stolen the dress. It was clearly made for her and her only, by the best of dressmakers.

She looked again every inch one of Miss Catchpole's young ladies, but someone more perceptive than Mrs. Britten would have realized that the lovely stylish dress had not changed the expression in the dark-blue eyes. Infinitely sad, and filled with caution for the sharp lesson, so sudden, that all the world was not necessarily her friend.

Her employer's hesitation was apparent.

"Am I all right?" she asked anxiously. "Is my dress all right?"

"Perfect," said Mrs. Britten absently. She herself had changed the djibbah for a saque of dark-green velvet that was little different, the big sandaled feet crushed into flesh-colored stockings and pointed shoes of patent leather. The cloud of rough, grizzled fair hair, no cleaner and apparently still unbrushed, was confined around her brow by a band of green velvet ribbon. "Quite divine," she said. "Come with me now to meet Lady Angela. As soon as she is ready, you may bring her down to lunch. We are all here today."

Ah, thought Isabella. The children.

As Isabella followed her along the passage, she thought of the pictures in her room. She had had a look at them while she was dressing. If they were Mrs. Britten's, then she could do better herself. Later she would learn that the family referred to them as Mater's daubs, and begin to have some compassionate understanding of the hours spent shut away alone producing them. For all the flowing clothes and the long cigarette holder and the sweeping gestures, there was something pathetically uncertain about the large figure, and Isabella watched her curiously around the edges of her own nervousness.

The old lady—what if she did not like her, and would have nothing to do with her?

She thought of going back a supplicant to Cubbington's and Mrs. Quickly, and clenched her teeth to stop them chattering from sheer panic: the familiar lump of fear constricting her stomach.

Mrs. Britten threw open a door ahead of her.

"Well, darling!" Her husky voice was bored and weary with false cheer. "All ready? Here's your new gel."

Lady Angela Britten was tiny. Like a ball of wool, crouched in a high-backed chair in a tangle of shawls and scarves crowned by wiry white hair puffed to the top of her head in the fashion of her girlhood. Minute feet in long-gone boots of gray cloth with buttons and leather toe caps stuck out beneath it all, and Isabella forgot her panic long enough to wonder whose would be the morning and evening job with the button hook.

She was overcome by how small she was. Like a bird under all the heap of wool. Somehow she had worked herself up into thinking she was coming in to face a masterful aristocrat, powerful and imperious.

"Where's my trumpet? Can't talk to the gel without my trumpet."

Sharp black eyes snapped at both of them, and the tiny lady was as demanding as anything Isabella might have expected.

An exasperated search by Mrs. Britten found the trumpet where she had dropped it the night before beside her bed, and she took it from her without a glance, fixing her big dark eyes on Isabella, shrewd and critical.

"What's your name, gel?" she said.

"Isabella," shouted Isabella into the trumpet. "Isabella Frost."

"From Chile," shouted Mrs. Britten brightly, and got a withering look.

"Not a bit," said Lady Angela firmly. "Very mild for the time of year. Arabella. Never knew an Arabella since my great Uncle Thomas's wife. Arabella."

She dropped the trumpet into the folds of shawls.

"Isabella," bellowed Mrs. Britten. "Gran, why not use your trumpet? She's always losing it," she said in an exasperated aside to Isabella. "And then when we find it, she won't use it."

"Lose what?" said the old lady. "What have you lost now, Selina? Always losing things. You're very careless."

"Time for lunch now, darling." Mrs. Britten would not forsake her terrible determined brightness. "Isabella will bring you down."

Lady Angela never even looked at her.

"When's lunch?" she said. "I'm hungry. When's lunch, Selina?"

Mrs. Britten retreated, and Isabella realized she was pink and raging. She beckoned from the door.

"She's only as deaf as she wants to be," she said to the girl, and could not conceal her irritation. "For anything she wants to hear, she has ears like a bull."

It had not taken Isabella three minutes in the room to realize this, and to realize the diabolical satisfaction it gave her to bait her daughter-in-law. She found it hard to keep a smile from twitching the corners of her mouth, echoing the bright satirical pleasure in the dark eyes of the tiny lady in the armchair. Poor Mrs. Britten. An easy victim.

Without much difficulty she succeeded in rescuing the ear trumpet from the tangle of wool and laying hold of it; and in gathering up the falling shawls and scarves as the old lady got. surprisingly nimbly to her feet.

"Handkerchief, Arabella. Top drawer."

"Isabella."

The old lady took no notice and for a few moments peered into her cloudy oval mirror, poking ineffectually at the bird's nest of hair that was beginning to fall from its tortoiseshell combs at the back.

Tentatively Isabella offered to do it for her.

"No, thank you, Arabella. Companion I wanted, not a nurse." Silently Isabella thanked heaven for that one.

"But you can give me your arm downstairs."

On their slow progress down she lost a trailing scarf of brown chiffon and a couple of large black hairpins, and faithfully Isabella gathered them up. This, she already realized, would be a large part of her duties.

But she could not resist a stir of grateful pleasure as they came down into the hall to the bright fire, the square room warm and comfortable against the dull day outside. She could pick up hairpins and be called Arabella till the cows came home to be allowed to stay in such a place.

She knew a moment's puzzlement that all the clothes thrown over the chairs and sofa were adult. A brown trilby on the long table before the fire. These must belong to the visitors. A bit daunting, children and visitors and Lady Angela all at once, but it had given the most immense lift to her confidence to be wearing again her own lovely dress, and to be back in civilized surroundings.

To be feeling again even something like Isabella Frost.

At the drawing room door, from behind which came the sound of lively voices, and Mrs. Britten's throaty laugh: eager, almost nervous, the old lady paused and looked Isabella up and down. There was something in the bright dark eyes that looked as if she liked what she saw.

And mischief.

"Well, Arabella, my girl," she said. "Now you get thrown to the lions."

"Isabella," said Isabella loudly.

"What? You must speak up a bit. I'm a little deaf, you know. Where's my trumpet?"

Isabella produced it from the spare hand with the dropped scarf and the hairpins. Tortoiseshell, with bands of gold. Rather grand, she supposed, if you had to have an ear trumpet.

"Now," said Lady Angela. "What is it?"

"My name. That's all. Isabella."

The old lady looked up at the tall girl with a pained expression, as if, disappointingly, she found her stupid.

"I know," she said. "My daughter-in-law told me."

Isabella did not miss the bright gleam in the old eyes that waited for her to get exasperated. Carefully she kept her face expressionless, but resolved silently never to protest again. Lady Angela could call her what she wished. Even in half an hour she had begun to realize why all the previous companions seemed to have left in such haste. In the half-blind vacuum of her old age Lady Angela had devised her own form of sport.

But Isabella had nowhere to go, and determined right from the start to give away as little of the game as possible.

There was a burst of laughter from inside the drawing room.

"Are you ready to go in?" she asked Lady Angela and did not raise her voice. The old lady nodded, and she opened the door. She did not regard a few children as lions.

They were all still smiling at whatever had amused them, and for a few moments it seemed to Isabella that their smiles were identical, pinned like masks to their faces under six pairs of astonished eyes. She was not to understand the procession of variegated young females who had stood where she stood now, beside Gran in the drawing-room door: waiting uncertainly to be presented to the family. Nor realize how totally different she was, beside Gran with quiet dignity, brown hair gleaming and the dress of slate blue silk impeccable from the offhand kindness of Brick: her one good pair of shoes fine and strappy over stockings exactly the color of the dress. She had plenty of stockings, thank goodness. Stockings had been easy for Effie to hide.

The corporate smile dissolved away around the drawing room and the people in it became themselves.

There were no children.

Only a silence, and all the eyes looking at her.

One pair mild and tolerant and faded.

One freely and coldly hostile.

One with warm immediate interest, looking her frankly up and down like a child with a new toy.

And three pairs with total indifference.

All of them looked at her through a haze of cigarette smoke, and the blue spirals from the pipe of the elderly man with the faded eyes. Clearly the father. The gentleman who came every evening on the train to Brighton. Mr. Peregrine Armstead-Britten, who had seen so many companions come and go, all of them smiling brightly until the rows started, when he thanked God it was none of his business, and retreated behind the pink pages of the *Financial Times* until it was all over and yet another had gone stumping down the garden path, suitcase in hand, leaving his wife puffing cigarettes and painting like a maniac. Something a little different here, though. This one did not smile: looking around the room with grave blue eyes as though they, not she, were the ones to be tried and approved.

The look of frank amazed hostility came from the youngest there, a girl little older than Isabella, bobbed hair falling in two gold curves around a porcelain face, doll-like with paint. She sat sideways in an armchair, one long leg in flesh-colored silk dangling over the side of it. The inevitable long cigarette holder poised in thin fingers with polished nails.

Immediate bright-eyed interest was clear from a dark young man with a boyishly endearing lock of black hair falling over his forehead, stiff white collar gleaming above a striped tie, dark blazer with flannel bags. Carefully and elegantly smart.

The indifferent looks came from the older ones, who like their father and father-in-law, for one was the wife of the eldest son, had seen enough companions come and go, and were in any case, like all the Armstead-Britten children, divinely concerned only with themselves.

With a big fire crackling in the grate and the Sunday papers strewn about the floor, and the sherry decanter sparkling on a small table, the room looked warm and welcoming and social. Isabella's heart rose and at the same moment Mrs. Britten got up from her chair with the sort of uneasy pride with which she always dealt with her children, who never failed to tell her when she displeased them.

There was something about Isabella, too, that unnerved her. Not like the ones that usually turned up for Gran.

"Ah, Isabella." Her throaty voice held too much welcome for her mother-in-law's companion.

"Let me introduce my children."

The young fair one lifted her eyes to heaven.

"My eldest, Algy. Algernon. And his wife Elizabeth."

A brief acknowledgement from a stolid face that would be like his father's in twenty years. Plus fours and brightly polished brogues and a diamond-patterned pullover in green and yellow. Isabella's eyes roamed greedily over every detail of this new world.

"Lunch ready yet, Mater?" he said as soon as he had made his perfunctory nod.

"Soon, darling. This is Jennifer."

Eyes lifted idly from a nail buffer polishing long fine nails. This in itself scandalized Isabella, who had been taught to do such things in her bedroom. Flappers, she thought excitedly. That's what they were. Flappers. The Bright Young Things whispered about so eagerly in Catchpole's.

In one inferior moment she realized that both her skirts and her hair were too long. Who would cut her hair for her?

"And this is Lance."

Dark eyes widening a little in something close to invitation. A carefully casual gesture pushing back the falling lock of hair. A charming smile.

"What ho, Isabella."

"And this," said Mrs. Britten hastily, "is Gwendolyn."

The fair girl swung her high-heeled scarlet shoe, and looked Isabella up and down.

"I imagine," she said boredly, "she will stay as long as all the others. Mother dear, when *is* lunch? Bendle said we *must* get on the court while the sun is on it. Probably the last game anyway. Perhaps the girl could help Cook hurry up."

Isabella was by now breathing a bit fast, and had the distinct impression that the tiny figure on her arm was shaking with laughter.

There was one person whom Mrs. Britten had not bothered to introduce, and she looked over to the heavy, mild-faced man in the armchair, ignoring all the others, and gave him a small formal bow. In Chile the head of the family came first.

Oh, Father. The pain could take her when she least expected it. Unbearable, so that she looked at them all for a moment, blindly, unable to do anything but try to quell it. Father, my father.

"Don't put me in one of those low chairs, gel," said Lady Angela. "Never get up."

Isabella realized that even had she wanted an armchair, no young one got up to offer her one. Only the pale wife smiled a wishy-washy smile, as though she had need to please everybody.

They all began talking again, and Isabella settled the old lady on a high-backed chair and stood beside her, since there was nowhere else to sit.

In a few minutes Gwendolyn looked out the window.

"Mother." The languid complaining voice cut the conversation. "I *did* say what about lunch. We'll get no tennis. You have got the new help, after all."

It was a few seconds before Isabella realized she was the new kitchen help. Then Mrs. Britten smiled her nervous-rabbit smile. This had been the moment of trouble with so many gels, but surely they couldn't think they got all that money for sitting with Gran all day. Some of them had even flounced off at that point. Surely not thinking that her own gels would go into the kitchen to help Brick on their own precious weekends.

"There," she said brightly, to soften the impact on Isabella. "You're quite comfortable, Mother."

"Smother?" said the old lady. "Why should I smother? Able to breathe as well as you." Gwendolyn gave her a look of pained distaste. "She's quite all right, now, Isabella. Will you please go to the kitchen and help Brick bring in the lunch?"

For a long moment Isabella paused, but unlike most of the others, she had nowhere else to go. Nowhere to storm home to. Mrs. Britten's smile remained fixed, the others went on talking, and Mr. Britten, used to such situations, had retreated behind the *Sunday Times*. Only Lance, presumably Lancelot, and what terrible names she called her children, thought Isabella, watched her with bright interest.

"I don't know," she said clearly, "where the kitchen is." There was no winning, but she would not give in too easily. At once Lance pushed back his lock of hair and got up.

"I'll show you," he said, and his mother's smile weakened, knowing that the house was not so big that Isabella could not have found the kitchen by herself. She did so hope there would not be *trouble* with Lance. That had been another reason for losing some of them.

He led her through a door at the foot of the stairs into a tiled back hall, two doors in it and a lot of cupboards; a narrow stairs going up between walls.

"There," said Lance. "On the left."

He gave her a warm, charming smile, pinning her a long moment with the compelling dark eyes. Then he was gone and she shrugged and put down her anger and went into the kitchen.

Brick and the cook moved like figures of ritual in a cloud of steam.

"Mrs. Britten told me to come and see if I could help you."

"She never did." Brick had an air of great surprise, and Cook gave a small quick cackle of laughter as she strained the potatoes that were causing all the steam.

"Here," said Brick, as they were tipped from the big cast-iron saucepan into a flowered tureen. She ladled them generously with butter. "Take these in." She nodded at the swing door through into the dining room. "Mind your dress," she added, with the laconic kindness she would barely acknowledge herself.

The smell of the hot potatoes, butter oozing through them, and of the big joint of roast beef coming out of the oven behind her in the kitchen, made Isabella realize sharply that she had not had a

square meal since Catchpole's, and it was all she could do, fine dress
and all, not to sit down in the empty room and simply start on the
potatoes.

She elbowed her way through into another bright room from
which folding doors opened through into the drawing room. She
could hear them all on the other side of them. A corner fireplace
with another bright fire and a lacquered overmantel decorated with
gold sheaves of corn, and small shelves full of china knickknacks
and ebony elephants. A big table was surrounded with heavy, high-
backed chairs, and the spotless damask tablecloth came almost to
the floor. There was the glitter of glass and silver and a pile of plates
on a candle warmer on the chiffonier, waiting for Mr. Britten to
carve the joint. All of it flooded with light from the long windows
onto the garden, the golden September sun rich on the dahlias and
chrysanthemums unharmed as yet by the cold fingers of the first
frosts.

Carefully she set down the potatoes and felt security and gratitude sweep over her. What matter if she proved to be maid of all
work, and the dear children seemed at first glance to be poisonous?
She would manage. After Quickly's she would put up with far more
than that. Glad and grateful to manage.

And it would not be forever.

Brick crashed in through the swing door with the meat.

"Where've you got to? Go and get the gravy and the horserad-
ish. Thought you'd gone to sleep in here."

She was barely an hour in the house, and the pattern was set.
But she went pleasantly, and did not tell Brick she had been re-
sisting the temptation to start wolfing the potatoes.

"Where, Mater, do you want the help to sit?" Jennifer asked
as they all streamed in from the drawing room.

"Why, darling, beside Gran, of course."

So she sat beside Gran, who snarled at every attempt to help
her with anything, and trailed her wraps in her lunch and lost her
trumpet and successfully put an end to most conversations by con-
fusing them beyond recovery. Isabella had to bend her head above
her plate to hide her smiles, but even she realized that it was her
first day, and that after a while she probably would not find it
funny, either.

And it was Isabella who must get up and ring for Brick for anything that was forgotten; Isabella who must clear the first course; and Isabella who rapidly realized she was expected to control, though goodness knew how, Gran's wilder flights of deliberate misunderstanding. And generally see she was not a nuisance to the family, who clearly had no patience with her.

They all talked at once in high self-certain voices and slang that was mostly too smart and modern for Isabella; except for the father, who, once he had carved, addressed himself in resigned silence to his roast beef, and took no part in anything.

"Gran!" cried Gwendolyn, when they had reached the trifle, which Mrs. Britten served and Isabella handed round. "Do hurry up or we won't get our game."

Gran looked up from the bowl from which she determinedly spooned away.

"Who's lame?" she said belligerently. "Good on my feet as you are."

"Game, Gran. Game," bellowed Lance. "Tennis."

"Don't shout at me," snapped Gran. "I'm not deaf."

"Why don't you use your trumpet?"

Isabella helped her dig in the heap of shawls.

"Now, what did you want to say?" said Gran with terrible patience. And dropped the trumpet in her trifle.

"Isabella," said Mrs. Britten in a voice of martyrdom, and it was Isabella who must take the jam-and-custard-plastered thing into the kitchen, where she was almost hysterical with laughter as she cleaned it. Brick looked at her almost pityingly.

"Won't be so funny when you've been here a week."

"I know."

Already Isabella was not only understanding why so many of her predecessors had left, she wondered they had even stayed a day.

There was a seething silence back in the dining room while Lady Angela finished a fresh bowl of trifle, the light of sheer malice in the old eyes.

"Mother," said Mrs. Britten, struggling to hold to the sweet husky tones, but ramming a cigarette into the long holder with shaking fingers. "Mother, now that Isabella is here to sit with you, we should let the children go, or it will be too late."

They did not wait for an answer, streaming from the room as though they were the children their mother pretended.

"Impossible," Jennifer was saying. "Absolutely impossible."

Gran lifted her woolly head and looked after them.

"Pack of spoiled brats," she said, succinctly.

Isabella found then who had to wield the button hook. Four times a day. The old lady sat with her boots unbuttoned until she came at the stroke of ten. Then they must be taken off for her afternoon rest, put on again, and taken off at night.

Eighteen buttons on each boot every time.

Patiently she did them on this first occasion, and saw the old lady settled comfortably on her sofa under a crocheted afghan.

"Thank you, Arabella."

Isabella said nothing, and had the pleasure of seeing her look a little put out.

This, thought Isabella gratefully, as she closed the door, was the time she had to herself. To catch her breath and come to terms with it all. Or them all. Before she had to face them again. The only decent one seemed to be Lance, whose dark eyes had flashed her several gentle messages of sympathy and complicity. The rest were horrid. Quite horrid.

Mrs. Britten caught her on the landing.

"Ah, Isabella." She was very bright, blowing clouds of smoke. "Gran settled nicely? Well, then, dear, perhaps you'd go down and tidy up the drawing room. They'll all want to come back in for cocktails before supper. And Brick has *so* much to do."

"Yes, Mrs. Britten."

It would be better when they were all gone. She had gathered that they came only for weekends. And a good thing, too. Except Lance. Lance, she thought, was rather nice.

Down in the drawing room the armchairs stood askew, and all the Sunday papers strewed the floor. The majolica ashtrays were full, and used sherry glasses still stood on all the small tables.

She set to work. Already she realized that many of the disagreements with her predecessors must have involved a definition of the precise duties of a companion. Or that, as Brick would say, she was being put upon.

By the front window she paused and looked down the garden

to the tennis court. They were all there, four playing, one watching, the legs of the girls flashing under their short white skirts, bandeaus round their hair and small white socks under their tennis shoes. Ankle socks, Isabella believed they were called. She sighed. In Catchpole's they had played tennis in what were called their sports skirts, suitably down to midcalf. No matter what had happened to her she was still herself, and even in her beautiful blue dress they made her feel elderly and dowdy. The dress was too long, and her hair still wound in heavy plaits over her ears.

Pain struck with the realization that there was no one to stop her cutting it now. Within her reduced world she was free to do about most things as she wished. Bitter, useless freedom, and she felt a deep resentment, which the hard life in Brighton had left no time for, that she should be standing there like the little match girl in the story by Hans Andersen. Watching them wistfully as though they were her betters, when she realized within a few minutes that she could outplay any of them. Both the girls were serving under-arm, and even in Catchpole's this was thought a bit dim. Although overarm serving did tend to reveal what Miss Catchpole thought to be a rather indecent length of leg.

She determined that at least at once she could be less of a dowd by shortening her skirts. Get one ripped up before the old lady woke.

As she put the last folded paper into the bamboo rack, Brick opened the door.

"Old lady's ringing for you," she said.

Bright, restless eyes met Isabella's as she opened the door.

"Don't want to rest today," said Lady Angela. "I want to go and watch the tennis."

"Oh, lord," thought Isabella. "They *will* be pleased."

"Want to have tea down there," she said. "Last time this summer. Got all this newfangled nonsense making it dark early. Something to do with the cows. Messing about with the clock for cows who can't tell the time anyway. God knew what time it was without all that. Might be dead next summer. Come on, help me, Arabella."

Isabella got her up and layered her into about three extra shawls.

"Take the afghan for my knees, Arabella."

Isabella's lips tightened, and she picked up the ear trumpet.

Down in the hall Mrs. Britten was putting on a soft white coat. Very smart, Isabella noticed, high collared and narrow at the hem. Only for a moment did she register exasperation, and then she controlled it.

"Coming to watch the tennis, Gran?" she said brightly.

"What?" said Gran.

"COMING TO WATCH THE TENNIS?"

The old lady looked at her as though she were an idiot.

"Of course," she said. "I told Arabella."

On the stone-flagged terrace along the side of the court, the September sun was still warm, but the first bite of autumn touched the air, and the elms along the lane were beginning to turn.

They were taking it in turns to play, the odd one changing at the end of every set. Algy was sitting out, phlegmatic in a dark-blue blazer with a silk scarf knotted in the open neck of his shirt.

Lance leaped around the court with calculated grace, a wide scarlet tie flapping about his neck, his flannels impeccably pressed.

The girls were all flashing flesh-colored legs and little socks, offering each other well-bred cries of encouragement.

"Oh, spiffing shot!"

"Well played, Gwenny!"

And Isabella sat there fuming that they had not even asked her if she could play, and even more to understand that however well she played, they would not want her. She was the Help.

She smoldered with resentment as she had never smoldered in Cubbington's, until it was Lance's turn to stand down. He came at once to sit beside her, flushed and elegantly handsome, his clear skin still faintly brown from the summer sun.

She was very aware of him, but still tart and resentful, and in no mood for respect.

"Isn't it a bit damp?" she said. "I should think your strings'll be going any moment."

He looked at her with an air of reassessment.

"You play?" he asked her.

She made an effort not to say "Of course," not quite understanding why this situation made her blaze with mutiny, where she had accepted all the worse that had gone before as simply the trappings of disaster.

"I have done," she said carefully.

Lance was all charm and enthusiasm.

"But how jolly. You must play sometime."

She did not point out that she no longer had a racquet—and where was that, by the way? Nor that the dark crushed marks on the grass showed there would be little tennis until the spring. And who knew what would have happened by then?

But she felt eager and anxious to keep her equality with this young man.

"I'd like that," she said, and he gave her the full strength of his confident and charming smile.

"Oh, Isabella!"

Mrs. Britten appeared like a fluffy white genie at the gate of the court. Isabella had not seen her come, had been entirely concerned with the pleasure of a few moments' chat with the one person who seemed to realize she was a human being. Perhaps one day she could tell Lance all about the earthquake and her father. She was jolted back to where she belonged.

"Isabella, *dear*. Will you be an angel and run in and help poor Brick bring out the tea? I think it's warm enough for one more time. And poor Brick has *so* much to do."

She flicked ash from the long holder and fixed Isabella with the rabbit smile.

All of which means, thought Isabella, that Brick has to bring out the tea and I have to help her.

As she moved toward the gate, she heard Gwen's high, petulant voice.

"Oh, *bother*, I've broken a string. Oh, *damn!*"

"Gwenny," cried her mother in routine protest, and the dozing old lady opened an eye.

"Gels," she said tartly, "cursin' and swearin' like troopers. Didn't happen in my day."

Brick greeted Isabella in the kitchen with no more than her normal sardonic glance, and gave her a laden tray, which she carried resentfully down to the tennis court, settling to the understanding that being a companion was no more than an extra parlor maid, with the old lady thrown in. Firmly she took herself to task. She would have to learn to live with it. She was lucky to have a roof over her head. And every day might be closer to the end of it all.

She managed to smile agreeably as she handed round the wafer-thin watercress sandwiches and the brown bread and butter, and the fruit cake, the family all flung exhausted into chairs, wrapped in their long, loose cardigans.

"One more game," Algy said then. "Just time for one more."

And they were gone, back to the court, both the hour and the season against them. Algy's pale wife and Mrs. Britten went up to the house, and she was left alone with the scattered remnants of the tea, and the old lady, cake crumbs all over her black shawl, watching her with bright malicious amusement.

The September air was taking on the sudden chill of late afternoon, and she decided firmly that she would do her job as a companion.

"It's getting chilly, Lady Angela," she said. "I'd better take you up to the house."

The old lady cackled as she helped her out of her chair, and gathered up the dropped purse, the ear trumpet, and one black shawl.

"She'll only send you back for those afterward," she said.

Isabella ignored her, but she was right.

She settled the old lady comfortably by her fire, and she demanded the game of solitaire from the drawing room. As Isabella came down the stairs, Mrs. Britten wafted across the hall, and looked at her in great surprise, as though she had not been looking for her.

"Oh, Isabella, Gran all right?"

"Yes, thank you, Mrs. Britten."

"Well, then, do be an angel, and get the tea things from the tennis court. Poor Brick is up to her eyes."

With what? thought Isabella. But she realized that Brick's vast laconic patience had to be cherished at all costs. Better a stream of companions who kept leaving, than have Brick being the one going down the garden path with her suitcase.

They were still all leaping around the tennis court as she made her two journeys with the trays, and she hoped meanly that all their strings would break. There was a sheen of damp on the grass, and the mist was gathering underneath the elms.

Autumn. Coming up to summer at home in Chile, she thought, and suddenly, unbidden, standing there on the chilly gravel with the tray, knew one of those moments that assaulted her close to destruction. She knew flaring violent hate for all young people calling to each other across tennis nets, their world secure, their home and parents still waiting for them there in the golden evening. And as far as she could see, this lot, and it made it worse, cared nothing for either home or parents. They were rude to their mother and the poor father might as well not exist, which appalled Isabella's South American soul.

Screwing her eyes to kill the hot and painful tears, she went on up and took the tray to the kitchen, where Cook was carefully crimping pastry in two shallow plates. She was barely out of it when they came storming back into the house.

"Oh, Mater! Get Brick to mix a cocktail or two. Then we must be off."

Isabella fled up the stairs. She could not mix cocktails.

But she heard the mother's plaintive voice.

"But, darling. Aren't you staying to supper? Cook will be so upset."

"Sorry, old thing. *Tempus fugit* and all that." Racquets and jackets were dropped all over the hall wherever they happened to be standing, and they trooped into the drawing room. "Going to have a bite to eat and shake a leg at the Ace of Clubs on the way back to town."

"Ace of Clubs?"

"New roadhouse. Top hole."

The drawing-room door closed and Isabella sneaked off gratefully to her room. Take a lot of companions to counteract that lot. In the kitchen, when Cook was told by a nervous and apologetic Mrs. Britten, she snarled as furiously as her round face could encompass, and looked into the oven, where two meat and vegetable pies were just turning brown.

"Be eatin' them all week," she said furiously.

But the chief beneficiary was Brick's elderly and baldheaded gentleman friend, who was the village postman, and who came up every night, slipping meekly through the kitchen door, when all Brick's work was supposedly done, for a cup of tea and a piece of cake: with which Brick never gave him either word or sign of encouragement. That evening he was astonished to get a huge plate of steaming pie, awash with rich gravy, slapped down with some inexplicable ferocity by Cook: and even given some wrapped up in newspaper to take home to his dog.

"Isa-bella."

Isabella heard the slam of the front door and the rumble of the two starting cars. During the day she had gathered they all lived and worked in London, except for Algy, who was a solicitor in Brighton. The gravel screeched with the urgency of their going, and silence fell over the house.

"Isa-bella."

"Ah, Isabella, dear."

She made her demands as though it were a privilege for Isabella to fulfill them, and then, with a flash of the rabbit smile, vanished through the door into her studio, not to be seen again until supper.

This time it was to clear up all the litter of the hall, and take the sticky cocktail glasses and shaker into the kitchen, where Brick received them without comment, already laying out glass and silver for the depleted supper.

Lady Angela's had to be taken up to her room. Isabella waited when she had settled her with her tray, not knowing whether to go or stay.

"What are you waiting for?"

"Is that all you need?"

"Heed," said the old lady. "Of course I'm taking heed. You just don't speak up."

Isabella sighed. She had had a small strange hope that the old lady would not play her games with her. Quietly she turned and handed her the ear trumpet, only to get a baleful glare.

"You can go." Her mind was already on her two poached eggs and toast. "Come up at ten."

They had supper in a small sitting room at the top of the stairs, and Isabella learned two more things. One, that as soon as Mrs. Britten was relieved of the pressure of being as young as her darling children, she had reverted immediately to the shapeless djibbah and the comfort of her sandaled feet. The other, sadly, that in the absence of his family, Mr. Britten was as mute and withdrawn as when they had been there. Isabella wondered if he even realized that they were gone.

At ten o'clock there was hot milk to be taken up and Lady Angela discovered sitting on the side of her bed in her nightdress and a fresh heap of pale-colored shawls, the black boots sticking out below it all, waiting to be undone.

Ten minutes exactly, reading from *David Copperfield*, left by some previous companion at the point where David reached Peggotty's house in the upturned boat on Yarmouth beach. At ten minutes a night she calculated she would be as old as Lady Angela before they even got him married to his darling Dora.

At least, she thought, when she stood at last gratefully quiet in her own room, looking out at the trees silvered by the full September moon, it could not be so bad during the week, when the so-called children were all away. She knew a small pang of sadness that Lance had not said good-bye to her.

The week was different only in that Mrs. Britten kept popping from her studio like a rabbit from its burrow, with her flood of requests that were instructions. She was never seen otherwise, unless wandering the house with some new, impossible oil, searching for a piece of empty wallspace to hang it.

"I do so like," she said to Isabella confidingly, "to get all my housekeeping over early in the day, and then I can dedicate myself to my Art. One simply cannot neglect a Gift."

Which meant ten minutes in the kitchen in the morning with Cook and Brick.

Except for—

"Isabella. Isa-bella."

"Poor darling Gwenny was too rushed to tidy her room when she was going. Always so busy, the darlings: could you put it straight, like an angel?"

Picking all Gwenny's discarded clothes from the floor and chairs, Isabella had the strongest urge to take them all downstairs and put them in the boiler in the kitchen. Already she sensed that

Cook and Brick were watching her with sardonic amusement, waiting for her to break.

"Isabella. Isa-bella. Just a few things from the village when you
take Gran for her walk." The few things would prove to be a couple
of stone of potatoes. "So much fresher from that little shop."

Gran's walk must always be the same, as there was no way for
Isabella to get her up or down the long hill to Rottingdean without
catastrophe. The first few days she was enchanted to be out, walking the autumn lanes high above the sea, keeping to the level that
led to a tiny hamlet, and the little shop for Mrs. Britten's few small
messages.

But very quickly she found out that the ancient, unsprung
bath chair sought out every rut and stone in the unpaved lane.
There was a long handle that steered a small front wheel, and
Gran's hand on it was uncertain. The whole thing was heavier and
more willful than she had expected, and several times, white with
shock, she only just succeeded in hauling the old lady up short of
the roadside ditch and the long wet autumn grass.

Mrs. Britten's small messages strung from the handle did little
to help the balance. (Why couldn't Harrods send the potatoes like
everything else, with the darling children? Or Overton's in Brighton, who apparently delivered weekly?) Daily she trudged gratefully
back up the drive with aching arms and deep relief that she had got
the old thing safely back once more.

"Isa-bella."

"Isabella dear, I see you have shortened your own dresses. So
clever. Look, Jennifer left this to have it taken in an inch. You're
obviously *so* bright with the needle, I'm sure you could manage it,
couldn't you?"

The rabbit smile and the vanishing trick, and Isabella left with
a wisp of pink bead-embroidered georgette that it would be absolute *hell* to put a needle in.

How long, she thought furiously, before she was asked to darn
the men's socks?

Smoothly she accepted everything. Common sense told her
she was well off where she was, no matter what, and her own fierce

pride would not let her show annoyance. At least she had a lovely room, and Cook's food was plentiful and marvelous.

The second weekend was much the same as the first. They all went to a dance on the Saturday night, strewing the house with their scattered preparations.

"Isabella!"

It was Lance this time, elegant in his dinner jacket, the ends of his black tie dangling. "I'm sure you're the kind of girl who can tie a bow tie. I can't for the life of me."

She had never done it in her life before, but her neat fingers managed it quickly, and she had the reward of the close warm smile of his dark eyes while she did it.

He touched her lightly on the shoulder.

"That's my girl."

On Sunday, lacking tennis, they all went for a long country walk, littering the hall with muddy boots and cold coats damp from the evening mist.

"Isa-bella." Dear Isabella.

The pattern was set. It must have been a couple of weeks later that the familiar caroling cry came from the studio door.

"Isabella!" Always rising on the middle syllable.

"Oh, there you are, Isabella." As though she had been away somewhere. Some chance, thought Isabella. On her days off she had to sneak out the back door to avoid a list of little messages in Brighton, where she had a standing arrangement to meet Effie at the gates of the Pier at two o'clock. For the last two weeks Effie hadn't come, and she felt curiously bereft.

"Yes, Mrs. Britten."

"The piano keys, dear. They look so yellow. And Lance gets so upset. He does like it taken care of. Brick will give you some lemon juice and fuller's earth."

Cook was putting something on to boil on the stove, and Brick had all the lamps of the house set out on the kitchen table, cleaning them and trimming the wicks and filling them. The warm room was full of the cloying smell of paraffin. Without comment she squeezed a lemon and mixed the juice to a paste with fuller's earth.

She searched a cupboard for a clean rag, and seemed to take it for granted that Isabella would not know what to do.

"There," she said. "Rub the keys well with that on a rag."

Maybe Isabella rubbed too hard toward the back of the keys, working more willingly because it would be Lance who would be pleased, but in no time at all the cracks of the black keys along the back of the keyboard were crusted with thick white powder she couldn't reach.

"Oh, *Lord,*" she said, and fled to the kitchen.

The lamps were gone, and the newspaper cleared from the big table. Cook dozed in her rocking chair with her big hands folded on her apron. Brick sat at the scrubbed table, her lips moving over a paper-covered novel of the type that would have been dubbed highly unsuitable at Catchpole's.

Their content was palpable, born of absolute indifference to the vagaries of the family they served. They lived in their own world, and after a long moment Isabella moved deliberately to join them.

As Brick looked up, she grinned broadly.

"I've messed up the whole piano," she said, "with dried fuller's earth. All down the cracks between the notes. A soft brush?"

"Oh, my lawks," said Brick, and Cook chortled quietly without opening her eyes.

The soft brush did it. Then they had to get a hard brush to get it all off the carpet.

"If she knew," said Brick on her hands and knees, "she'd never ask you to do anything again."

"I'd like to think so," said Isabella, and Brick came as close to a smile as she would ever permit herself. She went out with the dustpan and two brushes, and in the silent house, on some impulse Isabella sat down at the piano in Lance's privileged place. She felt warmed and a little less lonely for the brief moment of humanity with the two servants, and it never occurred to her to ask if she might play.

Idly she drifted into "Roses of Picardy," the poignant notes falling rich as the late gold sun into the quiet room.

Suddenly the studio door crashed open, and a second later Brick shot through the door from the hall.

Mrs. Britten's face was contorted, a frightening red, her mouth working.

"Stop it," she screamed at Isabella. "How dare you! Don't ever touch that piano again. Never. Do you understand me. Never!"

She didn't wait for an answer, the studio door slamming behind her. Isabella could only turn and look at Brick.

"I wasn't doing it any harm."

"She had," said Brick factually, "another son. Killed four days before the Armistice. It's not the piano. He always used to play that tune."

She closed the door behind her, leaving Isabella staring at the cleaned keys, touched by guilty compassion. How ghastly ignorant they had all been at Catchpole's. How locked into their own self-satisfied little world. Almost everyone she had crossed since she left that place had been touched by some sorrow, and she was only just beginning to understand that this might be what made them as they were. Even that horrible woman Quickly, with her dead son. Locked in her own griefs and loneliness, Isabella had only been able to see her unkindness. Here, there could well be forgiveness for a woman who slavishly idolized her remaining children, because, maybe, she had lost the one who mattered most.

Under the threat of loss, she realized that she herself had already deeply changed.

As she closed the piano lid, her mouth tightened. Pity for Mrs. Britten, but how shameful the young people who used her as they did.

She crept up the stairs, trying to avoid some other summons, shaken by the thought of Mrs. Britten with a wound still raw and terrible even after all these years. Trembling a little with fear as to how she would react if she were to find that her father and mother were really dead.

She had only to wait until the end of October for part of the answer.

As she took the letters from Brick's admirer at the door, she looked out and shivered at a miserable day: the tall elms skeletal, the leaves whirled off them by wild autumn gales; the grass and flowers bitten by the first hard frosts; the air bleak with an early winter.

Gratefully she turned from the door into the warm firelit hall, glad of the chance to look the letters over before she put them down on the hall table.

One for her. From Chile.

But typewritten. No loved handwriting.

Since it was too cold to go out, Lady Angela, mercifully, was dozing by her fire. On trembling legs Isabella raced up to her room, her hands shaking so much she could hardly open the letter. Mrs. Britten could have trilled and called until she ran out of breath, and she would never even have heard from her.

It was from the lawyer in Valparaiso. The man himself, who had long known her parents, back once more in his repaired offices, repaired himself from the injuries he had suffered in the earthquake.

His office, he said, while he was still recovering, had already written to Isabella in July, at her school. Her face flushed with a gust of savage anger against Catchpole. Only, wrote Sr. García, when she wrote with the new address at Rottingdean, did he realize she had never got the letter.

So it was his sad and difficult duty to write once again to tell her that her mother had perished in the earthquake.

Her face grew still. No wave of bitter grief swept her. Only a terrible sad and final acceptance. In her heart she had known it all along.

But not her father, not her father.

It seemed the hacienda where her mother was staying took the full run of the earthquake, and came down in a heap of stones and plaster and little more than matchwood. The people in the pueblo on the estate, whose cardboard houses had, as always, fallen round them with little damage, and the vaqueros, out in the open spaces with the cattle, had raced to the ruin and clawed it apart with their bare hands, but no one in it was left living. They had buried them immediately, as the heat demanded, all together, in a quiet corner of the ravaged garden, only the servants being taken back to the grieving of their village. The priest of the pueblo had said a funeral Mass, and had insisted that something distinctive be taken from each body as an identification.

From Isabella's mother he had got a deep bracelet of heavy

silver, inlaid with gold and turquoise. Isabella drew a sharp breath of pain. Well she knew it. Inca work. Most beautiful. Her mother wore it constantly. Had worn it constantly.

She went back to the letter.

He was giving the bracelet, the lawyer said, to a friend of his coming over to England, who would see that Isabella got it. As to the grave, when the relatives of the family were finally traced, they had decided not to interfere. There would already, he said delicately, be problems of identification, and in moving the bodies. They had, he said, cased the grave in marble, with the names of those buried engraved on it.

The lawyer hoped this satisfied Isabella, as the only available relative.

A slow tear ran down her face, and fell onto the letter. Yes, it satisfied her. Her mother would have been more pleased to lie like that, almost alone, than in some crowded cemetery full of marble angels. The great familiar sky above her. And a deserted garden would overtake it quickly after rain. Probably the morning glory had already swallowed it in a rampage of blue trumpet flowers, and the little yellow things like primroses that covered the whole world in spring. It may well be that she and her father would never be able to find it.

There was, the lawyer said, unfortunately no news of her father, and as her mother had left no individual will, her death made really no difference to the situation. It was a pity her father had not appointed a guardian for just such an eventuality.

"No," she said aloud. "No." Her mother would have left no individual will. My father's wife would not have been allowed to trouble her beautiful head about such matters. Nor would there be any question of a guardian. Her father was blithely certain of his own immortality.

As she was still certain. Not blithely, God knew. But certain.

Sr. García went on to say he was pleased she had found congenial and suitable occupation, and Isabella could sense him relievedly washing his hands of her. He assured her he would send on at once any news that reached him.

He could not understand why she had not got his previous

letter, although he had to admit that letters between the two coun-
tries frequently went astray.

Miss Catchpole had received the letter. Two days after she
had disposed of Isabella.

It frightened her so much that she had to sit down, her heavy
face crimson and the blood throbbing in her thin-skinned temples.
What if it was to say that the father was alive and coming? Even if
she raced down and retrieved her from Cubbington's and Quickly,
he would be told what she had done. And even worse, there were
certain things she had already sold, in anticipation of taking the
proceeds down to Gloucestershire. She was breathing very fast and
her pince-nez fell off her nose. Clumsily she rammed them back on
again. She had a right to know. A right.

With shaking hands she lit the little spirit lamp under the
elegant silver kettle with which she made herself afternoon tea, and
waited in little short of anguish until the steam began to hiss from
the slender spout.

She compelled herself to go gently with the steaming open,
but then she seized the letter and went feverishly down the pages.
The relief was almost as damaging as the fright. She felt quite faint
and her head was roaring.

The mother. Only the mother.

Calming, she put it carefully back in the envelope and reglued
it. She gave it to the housekeeper with instructions to give it to
Quickly, who regarded it with the sneer she reserved for everything
to do with Isabella. She put it in her apron pocket, never to think of
it again until she noticed the lump of pulp as she was putting the
apron through the mangle from the dripping suds. Contemptuously
she pulled it out and threw it hissing into the range.

Carefully Isabella put her letter back into the envelope. And
told no one.

Only Effie, whose small dumpy figure pleased her almost to
the point of tears when she saw her waiting outside the gates of the
Pier on the Wednesday.

They sat in what shelter they could find from the screaming
wind which was drying and whirling all the dead leaves, and thrash-

ing the bare trees in the country. Here it tore the tops off the gray racing seas that crashed like thunder against the pillars of the Pier beneath their feet.

"Well, Miss," said Effie, crouched back in the seat in her thin coat, her hands in a small moth-eaten muff. She was as matter-of-fact as experience had taught her to be. "You really knew that all the time, didn't you? Somehow you knew."

Sadly Isabella nodded.

"Different about your father."

"Oh, yes. I cannot, cannot, accept that he is dead. I'm sure he'll come back. But when, Effie? When?"

Effie looked at her out of her pale, elderly eyes. She was younger than Isabella, yet life had filled them with sad knowledge. Doing well, Miss Isabella was, she thought. Standing up well to everything, and stronger for it. She's always had it in her, that's what. Even in the rich days, she'd had it in her.

" 'Ow're they all gettin' on up at that madhouse?" she asked then.

She loved to hear all the stories about what she thought to be a spoiled and selfish household, and the mistress a bit off her head without a doubt. And that Brick, too. She seemed to be a card, with her gentleman friend coming every night. Puttin' on Miss Isabella, they were, without a doubt. But it seemed to be a nice comfortable house, and good food. Effie would have given much for a situation in a nice comfortable house with good food.

As she had hoped, Isabella smiled and launched into her bundle of tales of all the goings on in Newstead. She enjoyed to tell as much as Effie enjoyed to listen, making funny stories of it all, reducing for her the burden of their selfish indifference.

Who in that house could she have told about her mother? The old lady, perhaps, with whom she was developing a strange, very amiable relationship. The old lady would have patted her hand and called her Arabella, but the pity in her bright eyes would have been soft and genuine. But Isabella could not burden her.

Mrs. Britten would only have been concerned, only half-listening, lest she want an extra day off for the funeral.

And the young ones would have said, "Mother? Didn't know

she had one. Where's my shooting stick, gold dancing shoes: or that brown felt hat I left here a month ago?"

All except Lance. But she did not yet feel sure enough to go to Lance, whose warm eyes promised so much that she needed in kindness and sympathy. Sometime, when the moment was right.

"I have to go," she said to Effie. "I've got all this shopping, and I want to be back before dark."

Effie's eyes gleamed with mischief.

Isabella refused to go into Cubbington's, and Effie went for her, taking great pleasure with money in her purse, in running Beech off his feet.

As they crossed the wild, windswept open space opposite the Aquarium, Isabella for no reason recalled the long-gone day of early summer when all her world had been secure, and they had crossed here with Smith and Rumbold, silly asses. And that young man with the nice brown eyes had caught her runaway hat.

Even though little had been said about her mother, she felt better as she climbed up the high step of the omnibus in the cold gray afternoon. Always she felt better for seeing Effie.

Gwendolyn was down first that weekend, coming on the Friday evening by train with her father. Isabella could not help wondering whether she had spoken a word to him on the journey. Lance and Jenny were driving down on Saturday with the order from Harrods, and Algy and his wife were coming for Sunday lunch.

Isabella was changing for supper, more content with her shortened dresses and saving carefully so that she might actually buy a nice new one for evenings. Catchpole had left her so little that she had to spend almost every penny making up on clothes and shoes.

More content with her shorter dresses, but where could she get her hair cut off? She still felt a frump with her braided earphones, but at Catchpole's, a dancing little man had come down from London once a month, and she had no idea where to go in Brighton or how much it would cost.

There was some commotion. Always some commotion the moment any of the family arrived. Gwen was pouring out some high-pitched torrent of accusation, answered by Mrs. Britten's deeper defensive tones.

It was a minute or two before she realized that the row, just outside her door, concerned herself. She laid down her brush, meeting her own eyes in the mirror almost as an accomplice asking for help with a mixed tide of fear and fury. That girl would say *anything*. And Isabella knew she loathed her. If Mrs. Britten believed her, it could be the end of her position.

She was already facing the door, trembling, but furious, when Mrs. Britten opened it. She looked as nervous and unhappy as Isabella herself.

"Isabella. Have you by any chance seen Gwenny's sapphire ring? She left it in the bathroom, on the washbasin."

"She *must* have taken it. Don't be so polite, Mother."

Carefully Isabella kept her temper, where once she would have flared with rage.

"No, Mrs. Britten. It wasn't there when I went to wash just now."

"Oh, yes, it was." Gwen pushed past her mother into the room. "Oh, yes, it was. I left it there, and you followed me in and took it. Come on, Mother. Search the room."

Fear was gone. Her position forgotten. Nothing in Isabella's mind but cold anger. She no longer remembered she was an employee. Isabella Frost, daughter of Angus, stood ramrod-straight as Gwendolyn swept in and began to open her drawers.

"No." she said, and even Gwen paused at the authority.

"But, Isabella," said Mrs. Britten weakly, loathing her task, afraid of losing her, but terrified of her domineering daughter. "It *was* in the bathroom when you went in."

"No, it wasn't."

Gwen sneered.

"Oh, Mother, come on. And the sooner you throw her out the better. There'll be other things."

Why, wondered a corner of Isabella's mind, had Gwen so hated her, right from the first moment? Effie could have told her. Or Brick. The uncontrollable jealousy of a spoiled youngest for a girl even younger and more beautiful than herself. She was not going to be in competition with her grandmother's companion.

"You can search my room," said Isabella coldly. "On one condition."

They both looked at her, Gwen with unconcealed impatience. Mrs. Britten would take any way out. Isabella was the best gel they had ever had. And Gwenny could be so difficult with them.

"Send Bendle for Mr. Partridge. If he is present, you can search my room."

Mrs. Britten gasped. Partridge. The village policeman. Fourteen stone of slow-witted officialdom, living in a cottage down the lane. They never went near Partridge.

"And make it all public?" Mrs. Britten cried, horrified.

"I don't mind," said Isabella.

"Oh, Mother, take no notice. Search the room."

"If you search my room without him," said Isabella, burning her boats—if her place was gone, it was gone—"then I shall go to Partridge myself and say that you have been found going through my drawers, and there are some things missing."

"And what do you *have?*" sneered Gwendolyn, but in the steady gaze of the dark-blue eyes, Mrs. Britten knew she meant it, and fluttered like a captive bird, caught between her daughter and this self-possessed girl who suddenly seemed no longer to be her quiet employee. Someone quite different.

Isabella braved it further.

"Will you please leave my room, Gwendolyn? I hope you find your ring."

"Mother—"

"Leave it, Gwendolyn," Her mother answered with unwonted asperity. The very idea of having Partridge plodding round her house made her feel quite faint. And that little ferret of a wife of his spreading it all round the village afterward. There was nothing she didn't get out of Partridge.

"Supper in ten minutes, Isabella," she said, and more nervous than ever, the rabbit smile flashed as she almost pushed Gwen out the door before her, making it clear, like Pilate, that she washed her hands of the whole business.

Isabella collapsed into her pretty armchair with the flowers on it, shaking, her hands trembling, touched with unstable laughter at the sight of Mrs. Britten's face when she had said she would get Partridge. So frightfully funny. Impossibly funny. Then suddenly she realized that she was crying.

Poisonous girl. Poisonous. She had won this time, but would she always? Was her life going to be nothing but a battle, even in this house that on the surface had looked so serene and welcoming? Oh, Father, oh, my father. Had she not enough trouble without the burden of unkindness for which there seemed no need? Gwenny had never suffered like the older ones.

Next door the bell clanged in Lady Angela's room, and she wiped her eyes and got up to go and see what she wanted. Her supper, no doubt. The old lady loved her food. But also, deaf as a post though she might be, she would certainly prove to have heard the row next door and would want to know what it was all about.

Supper downstairs was difficult and silent, Gwen not speaking to Isabella at all, the angle of her fair head showing her contempt, both toward Isabella and toward her mother, who was barely able to eat with nervousness. Only the father sat in his customary vague way, oblivious of the atmosphere, making no more than his usual self-absorbed remarks about the condition of the City.

Isabella escaped to her room as soon as it was over, nor did Mrs. Britten try to delay her with any little jobs, scuttling off to her own studio with even more than her normal look of a frightened rabbit.

She came down to breakfast the next morning, tired from little sleep, frightened now at the stand she had taken, and terrified for her position. There was no way for her to know that her equally disturbed employer had also lain awake fraught with worry lest Isabella should leave. Gwenny was so headstrong and she might provoke the gel just too much. And the gel was excellent. Got on with the old lady and the servants and never sulked like all the others when she was asked to do the occasional small thing around the house.

Both she and Isabella arrived to the table weary and tense, but Isabella at least still reacted hungrily to the delicious smell of bacon and sausages floating in from the kitchen. She had never stopped being hungry since she'd left Quickly. Fear snatched at her that she might be on her way to somewhere similar.

Gwenny drifted in late in a dark-blue satin negligée edged with white marabout, the soft fronds framing her lovely petulant face, that gave no sign of a disturbed night.

"Morning," she said to no one in particular and picked up the Benares bell and jangled it for Brick.

She was halfway through her cornflakes in their blue-and-white plate with the Chinese lovers on it, when her mother gave a stifled shriek.

"Gwenny. Your ring!"

Gwen glanced idly at her hand, where the two small sapphires caught color from her blue kimono, and sparked and glowed with light. The ring had been a twenty-first birthday present, and she was very proud of it. She pushed away her plate.

"Oh, yes," she said casually. "I found it in the pocket of my dressing gown. Ring for Brick, would you, Mother?"

At Isabella she never cast a glance. Isabella glared across the table, fermenting with fury. No apology. Nothing. And it could have cost her her position. With sick insight she realized that that was probably exactly what Gwenny wanted. And all for a paltry little ring like that. She should see some of the things that Catchpole had pinched from her. Suddenly she knew that Gwenny would never concern her again, was not worth even noticing. Savagely attacking her delicious breakfast on the other side of the table, she doubted that it had ever been missing. Would the ghastly girl have gone so far as to have "discovered" it among her things, if she had been allowed to look? Probably.

In that moment, sadly, she felt thicken once again the defensive skin she had learned to assume from the first day at the hands of Beech. Even here she was at risk. In such a house, from the hands of such people as the smooth, graceful girl who had pushed away her half-eaten breakfast and was, with boredom, blowing smoke rings at the ceiling.

"Oh, Father, please," she said mutely to her plate. "Please come back while I can still stand it."

"Excuse me, please," she said then. "I have to see about Lady Angela's breakfast."

A few minutes in the hall, forcing back the tears she had learned to accept as useless, and she went about the day's business, answering the endless trilling calls of Mrs. Britten: preparing for the hurricane of the weekend.

Even though she knew they were all going out to some grand

ball in Brighton, she dressed with particular care that evening. Some sort of feeling of flying the flag against Gwendolyn, and also, there was always the unadmitted hope that she might run across Lance before they all went out; even if it was for no more than an approving flicker of his long dark lashes.

As she went down the stairs she could hear the piano; Lance getting into the mood of the evening with a jangle of ragtime. The fire, she thought, and smiled a little, not deceiving herself. And the lamps. Better see they were all right before Mrs. Britten came down.

Her dress was her favorite of the three that Effie had managed to hide for her. A bit grand for supper alone with her employers, but she was not interested in them. It was dark-green velveteen, with wide soft sleeves of palest green georgette, embroidered along their edges with dark-green beads. She knew it suited her and she felt smooth and confident in it.

And Brick had cut her hair.

Brick.

And done it beautifully, in a thick swinging bob. Perhaps in mutiny against being treated as a thieving servant, she had asked Brick where she could go to have it cut in Brighton on the following Wednesday.

Brick looked at the thick shining brown hair.

"Pity," she said. "But nice and thick. I'll do it for you."

"You!"

Her face showed her doubts, and Brick huffed at once.

"Done many things in my time," she said tartly. "Ladies' maid. Go and waste your money in Brighton if you want to."

Isabella made haste to placate her, and after lunch, wrapped in an old sheet beside the kitchen table, with Cook advising from the rocking chair at the fire, Brick cut her hair.

"Suits you, I must say," Brick said, carefully sweeping all the long bright hair from the kitchen floor. Isabella was enchanted, peering into the flyblown mirror on the kitchen wall: feeling the soft swing of short hair against her cheeks: stifling the moment's panic as to what her father would say.

Somebody must admire her.

Lance did, wholeheartedly. As she came in he stopped playing and stared at her with exaggerated surprise, his fingers still on the keyboard.

"Top hole," he said. "Absolutely top hole."

She felt herself blushing and made some feeble excuse about the fire and the lamps. He didn't answer, but broke instead into the sweet old melody of "Greensleeves."

"That's you," he said, "isn't it? And you are harsh to me, too. I can never get near you."

He held out a hand, and mesmerized, she went to him: incredibly handsome this evening in white tie and tails, the falling hair brushed back and oiled to stay there. The dark eyes on her, full of warmth and invitation.

As she came close to him, he took her hand in both of his.

"You're quite stunning, you know. We must get to know each other better, Isabella, don't you think?"

All the warmth, the gentleness, she had been longing for. The promise of companionship: someone with whom in the end she could relieve herself of her burden of sorrow and loneliness. Promise, perhaps, even of the love so shredded from her life.

"Oh, yes," she breathed. "I'd like that."

His mother's voice was in the hall. Turning the hand he held, he kissed it in the palm. Then he winked at her, bright and conspiratorial, and went back to the piano. Her left fist clenched as though to hold the kiss, Isabella went over and poked blindly at the blazing fire.

"All alone?" chirped Mrs. Britten far too brightly from the door. "Have you asked Gran what she wants for supper, Isabella?"

Isabella had, but she slipped out, nevertheless.

Behind her Lance was playing "Three O'Clock in the Morning."

In the frosty darkness at about that time, she heard them come back: tires throwing up the gravel: heedless shouting and laughing, indifferent to whom they woke. Happily she snuggled deeper into her warm bed, suffused with an excitement and content she had not known for months. Tomorrow she would see him. All tomorrow.

Sleep was just washing over her again when she heard the soft insistent tapping at her door. What on earth, she thought irritably, was the old lady up to? She had a bell immediately beside her bed, and clanged it loud enough to wake the dead. Shivering and reluctant, she sat up and groped for the matches to light her candle. Then for her dressing gown. The night was bitterly cold.

Without hesitation she opened her door, expecting to do no more than coax a wandering old lady back to bed. But the wavering light of her candle found her Lance, endearingly young and childlike in a big camel-hair dressing gown, his hair all over his face. But his smile was inane, and his eyes held some bright expression that caused her immediate nervousness: he swayed slightly as he stood with his finger to his lips.

"Sh—sh—sh," he said, making enough noise for a small goods train, and in her innocence, for she had no way of knowing differently, Isabella still did not grasp what it was all about.

"What do you want, Lance? Are you ill?"

He giggled.

"Never felt better, darling. Want you. Said you'd like to know me better, didn't you? Well, c'mon, let me in or the Mater'll hear us."

All her dreams fell about her in the chilly candlelight as she understood him. No love, no security here. Only panic. Frantically she looked down the passage to where Mrs. Britten slept. He wanted nothing but to get into bed with her, and her ideas of what that meant were little more than ignorant. Except that respectable girls did not do it. And that to be found doing it with Lance would mean the packing of the one suitcase there and then in the middle of the night.

"No, Lance," she hissed, desperate to get him away. She moved out and pulled the door a little behind her, to keep him from slipping past her into the room. He grasped the opportunity to grab at her, fumbling at her dressing gown, and she felt the hot wax fall on her hand from the shaken candle. "Oh, no, Lance, please. I didn't mean this. I just meant—"

The fatuous smile disappeared, replaced by a look of smudgy contempt.

"One of those, are you, Isabella? Lead a chap on and then come all virtuous. Don't be so high and mighty. You're only the Help."

She could have a baby, she thought wildly. She knew that much. And he was forgetting to whisper now, his face different, ugly, his eyes glittering in the candlelight. Only the Help! In a mixture of fury and panic she pushed him, and already drunk and unsteady, he went crashing against the door across the passage, with a noise fit to bring the household.

But Isabella had misjudged her household, as she stood trembling with her back to the inside of her door, the key turned in the lock. After parties and dances the Armstead-Brittens were well used to hearing their sons, and sometimes their daughters, crashing round the house at night.

The darlings were home, thought their mother drowsily. So dangerous, these motorcars. She heaved her vast bulk over, in the big double bed, and slept again.

But for Isabella there was no more sleep that night, shivering miserably in her bed grown cold, her hot-water bottle useless, feeling frightened, sullied, and bewildered, knowing no rules for such a situation. Far worse than Beech, and Lance supposed to be a gentleman, and what would happen if Mrs. Britten found out he even *thought* of it: not knowing, like the crashes in the night, that Mrs. Britten was well aware Lance thought of little else, and had been worried about Isabella from the moment she came into the house.

All the brief sense of security was gone. First Gwenny and now this. It seemed that for a girl in her state, nowhere in the world was safe. What was she to do? How long could she stay here? And where else could she go? Half her mind waited for Lance to come again, but at least now her door was locked. It was only when she heard the familiar and vaguely comforting noises of Brick down in the kitchen, and Bendle raking out the range, that she fell into unhappy and uneasy sleep.

Tipsy and sleepy, Lance had not had the energy to pursue it, picking himself up from the floor and weaving his way back to bed. Silly little tease. Ah, well. He'd get her another time.

To her astonishment he was, like Gwenny, exactly as always the next day: except for a conspiratorial gleam in his eye that frightened her to death: he would be back. It was she herself who was the pale one, heavy-eyed and filled with guilt, so that Mrs. Britten hoped irritably she was not coming down with the influenza.

Isabella could not wait to see them all go on Sunday evening. They had been round the house all day, too tired and hungover for their usual outdoor life, and at the last slam of a car door she breathed with relief and looked forward to her week of peace.

In the kitchen Brick eyed her shrewdly. She had seen that hunted look on the faces of other girls in this house, and they did not hesitate to say what caused it. Although some of them, different, had enjoyed it, and that brought yet another one going down the garden path. Brick knew a moment of anger, and wondered whether to speak. Sort of sheltered, this one, fallen on hard times, shouldn't wonder. Too much of a lady to know how to deal with these things. Then she closed her long mouth and went on with her lifelong policy of minding her own business: thus depriving Isabella of even the one small breath of confidence that might have made her less vulnerable.

"Isa-bella! Ah, there you are. Will you be a dear and go to the back hall to help Brick? She has to get out all the extra glass and china. It's dear Gwenny's birthday on Saturday and we're having a party."

Another, thought Isabella, did they ever do anything else?

Even a week ago she would have been enthralled with this new world she was only just learning about. The drive crammed with flashy little cars: the drawing room cleared and the rugs up and all the house full of firelight and noise and high laughter. Lance at the piano, and the room alive with flashing legs and smiling faces. The Black Bottom and the Charleston and the daring seductive rhythm of the tango. They all knew how to do them all, their smiles vanishing in their concentration: painted faces and glittering headbands and long ropes of pearls and the swing of fringes as they danced.

When Lance tired it was her job to wind up the small black gramophone in the corner. One of these new ones in which the music came out of the thing itself, and there was no horn. Sharp and tinny like the hectic gaiety in the room. But it ran down so quickly.

"You don't mind, do you, Isabella?"

Warm, encouraging smile from Lance, crinkling the dark eyes at her, but he did not ask her to dance. She was bitter. She was only the Help, not to be approached in public. Only fit for his secret and shameful pleasures. She had read that in a book somewhere, and it sounded right for what was happening.

"I'm Forever Blowing Bubbles" and "Three O'Clock in the Morning" and Mrs. Britten, beaming, throwing open the double doors and announcing supper.

Slowly, as they all streamed flushed and laughing into the dining room, where Cook and Brick had laid out a masterpiece of a cold supper, she took the needle off the last record and put it into its paper case. She should, she supposed, go in and take her place as the Help, and hand around the food, but apathy and indifference held her. Miserably forlorn and insecure, with no idea what to do about it. Effie had not been there on Wednesday, caught for something, no doubt, by old Catchpole.

About Lance she was definitely frightened. Either that his mother would find out, and she would be thrown from the house, or that some night he would not take no for an answer, and what then? Supposing, she thought in flaring panic, she should have a baby? A sick inadequate feeling niggled at her that any of these bright, chattering painted girls would have known better how to handle the situation. It was not one, she thought wryly, that her training in Catchpole's had ever included. Maybe these girls would think her both hopelessly ignorant and passé, even to want to say no. Her knee-length dress and swinging hair no more than a disguise for a frightened prude.

Which I probably am, she thought miserably, but where would I have learned to be anything else? Beech had thought she was a prude, too.

Sadly she sighed. Newstead was a bewildering disappointment: full of threat and trouble when she had thought it a haven where she could wait safely until her father came back.

Oh, Father. If only you knew what was happening to me.

In the dining room she smiled politely, held plates for glittering young people who talked across her face: gave them serviettes and silver, and stood staring without interest at the food, all her fine appetite gone, waiting only for the moment when she could go to her room and be alone with her unhappiness. With her door locked. Gradually she became aware of eyes watching her along the table, and looked up to meet them.

Brown, friendly, a tentative half smile, hair the color of the last leaves falling from the elms.

He was in no rush to reach her side, all his movements marked by a steady and thoughtful determination. Halfway through his slow way round the table, she recognized him. Unbearable memory of security so complete, she had not really realized it was there until she lost it. The blue windy day and the summer-colored sea.

"James Bennett," he said when he reached her, and put down his plate for a firm warm handshake, in itself an immediate statement of strength and dependability. "We've met before. Very briefly. Do you remember me?"

"I'm Isabella Frost. And, yes, I remember you." Her voice trembled slightly. "My hat blew off on a Saturday morning on school shopping. Outside the Aquarium. You brought it back to me."

chapter
7

The high Chilean summer was shriveling the mountain village.

El Perdido no longer needed the constant care of Sister Jesús María, who had gone back in holy and unquestioning obedience to nursing the sick of the village: trying to blot from her rebellious memory all the secret, sinful pleasure of the last weeks, when she had been so often alone with the doctor. Keeping between herself and her confessor the sad haunting of her mind, filled against all holy rule by images of tumbled dark-red hair falling over a high forehead: eyes that could blaze with intelligence and fun, or be shadowed and inscrutable with whatever sadness ruled his life.

Now, El Perdido was looked after by Groucho, who thought, under heaven, that he had enough to do already without this legless burden. In their charity the Sisters left the man his small, white-walled, peeling room, for in his state, where else could he go? Wordless, friendless and futureless.

They had all realized that behind his vacant eyes, a strong and unyielding character marked all he did.

"And b'God, why wouldn't it?" Liam said. "The man must be as tough as old hemp to be here at all."

He felt he had himself no strength of character at all, for if he had, he asked himself, would he not be somewhere else than in this godforsaken pueblo; and humble and fascinated, he watched and supervised the patient, painful task of getting the twisted legs to walk again. Even partly. Except that El Perdido had little patience, crashing to disaster so often that Liam was driven to rage that in his haste he would destroy his own months of tedious care.

The man even managed to make his own crutches, from two pieces of wood Groucho had managed to pilfer up in the village, searching long for something that would be long enough: El Perdido was a tall man. A giant to the short, deep-chested Indians.

"Give me the knife," he said to Groucho, and even in his weakened hands, found with it a skill that Groucho, who must make everything, had never known.

They brought him things then from the convent for mending, and Liam watched his neat economical movements: his innate knowledge of how to go about any job he was given. Not his usual work, Liam thought, the patching up of old chairs and kneelers: the neat instinctive weaving of mats from the cane fronds out of the fields below the village. Not his usual work, although he could clearly turn his hand to anything, even when he barely realized what he was doing. But when they had first brought him in, his hands had been anything but the hands of a carpenter or a weaver. Fine and well cared for. As Liam's own mother would have said, they were the hands of a gentleman.

Then, how could he whittle and carve and weave, and the very moment he could hobble onto the convent patio, be anxious to start gathering the fallen tiles and rebuild the roof? Without a glimmer of memory of the earthquake that had brought it down?

He wanted to get at the bell tower.

"Cracked," he said. "Come down any day and kill us all. What cracked it?"

How did he know all these things? An architect? Draftsman?

Frequently he was irritable and restless, as though driving energy consumed him, far beyond the bounds of his crutches and the convent walls. Impatient with everybody, filled with sullen frustration, since his damaged mind could not remember for him what he should do with the energy.

Sister Jesús María inquired about him every time Liam came into the dim unhappy ward to see the other patients: unnecessary words that lay on the conscience of her training. Nor would she face that same conscience with the question as to whether she really cared about El Perdido, or whether her inquiries were only for the bittersweet opportunity for a few short words.

"Liam," she had begun to say to herself in her mind, never allowing it to reach her tongue that would indeed have difficulty handling it. Strange foreign name that she had never known until the stranger had begun to use it. Before that he had been none other than El Médico. *Borracho*. Drunk.

"Physically," Liam said about the man, "he is remarkable. It was little help I was able to give him here, but he's recovered beyond anything I thought. Strength of character, Sister. Nothing else is holding him up on those legs. But his memory—" He shook his untidy red head. "We'll have to get that back before it's too late, or the man will be a vegetable. I'm concerned."

Father Ignacio would come padding down the long hill to talk to him, with some vague hope that he could reach his soul, where the others had not managed to reach his mortal mind. But El Perdido regarded him with less interest than he regarded the piece of wood and the tools in his hands.

"He is a child of God," the old priest would say sadly. "A child of God." Putting him on a level with all the small sad victims of inbreeding and malnutrition born up in his forgotten village.

But at Liam's words Sister Jesús María knew a sick, guilty pang of pleasure.

For her, El Perdido, the Lost One, had not been the only one at risk. May the good God pity the man if he had to be sacrificed to save the *médico*, and she must ask forgiveness and let him go. For she had noticed that in the battle for the life and health of El Perdido, Liam had, to use his own word, become concerned. Concerned. Although he would have been furious and abusive had anyone told him so, he was drinking less, even though there were still bad days. And to the sinfully caring eyes of Sister Jesús María, he had become a little less gaunt. A little less driven.

Concerned. Instead of the maudlin guilty tears when people in the village died when he was too far gone to help them. Perhaps with her perpetual battering at God, he would recover also, even though it cost her own immortal soul; pleading with God in a manner that all her training told her to be sinful, and putting her own eternal life at risk.

"I am afraid," she said to Liam, "I am unable to help him now. Reverend Mother will not let me even visit him."

Liam had tried, going to Reverend Mother and trying to explain that the man's mind needed healing as well as his body, and that the intelligence and understanding of Sister Jesús María could be of help to him.

Reverend Mother's ancient Indian face looked as though carved from teak, and the old wrinkled reptile eyes looked back at Liam as though he himself were mad.

"The man walks now," she said flatly. "He has no need of my nuns. His room he may keep, and Groucho will watch for him. No more."

Nor could he get more. She did not have the young nun's charitable view of Liam. A foreigner. Fortunate, she supposed, to have a doctor here at all, although in her view they had done well enough before he came. If the people died, it was the will of God. In her rigid eyes, from all she had heard, this foreign doctor was no more than a senseless drunk, and if asked to consider the pressures that had caused it, she would have been contemptuous. Her own life had contained no more pressures than those she had gladly embraced for herself, leaving a world little wider than the convent.

"No, señor," she said again flatly.

"Silly old Inca," said Liam in English, and went out.

Liam spent most days now with the man, for Groucho had his own work to do, although it was not often that El Perdido did not have some part of it in his strangely skillful hands.

"Señor," Groucho said to him one day, "he knows about the rocks. See him now."

The heat was monstrous, the yellow mountains beyond the valley trembling with it as though the earthquake had struck again: even the late afternoon sun intolerable, Liam's hair plastered dark against his head below his old straw hat.

He stood with Groucho in the narrow shade below the convent wall, from where he had kicked him awake.

"Idiot," he said to him as he stumbled to his feet, his poncho wet with sweat. "What if he falls?"

"He will shout," Groucho said philosophically. "I cannot have four eyes in my head all the time."

He was appalled in all his instincts that the light-skinned stranger, only now coloring from the sun, should feel no need of the siesta. How could a man live without the siesta in the high heat?

No wonder he had no wits. That was probably what was wrong with him.

"See him now," he said.

The man, unshaven now, with gray streaks through a thick brown beard, was sitting on a rock, his legs stretched out before him and his crutches at his side: wearing a patched white cotton serape someone had found for him, a tattered straw hat of Groucho's tilted over his eyes.

In his hands he held a piece of rock: turning it carefully over and over as if it held some message. In the end he threw it from him with a furious gesture, and in the hot silence it rattled down the hill.

Liam went over and sat down beside him, easing his angular bones to the sharp rock.

"Hello, there," he said. "How're the legs today?"

The dark-blue eyes were empty, but this was a question of the present and he could answer it.

"This one." He touched the left. "Better than that one. I can almost stand on this one."

"Don't rush it," Liam said. "You're in no hurry anywhere."

Distress and panic clouded the bearded face.

"But I should be. I should be. I should surely be going somewhere. And in a hurry now."

"Nothing remembered?" Liam asked him.

"Nothing."

"Not even about the rocks?" He picked up a small one and looked at it in his hand. Nothing there that he could see. Just rock, but he was no geologist. The man reached over to take it from him, turning it as he had before.

"They attract me," he said. "That's all I know."

Liam sighed. It could mean no more than that the fellow spent his life carving gravestones. But he doubted it.

"Tell you what," he said. "We'll play a game."

The blue eyes looked suspicious, wary. Fearful of the confusion, the actual physical pain of trying to push his unwilling mind.

"There's a fellow in Vienna," he said, "called Freud. Knows a lot about what makes your mind work. He has this idea that if you say a word to someone, you can learn a lot about them from what it brings to their mind. Will we give it a try?"

The man shrugged, nervous. Almost brutally indifferent though he was to his physical injuries, determined only to get back on his feet, his mental state filled him with fear. He was nothing. In a void. But somewhere he must have a world. Try anything.

"Why not?" he said.

"Why not indeed," Liam answered, himself almost as nervous. God only knew what they might unearth. Or nothing. And that would be as disappointing for the poor fellow as if they had never done it.

"I do not understand it," said the man.

"You will. Maybe. Now suppose I said to you the word 'table,' what would you think of?"

"Legs," said the man after a long pause. God, thought Liam, Freud himself might make something of that one, but it meant nothing to him.

"Clothes."

The man fingererd his patched and bleached serape and shrugged, the blue eyes empty.

They went on, one thing after another, and the only thing it made clear was that the man could find an association for most things present at the moment in his life. There was no past.

Trains, cities, the sea, the earthquake, anything concerning a wider life got only the same veiled blankness. But God dammit, Liam thought in frustration, a man in his physical condition with an expensive rifle and silver-mounted harness did not come from some pueblo on the other side of the mountain.

"Rocks," he said suddenly, but the man merely bent and picked one up, looking at it a long time before he threw it away without answering; but Liam knew a thrill of hope and excitement. There had been some moment of silent strain, and indeed the poor fellow now looked exhausted, as though the fruitless exercise had cost him something.

He tried a wild one. Real Freudian trap, he thought. Should touch the deepest memories. Tilting his wide hat to the back of his head, he looked closely at the man's face.

"Woman," he said.

The eyes met his, innocent of reaction.

"Sister Jesús María," he said.

"Ah, God, Fergus, a fine fellow like you can do better than that. And probably have."

He got his reaction. For one moment the blue eyes blazed and the man looked as if he were about to faint, hands beside him on the hot rock.

"Fergus," he said hoarsely. "Why did you call me Fergus? Fergus. It's not—it's not—."

"Well," Liam said carefully. "I was just trying out names to see if one belonged to you. That's a good Irish name. Is it yours?"

But there was no reaction now, the man staring over to the mountains where the hot shadows were gathering in the clefts. As though there he might find the answer to all he could not remember.

"I'm tired," he said limply, and looked it, his face ghastly under the beard. "I don't want to do more. It's no good anyway."

Liam clapped him on the shoulder.

"You did well," he said.

But the dark-blue eyes were vacant, devoid of excitement or hope.

Groucho came from the still-broken door of the convent, sagging now on one hinge. The stranger had promised that as soon as he could support himself he would mend it. That and many other things. Groucho did not want him to go away.

He smiled his wide amiable smile, teeth blackened stumps under the ragged moustache.

"It is your meal, señor," he said to the man on the rock.

Slowly he turned and looked at him, as if he were leaving the mountains with reluctance.

"What is it?"

"Beans and chili, señor."

"Is it ever anything else?"

Liam, going off up the hill, turned back sharply, and astonishment lit Groucho's face, swelling his protuberant brown eyes. He had long accepted that El Perdido was an idiot forever. God did not let a mountain fall on a man and then give him back his wits just like that. A useful idiot. But an idiot. He had treated him as he would treat a simple child of the village, laying his food before him and expecting no comment other than that he eat it.

Now for the first time, he had complained, and noticed what he was eating.

Liam turned back up the hill. Enough was enough for the moment. But with the sun still hot enough to burn his back, a great satisfied grin spread across his face: his being stirred by a forgotten excitement. Of hope and success.

On reaching the village, he did not go alone into his house, as had been his habit all the days he had sheltered in the village from the disaster of his life. He went instead to an unsteady table under the peeling pillars of the colonnade outside the dark cave of the cantina. And ordered his own beans and chili, for what else was there, and the bottle of *agua ardiente* to be brought to his table.

Darkness brought little change to the intense heat, taking away only the direct enmity of the sun. Nevertheless it brought the people from their ramshackle homes. Separately. The men in groups, those with a few pesos making for the cantina. The women around the fountain that in this arid world had never been known to run dry, pouring forever from the eternal snows that capped the Andes. They sat around the cracked rim, half-naked children squabbling and playing in the dust around their feet.

Father Ignacio came out, and from the crumbling steps of his church surveyed his small kingdom and found it as much as he could hope for, at peace.

But all round the sun-baked plaza dark heads were together and liquid astonished eyes looking at each other, questioning. Whispering. Whispering that after all this time, the *médico* sat among them like any other man: in the cantina, eating his beans and chili with a tin spoon, as they would eat themselves.

Had anyone suggested to him that his preoccupation with the injured stranger was helping to heal his own wounds, he would have snarled, and laughed uproariously, shaking his red head and reaching for the bottle, if only to prove them wrong.

Under astonished and disapproving glances from Mrs. Britten, Isabella spent the remainder of the party evening defiantly talking to James Bennett, expanding like a flower under his calm and deliberate kindness. Emphasized by the warm steadiness of his brown eyes.

Afterward she remembered little of what was said. It must have been all about him, because, still raw at her disappointment over Lance, she was reluctant to commit herself even to the most trivial exchange. Only in answer to his puzzled questions did she admit that her circumstances had changed, and she now had to keep herself. Nor did she add that it was only temporary. She was in turn puzzled by a fleeting expression that crossed his face when she told him this. Relief? Pleasure? Certainly a quickening of interest.

But why, she thought, should he feel any of these things?

She learned that he was a schoolmaster. One of three sons, two married in other parts of England, and he, when he was not at school, still officially living with his father, a retired brigadier, crippled with arthritis, and cared for with devotion by his old batman.

"He and Crumbles have a life of their own," he said without resentment, or even, she thought, much interest. "Chewing over old battles and old hates. They won't miss me when I go. Won't even realize I've gone."

A pang of pity touched her. Poor young man, was he as she was, adrift and unwanted anywhere? She felt close to him and full of understanding.

"Go?" she said. Lost as soon as found, this shred of kindness and understanding. "Where are you going?"

"I teach," he said, "in a very smart and expensive prep school in Brighton. Hate it. None of my own ideas. Only do as I'm told. Want to have more say in how the boys are taught, so after Christmas I'm taking over a country school. Real village school. Girls, too. All on my own. Do only as I think."

Except, he thought, for the School Board, who seemed to have some fixed and archaic ideas. But this evening was giving him his first glimmer of hope that he could get round them. It was not in his character to settle for any situation where he was told what to do.

"Where?" asked Isabella. Making conversation, because she did not want him to go away: an island of normalcy in the shrieking party.

"Suffolk," he said. "Little place called Brackenham."

Her heart contracted with pain, and for a moment she had difficulty breathing.

She even remembered it. Driving through it in the lovely lost days, deep with summer. Not twenty miles from Enderby. Enderby. Long cream-colored house with a pillared portico and great flower vases on the steps. Miles of green soft parkland where she would ride on early mornings with her parents, the mist still lying on the grass and the great elms heavy with shadow. And although it cannot have been true, it seemed in her memory always to have been perfect summer. As all her life was.

Dear God, when the wound was rubbed without warning, it grew worse, not better.

"I say. You all right? You looked jolly queer there for a moment."

They were dancing again. "Alexander's Ragtime Band." High tinkling beat from Lance at the piano.

She made herself smile.

"I'm perfectly all right, thank you," she managed to say. "But look—Mrs. Britten will be furious if I don't help Brick clear this table. I must go. . . ."

Reluctantly she helped the impassive Brick stack the plates among the ruins of the carved ham and the ribs of beef, the salmon mousse and the smeared remains of the jellies and meringues and fruit salad. She could not help wondering, and not for the first time, if Brick would have noticed at all if she hadn't come to help. If indeed, Brick's pressured life existed only in Mrs. Britten's mind, to give her the excuse to be always telling someone to do something. As a compensation for being able to tell her family nothing.

James Bennett went, equally reluctantly, she told herself, to stand at the edge of the noisy crowd. He did not dance, and since she had only just met him, her pang of pleasure that he did not seem interested in any of the other girls was quite unreasonable.

He came up to her again when she returned downstairs after seeing Lady Angela to bed. She was cantankerous and resentful because she had been firmly prohibited from coming down to the party.

"All that shriekin' and yellin'," she said. "In my day parties were for families. Didn't leave your grandmother upstairs like a pair of old boots. That gramophone thing. How am I supposed to get to sleep? You don't do all those fast dances, Arabella? Bad enough to cut your hair."

Isabella did not, not because she didn't want to, but because she had realized it was not what Brick would call "her place." Nor had any of them asked her to.

As soon as she came back into the room, James got up and came to her from where he was sitting alone in a chair just inside the folding doors. Compared to most of the others there, puffing their long cigarette holders and shrieking endearments and risqué jokes, he looked calm and steady and correct.

All qualities to which at the moment she was particularly vulnerable.

Also he was *very* handsome.

They talked then, and once again she had to go to Mrs. Britten's trilling call, but he was there again in front of her in the flurry of kisses and promises at the end of the party, Isabella inevitably searching for the wraps that had been thrown pell-mell around the hall.

"Look," he said. "D'you have a day out?"

"Yes," she said, and not so long ago would have been appalled at her lack of hesitation. Briefly she thought of Lance, but this, she felt sure, was no Lance. All she could feel was a sweet thrill of excitement and expectation.

"Capital," he said. "Capital. I have free periods on Wednesday afternoon. Games day. Care for a spin in the Norton?"

"The Norton?"

"My motor bike. Got a nice comfy sidecar. You won't be cold."

She wasn't bothered about being cold. The only quick pang was about Effie. But Effie would understand. And far from being like Lance, this young man had a wholesome stability that was like a clear wind to blow the ghastly taste of Lance from her mind. She also hesitated because it had occurred to her that in her strange position of being neither one thing nor the other, it might not be correct for her to go out with a friend of the family.

He smiled.

"Quite respectable," he said. "I've asked Mrs. Britten."

"You have?" Astonished. Back in some measure to the world she had known, where it was correct to ask permission to take a young lady out. Away from furtive fumblings behind a shop counter and the lecherous approaches of Lance at night.

Only the Help. It rankled.

"Mrs. Britten said yes?"

He nodded.

"Then, yes. I'd like it very much."

From that correct and careful moment she was his slave.

"Isa-bell-a."

He was the last to go, the haze of cigarette smoke drawn after him by the frosty cold outside.

"Bye, Isabella. See you on Wednesday."

"Isa-bell-a."

She knew what it would be. Scattered sheets of music and gramophone records: overflowing ashtrays with dirty glasses all round them and the rugs to be put back. Lance gone stumbling up to bed but all the others sprawling in armchairs discussing the party, ignoring her as if she were not there.

"And, Isabella, darling, will you please stay up last and open the windows to let the smoke out, or it smells so dreadful in the morning. And poor Brick is *so* tired."

Patiently she set about it all, not needing the piece about poor Brick. Poor Brick had the constitution of a carthorse, but knew when she was well off.

Tonight she could ignore it all, possessed by some conviction that a door had opened for her. Earlier she had missed her parents with almost the dumb blind suffering of an animal, sometimes appalled that she found it hard to see their faces anymore. Lately, as if to reassure herself as time passed, she had developed the habit, in empty moments, of talking to her father, telling him in her mind all the things she was doing. She had not told him about Lance. Thinking only of the love and care that she had lost, forgetting, in the lonely moment, the actual reality: of the strong dominant man who had carved life for his wife and daughter: with the certainty that there was no life for them except the one he chose.

"You would like him, Father," she was saying as she plumped

cushions and emptied ashtrays. One by one the family had trickled off and the bitter breath of the night came through the opened windows. Serve them right if it was freezing in the morning. "You would like him. Big and strong and steady. Bit like you, I think. And it's perfectly proper for me to go out with him if Mrs. Britten says I may."

Shivering, she closed the windows and went up herself, the thought of Wednesday a secret surprising warmth that she hugged to herself when once in bed, a cold frosty moon beyond her windowpanes and the stone-hot water bottle at her feet.

Her door locked.

The motor bicycle combination enchanted her: a black glittering machine that was clearly the pride and joy of James's life. He arrived himself in high boots and leggings and a leather coat: a leather helmet and goggles like one of those aviators. It all impressed her, and also his kindness in bringing a helmet for her also.

"Gets cold, you know, at speed, this weather," he said, noticing her glance. "Gets your ears."

"I'm sure it's immensely fast," she said reverently, and he swelled with pleasure. Closed into the neat sidecar it was marvelously snug, James having provided a rug, and a strangely benign Brick having filled her stone hot-water bottle from the breakfast kettle on the range.

"I'd like to see that one go out on her own feet," she said as Isabella left. "Not thrown out, like others. And not their fault, either."

Cook nodded.

"No house for a nice girl like that. But the Madam won't be pleased."

Madam was in a confused state as she watched them go, from her bedroom window. Goodness knew what they would do if they lost Isabella, but she had known James all his life and some weakly romantic side of her nature could not resist the situation; even though she felt darkly that she did not understand the young man, going for Gran's companion, with her own darlings showing no signs of falling in love with him or anybody else. She shied away from the realization that in their circles, love was out of fashion, and it charmed her to have had James come and ask if he might take Isabella out. She could not imagine he would stay with Isabella, and if he was in the courting mood would probably turn soon to Gwenny as more suitable.

She was so generally bemused by the situation that she forgot to give Isabella any little messages.

They went inland that first day, threading the bare winter lanes that wound among the downs between small villages empty of people in the cold: only the straight smoke in the windless air above their chimneys telling of life. In the end they got out to walk in the clear, cold afternoon, the sea slate-gray in the far distance beyond the treeless shoulders of the downs: scattered only here and there with the primeval tree rings dark and bare against the sky.

They talked of these and James told her of the long-gone tribes who had camped around the dew ponds, and lived their sullen superstitious lives around the marshlands in the valleys, planting these rings of trees on the high downs around their dead: told her more of England in the hour than she had heard before: told her many things, and much of his ambitions to own his own school. Talking always with the calm certainty of what he said, and that he would be listened to: taking her arm and pulling her close when she shivered suddenly in the bitter wind rising as the pale sun faded.

When they left, he wrapped her carefully in the rug, and apologized that her hot-water bottle had gone cold.

"I tell you," he said then, "one day they will make cars with heaters in them."

Isabella laughed.

"Have a little fire in a grate?"

"Heat from the engine," he said. "Why not?"

And Isabella knew already that if he said it, then it would almost certainly be correct.

The next Wednesday they went along the coast to Eastbourne. Twice during the week he had visited her, careful each time to ask for Mrs. Britten first to get permission to visit Isabella. So they had the drawing room to themselves until it was time for her to go up to Gran, although Mrs. Britten had begun edgily to wonder what he saw in the girl, with her own Gwenny there available. Had she

asked Gwenny, she would have been told that James was a pompous and pedantic old stick, and she wouldn't touch him with a
barge pole.

But by the time they had had their second outing, Isabella felt
happily that she had known him all her life: slipping so easily into
the pattern of his personality: forgetting that after months of sorrow and subservience, her own personality was drained away, leaving her ripe for any benign authority that took over.

Hourly she found herself growing more conscious of him. Hair
a little fairer than her own, that curled all round its edges, and these
deep, warm, steady eyes promising so much of safety and comfort.
Strong hands with long capable fingers.

She smiled more these days than she had smiled since last
May, when the letters stopped. Like Brick, she thought with
amusement, with her follower in the kitchen.

On the way back after walking the high windswept cliffs at
Eastbourne, he stopped for tea in a café just before Rottingdean.
Everything, she thought, an English tearoom ought to be. Oak
beams low enough to make James duck his head, and lots of old
prints, and what he called Toby jugs along a shelf and the wheels of
a farm wagon against the walls. Two prim ladies behind the counter
in colored smocks and a big warm fire glowing in a brick fireplace.
The cold shut out, and the world with it.

"Oh," said Isabella gratefully, her face frozen from the wind.
"How cosy. I could stay here forever. Forever."

Pulling off the leather helmet, the brown hair swung soft
about her flushed, windblown face. Everything he wanted, thought
James, looking at her with satisfaction. And marvelously beautiful
into the bargain. He could even, he thought amazed, fall in love
with her in the end.

The older of the two prim ladies in her pink smock was standing at the table, looking at them over her pince-nez in a manner
that said customers were necessary but evil, and she would do no
more than tolerate them.

"Set tea," she said, daring them to want anything else.
"Scones cream and jam bread and butter cakes Indian or China."

They blinked and sorted it out.

"That will do, Isabella?"

"Sounds delicious."

"Indian or China tea?"

Her mother sipping China tea with a slice of lemon in it from a cup as fine as paper. The fans going and the heat burning down outside and the sharp aromatic smell of the tea. But she didn't like it.

"Indian, please, James."

Her voice shook a little. The prim lady snapped an elastic band around her notebook and departed. James looked intently at Isabella.

"Something's wrong. What's the matter? Have I done anything?"

She shook her head and thrust down tears. It was the suddenness, the absolute lack of warning with which the pain could strike. Just some word said, some picture conjured up.

"It's nothing to do with you."

"Well, tell me anyway."

So, in the warm lamplight and the firelight, with the cold English wind whistling past the windows, she told him. First of all about the China tea, as though that were the most important, and then after it came a flood of everything. Chile and Enderby and Catchpole's and the earthquake and Cubbington's and Beech and Quickly and Mrs. Britten. But not of Lance. That she could not speak of.

"And it is only a couple of weeks," she finished with infinite sadness, "since I heard officially that my mother was actually killed. About my father I still know nothing."

Under the disapproving glare of the lady in pince-nez, he took both her hands in his across the table.

"Oh, my poor darling," he said. "Poor Isabella. What you have been through. My poor Isabella."

She felt light-headed with the relief of laying her burden down, tears still touched by the lamplight on the edges of her lashes. To no one had she told the whole sad tale. And no one through all these lonely months had held her hands and pitied her. Sympathy she had had from Effie, but it was brusque and practical, urging her to get on with life as it was. How to treat tired feet and wear protectors against Beech.

No one had held her hands and looked at her with tender brown eyes full of pity and consolation. Although as she was speaking, she had again seen this strange look of relief and pleasure cross his face. As though at times he were almost smiling. She forgot it, wrapped in the warmth of his gentle kindness. Drained with the relief of pouring it all out. In the great blue eyes James could read the total willingness of surrender, and his mind surged with satisfaction and pleasure.

Never was she to know that the board of the village school he so coveted had made it very clear to him that he had only been appointed provisionally. On his arrival actually to take up the post, he would be expected to be accompanied by a wife.

Unmarried schoolmasters in the village were frowned upon.

Hastily he had assured them that he was engaged, and would put his proposed marriage forward. But girls less vulnerable than Isabella all seemed to share Gwenny's view that he was a dull and pompous stick, and by the time he went unwillingly to the party at Newstead, he was almost in despair over the finding of a bride. A suitable bride.

Now there she sat across from him at the table, firelight and lamplight on her lovely face. Still a little tremulous. And he knew he only had to ask her. The father was done for, of course, as well as the mother, and in time she'd come to accept that. Just as well. He wanted no rich wife with a domineering father to interfere in everything. Any wife of his must be willing to live on what he had. And thanks to his mother, he was not poor, but always the saving for the school came first. But to Isabella as she was, even the most slender safety would be heaven.

Deeply he breathed with pleasure and satisfaction. He had found her. With a special license, just in time.

Isabella.

"Wantanymore?"

It was pince-nez again, in her youthful, unsuitable pink: looking as though she found them both distasteful. Holding hands in her respectable tearoom.

"Yes, please," said James. "Another pot of tea. Indian."

He warmed his eyes and devoted himself to comforting Isabella, full of tenderness and sympathy.

Would she be able, he asked her when he left her later on, to come out earlier next Wednesday? There was somewhere special that he wished to take her. Gently he refused to tell her where. Just somewhere special to him, and he hoped she would find it so, too.

"Yes," she told him. Properly, she had the whole of Wednesday off. Best thing to do would be to be early to breakfast, and then bolt upstairs to her room immediately: before Mrs. Britten tried to catch her to see to Lady Angela before she went. Or produced a string of messages. Somewhere special might have no place for messages.

Somewhere special.

Her eyes were still luminous with content when she went upstairs to Lady Angela at ten o'clock. Happy, she told herself. An almost forgotten feeling. Sheer happiness of having poured out all the terrible things that had happened to her: and having it listened to with sympathy and warmth. Of feeling wanted, and cared for.

The old lady peered at her shrewdly from a black shawl wrapped round her bird's-nest head against the draft from the window.

"Young James Bennett, I hear, Arabella."

There was no point in denying it, and the old lady nodded vigorously.

"No harm there." She cackled suddenly, an ancient witch in sable wrappings. "Wasn't always as old as you think, Arabella. Knew his grandfather in Delhi when we were both young. Not so steady as young James. Oh, dear me no." She laughed again and the old eyes were gone into the past.

"Good for you, Arabella," she said then, and Isabella had to evade all her curious questions as she undid the button boots and pulled the black woollen stockings from the scaly skeleton legs. She didn't want questions. Only to be alone and think about it all; and she had difficulty in remembering where they had got to with that tedious *David Copperfield*, who always seemed to take such a long time doing everything. Ten minutes a night made no headway at all.

Next Wednesday came in the middle of a spell of mild, unseasonable weather, the damp lawns green as emeralds and the sky a pale milky blue, full of treacherous promise of the spring that would still be long in coming. Perfect day, she thought, as she peered from her window before her race down to breakfast. Perfect day for something special.

"Off out early, then," said Brick, with one of her rare bursts of conversation.

Isabella looked with pleasure at the plump brown kipper set before her, yellow butter oozing over it in streams. Her appetite had come back even sharper than before.

"Better get off, then," Brick said when she was finished, knowing the dangers as well as she did herself. "Nice day for it."

Isabella felt a warm glow of content. What matter if all the ghastly family took no notice of her? Compared to what had gone before she felt surrounded by kindness and approval.

But even that bright feeling did nothing to prepare her for what happened.

"Going a different direction today," James said when he had folded her—and was it her imagination or was there really a new tenderness in his manner?—into the warm cocoon of the shining sidecar. The whole black machine shone and glittered to match the day, without even a speck of dust from previous spins, and she felt deep pleasant certainty that it had been cleaned and polished to impress her. She took a long happy breath of the damp mild air, blessedly far away from Beech and Quickly. And even Catchpole's.

A different Isabella, suddenly looking forward to life without fear. She smiled at James, her beautiful smile that had begun to appear again, warm with confidence: and James felt startled, his calm plans shaken by feelings he had never allowed for.

"Where to?" she asked him.

"You'll see."

Westward through Brighton, and she looked over at the Pier and knew a pang of guilt about Effie. Somehow next Wednesday she must see her. James smiled down at her through his goggles.

"Remember who met who just here?"

They kept along the dark-blue sea through Hove and out into the country, the downs lifting their spare beautiful contours to the pale sky inland. At Shoreham they clattered over the long wooden bridge and Isabella looked down at the wide estuary with all the houseboats moored along its shores, the quiet water bright with the winter sun. It would be nice to stop there, she thought, and explore the green meadows along the edges of the tidal water.

"Going inland," James shouted down to her as if he read her thoughts. "Not here. Road's too bad in from here."

They turned in only when they were humming along the back of what James said was Worthing; through prosperous wide avenues set with houses that reminded her of Newstead.

A country road then, winding between bare hedges and ditches heavy with wet winter grass, and Isabella thought how rich and lovely it must be in the summer, dark with leaves and starred in the ditches with wildflowers. There were roads like this near Enderby. Memory touched her, as it did, suddenly and with pain, for other roads and very few of them, thick with ochre dust and no green in all the passing world save the dusty spines of the prickly pears. Or in the winter, rivers of yellow water that could take the road away.

Her father in goggles, like James, against the dust.

James stopped, quelling the pain as she watched him run the combination off the road and onto the beginnings of a muddy track at a farm gate.

"And what if the cows want to come out?" she said.

"They'll have to go round it, won't they?" James did not put himself out for others. "Come on, out you get. We're here."

His eyes were bright with some secret plan, but here seemed to be nowhere, except with enough mud to make her very glad she had put on the old shoes she had worn in Cubbington's. Nowhere, except for a great green hill, tree-crowned, rising immediately at the side of the road.

"Up there?"

"Yes." He finally settled the Norton to his satisfaction and buttoned the top on the sidecar. "Keep the warmth in for you," he said, and she glowed at his thoughtfulness, soft with gratitude and immediate devotion.

She's like a dog, thought James, that had been kicked for months, licking eagerly at the first hand that stroked it and gave it a biscuit. Ready to follow at the snap of fingers, the owner of the hand. All he had to do was to be kind to her. Because she was right for him.

Taking her arm, he led her through the gate. Away above them bare branches of immense trees crowded the sky, and underfoot the mild day had thawed the frost to mud, so they must pick their way along the rough green edges of the grass. In the shade and underneath the hedges, it was still stiff and touched with rime.

At the top of a long slow climb they went into the trees. Into a shadowed world where even the bare silver branches of the beeches were interlaced, holding out the light. Pale trunks rose round them, straight and regular as the pillars of some ancient cathedral, and here and there dim random shafts of sunlight lit to dead gold the fallen leaves of timeless summers.

Isabella fell silent, awed by the stillness and calm beauty, and it made it all the more beautiful when James took her hand, watching her entranced face.

"What is it?" she asked him at last, thinking it at first no more than the careful planting of some country house. Like the planned grouping of the elms at Enderby.

"Chanctonbury Ring," he said. "I told you about the old burial grounds. This is the biggest. And they think, the oldest. No one knows how old."

"I feel it," Isabella said then reverently, child herself of an ancient, timeless land. "I can feel it. Feel time. As though it has been here almost forever."

Their footsteps as they walked were silent on the carpet of dead leaves, and no bird sang. The silence absolute.

"Oh, James," breathed Isabella. "This is a magic place."

"I hoped you would think so," said James, and felt he sounded utterly sincere.

Her blue eyes were enormous, full of wonder, and the practical and careful James, who had planned it all, looked at her and knew a moment of surprised delight. Could he indeed be falling in love with her, he thought, confused by the tenderness and pleasure of his emotions, not allowed for in all his careful plans.

There was light between the silver trunks, pale winter blue of the sky beyond, and a stile in an overgrown hedge. He helped her over it and in the close moment smiled at her, and Isabella knew she was trembling, already touched and shaken by the strange primeval majesty of the place they had come through. She looked back through the shadowed trees.

"There," said James, and turned her round, shearing the words at her lips.

They were on the side of a sharp steep hill, and to her astonished eyes it seemed half England lay below them.

"James."

"Not much good today," James said apologetically, as though he owned it. "On a clear day you can see seven counties."

So mild a view. So gentle. So completely English. Small houses nestling in their sheltering trees: sheep and cattle in hedged green fields, brilliant with the thaw: long calm sweeps of ploughland, filled with the seeds of next year's harvest. Rich and fertile country that touched her mind again with the contrast of standing on such a hill in Chile. Nothing to be seen but barren ochre ground and the endless folds of other mountains.

"All the riches of this land," her father had said of Chile, "lie under it."

So to her touched and tender state, there added memory and sorrow, and when James took her hand in his, she turned to him, utterly pliant.

"Beautiful, James," she said. "Utterly beautiful. Thank you for bringing me."

James had set his scene with care.

"Told you," he said, "it was somewhere special. And I brought you here for a very special reason."

"Yes?"

The brown eyes fixed her, somber and dark. Oh, God, thought Isabella, he is going to tell me kindly that I have been a mistake. That he will not see me again. Panic ran through her at the loss of the frail security she had begun to cling to. Back to loneliness and struggling with it on her own. Sick with misery, she stared out at the gentle land. Never could he have found her more vulnerable.

But the grip of his hands tightened on hers.

"I want to ask you, Isabella, to do me the honor of marrying me."

She knew she was gaping at him, eyes and mouth wide, and James raced on.

"I know I'm going very fast. But you see, dear Isabella, I have to. I am going to Brackenham just after Christmas, and I have realized that all I want in the world is for you to come with me. There's a nice little house with the school, and since I set eyes on you, I have thought of nothing but to have you share it with me. With a special license, we could be married by Christmas."

Still she stared at him, all her heart and loneliness crying out to say, yes, yes, yes.

James thought she needed persuading.

"I won't always be a village schoolmaster," he said. "That's just to get practice in having a school of my own. When my father dies, I shall be quite rich, and have my own prep school. I won't let you down, Isabella. But I love you, and can't let you go."

"You *love* me?"

How could she believe anybody loved her, after the ghastly misery of the last few months?

"Of course I love you, darling Isabella. That's why I'm asking you to marry me, you goose. Having met you, I can't face going off to that place on my own. Don't you care for me at all?"

The blue eyes filled with a dependent adoration. This was no Lance, out only for what he could get. The idea of leaving all the gang at Newstead, and settling down in a little house with James, did not seem far short of paradise.

But.

"My—my—father," she said, leaving all his strong opinions unspoken. However much she might love James, she knew in her heart that Angus Frost would not consider her as the wife of a village schoolmaster.

James bit back the desire to tell her to forget about her father: that he was almost certainly dead: that people got buried, untraced forever, in earthquakes.

"He's not here, my darling," was all he said carefully. "You've had to decide everything for yourself since that woman threw you out, so surely you can decide this, too. And I'm sure he would be happy to see you secure. Which I promise you will be with me."

Oh, yes, that was true. He's good and dependable, she told her father in her mind. I can see that. And as safe as the Bank of England. And, oh, dear, yes, I love him, even in so short a time.

It was irresistible. No more dealing with people she loathed. No more Lances. No more insecure terror of being jobless and homeless in the streets. Only James, loving and competent.

It took a while more of careful talking before the look of astonishment on her face was replaced by one of excited radiance. Her cheeks flushed, and the great blue eyes grew luminous.

God, she was beautiful, James thought. Beautiful. Everything he could want, and there for the taking.

"But can we, James, so soon?"

"Oh, yes," said James, who had already inquired into it all. She had not said no.

"We can get a special license. I can arrange all that and you are accepted as being without relatives."

That hurt, but James went blithely on.

"We can get married before Christmas in the Registry Office in Brighton."

For one fleeting moment she thought of her wedding as she had always assumed it would be. In some grand church with her mother in charge of everything. A beautiful white dress and clouds of veil, and some fine young man of her parents' choice. The church full of rich and well-dressed guests.

Who would come now to see her married?

Effie, probably.

She fought it all down. As she had so bitterly learned in the last months, today was not yesterday. And when her father did come back, he could buy James the school he wanted, and everything would be heavenly.

"Yes, James," she said, a little breathless. "I'll marry you."

She felt stunned and a little frightened, but blissfully happy. As they walked back down to the Norton round the sunny side of the hill, James's arm protectively about her, she looked up at the great old circle of trees against the sky, and knew she would remember it all her life as the place where life grew safe again.

At Newstead her news was not well received.

Mrs. Britten did her best to congratulate them. She had encouraged it from some foolish sentimentality, but now she realized it meant the loss of Isabella, and the rabbit smile was false and irritable.

"And just how long can you stay?"

Gwenny looked at her at the weekend as though she was some poisonous upstart. The others took no notice at all.

But the old lady cackled and patted her hand.

"Well done, Arabella."

And in the kitchen there was a warm air of satisfaction.

On the Friday, Isabella got a letter. In a grubby envelope, her name and address in difficult and ill-formed letters. Nervously she opened it, not yet secure from the feeling that everything out of the ordinary was a threat.

Dere miss [it said],
    pleese to meet Effie at the peer Wensday. She need you.
                Respecfully. Sara Jones.

It must be Effie's mother. She had written down her address for Effie in case it was ever necessary for her to get in touch with her. Equally nervously, she showed it to James in the evening, reluctant to break their Wednesday outings, but deeply aware of all her obligations to Effie. To her surprise James agreed easily.

"Certainly, my darling. She seems to have been very good to you." He was being carefully benign and indulgent until he was quite sure of everything.

"I'll drop you off there in the Norton, and go and see my father and tell him about us. Then next week we can go and see him together. He'll love you."

By the Wednesday the mild spell was gone, and where Effie waited in front of the Pier gates, she looked pinched and miserable, her sallow face blue, watching Isabella get out of the Norton as though somehow it increased all her troubles.

"Who's 'e?" she said.

"I'll tell you all about it," Isabella said happily, but she was concerned for Effie.

"Effie. You do look unhappy. What's wrong?"

They paced the damp boards of the Pier on the side where a

pale sun tried to lift the cold. Now it was Isabella's turn to listen and give help.

"I was wondering, Miss Isabella, if you could ask your lady if she knows anyone wants a maid. Live in."

"Why, Effie? What's wrong with Catchpole's."

"Nothing. The old whale's as good as ever. No, Miss. It's me 'ome. I've got to find somewhere else to live. An' I can't afford no lodgings on what Catchpole pays me."

"What's gone wrong, Effie?"

Effie flushed and looked unhappy and embarrassed.

"Well, Miss Isabella." They turned round and walked back again toward the dull flat sea. "Me mum married again, see. About a month ago. It was good fer her. She was lonely wiv nothing but a pack of kids. And she had to keep them all. But me stepfather—"

She hesitated.

"Oh, is he cruel to you, Effie?"

Lord, thought Effie, does Miss Isabella even know about these things? Someone better tell her soon if she didn't. How should she put it?

"Well, Miss, it's all right wiv the little ones, but me—well, he thinks he should get me thrown in wiv Mum. Never leaves me 'lone. Coming nights even wiv the other kids in the room. Drunk an' all."

Effie was telling Isabella nothing. Vividly she recalled Lance's blurry face in the candlelight, the inane smile pinned to his lips. He thought she should be part of the general deal as well.

"Oh, Effie."

"I can't stand it, Miss. Great brute he is. I got to get out. And me mum isn't all that pleased. Thinks I egg him on."

She snorted in disgust.

In Isabella's mind an unbelievably blissful idea was forming. And it seemed James would refuse her nothing, although it seemed too much to hope for. Still, there was no harm in trying.

"Effie," she said, breathless, "I have something to tell you. Maybe, just maybe, we could put the two together."

Effie looked at her, aware even through her own misery of some change in her. Her face alight as it had not been for months, she took off her glove and showed Effie the modest sapphire between two diamonds, that James had placed on her engagement finger.

So great was her translation from one world to the other that she did not even stop to compare it with the fabulous glittering rings her mother used to wear. Nor even with the youthful and suitable ones that Catchpole had taken from her.

It came from James, so it was perfect.

"And we're getting married before Christmas. Something called a special license, so you don't have to wait."

Effie's face was bleak.

"I'm very happy for you," she said. "Very happy, Miss Isabella." Privately she wondered if the arrangement would please the handsome firm-faced man in the photograph that used to be in Miss Isabella's room. And who might still come back. "You think," she said, "that I should go for your position. Would you reckon I'd be suitable? Wouln't they need more of a lady?"

"Oh no, oh no." Isabella was excited now, her cheeks flushed, full of her idea to make everyone as happy as herself. "I thought we should both go and meet James, and see if we do not want a maid for ourselves." Even now, in her mind, everybody had a maid. She just had not thought of it. "All I don't know, Effie," she said, "is how big the house is. I just don't know if there's room."

Effie looked as though a glimpse of heaven had opened, brilliant in the dark day.

"Oh, Miss. Miss Isabella," she said earnestly, "if I came to work for you, I wouldn't want no wages. Just me keep. That'd be all I'd want. But what'll your young man say?"

"We'll go and ask him," Isabella said determinedly.

She knew it was an offer that James could not refuse. It was his responsibility to find someone to clean the school.

They sat in the café where Isabella had arranged to meet James, Effie unhappy and on the edge of her chair, unused to such places and only anxious to be gone as soon as the wonderful arrangement had been made. Having listened to the whole story, both girls sliding with embarrassment over the real reason for Effie's leaving home, James, to Isabella's delight, was willing and expansively pleased, lavishly buttering a crumpet, and she was not to realize that even as he did it, he saw another good reason for having this girl. He loved his food, and as far as he could understand, Isabella had never boiled a saucepan of milk in her life.

"Is there room in the house, James?" she asked him eagerly. "Is there room in the house?"

"Oh, yes," James said handsomely, enjoying playing the philanthropist. "There's a good-sized kitchen downstairs where we would eat, and a little parlor. Then upstairs there's one good bedroom over the kitchen, and two little ones. They expect schoolmasters to have families," he added, and Isabella blushed.

"Then Effie can come and be our maid?"

"I'd ask no wages, sir." Effie said what she had said to Isabella. "No wages. Only me keep, an' I don't eat much."

Indeed, thought James, satisfied, she was little bigger than a sparrow. He hoped that she was strong.

And he smiled warmly on them both. Anything his darling asked, his manner conveyed, would be his to give.

"I think it would be a jolly good idea."

Effie was trembling with relief and pleasure.

"Thank you, sir. Thank you, Miss Isabella. I'll never stop being grateful. I have to go now, or Catchpole'll be after me."

Isabella heard the name Catchpole like some distant chord of unhappiness she could barely identify, swamped with happiness she thought lost for ever. Everyone she cared about—except her father —together under one roof.

"Oh, James," she said when Effie had threaded her diffident way through the tables to the door. "Oh, James, you are so kind."

She leaned over quickly and kissed him on the cheek.

"Hey, come on, old girl, not in public."

But he, too, was smiling. He, too, thought he had done rather well for himself.

There was a difficult and inconclusive interview with James's father, who made it clear that he was more interested in his game of backgammon than in any girl his son proposed to marry. And the batman Crumbles looked at them both with active dislike, conveying probably his thought that if there was any money going when the old man died, he deserved it more than any son who wanted to go flittering it away on a wife.

"Sorry," James said as they left the house, in which all life,

such as it was, was confined to the one airless overheated room.
"But we had to go."

Even he seemed reduced: the gloss gone from his fine self-confidence.

"Is it always like that?" Isabella asked him, trying to understand what it was like to have a father who did not care about you.

"Since my mother died," he said.

"We are both," said Isabella softly, "very much alone in the world."

James tucked her arm in his.

"We have each other," he said.

They were married on December twenty-third, in the Registry Office in Brighton, James having coped with all the arrangements and legalities with his usual calm competence, and to Isabella's pleasure and astonishment, Mr. Britten announced his intention of taking her down there in the Bentley and standing witness. His wife stared at him as if he were guilty of some dreadful treachery.

She rushed to speak, all gushing contrition.

"Isabella, darling. You know I would adore to be there. But with you gone, I simply won't have a moment. I don't know what will happen to my Art."

She would never forgive her for leaving, having made life so easy.

The old lady gave her a garnet ring from her own finger, and Isabella hid it, knowing Mrs. Britten would probably take it back.

"Well done, Arabella. Give me a kiss."

Brick and Cook gave her a fine new suitcase, a grand surprise when she began to pack her meager belongings the evening before.

"Keep the upper 'and on 'im," was all Brick said tersely, but Cook was all pastry-smeared benevolence, transferring a good deal of flour to Isabella's clothes as she kissed her, in the hot kitchen that Isabella had come to know as the happiest room in the house.

On the actual morning of the day, when Brick's admirer thumped the knocker in the gray light little beyond dawn, there was a small square parcel for Isabella.

"Wedding present, eh, Miss," he said. "Good luck to 'ee."

Wedding present. From whom? It was the merest chance, but

the lawyer in Santiago had kept his promise, and in a small white box on a layer of cotton wool lay her mother's silver and gold and turquoise bracelet.

She cried a little then, and over the breakfast table Mrs. Britten looked pained. Bad enough to have the gel going without this sort of fuss. But clasping it on her wrist, torn with memories, Isabella was glad to go to James with even one lovely thing of her old life about her. It made her feel a little less humble and obliged.

"Very nice," James said when she showed it to him. The only Isabella he wanted to know about was the one he was creating.

It took so little time to become Mrs. James Bennett. Only minutes, and then they were out again on the windy pavement. They got her new suitcase and strapped it with James's own on the pillion of the Norton. He had sent two trunks by Carter Patterson and taken Effie down to the house a week ago with another suitcase, to have everything ready for them. Mr. Britten bent his mild face and kissed her.

"Be happy, m'dear. Liked having you round my house."

There was no time for more than astonished pleasure, and he was gone again into the Bentley.

As if to join in their own personal celebration, all the shops were bright with Christmas: tinsel and holly and cotton wool snow, and every butcher's window framed in hanging turkeys: the toyshops a child's dream of heaven: lights blazing in the chilly day.

With an air of finality they left it all, and went north out of Brighton, all their possessions with them, and along the stark line of the winter downs: nothing but the road between them and their own Christmas.

Liam walked up the long hill from the convent to the village, wiping the sweat from under his ragged hat and fretting.

All the years of his apathy he had cared for the sick of the village with a sort of blind, automatic efficiency. Fighting always, unless he was incapable, for life, but unable, from his lonely state, to feel involved if it were death.

He kicked a stone from his path and cursed richly when he hurt his toe. Why was he going mad with frustration because he was failing to heal this man's mind? He had healed his body as well, God pity him, as it would ever be healed. But failed with his mind, and a great fear, that he resented as some sort of intrusion, was taking him that it was already too late. That the fellow would never be more than the strangely capable child he was now, regarding with sad and vacant eyes a world he could little understand. Groping in an empty mind for a past that was gone forever.

There was only one more thing Liam could think to do, and he cursed himself even for the thought. For being so weak and sentimental as to do it. The only thing he had valued in these last years was his solitude, blinding himself to a world he did not want near him.

Now he was thinking of smashing his mold to help some fellow who meant nothing to him. Railing at his own foolishness, he knew nevertheless that it was inevitable: as inevitable as that this crucifying sun would go each day across the sky from east to west: from mountaintop to mountaintop. Some compulsive step he could not refuse to take, leading to God knew where.

This vacant fellow, with no more than a child's conversation, was making demands on him.

When he whistled outside the convent door an hour later, he was leading a llama on a bit of frayed rope, its disdainful head held high, as though it despised any part of what it was doing.

El Perdido limped out on his crutches: "What's that?"

"That's a llama. They use them up the mountain on their few acres for carrying crops and water. Have you never seen one before?"

The man stared a long while, his brow furrowed.

"No," he said.

Liam sighed. The man hadn't been riding through the foothills of the Andes without having ever seen a llama. But he had not seen it yesterday, so for him it did not exist.

"Well, you're going to ride him today," he said. "You don't get enough talking or thinking down here. I'm taking you up to my house, if you'd give it that good name, and you'll have more company. Groucho couldn't raise the living, let alone the dead."

"Up there?" said the man, and looked up the mountain as though it were the end of the world.

"In the village. Yes."

"And I will ride on this?"

Liam knew a small sudden flicker of hope. The prospect of change had surely brought a small stir to the blue eyes. The faintest possible flicker of interest.

"GROUCHO!" he bellowed then, to bring him from wherever he would be snatching his secret sleep. The man, as pliable as a child, was stroking the rich wool of the animal.

In the hospital room Sister Jesús María heard him shout. She was still too disciplined to lift her head, but her hands trembled on the bandages she was winding round the suppurating wound from a machete. God forgive her the burden of her sin, but she could not get him from her mind: living over endlessly there those long night hours when they had sat together with El Perdido, nothing in the black silence save the whir of moths around the tiny lamp, and the call of the convent bell, which she had been given permission to ignore. She sighed and breathed a prayer of penance and bent again over her bandaging.

Groucho came running when Liam shouted, startled from some patch of shade with half-shut eyes.

"Help me get him on the animal," Liam said.

Groucho blessed himself, appalled.

"Señor. His legs!"

"That's why I don't ask him to walk. Come on."

Somehow they manhandled the man, with some terrifying moments but no disaster, sideways onto the llama, his poor legs dangling, and his apprehensive fingers tangled in the long thick wool.

"What happens if I fall off?"

Now there was feeling in the blank eyes—pain and suffering were recent and he could remember them.

"You'll break your legs like matchsticks," Liam said cheerfully. "So you'd better hang on."

"Señor! Where are you taking him?"

"To my house," said Liam grandly.

"Aiee-ee." Groucho looked up at him sadly, pulling on his moustaches. The convent door had not yet been mended and El Perdido seemed the one to have been sent by God to do it. He brightened. If the mad El Médico could get him up the mountain on the animal, then no doubt he could bring him down again when the man was ready.

He yelled after Liam as he started up the mountain.

"Señor! In five days I go to the town. Do you want me to see your friend?"

Liam did not look round, only raising a hand in acknowledgement, too preoccupied in leading the llama carefully round the worst of the rocks. He didn't really want the fellow to fall off.

Against all rules, when Sister Jesús María heard his voice, she opened a shutter to watch him go. He was taking the man up to the village. Then he would come even less often to the hospital, for he often looked in when he was down to see El Perdido. Or if there was nothing more, there was the sound of his voice as now, shouting at Groucho beyond the walls. Something. Anything. Dear God, if it was sin, it brought its own punishment.

Her beautiful young high-boned face grew pinched and bleak, rigid with hopelessness, and she closed the shutter and came back down the shadowed broiling room, her mind, as Liam's had once been, blind to the sufferings and sorrows of the patient people sweating on the cots. One sorrow could obliterate the world, and she could bear no longer to be faced with it on every sinful day.

She had heard what Groucho shouted.

In a week or so he would be going into the town.

chapter
8

With the steady and calculating competence that James brought to everything he did, it was no surprise that the first days of Isabella's marriage brought her to an ecstatic happiness, full of tender gratitude to this flawless man who had snatched her forever from the pit of misery. James in his turn was bland, a small satisfied smile curling the firm lips under his soft moustache. He had judged rightly that Isabella would be no shrinking miss, and that properly led would bring to her marriage the same candid directness that shone from her blue eyes over everything else.

So it came as no surprise, either, that she found almost immediately that she was pregnant.

"James. So soon!" she said, almost a little embarrassed, when she told him. It did not seem quite respectable. "So soon!"

James kissed her.

"Not a moment too soon for me!" he said, and his expression of contentment deepened. The child would bind her to him even more securely: at the back of his mind always the thought of some rich and disapproving father coming back from nowhere. Also, for the school of his dreams, his mind held the clear picture of the green lawns walked by Isabella with at least two or three children at her side. It gave the parents confidence. All was working out very well, and the children of the village found their new schoolmaster a benign and cheerful fellow in these snowy months of the early year of 1928.

Isabella was also thinking about her father, delighted to have the coming child to offer him as a proof of her happiness and to show him how well she had managed to settle herself when thrown on the world alone. She was proud and satisfied and deeply happy, and in the first days in Brackenham she had written to the lawyer in

Santiago with her new address. Any news now would be direct. No more relying on other people like Catchpole and Quickly. Mrs. Britten had been so totally disinterested she had not even bothered to give it to her, knowing she would write herself in days.

"Dearest," she said, "would you take this to the little shop in the morning to catch the post?"

Every morning even in the deep snow, lit to blue and rose by the early sun, James took a walk before his breakfast in the snug kitchen. Isabella smiled indulgently. Already she knew that James was a man of habit. He chose his habits himself, and nothing would shake them, although if other people had habits they must be changed at once to please him.

Effie thought he was a little mad, watching him climb into his boots in the bitter morning as she opened the dampers and raked out the ashes to get the stove roaring for the new day.

"Three rashers and two eggs, Effie, please," he said.

That was habit, too, and she had begun to realize he would never eat anything else, but still he instructed her every day.

"I'm going up through the village with Madam's letter," he said, partly to fix it in Effie's mind and partly in his campaign to make Effie call Isabella Madam. She was no longer Miss Isabella. The girl couldn't seem to realize.

"Yessir," said Effie.

All contact with the outside world came with the postman, who cycled the six miles from Lavenham every morning, even through the ice and snowdrifts, to collect and deposit letters in the one tiny village shop, and James set off up the rambling street in the clear beautiful, bitter morning. The snow had come the day after they arrived and James realized he had far from his full quota of children yet, as the ones from outlying farms were unable to get in to the school.

He fingered the letter in the pocket of his oilskin. He had no intention of posting it whatever. Isabella was the perfect complement to all his plans, and they were all working out exactly as he wished them; Isabella dependent and grateful, and all the future mapped out step by step. Her father would be dictatorial as all rich men were: interfering. It was the last thing James wanted. Firmly he strode up the long street, the snow hard under his feet, consciously taking His Walk. From every haphazard cottage a plume of smoke rose straight to an icy brilliant sky, as like Effie people kindled the fires against the bitter morning, snow piled against the windows where lights still glowed in small dark rooms.

James marched past them all, and through the small panes they looked up from the fire or the children, or where they shaved in their braces before a fly-blown kitchen mirror, to see him pass. In their view the new Schoolmaster was a strange man, but then in their view all schoolmasters were strange men, and they sent their children to them only because if they didn't, the attendance man from the county would come hammering on their doors! They themselves had managed with little learning, and thought it of doubtful value to their children.

James had found a lane at the edge of the long street that would bring him back out onto the wide space of the village Green, where great oaks and elms stood skeleton against the snow. Across the green, set at an angle, would be the Schoolhouse, and Isabella waiting with his breakfast.

In the lane, snow banked high in smooth lovely dunes along the hedges and barely trodden underfoot, he stopped and took Isabella's letter from his pocket. Carefully he tore it into small pieces and stuffed them deep into a snowdrift, covering them with snow. Satisfied, he went on: by the time the snow melted it would be mushed and indecipherable. Best thing to do.

Benignly he came in through the back door of the Schoolhouse, taking off his wet boots in the scullery and banging the clotted snow on the floor for Effie to mop up, putting on the warm slippers Isabella had left for him. Rubbing his hands, he came on through, up the step into the kitchen, and kissed her, where she stood at the stove, turning the heavy, ancient pan. Effie was sweeping out the freezing schoolroom and starting up the stove in there.

"Well, my sweet," said James to Isabella. "What's for breakfast?"

"Three rashers and two eggs," said Isabella, still charmed by James's smallest want. Not yet noticing habit and monotony.

"Good," said James, as though it surprised him. "Good."

He sat down at the snow-white cloth with which Effie had laid the table, and Isabella waited on him.

Isabella was happy through all that spring and summer carrying her child: deeply and tranquilly happy, nagged only by the ceaseless prick of grief about her father. As time passed, she knew a certain surprise that the lawyer had never replied to her letter, but comforted herself that he would certainly write if he had something to tell her. He had her address, and every time she thought of that, she hugged to herself the pleasure that it was her own home and that she was no longer dependent on anybody.

Except on James, of course, and that was different.

She was charmed by the simplicity of living in the village, where, if she fancied, she could walk up the straggling street to the little crowded shop that smelled of meat and candles, and provided for the most primitive wants of the village.

But she preferred to do her shopping at the door. At Enderby she had had no idea where food came from. It was always on the table, and all the necessities of life available. In Brackenham there seemed always some patient horse standing at the door, having plodded bravely through the snow. The Oil Man, the Bread Man, the Meat Man, and the Thread Man between them left little she could want.

The Oil Man brought yellow soap and Bathbrick and Reckitt's Blue and Robin starch: candles in bundles with brown paper bands around them; all stacked as in a cave in the dark recesses of the cart: at its back the tank of paraffin, strong-smelling, dripping yellow into the snow as the can was filled by his frozen fingers.

They brought news and gossip from the villages around, although Effie got more out of them than Isabella did. They felt something vaguely wrong about Isabella, who belonged, they felt, in one of the big houses outside the village, where they came always to the back door and never saw the mistress. Not standoffish, she wasn't. But different.

The Thread Man was a gypsy, his hooded cart a brilliant red and yellow, and as well as needles and thread he had bolts of cloth and cards of lace and stockings and blouses and underwear and even the occasional dress, and would, with his white flashing smile, willingly bring anything else he was asked to.

The Bread Man came from the neighboring village of Brecon, and his pale fat face looked like his own uncooked dough. His name was Barker and all the children ran after him singing, "Baker Barker Brecon bakes brown bread." "Tee-hee-hee" was all he would say, grinning his fat grin. "Tee-hee-hee." Isabella thought him a bit simple, but his bread was gorgeous.

The Meat Man came when he felt like it, or had anything to sell, and the same with the Fish Man she had only seen once.

Isabella knew she should let Effie deal with them, but could not resist putting on her coat and wrapping a warm scarf over her head, and coming out to pick over the treasures of their carts.

James told her it wasn't suitable.

If also, as time passed, she began to understand that James was not so much dependable as dogmatic and obstinate, measuring no opinion but his own, she was still so much in love with him, and so grateful, that she took it only as an endearing trait. For her in that lovely summer, everything James did and said was perfect, and she carried his child like a treasure.

And kept his house like an adoring slave. Not that she had a great deal to do, for Effie forestalled every effort, telling her to rest and look after the baby. Nor did Effie look at James with the same uncritical eyes, and came to the conclusion very rapidly that Miss Isabella had married herself a tyrant: although, God be praised, she didn't seem to notice it much yet. And when the baby came, there would be that to keep her happy.

James in his turn disliked Effie, not finding in her pale protuberant eyes the approval he demanded and expected. But he was aware that maids for nothing did not grow on trees, and he doubted Isabella's ability to manage on her own. So, both of them, loving Isabella, held uneasy truce, and between them Isabella bloomed, tranquil as a rose.

The Schoolhouse stood at an angle that allowed it to look down the straggling length of the village street of thatched and slate roof cottages of all shapes and sizes: and also to the right over the expanse of the village Green, where great elms and oaks spread their green shade and the children played and tumbled and shrieked and old men sat and gossiped on wooden benches and on the rough grass there was the occasional cricket match with a neighboring village. The first thing Isabella watched there was a great snowball fight on the day after Christmas; the men of the village dividing into two, and all the women and children coming out to watch and cheer them, wrapped like bundles against the cold: dark against the fresh snow. And several of the men wearing their tin helmets from the Great War. It seemed they did it every year.

She longed to go out also, and watch and cheer herself, and thought it a good opportunity to meet the villagers. But James would have none of it. She would, he said, catch cold. But in reality he thought it beneath his dignity, watching with distaste the shouting, tumbling figures in the snow. No place for him.

A huge horse chestnut spread its bare fingers over the red Schoolhouse roof, taking up most of their tiny garden, and the school ran back at right angles to the house, so that only Effie in the scullery and the yard knew anything about it, and the playtime bedlam of the playground. After her first visit Isabella was not allowed in the school. She had thought it bleak and empty in the cold snow-light, and thought there was much that even she could have done to make it brighter and more cheerful for the children. She could draw and paint quite well, she said. Could she not get the Thread Man to get her some paints and paper, and she could do some big cheerful pictures that children like. Could she and Effie perhaps not even paint the woodwork something other than that awful brown?

But again, scandalized, James would have none of it. The school in his mind was the pattern of the one he would have in the end, where his wife would only be seen walking the lawns with his children. Through the eyes of his future he did not really see the crowds of red-cheeked country children huddled unwillingly on the benches of his bitter schoolroom, with its bare walls.

He would at least talk about it, and she loved to see his calm face kindle with his enthusiasm.

"I don't want to teach them just the Three R's," he said to her, sitting over the warm fire in their tiny parlor, the snow piled on the windowsill beyond the curtains. "I want to tell them of the world, make their minds reach out. I want to tell them of the Pyramids of Egypt and the Taj Mahal; the Sahara Desert and the Andes."

Isabella could not understand that he wanted to broaden their minds to things they would probably not believe in, but would not allow one single picture of something they might know and enjoy.

"They will think you mad," she said, thinking of the little she had already seen of the bucolic villagers and their children. "I could tell them of the Andes," she said then reflectively, ripped by a sudden heartsick memory of the great dark snowcapped bastion against the sky beyond the desert.

"You?" James halted in surprise.

"James! I have told you where I lived. Of course I knew about the Andes. My father took me on expeditions into them. I have told you."

James only grunted and in a moment went back to his own ideas. Isabella knew a glimmer of sad nervous understanding that he did not really care where she came from: that a girl without background was exactly what he had wanted. To place her in his setting, and mold her to his taste. Like the children. A prickle of fear touched her as to what it would be like when her father came back, and without any option her world would be thrust on James. Enderby was only twenty miles away, and her father was not one to be ignored.

But James had gone on talking, and she lost her moment's fear in the warm enthusiasm of the brown eyes, and in her own excited certainty that he would accomplish everything he planned. He was wonderful. Wonderful. So strong and determined. Of course he would get on with her father. And then he could have his school.

It was James who ran the school, and Effie who did the housework and most of the cooking, but it was Isabella who managed all the little touches that turned the tiny Schoolhouse with its nondescript furniture into a home. Conjuring some comfort, and elegance even, out of nothing, so that James preened himself, and saw his dream of the future perfect. He had chosen well.

She got on, too, with the village people, piercing their reserve with her candor and friendliness, never waiting to be spoken to first, but speaking herself with her beautiful wide smile, capturing them so that although they said among themselves that she seemed too much of a lady to be Schoolmaster's wife, they soon accepted her. And James, with greater reservation. Thought a little bit too much of himself, did Schoolmaster, they decided. But she was lovely. And expecting so soon, poor thing.

The wind turned soft to the west and the snow melted, and in the playtimes she could hear the children shrieking and yelling in the playground at the back, released, themselves, from the bondage of the snow, her days punctuated now by the piercing sound of James's whistle as he called them in from play.

March stretched into April and the lanes around the village were starred with primroses and violets. Charmed with them, Isabella picked them with delight, coming home with great fragrant bunches to set on the windowsills of her parlor and kitchen, watched indulgently by the people of the village, who took the coming of their flowers as they did the coming of their lambs, simply a marking of the turning year.

James looked at the tiny perfumed flowers, bunched into teacups, for the Schoolhouse made no provision for such frivolities as flowers.

"When the weather warms," he said, "I shall take the children on nature rambles. Teach them to see such things properly."

"What do you mean by properly?" Isabella asked him, touching the soft petals with her finger, loving them only for their color and perfume, and delicate perfection.

"As part," said James, "of the Grand Pattern of Nature."

"But, James," she said, and could not help a smile. "In a village like this, even the children you teach are part of that, never mind the flowers. They take it all for granted."

"Not as I shall teach them to see it." James was pompous and a little annoyed. Isabella's place was only to admire.

She kissed him on his nose.

"My darling James," she said, "they will think again that you are mad."

It did not take Isabella long to realize, nor did James need to tell her, that she must let down her skirts again, and she thanked heaven that she had not cut them off. The Bright Young Things of Newstead had no place in Brackenham, which would have been shocked to hostility to see the knees of Schoolmaster's wife. They even stared at her hair and obviously thought it fast, but accepted it because they liked her, and she came, so the whisper went round, from some heathen foreign country, so she must not be expected to be like other people.

The huge horse chestnut over their roof bloomed with great pink candles that scattered petals like a second snow across the tiny garden. She looked up at the blossoms and laid her hand on her body, thinking that when they turned to the shiny brown conkers that the children loved, her own child would be born.

She was actively and tenderly happy with her husband and her coming child, and the sad pain over her father had sunk to a dull ache of acceptance; almost acknowledgement now, that he might never come back.

But James had removed the nightmare of insecurity. Tomorrow was as safe as today, and mornings for walking with pleasure and content. Inevitably her love for her husband was rich with gratitude.

Effie watched them both with her shrewd pale eyes and pursed her small mouth. She, too, had everything to be grateful for to James, for had he not taken her away from the intolerable situation at her mother's and given her a home? But unlike Isabella, she had no illusions but that he had done it only to please himself, with Miss Isabella unable so much as to boil an egg properly. He was not worth, she thought, Miss Isabella's little finger, and deep inside her she felt a certainty that he would one day bring her to unhappiness.

Isabella felt the child to be growing with the year, through the high summer, as her body became heavy, and at the same time flowers spangled the long rich grass in the ditches as she walked slowly through the village, returning the benevolent smiles of the women. She had looked forward to having many jaunts in the Norton once spring and summer were come, but James would have none of it, lest it shake his son.

"My son," he called it all the time with certainty. James was the kind of man who felt he had failed in his masculinity if he did not have a son. Daughters were for weaklings, and Isabella would do nothing so unsuitable as to have one.

"And what, James," she would say to him, "if it is a daughter?"—not believing he would mind as long as she safely bore his child. But James would look at her with something close to anger that she should even think of failing him, and a hint of nervousness entered into her waiting. He could not really mind so much.

"My son," he would say. "My son."

"Our child," she would answer, lest his own foolish determination should disappoint him.

Reluctantly, in the Easter holiday, she had persuaded him to take Effie in to Bury St. Edmunds to buy materials for the baby's clothes, and through the sunny days she sat by the window of the kitchen and sewed while Effie cooked. James disapproved of this. She should sit in the parlor and keep Effie in something called her Place. But Isabella could never forget the terrible time of her life when Effie had been her only friend, and would not change toward her. The parlor was hot and stuffy in the summer anyway.

She looked with pleasure at the small fine clothes she was so beautifully stitching, and the tucks of the feather stitching and the fine French hems: the minute and perfect buttonholes.

"At least, Effie," she said, "I'm making use of something Catchpole's taught me."

Effie snorted even at the name, up to her wrists in flour. She looked over at what Isabella was sewing.

"You'll need to have a girl, Miss Isabella, to show those off."

Isabella looked appalled.

"Oh, Effie, I wouldn't *dare*. Mr. Bennett wants a son."

The corners of Effie's mouth drew down.

"He's not God."

Isabella said nothing, because she realized that in his own small world, this was precisely what James was, with his schoolroom full of children to whom his every word was law, and his two dependent women, both of whom he had, godlike, snatched from some disaster.

Dear James. Although she had begun to understand him and to realize that he wanted his own school simply because he could not take orders or suggestions from anyone, she would not have him otherwise. Strong, decisive, and the bulwark between her and a world grown hostile. She had learned to subdue her own strong personality and channel it into ways of getting James to do what she wanted by convincing him it was his idea in the first place. With a glimmer of understanding she had not had as a child, she felt it very possible that her lovely and gentle mother had had to do just this with her father.

James and her father, she reflected, were really much alike, except that James was more sober and down-to-earth. No doubt, she thought contentedly, that was why she loved them both so much.

She sat with him through the warm evenings of high summer, on the bench in the little garden at the side of the house, among the tangle of small country flowers that she promised herself she would turn into a real garden next spring. Stocks perfumed the heavy air and in the falling dusk the swifts swooped low over the Green across the road, where the great trees massed summer-solid against the limpid sky. Peaceful time of day, wearied now by her heavy body in the August heat: anxious to have it over and the child in her arms.

But it was not until the great gold hunter's moon of October was swinging over the elms by night, that she suddenly grew still one morning at breakfast, her eyes fixed on James's face as though he could do something to avert it now that it had come. He who had absorbed everything that troubled her.

James noticed nothing, finished his breakfast, and stood up, blotting his mouth methodically with his napkin.

"James, don't go." Her voice was sharp. "I think the baby's coming."

James beamed paternally.

"And high time, too. There's nothing to be afraid of, Isabella, I've told you it's all perfectly natural. I'll send Effie for Mrs. Pickup, but I have to go into the school."

"James. Don't leave me."

"Sweetheart. It's not like you to be foolish. Women have babies every day. Effie will only be gone ten minutes." He bent and kissed her. "My son," he said. "My son."

"Your son!" thought Isabella with a burst of mutiny, torn by another pain. But you are not the one going to have it. She was suddenly frightened. There seemed nothing natural about the pain that was ripping her. So soon. Took a long time to work up, Effie had said. Hours before it really bothered you. First baby could go on all day and nothing to it. But not this. Not this.

Effie could have delivered the baby herself: seen enough of it, goodness knew, but then her mother had them, as she said herself, like shelling peas. One look at Isabella's face told her that right from the beginning this was different. She waited only to see her back into bed before going straight off through the cool fresh morning for the village midwife.

Mrs. Pickup was not the conventional blousy midwife: a tall, lean, spotless woman of great calm and experience, whose ill-fitting dentures clacked like the castanets of Isabella's childhood. She came at once, curious, as all the village was, to get into the home of Schoolmaster and his foreigner: coming in to Isabella with her bright china smile, and her air of quiet confidence and knowing what to do.

The hunter's moon was sliding down behind the elms and the night grown still around the village, when with Isabella, gaunt and sweating and screaming for her mother, and clinging to Effie's hands fit to break the bones, she came down to James who sat beside the kitchen range. Already he was feeling things had been mismanaged, since he had had no supper. He did not like to hear Isabella screaming. Surely even childbirth should be handled with dignity.

"Well, Mrs. Pickup? My son? It's been very slow."

"Sir." She tried to keep the panic from her eyes. "Sir. I think you should go to Lavenham for the doctor. In that machine."

And quickly, she wanted to add. Quickly. Or you could lose her. The deliberation with which he put on his leather coat and helmet maddened her. The man seemed reluctant to go. Did he not understand? She clamped her clacking mouth and glared at him.

James did not really understand. His firm mouth tightened as he kicked the Norton into life, almost more with annoyance than fear. Nothing could happen to his son, or indeed to Isabella, simply because they were his. He did not approve of this uproar and inefficiency that was only delaying things.

The doctor came at once, and they roared back through the cool misty night. But the kitchen was light, and flushed with dawn before he came back downstairs to James. A young man like himself, looking at him with a careful and considering eye. Tired, his thin fair face drawn.

James had heard the child cry and forgot there had ever been any difficulty. Ready now for the congratulations.

"My son?" he said. "My son?"

The doctor paused a long moment, looking at him.

"You have a daughter, Mr. Bennett. Also you have a wife, in which you are very fortunate. You may go and see her for just a moment, and then I would be grateful if you would take me home." James's mouth opened and closed like a fish's, ready for a moment simply to berate the doctor. Then it shut and a look of outrage took his face, with the realization that real disaster could actually overtake him.

He turned and pounded up the wooden stairs.

Isabella looked worn and shocked in the pale light, but exquisite, her brown hair already brushed, spread out on the pillow, the lids falling in exhaustion over the great blue eyes: pools of anxiety and apology that waited only for James. The baby, wrapped in one of the shawls she had so tenderly knitted for James's son, lay sleeping, crumple-faced, in the crook of her arm.

Effie and the midwife busied themselves about the washstand and did not look at him, whispering together. He glared at them as angrily as if it were they who had made the offending daughter.

Then he made himself, rigid with disappointment, bend to kiss Isabella. She was young. There would be other chances. There would be his son.

"Oh, James," she said. "I'm sorry. So sorry."

Before he could find anything to say, the lids had fallen over the exhausted eyes and she was asleep. He barely glanced at the baby, turning back downstairs to the kitchen, where the doctor waited for him, his back to the welcome fire.

"I would be very pleased if you could give me a cup of tea, Mr. Bennett," he said, and knew that if he did not ask for it, this smooth self-centered character would send him off with nothing, even after the long night hopefully saving the life of that lovely creature upstairs.

"Effie!" shouted James, and the doctor moved to look abstractedly out the window, turning round only when Effie held out the steaming cup. She avoided his eyes.

"I will be back, Mr. Bennett," he said as he sipped his tea gratefully, and although the great trees on the Green still loomed like ghosts in the breaking mist, the first sun of the day warmed the back of his neck through the window. "I will be back tomorrow to see them both."

James looked black.

"Is it necessary, Doctor? Has she not the woman there?"

Tonight would cost him half a crown at least. More.

"It is necessary," the doctor said, but James was oblivious to his look of distaste, thinking only to get him away as fast as possible so that he might be back in time for his morning walk before school.

Isabella slept through most of the day, waking only to take the wrapped-up baby that Effie gave her when it was time to feed it. James, ever mindful of his picture of himself as fair and just, put aside his first disappointment conscientiously and was kind to her, bringing at last the true radiance of her motherhood to her tired face.

"Oh, James." She smiled weakly up at him, blue eyes full of gratitude that he should not be angry. "I know she is a girl, and it's a great disappointment to you, but she is *very* beautiful."

He managed an indulgent smile.

"She is your baby," he said. "Soon you will have a son for me."

"Several, James dearest. Oh, several."

Tenderly she smiled down at the tiny creature in her arms, and Effie, coming in to take the baby, caught the expression on her face, and the careful benignity of her husband's. Turning, she clattered back down the wooden stairs, and stood in the kitchen, blindly poking the glowing stove and wiping the tears from her face with the back of a sooty hand.

"Oh, my lawks," she said to no one, despairingly. "Oh, my lawks. Poor Miss Isabella."

And James came down and told her to wash her face and hands before she served his supper, nor did he even question why she should be weeping like this alone, in what should be a house of happiness.

In the dusk of the October day, and the first lamplight, the doctor's gig drew up outside the door, the black horse itself like a shadow of the evening. Curtains stirred in all the windows of the nearby houses, for the news from the midwife had run like wildfire through the village. They all knew already what James did not know, in the complacency and tolerance upon which he prided himself. Who, they wondered, would be the one to tell him? And the poor girl.

He let the doctor in, bidding him as patient a good evening as he could manage.

"And how is she?"

Damp rimmed his beaver hat and he took it off and laid it on the table.

"Well, Doctor, well."

As though it was only to be expected, this visit unnecessary. Why shouldn't she be well? Isabella was a strong healthy girl.

"And the baby?"

James did not understand why the man was examining him so closely. Cold gray eyes, with the sparkle of the lamp in them. He shrugged, smiled a man-of-the-world smile, trying to crush irritability and an infuriating feeling that this sad-eyed man was finding him inadequate in some way.

"As babies are," he said.

The doctor turned and, without another word, went up the narrow stairs. It was a long time before James heard him coming down again; slow, deliberate footfalls on the high, uncarpeted treads. He came into the kitchen and put his black bag on the table beside his hat. James was only waiting for him to go.

"May I sit down?"

Grudgingly James assented, and across the rag rug the gray eyes looked at him again carefully, in the lamplight.

"Everything *is* all right?" James asked, and knew a pang of real fear that surprised him. The man looked so grave. Of course everything was all right.

"No, Mr. Bennett." The doctor steepled his fingers and watched him over them. There was a hint of frost in the evening, and the range glowed scarlet. "No, Mr. Bennett, I am afraid everything is not all right."

James sat immobile, the fire-glow on his face, his eyes fixed on the other man. Things did not go wrong for James Bennett. Young, strong girl, to have his sons.

"As you know, it was a very difficult birth. It would be most unwise, I think, for your wife ever to try and have another child."

Even as James reeled under the loss of all his sons, gaping, the doctor spoke again.

"And I am afraid there is," he said slowly, "something wrong with the baby."

Winter was coming to the high village: clear beautiful wind-washed days, and nights of bitter cold: sudden outbursts of teeming rain, the torn clouds so low that mountain peaks and even the village itself thrust through them with an air of darkness and mystery.

Liam was well pleased with his idea of bringing the man up from the convent and into the village. No memory yet: only the occasional stillness of the eyes, as though he were groping for something and, not finding it, going back to vacancy.

But he was less irritable: talked to the dark patient people of the village and helped them make their simple furniture and re-build their poor fallen houses when they were washed away by rain. Teaching them how to strengthen them so they might stand against the next flood. Working as hard as his legs and his crutches would allow him, clearly finding in the work some relief from the tensions aching in his empty mind.

Liam watched him, and carefully pieced together all he saw, never pausing to realize that for the first time in three years he was thinking more of someone else than of the morass of his own blind griefs and sorrows.

He listened to him, too, as they sat together in the small adobe house that the priest's housekeeper looked at with increasing approval. There had been long times when she had not dared even to venture in to try and keep El Médico from living like an animal: when the food she brought would be left outside the door uneaten or even thrown against the walls.

Now El Médico was changing, the dark rage, whatever persecution of God had caused it, was going from his eyes, and he saw again how he was living. As for the mindless one, he was neat and careful and everything must be placed about him so.

So Liam talked to him, in the newly tidy house, or on the benches of the cantina in the fading summer when the children rolled and scrambled in the dust and the last of the golandinas flashed their yellow throats against the purple sky.

From the blank wind came snatches here and there, vague, disconnected, flashes of faint light in darkness. Liam carefully pieced them all together.

Groucho came to him, the light of his expedition into the world bright in his bulbous eyes.

"Señor Médico," he said, "I am going to the town. You will want me to get these medicines from your friend."

"I will, Groucho. And I want you to give him a letter."

Carefully he worded the advertisement. Physical characteristics: well-cared-for body when he was found. Fine hands. Could possibly be an engineer: a geologist. Probably a man with a family.

Then he begged pen and paper from the priest and wrote it out, with a note asking his friend to place it in the biggest newspaper in Valparaiso. With the help of God that might get the fellow back where he belonged. There hadn't been enough to say before— just a statement that there was a man injured in the earthquake could have brought too many people on the long weary journey to the village only to have their hopes dashed when they got there. Now that there was more to tell, they might place him. Although, Liam thought sadly, no one would be looking for this bearded wreck with the shattered legs. Anyone looking for this man would be searching for someone rich and handsome. Whatever the outcome, there would be grief.

In any case it was a year. People would have stopped looking. But he must try.

It was a cool day with the first wind of winter whipping off the snows. He walked down the hill to give it to Groucho.

"Ah, señor," he said as he took it. "I thought you had forgotten. I was almost off. I am just waiting for the Sister."

"The Sister?"

These nuns never went anywhere. What Sister?

Groucho's goiterous eyes were bulging with his news.

"The Sister Jesús María. She is going back to the world. Indeed, señor."

Liam gaped at him.

"And what in Jaysus prompted that? For good?"

"I do not know, señor. I have only just been told."

A girl came out of the convent, alone, carrying a small wicker basket. No one stood to say good-bye and the door closed sharply behind her in her ill-fitting clothes: obviously dragged from some convent cupboard. But they could do nothing, he thought, amazed, to disguise the rich beauty of her figure. All this, he thought, beneath that convent habit. And those great green eyes. He stared, hypnotized. Some man was going to be glad to get Sister Jesús María back into the world, the lucky fellow. But what was it all about?

She seemed to have difficulty coming to the wagon, and when he spoke to her she blushed scarlet, distress clear in her face, sculpted in fine bones under the colored scarf that wrapped her shorn head.

"What's this, Sister Jesús María? What will I do without you?"

"I have decided," was all she said, and would not meet his eyes, climbing dumbly into the wagon. He looked at her, full of certainty there was something he did not understand. Angry, without knowing why. There was only one thing he could think to say and do.

"For the love of God," he said, "is that all the clothes you have? A cotton dress for the cold nights? Here, take this."

He pulled off his woollen blanket and thrust it at her, and from the rickety wagon she took it in her hands as if it were a sacrament, the green eyes above it brimming with tears. Holding it tenderly between her fingers.

Groucho shouted at the mules and the wagon lurched away, and still she looked at him. As if saying good-bye to life itself.

Liam shivered in the cold wind, and watched her go, bothered by the feeling that there was something he had missed. Something important he had failed to understand. Maybe he should have talked to the girl.

The wagon lumbered down into the valley and on the wind he

could still hear Groucho cracking his whip and shouting at the mules. Sister Jesús María looked no more than a bundle in the back, the blanket still between her fingers.

Frowning, he turned back up the hill to beg another blanket from Father Ignacio's housekeeper, briefly wondering about the patients in the makeshift hospital: distracted then by a sudden and unbidden presentiment that he would not be there much longer himself, to care for them.

One day in April when the whole village was in danger of sliding down the yellow mountain from days of torrential rain, Liam saw the last of his grateful patients splashing through the puddles down the path from his doorway. He cleared up after the morning and reflected on another aspect of having El Perdido to live with him. The small room was immaculately clean and tidy, the blankets straightened on both beds, and from somewhere the man had begged a worn rug to cover the earthen floor. God keep him, he was a compulsive housekeeper.

What surprised Liam was that he had to admit he liked it, and put his own things away that much more carefully on his solitary shelf. Nor did the bottle of *agua ardiente* alone in the hut appeal to him anymore. He took the blanket with the hole in it from his bed, and pulled it over his head to go across the plaza to the cantina. Although the rain had stopped, the very air was wet with its own chill: the adobe buildings dark with soaked water and the torn clouds floating like wraiths away below the village.

He stood between the crude pillars of the colonnade of the cantina, unwilling to go inside, and unwilling to sit on one of the sodden chairs outside. Gratefully he felt the warmth of the *agua ardiente* go down into his chilly stomach and regarded the plaza. Apart from the few bedraggled hens pecking around the bench in the middle, it was empty, but as he stood there, he could hear them, whatever it was they were all up to. The whole village was somewhere and creating bedlam. And banging away at metal, like an old forge.

He took the bottle from the stained counter, and the glass, noticing the half-blind movements of the old bartender. The man had two cataracts, and what could he, Liam, do about that? For a moment fury flared against the inadequacies of his resources in the village, surprising him who had been willing to plod mindlessly along with what he had, helping those he could and leaving those he couldn't. As though struck by an enemy, he thrust aside the thought, and went on down, glass and bottle in hand, to see what was happening on the mountain, where all the noise was coming from.

The center of the village was the long square with the few decent adobe buildings that the place possessed, the church with its cracking steps and rusted bell; the house of the *Alcalde* that even had the high grace of a balcony, the priest's house, and a few more single-storied dwellings built from the mud of the mountains by the less patient, who were weary of being washed away.

From the square the narrow, muddy alleys of shacks spread out like tentacles in both directions along the mountain, and down below lay the hectares of cultivated fields. Water from the endless spring poured out into the tiled trough where the village drank and washed and did its washing under the fountain and in the tiled trough itself, and the water then poured on out through a pipe in the base to irrigate the fields below. Should they want water elsewhere in the village, they carried it by hand or rolled it in a barrel that trundled on its own axis on a wooden pole.

There were not even any women slapping and beating their washing at the trough as he passed the end of the straggling plaza. But he could see and hear them all below him, a dark mass in their ragged ponchos and felt hats, many still wet from the rain, all gathered down the rough steps beyond the fountain: men, women, and children all gathered in the sliding mud, chattering with excitement at the diversion in their soft un-Spanish Spanish. Another *loco*—

All watching El Perdido.

He was nearly finished. From somewhere he had found a long sheet of rusty corrugated iron. Probably, thought Liam wryly, pinched someone's roof. Even without his memory El Perdido was a formidable character.

The banging was explained. He had had it hammered into a V-shaped channel and now, crutches and all, was up to his shins in dirty yellow mud, yelling directions at three men who were digging the end of it into the hillside underneath where the water cascaded from the base of the fountain falling some meters down to the flooded earth beneath.

He shouted and gesticulated and browbeat them, sending them for rocks to support it, until the water flowed steadily down instead of dropping like a waterfall to flood the ground.

Liam reached to help him out on to dryer ground.

He was soaked, sweating, and gray with exhaustion, but his eyes were alive, blazing at Liam and the gathered villagers. The men were already beginning to do as he had told them, and were digging the first irrigation channel from the end of the trough, so that all the water went straight to the fields.

"Fools," he cried to Liam, heedlessly wiping his muddy hands on his sodden poncho. "Couldn't they see they were losing half their water there where it fell from the pipe? There was so much soaking in there, it could make another spring lower down. Wasted. All wasted!"

Liam regarded him with carefully held excitement, still holding his bottle and his glass.

"And how, Fergus," he said carefully—he always called him Fergus, as it was the only name to which he had reacted—"how did you know to do all that?"

Know? The bright eyes clouded and grew vague. "Know? I don't know how I knew." Already he was looking at the flowing water as though it had been nothing to do with him. Spent and uninterested.

But hope flew in Liam's mind.

"A great piece of engineering," he said.

"Engineering!" The dirty hands gripped the crutches and again the eyes flared. Liam watched them carefully. Nothing yet was getting as far as speech, the awakening impulses showing only in the eyes. This one lasted no longer than a second, and then he was again an exhausted, dimwitted cripple.

"Come on up," Liam said, and pressed him no more. "Come on up to the fountain and wash yourself and we'll see if we can get you some dry clothes."

He and the man together, he thought, stumbling toward something, and almost as difficult for both of them. He flung the glass away and put the bottle of *agua ardiente* to his mouth. When

Father Ignacio's housekeeper came to them later with a bowl of chili, he was drunk.

"*Borracho, padre,*" she said sadly to Father Ignacio when she went back, placing his own food before him with old hands as gnarled and withered as dried wood. "*Borracho* again. He has not been that way lately."

"It is to be expected," the old man said wisely. "All cannot happen overnight, for either of them. Or, please God, for both."

Change. Change. The nun had gone, and only he in the confessional knew why and pitied her. Occasions of sin. Soon these two would go as they had come, and the village would turn in upon itself, with only the things they had done to remember them by. And that not for very long. Children growing, who might have died and would die the next time. And the clever new thing with the water would be allowed to rust and rot until it collapsed and the water fell again as it had always fallen, wastefully onto the mountain beneath.

He sighed and broke off a piece of tortilla, looking at it distastefully. Maria was no cook.

The stranger woke early a few days later, the sun of a bright clear morning coming in shafts of brilliant light through the broken shutters. He lay and watched the light, and unbidden, wandering into his mind, came the knowledge of another window where the light also came in through shutters in the morning. But there were soft white curtains round it and the sun fell on, fell on—

"Liam!" he yelled.

But by the time Liam was awake and aware, the man was defeated, weeping, already unable even to remember the memory.

For another week he groped and searched after fragments that danced through his brain like the fireflies above the fields at night. Hopeless and desperate with frustration.

"Tell me everything," Liam urged him. "However small. Tell me every single thing you remember. That helps to hold it."

But he could never get the images that stormed into his brain as far as words, only the anguish in his blue eyes telling of his fearful battle.

Liam could do no more than encourage him, and the high-boned Indian faces stared at him as they would at a statue that had spoken: for word had flown through the poor shacks of the village that El Perdido was loosing the curse upon his mind, and remembering who he was.

They blessed themselves when he limped past on his crutches through the cold winds, and did not know what to expect or pray for.

Liam was sleeping little, alert night and day for any hint of returning memory, trying desperately to build on it, forgetting about sleep; forgetting the *agua ardiente*, bent, he thought, on a long, slow job of coaxing back the dead mind.

He got up one morning, in a brilliant beautiful dawn from which wind had swept all clouds, leaving clear purple sky; every line and shape of the tumbledown plaza etched sharp against it. There was no one yet stirring: even the hens slept, roosting on the rotting beams of the colonnade. Only Maria, the priest's housekeeper, was already at the fountain with her lump of yellow soap, banging and slapping at the laundry of both priest and church, and indeed of Liam and El Perdido as well, when they could spare anything to be washed. Her tiny emaciated figure was all that moved in the bright still day, touched yet with some cool shadow of the night. Black as a bent old bird above the water.

Surprised, Liam found himself aware of the morning and the silence with a sharpness he had lost for years; the world became something he walked through, even in his rare moments of sobriety, unseeing, and uncaring. Save when his hands and his eyes found sickness, and all his deepest instincts could not help responding: some part of him still fighting where he met it, the death he had so longed for for himself.

Now suddenly he was aware of the sharp exquisite morning and the new day that it implied. No longer a burden but a gift. He gave the lopsided grin that so few people in the village had ever seen.

"B'God, Liam," he said aloud. "You must be going soft."

There was no more time to think about the state of his own mind. Behind him there was a hoarse shout and a heavy thump on to the hard earthen floor: a cry of pain. He whirled back into the room and from the ground, his legs crumpled under him, the stranger blazed at him with confused but furious blue eyes.

"My legs," he shouted. "God dammit, what's happened to my legs?

"And where am I? What is this hole?"

He glared round the miserable room.

"And who are you? What has happened? I tried to get out of bed and fell down. What's the matter with my legs?"

Panic filled his eyes and his voice was rising, sweat breaking suddenly on his face.

"First things first," said Liam, and hoped he could match himself to the moment. To hold it, and not find it gone back in minutes to the same cloudy vagueness. He helped him from the floor back onto the bed and examined his legs, talking quietly all the time.

"No harm done, I think, but I can imagine it hurt you. You were in the path of an earthquake. Smashed both legs and smashed your head, and lost your memory. Been here in this village almost a year. I'm a doctor. I patched you up as best I could, but you'll not walk again without sticks or crutches."

The man growled at that, but his mouth was open, gazing at Liam, trying to accept all he had told him.

"A year?" he said, and now his voice was hoarse. "I was going with Gordon to look at a new mine site. Where's Gordon? Where's my friend who was with me? What village?"

Correct, correct, correct, thought Liam jubilantly. If the first thing he remembers, so quickly, is the last thing that has happened to him, then there is every hope he will be all right. He sat down on his own bed and carefully asked the big question. Trying not to force him.

"Do you know who you are?"

The blue eyes bulged with the effort and the sweat ran down into the man's beard.

But the answer came.

"My name," he said, and every word was an effort, "is Frost. Angus Frost," he added, and Liam realized how close he had been with Fergus. "Angus Frost. I am a mine owner and engineer in the north of the Atacama Desert. I am—"

A note of authority had begun to creep in and show a little of the real man, but suddenly again fear and panic filled his eyes. He tried once more to scramble from the bed and Liam held him back. He clutched Liam's arm, fingers digging to the bone, shaking from head to foot.

"Clara," he shouted, shaking Liam as he was shaking himself. "And Isabella! Dear God in Heaven. Clara and Isabella."

"And who are they?" Liam asked him, trying to ease the crushing fingers on his arm. "Who are they?" he said quietly.

Angus Frost looked at him as though it was he that was mad.

"My wife!" he shouted again. "Who else? My wife and daughter!"

chapter
9

"But, James! The doctor says she can be cured!"

Coming up to Christmas, the child in the house should have made all the celebrations more perfect and tender. But James would barely look at the baby, treating her with exactly the same self-righteous conscientiousness as he treated Effie. He had acquired her and would do his duty by her, but no more.

The baby grew more beautiful every day, with a face like a small exquisite flower and Isabella's great blue eyes. A happy child that gave little trouble, and rarely cried. But to James she was a girl and she was flawed.

Something of James Bennett's that had the unpardonable fault of being less than perfect. Unforgivable.

It was a situation that in the dark nights he found impossible to contemplate. What now of the vision of the school with Isabella walking among the parents on the lawns, her shining children at her side? One child only, and that one a girl dragging her leg behind her. How had it happened to him? She would have to be kept out of the way. Bad enough now, to have all the village looking at him as though they pitied him.

It was with great difficulty that he managed the scrupulous fairness on which he prided himself. He never actually blamed Isabella, but his disappointment was so plain that her grief over the baby was edged with desperate guilt: lying stiff on her side of the bed with hot silent tears running down the sides of her eyes as James ostentatiously composed himself for sleep on his side; saying as clearly as if he spoke the words, that there was no point in lovemaking, since she could no longer make a child.

She had failed James, who had given her so much. She had not managed to give him the one thing he had set his heart on. Still loving him and still filled with gratitude for all he had done for her, she was too selfless to blame James for failing her, leaving her in lonely and guilty sorrow with only Effie for comfort. Effie in her turn thought of him no more nor less than she had expected. Bone-selfish and thought the world of himself. Poor Miss Isabella. All that terrible labor and her nearly dying and now the baby crippled, and all he would still talk about was what he wanted for his dinner.

"And how is the child?" he would ask conscientiously once a day and never listen to the answer.

Men! Thank the Lord it was a good baby, or no one would be able to live with him.

And mean, he was, mean. Effie banged the broom around the knotted schoolroom floor, raising clouds of chalk dust to settle on the benches. Mean! Miss Isabella had told her the baby's leg could probably be cured but it would cost a lot of time and money. If he loved the baby, he would find the money somewhere. He must have it somewhere with all his posh clothes and his father some kind of a high soldier.

She shook the blackboard duster out the playground door as vigorously as she would like to shake James himself. Sell that great roaring motorbike for a start, he could. Poor Miss Isabella. Nothing didn't seem to go right for her.

The winter was mild with little snow, but gray and sad like Isabella herself. There were hours of happiness as the baby, Clara, wrapped in her warm shawls, showed no sign of anything wrong. Isabella had called her after her mother, James having made it clear that the naming of a girl child was of no importance to him. The big blue eyes were growing intelligent, smiles coming for Effie and Isabella and the sympathetic clucking villagers in the streets: small fists grasping strongly at her new world. A baby that anyone could love.

But every time she was undressed, there was the poor little dangling leg.

The young doctor had been very kind, carefully explaining what was wrong. The hip joint was like a ball fitting into a socket, but in Clara's tiny hip the bone at the top of the leg was loose and kept slipping out of the socket. It was a result of the long difficult birth, he said. He did not say that it was actually the direct result of

Mrs. Pickup's well-meaning efforts to drag the breached baby into the world before he came.

"You see." Gently he manipulated the two parts of the joint together. The baby laughed. "She has no pain and if I hold it like this, then the joint is perfect. That is what must be done. It must be held like that by a splint for six months. She would need to go to hospital. Or to have a nurse at home."

Isabella thought at once of the cost. She had learned that James did not part with his money easily.

"Couldn't it be done at home? *I* could look after her."

"You are a nurse?"

"No." She shook her head and her heart was cold.

"Then I am afraid not. It needs professional nursing. If the splint becomes displaced, then it would only make everything worse."

She was silent. Money. James only wanted money for one thing. If it had been a son, it might have been different. Or, her father. Her father with all the money in the world.

The doctor patted her hand.

"There's no hurry," he said. "It won't get worse. Wait until the spring and then take her to the hospital in Chelmsford and see what they can do for you. Or even London."

There must be parents somewhere who would help, he thought, sadly familiar with this hesitation in the face of some necessary, costly, operation. As he came down the stairs he wondered again what such a girl was doing married to that pompous and self-centered prig.

It was only Isabella who did not see James like this. To her he was still the same James whom she adored. It was she and her poor little baby who were wrong. All winter she gave him his favorite foods and poured on him all the natural tenderness of her nature, and tried to interest him in his sweetly developing daughter, but his only response was to immerse himself more than ever in the school he had, and to talk more constantly of the one that was to come, as though painfully now, it was all he had to look forward to in life.

Isabella grew thin, the great blue eyes enormous in her face, and in the scullery Effie slammed the dishes in the stone sink and would have liked to slam them on James Bennett's head. None so blind, she thought, watching all Isabella's efforts, none so blind as those who would not see. If only that father would turn up, though there seemed small chance now of that. Dead as mutton, she reckoned, long ago.

Both of them were dumbfounded when, in the middle of a windy March when the world seemed scoured by the clear spring light, and the branches of the horse chestnut clashed and rattled above the roof, James announced his intention of taking the baby to Guy's Hospital in London.

"Best hospital," he said to the gaping Isabella. "They'll tell you exactly what you can do and what you can't do."

"Is that the one where your brother was, before he went to Birmingham?"

James didn't appear to want that side of it mentioned.

"Nothing to do with him," he said shortly. "Just get the best opinion. I'll get an appointment."

Now Isabella chattered with Effie in the kitchen, and sang to the baby around the house: little old soft Spanish songs from Chile, and Clara laughed as though the sound of Isabella's singing were the funniest thing she had ever heard, reaching up to bang her mouth with small determined fists.

"She doesn't think I have a voice, Effie," said Isabella, laughing in her new happiness, and Effie laughed, too, but did not trust James Bennett and whatever he was up to.

Nor did Isabella quite understand why, with this new generosity toward the baby, he still did not seem any more interested in her; or indeed in Isabella herself, save as Schoolmaster's wife, and all that represented in the village.

Their appointment was early, and they had to leave before it was full daylight, Clara bundled in every shawl that Isabella owned, and well down on her lap so that she would escape all the draft in the sidecar. Clara slept on as peacefully as if she were in her own wooden cradle that James had picked up secondhand in the village, and that Isabella had lovingly repainted. Slept through all the ghostly lanes of Suffolk, where ancient trees loomed in the dead half-light: and into the flat, open land before London, the pale sun catching the faint green bloom of spring across the wide fields.

Isabella tried not to think of the times she had come this way before, in her father's Humber, when they would leave Enderby for a couple of weeks of the London Season. Nothing mattered now, nothing, save that James was actually going to do his best for Clara. Warm love for him filled her and remorse that she had misjudged him. And failed him. Dear God, and failed him. Perhaps if she was a very good wife, he would in time forgive her. For one child and that a girl. Even if she grew to walk perfectly.

Clara was awake, looking up with big sleep-darkened eyes at the rushing world. In through the drab endless streets of Eastern London—her father would never come that way, coming in through Thaxsted and down the Cambridge road, to allow her mother the most pleasant entry into the city. All streets led now for her to the grimy pile of Guy's Hospital, beside the sluggish winter-cold river. Her mouth was dry and she held Clara to her as closely as if even to heal her, she would never let her go.

They only glimpsed for a moment the great tiled waiting room lined with benches and poorly lit by dirty windows, like a railway station, thought Isabella. Then they were led through a swinging door into quiet corridors with mahogany doors. All Isabella could think of while the doctor was examining Clara, closing her mind to what was actually happening, was of James's generosity in not allowing her to sit and wait her turn in that gaunt place downstairs: paying instead for this quiet room, and the austere but gentle man who was handling Clara so kindly, smiling at her bubbling conviction that he was only playing with her.

My poor little Clara, she thought then, and could have wept. She who so loves life, please God let her enjoy it to the full.

James was seeing to it. She longed to take his hand, but James was sitting impassive in his blue leather chair, waiting for the examination to be ended.

"A lovely child, Mrs. Bennett," the doctor said then, looking over his shoulder as he moved to wash his hands in a small washbasin. "I see no reason why she should not be completely normal."

"Oh, James! Oh, Doctor!"

Relief flooded Isabella, and the roar of London beyond the windows was suddenly a jubilant thunder.

"When—" she began, but James stood up blandly.

"Isabella!" he said. "I am sure the nurse can find you somewhere to feed Clara and whatever else you have to do, and I will talk to the doctor. I'll come and find you."

"But—"

She looked from one to the other. The doctor neutral, James determined. Already the nurse was picking up the tumbled white bundle that was Clara.

"This way, Mrs. Bennett," the nurse was saying cheerfully, a bony young woman with a face like a horse to whom she took an immediate dislike. Herding her out like a child. But there was nothing to do but go, remembering her manners to thank the doctor: just one reproachful look at James that he didn't even meet.

He came to her as she was still feeding Clara, a benign smile on his face.

"Well, my dearest Isabella. You must be happy now. They can have her running like any other child."

"Oh, James, oh, James."

Tears edged her lashes as she looked down at the happy guzzling baby. Then she looked up at him.

"But when, James? When? Do I have to leave her now?"

James shifted a little in his chair.

"Ah, no. There's no hurry, Bradford said. When she's about two we should be able to manage it."

"*Two!* Why do we have to wait? If it's done now, she'll know nothing about it. At two she won't want to leave us. Why not now, James? Why not now?"

He looked irritated.

"The price is too high."

"Too high! There is *no* price too high. To see her walk and run. *No* price too high!"

Frantic blue eyes blazed at him.

"Sell the Norton!"

She realized from his look of horror that there was no hope there. He tried for his kind patience.

"My dear Isabella, and you are down in Brackenham without the Norton, how do you get anywhere? You are not one of the locals to get lifts in carts. How do you get the child to the doctor if it is sick?"

That touched her, but "it," she thought. Not even "she." Not Clara.

She shook her mother's bracelet at him, worn today as a sort of talisman; James looked at it disparagingly.

"I wouldn't think that would fetch much."

As she buttoned her blouse she thought wearily that her father would never have on her mother's wrist something that would not fetch much. But how could she go about selling it? Or arrange for Clara on her own?

Magnanimous in victory, James patted her shoulder.

"Only eighteen months, pet," he said kindly. "We should be able to spare it then. Have it done when she is two."

And with that, Isabella, bleakly, had to be content, too sad for tears, wrapping her crippled baby in her shawls and going down again past the echoing caverns of the general hospital, to the precious Norton, over which James ran a duster before he would even take it farther.

"Have to go and see a chap for my father now," he said. "It's in Horse Guards, so you can walk in the Park while I am gone. It's nice and mild."

All genial again now he had had his way. Why, she wondered, had he bothered in the first place?

In the soft bright day, under the swelling buds of the trees, she sat on a green chair in St. James's Park, and let the charmed and chortling Clara watch the ducks, streaming backward and forward across the lake with all the urgency of spring. There were daffodils in yellow drifts below the trees, and happy sparrows chittered after crumbs along the gravel paths.

She saw none of it, thinking blindly now of her parents. In this very park she had walked with her mother: fed the ducks herself as a child, going back across Green Park in the English sun they thought so gentle. To Brown's Hotel in Half Moon Street, just across the Park. They came in for the Racing. The Derby and Ascot, and on the way back to Enderby the July Meeting at Newmarket. And all the delights of summer London; dancing their nights away in striped marquees set up in lamplit gardens.

Rich and handsome and splendid. And young. Young even now that they were dead. She had been going to go to all these places with them for the first time last summer. All these balls. Coming out, they called it here, even if you did not do the feathers and the King and everything. It was a joke that her father wanted to catch an English lord for her.

And she had married for love, a village Schoolmaster, leaving her here on this green chair with a crippled baby and no money to heal her. She had not cared about the money for herself. James was all she wanted, and had this been a healthy boy, no doubt all would still be well.

But now she needed money for Clara.

The grass and daffodils shimmered to a green-and-yellow cloud before her eyes, and her baby laughing in her arms, she wept for them then as she had not wept for months, indifferent to the pass-ersby.

If they were here, Clara would be running by the time she was two. People probably think, she thought wryly as she wiped her eyes in the end, that I'm weeping here over a fatherless child. And I might as well be, for all he cares about her.

Effie had no illusions about what James was up to, taking the now tired and fretful baby from Isabella when they reached home.

"Why wait until she is two?"

James had gone into the school and they had the kitchen to themselves, Effie furious, Isabella tired and white.

Isabella told her everything, and Effie's sharp little mind rushed angrily to its conclusions.

"Friend of 'is brother's, was it?" she asked.

Isabella nodded wearily.

So, thought Effie, the mean pig didn't have to pay for it and now all he has to do is keep promising. When she's two, it'll be for when she's four. It'll be never, poor little thing.

"He said the price was too high," said Isabella.

"No price too high, Miss Isabella." But Effie knew from her own hard world that often the smallest prices were too high to be paid. But she didn't believe this of James Bennett. He just wanted his money for other things.

"That's what I said to him, Effie." Isabella's voice was small and tired. "There is no price too high for that."

Effie looked at her.

"Cheer up, Miss Isabella. She'll be two in no time at all. Now look, you feed Miss Grumbles here, and I'll make you a nice cup of tea. It'll all come right, you'll see."

But as she filled the old black iron kettle at the scullery tap, she shook her head.

"Men," she said to herself. "Men." And particularly James Bennett.

James was pleased with himself. He had done his duty, and his sense of duty was very important to him, and, he felt, restored the harmony of his home.

All that Isabella could do was settle down to wait, asking herself if her life was ever again to be anything but waiting: and asking God to help her not to hate James, because she loved him. Trying then to understand the terrible mixture of her feelings; wanting to believe in him for the love she still bore him, but certain that had he wished to, he could have found the money to put Clara into the hospital. Hating him for that.

As the baby grew more active the little trailing leg was more noticeable, and she found it almost impossible to bear. Had it been incurable, she would somewhere, she told herself, have found the strength to bear it. But not this. Not this.

Through all the soft days of spring the peace of his house that James prided himself on was fragile: held by the strength of Isabella, who had learned dignity and discipline if nothing else from Catchpole, and laid all her feelings away behind a careful smile, keeping his home and his life as she had always done.

"Don't know how you can be so nice to him, Miss Isabella," Effie said. "Meself I'd like to take the meat chopper to 'im."

Isabella smiled at the fury and loyalty in the small pale face. What would she do without Effie? But she answered her seriously.

"Duty, I suppose, Effie," she said. "My father was always very strong about duty. When you take on a responsibility, he said, you have to see it through, even if it isn't all you hoped."

"Yes, Miss," said Effie, and went on cutting the meat on the kitchen table as though it were James Bennett. She didn't quite understand Miss Isabella, but realized she was just being herself. Follow that stuck-up fool to the end of the earth, she would, just because she'd said so in her marriage vows. Too good for him by half.

At the beginning of June each year Brackenham held its annual fête to make money for the care and restoration of the crumbling old square-towered Saxon church across the village Green.

For days the village had been in a ferment, the children racing across the road the moment they were let out of school, to watch the stalls going up. Frail structures of laths and canvas belonging to the local people, who would give all they made to their little church. Stronger structures in bright red and yellow paint, piled on the bright carts of gypsies, who would give only what they had to pay to be allowed to come.

And lastly the long-awaited marvelous moment when the children caught the rumbling across the country silence and raced shrieking to meet the great traction engine, shining green and polished brass, its tall funnel belching steam; behind it the stacked wagons of the merry-go-round, the spotted horses stacked in rows, their wild flaring eyes with inch-long lashes looking as though they wondered what had happened to their whirling freedom.

Behind them the blue-and-yellow canopy was packed in sections like great slices of colored cake, and there was not a child above five who did not feel he could have assembled the whole thing himself, so avidly did they watch, year after year, as it was put together.

John Peter Burgess, whose name was painted on the canopy with the fine French word "Carousel," beamed at all the children through his drooping whiskers and waved his hat to them as though they were the first children he had ever seen: patient with them and putting them tolerantly out of his way, for although he had been working since he was a nipper with his father, for him, too, his carousel had never lost its magic. He, too, could have cheered with all of them as the first horse was slotted onto its brass pole: as the steam got up and the first music blared into the evening, scattering the swallows and filling the eyes of the children with delight.

Every horse flawlessly painted, and they all had their favorites as they went up, their names painted on their shining flanks. Dobbin and Dasher and Daisy and Paul. Chestnuts and shining white with chestnut patches: or dapple-gray.

The children forgot their homes and suppers until the Green was full of mothers crying their names: trying to drag them away by the hand, scolding for the forgotten supper and the coming dark. But many of them, when they found them, were caught themselves by the spell of memory: the one bright day of summer magic of the merry-go-round. Children themselves only yesterday, and John Peter Burgess and his painted horses not changed one whit. They, too, forgot time and supper and stayed to watch, drifting home in the end between the naphtha flares around the half-made booths. Chattering: already caught by the air of holiday for tomorrow.

Outside the church, where the crooked lych-gate led onto the Green, the Vicar himself stood, listening to all the hammering and the hiss of naphtha and the rumbling roar of the traction engine as John Peter worked a head of steam to test the carousel. Anxiously the Reverend Cotwood scanned the sky, fearful of even the smallest cloud that might speak of rain tomorrow: desperate for every penny for his small exquisite church, where the dry-rot and the deathwatch beetle were eating away at the ancient beams faster than he could find the money to restore them.

He stood as Father Ignacio stood in the first darkness, his eyes roaming the ragged peasants taking their poor hour of ease in his long bedraggled plaza. But the mind of the Reverend Cotwood tonight was on the rich from the big houses in the country round the village, slumbering under their sheltering trees in the rich Suffolk fields.

These he wanted with open hands and open purses. His own village people, God bless them, would come even if the heavens opened, but they had little to bring to the day save their own passionate enjoyment. He needed the rich.

Like Father Ignacio, he looked at his small world and knew he could only do his best for it, turning in the end to go in to where his housekeeper waited reproachfully with the supper that even he had kept waiting.

Across the Green James firmly pulled the curtains across the parlor window. Isabella accepted sadly that they no longer sat together on the garden bench among the stocks and mignonette and pansies that Effie had brought to discipline in the tiny garden: the rambler roses taken from the ground and carefully trained along the schoolyard wall. Isabella felt guilty and useless, unable in the autumn after Clara's birth to rouse herself to the effort of the garden.

Not that James seemed to want it anymore. But tonight she protested at the curtains drawn against the purple evening, splashed all across the darkening green with lights.

"Oh, James. Do you have to close them? I like to see it all happening. Couldn't we," she cried, "go and sit on the bench in the garden and watch?"

"Isabella, you are a child. Who would want to watch this foolish bedlam? Thank God there is only tomorrow and it will be over."

"James! We *will* go?" cried Isabella. Last year he had not thought it proper because of her pregnancy and she had sat all day watching from the window like the captive child she was.

"I love it," she cried, the Latin in her responding eagerly to the lights and the excitement and the rising tide of the festivity.

Effie slowed her collection of their teacups, waiting to hear his answer, the mean-minded prig. She'd get Miss Isabella to the fête if it was the last thing she did, but truth to tell, she'd rather go alone. There was a young farm lad giving her the eye around the village this last week or two, and if that wasn't an invitation for the fair and all that went with it, she knew nothing about anything. Get him on that merry-go-round, where she'd have to hold tight round his waist, and they'd be off for the day. Nothing like that for Miss Isabella, but she should have a bit of fun, too, poor thing.

"Well of course we'll go," said James testily. "The Vicar has asked me to be on the platform with Lady Lyndly when she opens it. It's my Position."

Lady Lyndly.

"James, I don't have to, do I?"

"You should, you should. But as you have insisted on giving Effie the day off, you will have to watch with Clara."

"Everyone has the day off for the fête, James," was all she said mildly, but she was thinking of Lady Lyndly. She came from one of the big houses out in the country, but still Brackenham parish. Her husband was the local member of Parliament. Of course she would not recognize her. Who would see in a thin woman with a baby and the poorly cut hair, for Effie was not as clever with the scissors as Brick, the cherished young girl who used to come down for a chat with her mother's guests for tea and dinner at Enderby?

She did not want to be recognized. It was not, she told herself, that she was ashamed to be where she was: married to James. She just hated to have people being sorry for her. She had not yet realized that she was beginning to be sorry for herself.

Although the merry-go-round was braying soon after dawn, and the children gathering soon after that, the fête was not officially opened until two. Not to end until the last tired child had been dragged home across the trampled grass, and the last drunken husband had come rolling in, clutching his coconut, or his china mug for winning the tug-of-war.

Isabella thought James looked marvelously happy up on the flag-strung platform in his alpaca jacket and his Panama hat: the English gentleman on a summer day: no different from Lord Lyndly, with his Tory cornflower in the buttonhole of his jacket, gallantly applauding his wife's few well-bred words.

All the villagers applauded lustily, too, but only because they knew they had to go through this before they could get to the proper business of the day, and they amiably understood that the upper classes liked to be allowed to stand on platforms and make speeches.

So everybody was pleased with everybody else, and the bright crowd filled with excitement and the air of festival, the day as blue and hot and perfect as the Vicar could have prayed for: dark spreads of shadow underneath the trees where the school benches had been put out for the old ones to sit and rest, and talk of all the other fêtes that they had seen: minding the babies, and letting the mothers free for one carefree afternoon.

The very moment the fête was declared open it burst into life, the people swarming from one stall to another on the trampled grass, jostling good-naturedly for their turn to throw rings over cheap bottles of perfume and pomade: the children to make their agonizing choice between a hundred strings, to pull one that would bring a tiny present: coconut shies, and throwing sticks at a grinning man in a barrel, and a queue outside the fortune-teller's tent, although everybody knew that it was only Vicar's wife dressed up in shawls and earrings, but very good at it, she was, and you could almost believe every word she said.

Over and above it all the merry-go-round bawled out its raucous music. "Daisy, Daisy" and "Lily of Laguna" and the "Blue Danube" and the "Skaters' Waltz" and a couple more: and then round again to "Daisy, Daisy," and beyond the stalls on the other side of the Green the excited children were being lined up for races, and the first teams of brawny villagers were being lined up for the tug-of-war, the village blacksmith as anchor man for Brackenham, whose team he had kept undefeated for seven years.

Isabella loved it all. She stood with Clara beside the merry-go-round, the baby securely strapped into her carpet-covered go-cart, and Clara's delighted smile was no wider than her own. They all looked so happy up there and she couldn't help reflecting it: all the spotless painted horses going round and round to the thumping music, and up and down on the glittering brass poles: graceful, charming: all their riders clinging on for dear life: beaming or shrieking according to their age.

Effie had wasted no time, and Isabella laughed to see her sitting sidesaddle behind her man, her old-fashioned ankle boots dangling and her arms gripping tight around his waist: the expression of delight and satisfaction on her face touched with not a little terror. Up and down and round and round, on the dapple-gray, not daring to take away a hand to wave to Clara.

Daisy, Daisy give me your answer do.

"Isabella! Why are you standing there grinning like an idiot?"

James was beside her. No victim here of the simple happy atmosphere. His handsome face was clouded with disapproval.

"I have a certain position in this village, you know. You should have joined the official party when we left the platform. They wouldn't have minded about Clara."

Kind of them, Isabella thought, with a sudden flash of spirit, and for one moment, just to annoy and confuse James, she was tempted to make herself known to Lord and Lady Lyndly. Remind them of Enderby, and the times they had sat at her parents' table. But it would not do. Were there to be any life with James after the manner in which she had disappointed him, then it would have to be on his terms.

"I'm so sorry, James," she said. "I was watching Effie."

Too much to tell him that she was longing to be up there herself, rising and falling on the dapple-gray, the music swelling round her and the painted canopy against the dark-blue sky.

"They think it very strange," said James, "that I appear to have no wife." His voice was cold.

"I will come now, James," she said, and turned the heavy go-cart on the rough grass, James making no attempt to help her.

Nor did she think anyone had actually missed her.

The Vicar smiled his vague sweet smile at her, and she paused to think that his own wife was in a hot tent in an Indian shawl and a pair of golden curtain rings in her ears, just to help on the day. James was wrong, somewhere.

Nor, on his pressing introduction, or rather, she thought, presentation, did Lady Lyndly appear to remember her. If she looked at her a little long, it was only because she was wondering what this elegant and beautiful young woman was doing married to this pompous bore of a schoolmaster.

Even with her ill-cut hair, and the flowered cotton dress that Effie had run up on the sewing machine, there was something that made Lady Lyndly look at her twice. Pausing.

Some subconscious memory that made her ask, after the formal words, "And are you English, my dear? You look a little foreign to this village."

"South American," said Isabella carefully, glancing at James, and to his obvious relief the Vicar came up with his two hands filled with wooden balls.

"A coconut, Lady Lyndly! Take home a coconut."

"But, my dears, I *have*," she cried a few moments later, in her clear bell-like voice. "I've actually hit a coconut. I *must* take it home to the children."

"I would like to try, James," said Isabella, plucking at his sleeve, but James pretended not to hear her, clapping and praising Lady Lyndly and more than a little put out when her ladyship turned back to Isabella, her brown hairy trophy in her delicate hands.

"I was just about to say, my dear," she said, "what a most beautiful baby you have. As lovely as her mother."

"People say," said James quickly, "that she is just like me."

"Oh, no." The tones of authority would have no contradiction. "*Just* like her mother. You must be *very proud.*"

She floated off after her husband, and James scowled and Isabella did not know whether to laugh or cry.

They trailed all round the fête and with beautiful professionalism Lady Lyndly did everything, even to blissfully having her fortune told by "Madam Bella" and buying striped sugar stick from a gypsy who was cooking it in a big black wooden bowl; and then pulling the cooling mass into sticks with strong muscular hands, across a hook.

"I adore the stuff," said Lady Lyndly, and flashed her wide self-assured smile at the Vicar. "But then I adore fêtes."

Isabella, watching her, thought this was true. A nice simple woman, with the almost forgotten assurance of wealth and position, who did exactly as she wanted to do. If she herself had asked for some sugar stick, James would have said that the gypsy's hands were dirty. And that she must remember her Position.

Then Lady Lyndly looked at her little gold fob watch, and tilted her head ruefully at the Vicar, the sun catching the diamond aigrette flashing on the side of her blue silk turban.

"But now, dear Vicar, we have to go. Cuthbert!" She beckoned her elegant moustachioed husband, who had followed amiably in her wake all afternoon. "Cuthbert! Your meeting! We must go."

"Cuthbert has a meeting at five," she said, as if he could not say it for himself, and within minutes she had swept the whole party into their motorcars.

Her glance lingered on Isabella in her clear good-byes, the job done, ready to move on to the next one.

"Good-bye, my dear," she cried. "Look after your lovely baby."

Isabella was silent, every such remark about the shawl-wrapped baby a knife in her heart. What about a little later when she should be showing two firm little legs in white shoes and socks?

The cars were bumping off the village Green and away between the summer hedges.

"Can we give the Vicar a cup of tea, Isabella?" James said. "Vicar, would you like a cup of tea?"

"Indeed, indeed I would." The Vicar smiled as he looked over at the queue outside the fortune-teller's tent. "My wife is otherwise occupied, I am afraid. And I think that the rest of them can get along without me for half an hour. Most kind of you."

As they made their way across the blackened and trampled Green toward the Schoolhouse, Isabella was allowed to buy one thing. There was a rough stall set up, covered in produce that the actual village people might not have in their gardens, a plump rosy woman from one of the outlying market gardens behind it.

"Oh, James look. Mrs. Primrose has got rhubarb. I'd love some rhubarb."

"Very good for you," said the Vicar with a grin.

But James loved rhubarb, too, and there was no room for vegetables in their tiny garden. Carefully he gave her the necessary tuppence.

"A bundle of rhubarb, please, Mrs. Primrose."

The woman gathered up the soft pink sticks, slapping on an extra one with a gap-toothed smile at Isabella.

"There, me dear," she said in her soft Suffolk accent. "I'll even wrap it up for 'ee. Took a lot of newspaper from the Fish Man when 'e come yesterday."

Isabella took the wrapped bundle and put it into the bag on the back of the go-cart, reflecting that she had not seen a newspaper since she had left Newstead. News filtered to the village through the traveling salesmen, mostly the garrulous Thread Man who seemed to feel it his duty to keep them all informed, in his garbled fashion, of the doings of the world outside.

She caught up with James and the Vicar at the front door.

"Take the Vicar into the parlor, James," she said. "I'll just lay Clara down to sleep and then I'll make the tea." She smiled at the Vicar. "Effie is off to the fête with her young man."

"Like all the village," he said.

Clara did not feel in the mood for sleep, and was screaming her head off at being banished as Isabella came back downstairs. She lifted the heavy old black kettle onto the fire, and turned back to the table to unwrap the rhubarb and get it out of her way, smoothing out the newspaper in an irresistible desire just to glance at it.

The London *Times*. On the back page. The Personal Column.

They heard her high strangled cry through in the parlor, and it was the Vicar who leaped to his feet: but Isabella was already in the door, the crumpled newspaper in her hand, her face chalk-white, and grasping helplessly for the doorpost as she slid to the floor.

They got her up and sat her in a chair.

"Put her head down between her knees," cried the Vicar, and it was only moments before she struggled to come up again, looking at them both with wild eyes, still unable to speak.

Then she began to cry, great gulping sobs, tears pouring from her eyes.

"What's the *matter?*" James almost shouted. "Is anything wrong with the baby?" Such an exhibition before the Vicar, who was rubbing Isabella's hands and making gentle soothing noises.

She shook her head, and managed to point to the paper they had trampled on the floor. James gave it to her, and with shaking fingers she found the place for him, the first unbelieving happiness in her swimming eyes.

James read it in silence.

Mr. Angus Frost of Valparaiso, Chile, seeks information concerning the whereabouts of his daughter Isabella. Last heard of in Miss Catchpole's Academy for Young Ladies, in Brighton, two years ago. Please write.

And there was a box number.

"Why a number?" Isabella had found her voice: frantic. "Why a number? Why not say where he is, so that I can go there at once?"

It was the Vicar who answered, James still standing dumb, trying to assess this fresh upset in his plan for life.

"Well, Mrs. Bennett, if he did that, all sorts of people who aren't you would be descending on him, if you understand me. This way he can sort things out."

He was too experienced and kind even to ask what it was all about, although there had been rumors in the village that this girl was without any family through some tragedy.

"It was an earthquake, Vicar." She had begun to babble, excitement shining now in her tear wet eyes. "My mother was killed, but I didn't even know that at once and my father was missing. I thought he was dead, too. We couldn't find a trace, could we, James? I haven't even heard a word from his lawyers. You'd think they'd have told him where I was, wouldn't you, James? They know because I wrote and told them."

"Yes," said James, and thought of the letter in the snowdrift. All for nothing.

The Vicar in his simple goodness was almost as delighted and excited as Isabella, both of them oblivious of James's dumb annoyance.

"I must write a letter," cried Isabella. "At once. But look, my hands are shaking. But I must. Oh, Father."

"Yes, you must," cried the Vicar. "Mr. Bennett, do you have paper and a pen for her, of course you do, you are the schoolmaster." He and Isabella both laughed as though it were the greatest joke in the world, and James glumly opened the cupboard for the pen and ink.

"I will wait while you write the letter," the Vicar said, "and I have friends going home to Long Melford this evening. I will give it to them to post there. That way it will get off first thing in the morning."

James thought again of the letter in the snowdrift, but realized he could not do it twice. He did his best to smile and look at least as delighted as the Vicar, laying down the notepaper for Isabella and putting the pen into her hand.

"He will think," she cried happily, "that I have some illness. Look at my writing, my hand is shaking so much."

Darling Father, she wrote, and looking at the words, she knew that in her heart she had never hoped to write them again.

Darling Father.

Late into the night there was dancing out on the destroyed grass on the Green, the scrape of fiddles and the surge of the accordion coming thin against the ceaseless braying of John Peter Burgess's Carousel, that would carry on until the last exhausted reveler had staggered home, winding down only into the empty night.

.Isabella did not mind the noise. She could not in any case have slept, lying wide-eyed beside the slumbering James, staring at her happy future. Everything would be perfect now. Her father would give them the money to buy the school of James's heart, and he could do exactly as he wished with it. Surely then, with everything he wanted, he would forgive her about Clara and no more sons, and they would be happy again. With Clara running about like any other child.

With her father.

Long Melford, the letter said when it came, surprisingly quickly. For days Isabella had been at the little village shop, waiting for the postman on his bicycle. Sleepless. Counting every hour of twenty-four.

Long Melford. My dearest, dearest Isabella, thank God to have found you. Come at once. I am staying at the Bull at Long Melford, waiting for them to open Enderby for me.

Dear child, come quickly—but just for this first time, come alone and let me have you to myself.

"Long Melford." Oh, so close. "I can go today. I can cycle. Oh, Effie, I can go today!"

She looked down at the letter and laughed, her face full of delighted love.

"He must have been as excited as I was when he wrote. Look, Effie! His writing is even worse than mine. Oh, Effie, wait until you see him. He is so *handsome*. But I wonder why he didn't come at once to see me? It's not far. He must have a car. Why did he not come at once to see me?"

No presentiment touched her, the earthquake forgotten.

"Oh, James," she said, the letter in her hands, smiling as though she could never smile enough: her eyes brimming with tears. "Oh, Effie—my father. James, you do not mind if I do as he asks, and go this first time by myself? It is only that we will have so much to say to each other. Then we will all be together."

chapter
10

In the first days of his returned memory Liam found Angus Frost almost impossible to deal with. He was excitable, intractable, swinging between exalted high spirits at his recovery, and deep depression at where he found himself and his helplessness to do anything about contacting his wife and daughter.

He blamed everybody.

"But there *must*," he shouted at Liam, "there *must* have been something to identify me. My name would be in my wallet."

"And your wallet?" Liam asked him.

"In my jacket pocket, of course. These flat-faced imbeciles must have stolen it. Where *is* my jacket?"

Liam tried to keep his patience.

"These flat-faced imbeciles," he said coldly, "have fed you and clothed you for a year, and it was one of them that nursed you back to health. And your wallet went with the rest of your clothes, stripped off you by being rolled down the mountain in the middle of a ton of rubble. You had little on you when they got you but the belt around your waist and a bit of shirt hanging round the collar. Father Ignacio has a few bits of silver, off the shreds of harness left on your mule."

He looked at Angus Frost, thinking of Sister Jesús María and her abrupt departure. The cantankerous personality was not unexpected. A severe blow on the head could cause major changes in a man's character, but God help the man, he even looked a wreck. No way of knowing anything.

"How old are you, Angus Frost?" he asked him.

"Forty-five. No. Forty-six by now, I suppose."

The answer came without hesitation, but the poor fellow looked sixty, and if Liam was any doctor at all, then he would not add many more years to the ones he had now. But he would have been a man, in the barren life of the nun, and who knew what upset that had stirred in her?

Angus Frost was banging on the floor with his crutch.

"I have to get out of this place. I have to go at once. I want you to arrange to get me out of here. Do you not realize, man, I have to get back to my wife and daughter? I have to get back to my business. God knows what's happened to the mines. Isabella should be back from school, in Chile now. They will think that I am dead."

His mind was swinging wildly between his business and his family: unreasonable, almost hysterical.

"You have to get me *out.*"

"Will you walk?" Liam asked him. "Or take a llama from the fields?"

"*Walk!* How can I walk?" He could not even see the nonsense of the suggestion in the desolate mountains lost to everywhere. "Why didn't you get me to a hospital where I'd have got decent attention and I wouldn't *be* like this?" He glared down at his withered and twisted legs. "I've *got* to get in touch with my wife and daughter. I'm Angus Frost!" he shouted, as though that answered and solved everything.

"And I'm Liam Power," answered Liam, and did his best to keep his patience, thinking of the long hot days and the black nights in the little room, the moths whirring round the tiny lamp: Sister Jesús María talking to him all those endless hours to try and talk him back to living. "And Angus Frost is a very lucky man to be alive. Until Groucho comes back with the mules we can do nothing."

"And when will that be?"

"I have told you. Only days now. Look, I'm going out. Try and calm down and rest. You're doing yourself no good."

"Calm down! All this and you tell me to calm down!"

"You'd be calm enough if you were the last year dead," Liam said curtly, and went out and down the path to the windy plaza. It was cold, and he huddled in his blanket on the bench outside the cantina, the *agua ardiente* slowly warming him against the chill. He had found lately that he could no longer stand the shabby darkness of the inside of the cantina: the crumbling walls with the few withered pictures stuck up long ago in a forlorn attempt at decoration: the chipped and battered counter and the endless smell of stale oil and chili. Time was he hadn't minded. The cantina was just the necessary source of *agua ardiente* and he saw none of it. But he minded now and, preoccupied with Angus Frost, did not stop to ask himself why, preferring to shiver where he had the view down the open end of the plaza and across to the cold yellow mountains on the other side of the valley.

Even when Groucho came back, what were they to do about Angus Frost? He had said that he came riding direct as the crow flew, from the railway, where there was a small town. That would be closer than the larger one where Groucho went, and if it was on the railway and had a station, then it must have a telegraph. Someone must go there with the mules, and get in touch with all the man's relations.

Someone. He reached for the bottle and took a deep gulp of the warming spirit. In the dark nights since Angus Frost had got back his memory—sleepless, with the wind howling like a banshee along the mountain—he had come to terms with who that someone would have to be. There was no one else. And what matter? he told himself. What matter? He could arrange everything for the man and then come back here, and his friends could come and get him. He would come straight back here.

Days. It was not like going back to Valparaiso.

He could handle it. Just days.

He saw the old woman going over from the priest's house with the tortillas for their midday meal wrapped in a white cloth, and a steaming jug of coffee in her hand. Suddenly the coffee seemed more appealing than the *agua ardiente*, and he threw a few pesos on the table and followed her.

Angus Frost stared in distaste at the heavy tortillas.

"There is never anything but these and beans and chili," he said morosely.

Liam grinned at him, caught in some unreasonable high spirits since he had decided that he would have to be the one to go to the railway and the telegraph.

"It was the first sign we had that you were getting better," he said, "when you began to grumble about what you got to eat."

For the first time ever the man smiled, startling Liam with a sudden charm and candor. Well, he thought, Rome wasn't built in a day. They'd probably have to wait a while for the whole man.

"I was always a man," said Angus Frost, "who liked good food."

"Tell me about it," Liam said carefully. "Tell me about your life."

They were still there after it was dark, the lamp unlit, some dam broken in the mind of Angus Frost. He spoke of his mines and the house up there within sight of the smelting chimneys, that his wife did not like, preferring the wide spaces of the hacienda farther south, where she would ride the herds like any vaquero. Or the cottage that they kept along the coast, where they could walk from the flower-filled garden straight on to the shore of the warm Pacific. He spoke of the town house in Valparaiso and of Enderby every second summer: of his worldwide business interests, and quietly now, natural anxiety concerning it all.

"And Isabella," he said. "We were just about to go to England to meet her. She was leaving school. I imagine she will have come back here to my wife. Valparaiso, I imagine, where they can get news most easily."

He paused a long time.

"I wish I had a cigar," he said.

"They roll them here from palm leaves," Liam said. "And their own tobacco."

Angus made a face of distaste, then he went on speaking.

"But you," he said. "I now remember every detail of my life, but you, who I understand saved it for me, were a stranger to me when I got my memory back."

Liam nodded.

"The most distant comes first. I'm surprised you didn't tell me about your old mother and your childhood."

The wide candid smile came again.

"They were there, jumbled up with everything else."

"You probably," said Liam, "won't even recognize Groucho when he comes back, and he's been looking after you for months."

Angus was quiet, somber.

"I owe a great deal to the people here," he said. "Apart from my life."

"Well, you did a bit in return. You gave them their irrigation system and with it a whole new slice of land."

"I did? I don't remember."

"You will."

"I have to thank them somehow," Angus said.

He fell silent then, and Liam saw that he was very tired.

"Give the poor head a rest now," he said. "That's enough for today. Come on in and watch me play chess with Father Ignacio."

"I think not," said Angus. "I'll just sit here and think about it all."

When Liam came back, having walked in the empty plaza for a while first, in a black world ablaze with stars, he was asleep where he had left him, sitting on the bed. He heaved up his feet and threw a blanket over him and Angus Frost never stirred, prostrate with the exhaustion of bridging his two worlds.

The next day the moment of release and peace had passed, and he was irritable again and dictatorial, almost ignoring Liam, intent only on the world he had left, and wanted to recover.

"I am like Julius Caesar," thought Liam as the months went by and all the pattern of Angus Frost's return to life took shape. He was always foreseeing that that which did happen was about to occur. Liam had foreseen that the man was not as strong or clear-headed as he thought he was, and when it came to it, he would take no step out of the village without Liam at his side.

"You will come with me, Liam," he said urgently when all the preparations had been made. "You will come with me. You are wasted, wasting your life up here in this place. Wasting it, Liam. I will help you start whatever you want to do."

Pretending that it was for Liam's sake that he asked him to come, and not because fear seized him at what he might find out. Liam looked back at him, gray eyes full of dark self-knowledge, and said yes, that he would come. Knowing his own fears, and knowing that Angus Frost was not the only who would need a crutch to help him back into the world.

"I will come," he said. "For a time."

"Stay with me? Care for me as you have cared for me here? I was unreasonable at first, but I know that I owe you my life. And the use of my legs, or what's left of them."

Liam looked at him, the dark-blue eyes alight with the man's indomitable spirit, but little more. Too much damage had been done, and more would be done by the strains he would undoubtedly have to face. Coming back from the dead, he thought wryly, could not have been easy even for Lazarus.

He had grown to an affection for this fierce, difficult man, who had probably been genial and charming before his injuries.

"For a time," he said again, and knew a real sorrow in his knowledge that time would not be for long. Please God, everything would go well for him.

So it was Liam who, when Groucho came back, turned him round as soon as he had unloaded his supplies, and headed the wagon eastward toward the railway and the sea. As they skirted the fallen mountain, he looked at the avalanche of stones. Angus Frost had wanted them to go and dig at once for his buried friend, but they had persuaded him that he was best left where he was.

"A cross, then," he had demanded. "A cross at least."

"Then, carve him one while I am gone," Liam said.

"I? Carve him one?"

Angus Frost looked at his hands. He did not carve crosses. He ordered them.

"Try it," said Liam laconically, and when he got back from the railway town, the cross was ready, exquisitely carved from a broken kneeler out of Father Ignacio's church. Father Ignacio had blessed the spot and Groucho had erected it.

Without words to himself or anybody else, Liam understood that this journey to the telegraph office was only a beginning. That he was contracting to see Angus Frost through all that he must do.

So it was he who had to come back up to the village, when all arrangements had been made for a suitable sprung and covered wagon to come and collect him—to tell Angus Frost that his wife was dead and his daughter apparently vanished without trace.

Angus looked a long time out across the farm where they stood together at the head of the fields, and although he gave no sign of

grief, his face grew on the instant more ravaged, and Liam knew it
yet another shortening of his life.

All he said was—

"We will find Isabella."

As though he were counting what was left to him.

It was Liam who had to suffer the appalled shock of the people
who came to get him, and saw where Angus Frost had been living
for a year: their faces when he said it was his home. Angus himself
was short with them.

"Were it not for Doctor Power and this village I would be
dead," he said, and Liam knew a queer shock. El Médico *borracho*,
the drunken doctor, was leaving, and it seemed that Doctor Power
was coming back to take his place. It was easy and natural, now the
time had come.

As they helped him into the wagon outside the convent, having brought him down as Liam had brought him up, on the back of
a surefooted llama, Angus said suddenly, "I remember the nun
now. A beautiful girl with green eyes."

Liam nodded, feeling sure he knew why Sister Jesús María had
gone.

The time up at the mines was boring for Liam, once the
marveling and the rejoicing was over. Angus was in his office from
dawn to late evening, reestablishing his kingdom with a torrent of
uncertain telephone calls and a mountain of cablegrams. He was
fortunate that his manager at the mines had been loyal and consci-
entious and had continued to operate them on the basis that he
would come back.

Many of the cables concerned Isabella.

"I don't understand it," Angus cried over and over again. "It
seems the poor child went to work because she had no money. My
lawyer established that much. He last heard from her in some house
where she had gone to be a companion. Isabella—a companion!
From then on there is nothing. Why could *someone* not have
helped her?"

Liam thought wryly that there were not many who could afford to take on a millionaire's daughter. He was slightly stunned at
the wealth and comfort in which Angus Frost lived, even in what

he called his "working house." What of the hacienda down in the country and the house by the sea, and the town house in Valparaiso?

All he could do was try to soothe the man's furious anxiety.

"I am sure," he said, "you will find her in England."

"We will go as soon as I am finished here."

But it was months, and Liam had occupied the time with Angus Frost's tailor. Like a man come back from the dead himself, he felt, as he wrote to his bank manager in Valparaiso for money. So that it was very much Doctor Power who left at long last for the tedious train journey down to Valparaiso, tall and elegant in his light, beautifully cut suit. Feeling its constrictions, he was not sure he did not prefer the freedom of his ragged blanket. But those days were gone as surely as if they had never happened. A hiatus in his life that must now be healed.

He waited with patience in the splendid white Mercedes on the tree-shaded road of the hacienda, where the wild roses and the morning glory had almost smothered the ruins of the house. The young couple who had inherited it were going to clear it away, they said, and make a garden, especially to surround the grave to which Angus Frost limped painfully across the grass. In the great flat distances the cattle browsed and the blistering sun of early summer beat down on the green-lined hood of the car: and Liam wondered how, after all these years, he would find England. And Ireland.

As they passed the south coast of it in the *Aquitania* on a bitter day in February, he stood at the rail and watched the green humps of the misty headlands go past: picking out the small white pillar of the lighthouse on the Old Head of Kinsale.

Angus came to a crashing halt beside him and Liam patiently forebore to tell him to be careful with his crutches on the slippery decks. Angus Frost would be patient with nothing. He saw only what he wanted and went for it, and the devil take anything that got in the way. Even if it was his own infirmity.

"What are you doing here?" he asked Liam now.

"Exercising the right of every Irish exile," said Liam, "to grieve a little for my country."

Angus had little use for this.

"Well," he said brusquely, "I said you could go there once we have found Isabella."

And once again Liam patiently forebore: from telling him that he neither paid him nor owned him. That he was beginning to understand that this time of recovery was as necessary to him as to the man beside him. But that he would go where he wished.

The habits of Angus Frost had reasserted themselves. At Southampton they were met by an enormous light brown Humber, brass fittings gleaming in the pale English sun. It appeared to have materialized from nowhere, and the driver knew without instruction to drive up through the winter fields, to Brown's Hotel in Half Moon Street in London, where their rooms were ready waiting for him.

They dined together in the old-fashioned dining room of rich mahogany, and Liam knew a side effect of the whole strange quest, that brought a quirk of pleasure to his mouth. A plate of good lamb chops, with cabbage and potatoes, such as he had not tasted since the day he had sailed with his new bride from Queenstown for Santiago.

With a hollow feeling of astonishment and relief he stared at his chops and realized that now he could remember that day with little more than the love he had held for her. The promise of their new life. Grief and guilt were healing.

Who was helping whom? Angus Frost, who had begged him to come and support him through all he had to face, was staring blind-eyed at his food, unable to eat.

When they went back up to their suite, Liam persuaded him to have a brandy, understanding with compassion from the man's ravaged face that having come all this way, he was afraid he might not succeed. That Isabella might be gone, like Clara, forever. But Angus Frost struggled suddenly from his chair, the balloon of crystal in his hand, and parted the velvet curtains to look down into the London street, where traffic and people alike splashed now through driving rain; lights shivering in the dark wet.

He let the curtain go, and the driving determination in his

eyes belied the ravaged and crippled body that limped on crutches back into the room.

"We are here," he said to Liam, who wanted to take the shaking brandy glass, but did not dare. "We are here, and we will find Isabella. And by God, I'll start with that woman Catchpole."

Liam did not know about which one, as a doctor, he should be most concerned. The thin-skinned, overstuffed woman, clearly suffused with guilt and terror, and a natural victim at any moment for a stroke; confronting Angus defiantly across her desk in what seemed to be a very high-class school. Or to Angus Frost himself, who was being reduced by the woman's evasive answers to a state of rage that threatened to shake his fragile frame to pieces.

"What d'you mean?" he roared. "Found her suitable employment. My daughter didn't need employment. *What* suitable employment?"

Miss Catchpole's hands were shaking uncontrollably. She put them in her lap and did her best to glare back into the furious eyes, convincing herself that what she did was right.

"Cubbington's. A local draper's emporium."

"A local draper's!" Angus was beside himself. "Dear God, woman, what did you do that for? Isabella was in no need. I hold you responsible. I hold you responsible for whatever may have happened to her. Fool! Fool of a woman. For God's sake, where is she now?"

Bravely, because she did not know what else to do, Miss Catchpole tried to justify herself.

"There was nothing else to do," she said. "Nothing else to do."

But Angus would not listen to any of it, raving on the other side of the desk, thumping it and shouting at her. Liam looked from one face to the other. One gray as death with his rage and disappointment, the other suffused with an ugly red, the blood clearly throbbing in her temples. And which one, he couldn't help thinking as he listened to them, should he reach to catch, if they both went together? As, God help us, was all too possible.

When they had gone, with the address of Cubbington's in Angus's pocket, Miss Catchpole could not rise to see them out, but let them go: and sat listening to the thump of crutches and the uneven slithering footsteps along the oilcloth passage from her room. Her heart was hammering and her mouth dry, and she thought at any moment her head would burst.

If he should find Isabella, then he would learn all that she had done. All that she had sold and kept. She had felt so *sure* the man was dead.

Next there was an interview with an obsequious man in a big draper's shop in the middle of Brighton, who seemed to be brought to almost speechless subservience by the arrival of the huge Humber outside the glass doors. He put his small feet together and inclined his large frame respectfully toward Angus, quivering with the desire to please. What possible order could these two ill-assorted men be wishing to make in his shop?

Angus was quivering, too, from rage with Miss Catchpole and the agony of getting himself from the car. He indulged in no polite preambles.

"My daughter," he said. "My daughter, Isabella Frost." Frantically he looked round. None of the faded ladies, nor the oily youth behind the cotton reels, remotely looked like Isabella. "The woman Catchpole told me she had found her employment here. Where is she?"

Mr. Crump glanced out at the glittering car, and saw the authority in the emaciated man before him, and a great pleasure suffused his anxious person. Whatever that Miss Catchpole had been up to, it was coming home to roost.

"Miss Frost *was* here, Mr. Frost," he said, and now his voice and his regret were genuine. Sooner her father found her the better. But it was no harm to try and make a bit of trouble on the way. "I always knew it was unsuitable, *quite* unsuitable, sir, but Miss Catchpole intimated to me that if I did not take her, and I had no real vacancy, sir, then she would withdraw the custom of the school. Not that the numbers mattered, sir, it was the cachet. It seemed Miss Catchpole no longer wanted her at the school. The cachet," he repeated, emphasizing the value of it.

Angus could barely wait through it.

"Where is she now?"

He shifted irritably on his crutches. Strange how his legs hurt more when he grew angry or upset.

Crump spread apologetic hands.

"I have no idea, sir. She told me she had got a position as a companion to an old lady out in the country somewhere. I was pleased for her, Mr. Frost. Pleased for her. It was more suitable."

Angus looked round the dark and fusty shop, struggling to accept it all.

"A very nice young lady, sir," said Crump. "A pleasure to have her in my shop. But not suitable."

"And where," barked Angus, "did she live, if that woman had thrown her out?"

Only Liam was aware of some fearful anxiety in the lank youth behind the nearest counter, staring at Angus Frost like a rabbit at a snake, his unhealthy face the color of ash. Avid to listen to anything unusual, Beech had realized that the man on the crutches was Isabella's father, and like Miss Catchpole, he was swept by the terror of retribution. Cost him his job, it could, if that uppity miss complained. He tried to efface himself behind a stand of laces, listening in the hope that it would all come to nothing. Probably, thought Liam correctly, given her hell while she was working there. At the beginning he had had small interest in Isabella as a person, caring only to see Angus Frost with his life restored as much as possible. Now he was beginning to understand what had happened, he was growing concerned and alarmed. Thrown out of her fine school by that imperious old woman: put to work here where that pimply youth would have baited the life out of her. Guilt was written all over him.

How had she coped with it? Would they find her, if they found her, destroyed as her father was destroyed? Foundered in some way in a life and world she could not handle. He began to feel a sense of urgency and anxiety.

Angus Frost had sent Crump to the book where he listed the names and addresses of all those that Cubbington's employed. He came back with a small piece of paper and a doubtful and embarrassed expression. Mr. Frost would have a seizure when he saw where his daughter had been living. He wouldn't like to be in that Catchpole's buttoned shoes.

He came to the door with them and stood, the spring sun gleaming in his oiled hair, to indicate to them how they should find Mrs. Quickly. He took his time over it, so that as many people as possible should see the fine motorcar outside Cubbington's and the two well-dressed gentlemen he was talking to.

Angus didn't want to listen to half of it, signaling the chauffeur to help him back into the car.

It was Liam who listened, understanding that no car could get to where Mrs. Quickly lived, wherever that might be. And that Mr. Frost probably could not get along the cobbles on his crutches, and that Miss Catchpole was a tyrant, actually threatening him if he did not take Miss Frost. Threatening him, and he knew it was unsuitable. She—

Liam cut him short. For the pale-faced man in the back seat of the Humber, every step might be the right one to find Isabella, and no one must keep him waiting. Crump was still bowing as the motorcar moved away.

And because of the car and the crutches, it was Liam who found himself appalled in a grimy little cobbled street, where he fully expected he might get the suit torn off his back for whatever was in the pockets: where women peered at him through dirty windows and ragged children followed him, jeering.

The number was almost gone from the peeling door, and he had to edge his way around a wooden handcart that stood up against it.

He was beginning to feel acute and horrified pity for Isabella Frost.

The door was opened by a little woman with a face like a ferret's and an enormous set of ill-fitting china teeth. Her hand went to her mouth at once as though to take them out.

"Thought you was one of my customers," she said without preamble, then suspicion took over. Men in good suits meant only officialdom and trouble in her world.

"Wot you want?"

She had closed the door to a crack, ready to slam it.

Quickly Liam explained what he wanted, and the door opened wider. Through it he got an overpowering smell of wet washing and hot ironing. Dear God, Isabella had been living with a washer-woman. Angus must not know that.

" 'Er," said Mrs. Quickly. "Oh, she's gone. Eighteen months she's been gone. I've got another lodger now. A gentleman. Ever so nice. Stuck up, she was. Never wanted her, but that Miss Catch-pole said she'd take away the school washing if I didn't 'ave 'er."

That Miss Catchpole, thought Liam, is quite a lady.

"And do you know where Miss Frost is now?"

"That Effie told me."

The china teeth clicked like teacups.

"Who's Effie?"

"Maid up at Catchpole's. Used to be Miss Frost's maid. Ever so thick, they were. Not there anymore, though. She left, too."

"Effie," said Liam. "Effie what, and where did she go?"

Mrs. Quickly shook her head.

"No idea. Just went."

Effie in her devoted loyalty would not discuss Miss Isabella's affairs among what she thought to be her enemies.

Betterin' meself, was all she said, and in Mrs. Quickly's words, just went.

"And what did Effie tell you?"

She was full of importance now and ready to pour it all out, the smell of overheated irons rising behind her.

"Rottingdean. Up the hill," she said. "Wiv' a posh family. Suit that Miss Frost, it would. Thought herself too good for 'ere."

And was, poor girl, thought Liam. And was.

"No address?" he asked.

Mrs. Quickly shook her tatty head. She wasn't going to tell him she had long lost it.

"Rottingdean and up the hill," she said. "Got to get back to my irons." And the door closed. And as well, Liam felt, before the house went up in flames.

"Nothing more?" Angus said as he climbed back into the car, and Liam shook his head, and told him all he knew.

"And what was it like, where she lived?"

Liam thought a moment.

"Clean," he said. "Poor but clean."

Angus was silent, sunk back into the corner of the car, something very near despair on his thin face.

"That leaves us back at Rottingdean," he said. "We have that one. Cable said she left with no forwarding address."

Because of the possessiveness of James Bennett, and the torn letter in the snowdrift, Angus Frost sat that bright day in the car in Brighton, oblivious in loneliness and grief to everything about him, and Liam could see the man was very close to tears. If he had seen the washerwoman's house, he would be closer, the limits reached even for his strong and resilient character.

"Well," he said, for he could think of nothing else to say. "Let's go to this house, anyway. There could be something they remember that might lead to her."

There was nothing, because the extraordinary woman who inhabited the house called Newstead seemed determined to be of no help to them. Billowing in some voluminous paint-stained garment, with a cloth round her untidy hair and blowing smoke at them from a long cigarette holder, she still seemed preoccupied with her own wrongs.

"I have no idea where she went," she said, aggrieved. "She told me nothing, just left me in the lurch with my mother-in-law to care for. I did *think*, that when I got one of Miss Catchpole's gels, she would show more consideration. But these gels are all the same now, wherever they come from."

She seemed to have no thought, or even understanding, of the feelings of the heartbroken, crippled man who sat in her bright comfortable drawing room looking at her with distaste. Once again Liam was thinking of Isabella. There were photographs of her all over Angus Frost's houses: no more than a very beautiful girl, still little more than a child, with enormous eyes and a smile of great openness and candor. How had she managed through all this? That fearful lodging and now this rabbit-faced female, whom he bet would have squeezed every waking hour of work from her. What would all this have done to the girl reared in all these fine houses, and in the high-class school run by that monster?

What would this girl Isabella be like if they found her? Would she be as damaged as her father but in another way? Would her state be the last straw to break her father?

"Can you tell me," Angus Frost was saying irritably, "exactly when she left you?"

"Oh, dear, yes." Another cigarette from the black-and-white box was fitted deftly into the holder by the paint-stained fingers. "Oh, *dear*, yes. It was just before Christmas, can you imagine that? With all the work of Christmas, and I only have one elderly maid, poor thing, and all my children coming. I simply had to abandon my Art. So inconsiderate. You would think they could have waited until after Christmas, at least."

"They?"

Angus grew rigid, and looked at Liam.

"What do you mean by 'they'?" His voice was hoarse.

"But my *dear* Mr. Frost, didn't you know that she was married? Quite well, I thought, in her circumstances. A young schoolmaster. *Quite* respectable. I knew his father. But thoughtless of them. Thoughtless."

It was a long time before Angus could speak, the bright sun falling through the open window on to a face gone rigid with shock.

"Married?" he said then. "Married?"

Ah, God, thought Liam, as though the rest of it wasn't enough. Poor devil.

"Ah, yes," the woman was saying. Mrs. Waxwork Benson or something like that, she called herself. "Ah, yes, but all *quite* respectable, Mr. Frost." There was something in the man's face that made her rush to placate him. He looked as though he might hit her with one of those crutches. She did so *hate* crippled people. Always difficult. "I do assure you that I saw to it that they observed *all* the proprieties. James came and asked my permission," she said as though that was all that was needed.

"And you gave it? You didn't stop them. You knew her circumstances and you didn't stop them."

Angus was shaking from head to foot and once again Liam feared for him. It was beginning to look as though the job might be to keep the father alive until they found the girl.

"My *dear* Mr. Frost." She had got her courage back. "These

gels come and go, although I *did* think your daughter was different."

"My daughter *was* different."

"But she told me nothing. Nothing. Only that her circumstances had changed and she needed the job. I thought her parents were dead."

"So I have been," Angus said tartly. "Is there no one else in the house who might know where she went?"

"I'll ask Brick," said Mrs. Britten eagerly, anxious to be rid of him and the red-haired young man who said nothing, but looked at her as if she were something from a zoo. Liam, like Isabella, was noticing that her feet were dirty.

The bell was answered by the tall lugubrious maid who had let them in, preserving her impassive face, and then racing back to tell Cook that Isabella's father had come from nowhere.

"Madam'll have nothing to tell him," said Cook darkly. "That girl kept herself to herself. Not like some."

"Brick," Mrs. Britten said, and again, like Isabella, Liam grinned secretly at the name. "Brick. Do you know where Isabella has gone to live? You remember Isabella?"

"Yes, ma'am." Although there had been so many since, she could be forgiven for forgetting. "I don't rightly know, Madam, but I think it was Norfolk. Yes, Norfolk. A village school, if I remember. That's it. A village school in Norfolk."

"A village school," said Angus Frost to no one. "Dear God in Heaven, my Isabella in a village school."

Brick went, and after a pause, he said to Mrs. Britten, "And the name, Madam. The name of the man she has married."

"Oh. Bennett. James Bennett. A very nice young man. I am sure you will like him."

But Angus Frost was already struggling to his feet from the chintz-covered sofa, and Liam reached to help him with his crutches. He did not speak or look again at Mrs. Britten, staring stony faced ahead of him when they had got him into the car.

Mrs. Britten stood on the doorstep, rabbit smile pinned to her face, and plain fear in her eyes. What a dreadful man. She hoped he would not come back if he found Isabella. Complaining, or anything like that. How could he? She had treated the gel properly.

As the Humber reached the front gates, the side screens open to the mild day, the chauffeur had to stop to allow in a harassed-looking girl, red in the face, maneuvering an old wicker bath chair over the rough patches of the drive. In it an old lady peered out from a bundle of black shawls, and a couple of shopping bags swayed from its handles.

They passed without interest, Angus Frost immersed in his own shock, and so left behind the one person in whom Isabella had confided.

"I don't forget things," Lady Angela could have told them. "I don't forget things. Brackenham, she said. To a village school. Brackenham. In Suffolk. I liked Isabella."

Between shock at Isabella's marriage, exhaustion and frustration, and the weakness of his injuries that would never leave him, Angus Frost went down the next day with pneumonia.

For six weeks he lay in a clinic in Welbeck Street, and Liam, helpless before the resident staff, could do no more than sit beside him, watching the plane trees beyond the window reach the full green of summer, even though the sun was fitful and inconstant, and the sharp showers were as he remembered an Irish April.

He looked at the glittering drops cascading down the window, blurring the façade of the drab buildings across the road, and thought of the first nights when, on occasions he had been sober enough, he had lain on the dirt floor beside Angus Frost's bed. With that little nun. Waiting for death or dawn, whichever came first.

Watching now the same flushed suffering face on another pillow, he knew that although he had said he could be with him only a short time, he could never leave this unhappy man who had unwittingly dragged him from his own self-inflicted death.

"I will be gone a few days," he said to the doctor. Better go out and try and find a reason for Angus Frost to live than to sit here and watch him die in sorrow.

"Tell him," he said, "that I will come back."

He bought a map, and took the great glittering Humber and the idle chauffeur who was only too glad to be on the road again, and carefully and systematically toured the village schools of Norfolk: the dark cloud masses piling the immense skies along the sandy wastes of the coastline: rain drumming on the hood through the pine-shaded roads around Sandringham, where the village school of the King of England did not hold Isabella Frost any more than any other. At Wells-by-the-Sea he looked astonished at flood marks on the edges of the estate of the big house, and took a little time to walk alone on the vast miles of sand, looking at the distant sea, and marveling at the fearsome power that had driven it so far inland.

But in the little red school in the estate village, no one had heard of Mrs. James Bennett.

Wakingham and East Dereham and Watton and New Buckenham and the devious, intruding sea at Horsey Mere, with the skies clearing and the summer coming and the buttercups and Queen Anne's lace white and yellow in the ditches. In the end he did what he realized he should have done in the beginning, and went to the County Hall at Norwich. But no, they were polite and helpful, but had no record of the name of Bennett in any school in Norfolk.

"But you will understand, sir, that there are many schools not under our authority. We would have no records of these."

"I think," said Liam wearily, "I have been to them all."

He went to the police at Scotland Yard, not sure Angus would approve, but he was in no state to know, and both as doctor and friend, he knew how it would increase the chance of Angus living, if he could bring his daughter to his bedside.

Earlier they had spoken of a private detective, but Angus had tartly rejected it. He did not want, he said, any prurient sleuth poking his nose into Isabella's life. He had been sure then that he could find her for himself.

Like the man in the County Hall in Norwich, the police in their red-turreted building above the Thames were polite and kind but of no help.

"No one could say, sir, you see, from what you tell me that the young lady has actually gone missing in any suspicious circumstances. Seems to me she just got married and went off with her husband."

The elderly sergeant assumed a wise and experienced expression.

"Could be, sir, you see, that she wanted to get away from her family. Some girls do, sir, in marrying."

Liam looked at him civilly.

"Thank you, sergeant," he said. "I'm sorry to have taken up your time."

"It's like Bo Peep's sheep, sir," the sergeant said cheerfully.

"Like what?"

"Bo Peep's sheep, sir. Leave them alone and they'll come home. And as like as not, dragging their tails behind them."

"Yes, sergeant."

"At least," said the sergeant, remembering belatedly a little more of the truth of his profession. "Many of them do."

Liam walked out through the pillared gates, and crossed the road to walk under the plane trees of the Embankment, fresh with their young leaves: above the fast-flowing spring river where the barges moved in strings and the old shot tower pointed its red finger to the sky above the grimy buildings on the far shore.

He paused at a bright-red telephone box and rang the clinic.

"No change, Dr. Power," the Sister said. "But he is holding his own."

She added the bright note of hope.

There was only one thing more that he could think to do, and he did not know if Angus would approve of it, but as he walked on down the Embankment in the direction of Fleet Street, he could not help marveling at his involvement. He who had lately and for so long refused to be involved with any one at all. Who had left the world more severely than any monk, his mind closed to all the pains and passions. The existence of joys he did not yet admit to. There was enough in his forgotten pleasure in the fair English day, the colors of the river and the sky and the brilliant barges. And that he was committed, by no driving will of his own, to the man who lay gray-faced and searching for his breath, back in the clinic.

He thought of the sergeant's words and hoped that Isabella would be worth it all if they found her. It would break Angus Frost, indeed probably kill him, if all they found was a girl secure and satisfied with her own married life. Who had indeed married to get away, indifferent to her father?

His steps slowed on the crowded pavement of Fleet Street, the traffic thundering past him from Temple Bar down to the slope of Ludgate Hill. But Angus, he reasoned, had a right, if possible, to know. Firmly he turned in through the bronzed glass doors of the London *Times*.

"I want," he said to the girl behind the desk, "I want to place an advertisement. In the Personal Column."

The following day, with the same ruthless determination to live that had brought him through his injuries, Angus had taken a turn for the better: safely through the crisis of the pneumonia, and slow, tedious recovery in sight.

There were six answers to the advertisement, and even before he showed them to Angus, Liam knew that they were none of them from Isabella. Unscrupulous girls, all hoping, God knew how, to pass themselves off as Isabella, for anything that Mr. Angus Frost might have to offer.

Sadly, after waiting a few days until he was stronger, he showed them to Angus, who had made no comment when he had told him what he had done: too weak anymore to question the methods, as long as he found Isabella while he still held breath.

His tired hand dropped the letters on the bed.

"How could they think," he said, "that I would not know her when I saw her?"

Or she know you, thought Liam. With the gaunt face of a man ten years older, and the grizzled hair. There had been photographs, too, of Angus Frost, around the houses, and Liam understood clearly that the emaciated creature in the bed was not what Isabella would expect to find.

"She might," he said carefully, "have changed. It is two years."

"She cannot," said Angus bitterly, "have changed as I have, but my daughter will know me. And I will know my daughter."

He was silent a long time, the blue eyes that had lost their brilliance staring out at the purple dusk beyond his window: the lights coming on in the buildings across the road: the rumble of homegoing London loud in the streets below.

"As soon as I can be moved," he said, "we will go down to Suffolk, where I will get better. We will take Enderby. Will you write me a letter, Liam, and see when we may have it?"

There had been pictures of Enderby, too, and Liam wondered what he and Angus were going to do rattling around in that elegant barn. But the man had a right to do what made him happy.

"I suppose," said Angus then, "that you are right. It is possible that she will have changed."

The newspaper given to Mrs. Primrose by the Fish Man, for wrapping her produce at the fête, was old. So that it was a month after Liam put in the advertisement that Isabella climbed on to Effie's bicycle to set out for Long Melford. James had made no offer to close the school and take her on the Norton. She had wanted to go to the village shop and telephone, the moment she got the letter in the morning, but James had thought it a ridiculous waste of money.

"Certainly not," he said. "It is only an hour or two until the afternoon."

The whole thing displeased him. Enough had gone wrong in having a barren wife and a crippled child. If his brother had not got him that free consultation in Guy's Hospital, where the doctor had rather reluctantly agreed to say as he wanted, she would still be nagging him night and day for money to cure a daughter he did not particularly want. The advent of a father, who could do nothing but interfere, annoyed him excessively. After two years he had thought that they were safe. All he wanted was to keep Isabella to himself, and shape her to what was left of his plan for living. She still had much to recommend her. Very good with the Vicar, and Lady Lyndly, and people like that.

He was testy and irritable all through their midday dinner, prolonging it as much as possible. When Isabella at last got ready to go, he asked her in the tones of a loving father if she was not going to feed Clara.

"Effie can do that," said Isabella, nervously pulling on her gloves. She never wore gloves round the village, but knew her father would expect them.

James looked pompous and displeased.

"I would have thought you would have wanted to feed your own child."

From behind her, Clara in her arms, Effie nudged her out the door, her small mouth, not for the first time, compressed in fury at James Bennett.

"Oh, Effie." Isabella took the high rusted bicycle from where it leaned against the wall, and put her purse into the basket. "Oh, Effie. I'm so nervous."

"Nothing to be nervous about, Miss Isabella. It's yer father, isn't it? Love him, don't you?"

"Oh, of course! But he's so handsome, Effie. So splendid. He might think I have changed."

Effie looked at her compassionately, remembering the shining girl at Catchpole's.

"No, Miss Isabella," she said. "Course he won't, and even if he did, he'll still love you."

Now Isabella's smile was radiant.

"Oh, yes, Effie, of course. He'll still do that."

But her mouth was dry as she cycled the miles to Long Melford, through small gentle roads where the hedges tangled with the long briars of wild roses and the soft white flowers of traveller's-joy: the ancient trees were heavy with the fresh leaves of high summer, and in the ditches the long lush grass was drenched with flowers. Isabella saw only the front wheel of her bicycle, eating up the dusty road until after what seemed a thousand miles, she coasted down into Long Melford, past the wide green space before the village, and at last into the wide, gracious, rambling street.

The Bull at Long Melford. She looked up at the windows, wondering if he would be watching for her, but they were all blank. Many times they had come here when out driving in the country: for lunch or evening dinner. Warm familiar memories of childhood.

She wheeled her bicycle into the cobbled yard where once the coaches had swung in under the great beamed archway, but when she faced the girl at the desk in the hall, she could not find her voice.

"Mr. Angus Frost," she managed to say in the end.

"Oh, yes," said the girl in the tone familiar to Isabella, that implied that anything to do with Mr. Angus Frost was important. "You'll find him in room six. He's had it made into a sitting room."

Polished oak stairs, rose carpet on the landing, and flowered chintz lifting at the windows in the quiet breeze.

She never even thought to knock, rushing now to open the door.

He was waiting for her, leaning on his crutches in the middle of the room, as though to make his crippled state clear at once. She saw an elderly, gaunt-faced man with grizzled hair, snow-white across the top of his head on the line of a scar: all his weight on his crutches, showing the uselessness of his legs and of the feet in their beautiful, highly polished shoes.

Only the dark-blue eyes blazed with something she could not define: excitement, or defiance of all that had happened to make him what he was: incapable of rushing to take her in his arms. Waiting for her reaction.

In his turn, waiting for his shining and self-confident Isabella, he saw a beautiful, tired-looking girl, with enormous eyes darkened by sorrows: in a cheap cotton dress, with ill-cut hair hanging like a fringe below her hat of faded straw.

Isabella was the first to weep, choking on her shock.

"Oh, Father, Father! What has happened to you!"

She could not even move to go to him, staring appalled, weeping as if he were already dead, and then he, too, began to weep, and they stood there looking at each other in tears, both of them in a state of distress by the change in the other.

It was raining a thin gray rain as she rode home, the sun gone with all her radiant anticipation, and she was wet through her thin dress by the time that she got there. James was not very concerned about this, nor indeed about her father, whom he was determined should interfere as little as possible with their lives. Even this first evening his supper was late and that displeased him. He asked her little, and through their silent supper she tried, and failed, to speak of all she had to tell him.

Or to speak even of her own sorrow and distress. She told him only that her father was coming to visit after school the next day, and although it clearly gave him no pleasure, not even James could be churlish enough to refuse.

Only when she went up to Clara after supper, and Effie came with her, was she able to talk of it at all. Effie had been looking at her with concern in her pale eyes, showing it only by bringing her a dry dress, and stuffing the straw hat with newspaper so that it should not lose its shape. She sighed as she ladled out the soup, Miss Isabella should have come back radiant, but she looked as though she had more troubles than ever on her shoulders.

Isabella laid the drowsy baby down after she had changed her and moved to comfort the little leg that could not move itself. She laid the blanket round her, and only then lifted her distressed eyes to Effie.

"It all went wrong, Miss Isabella?"

"Yes and no, Effie." She was near again to the tears she had managed to hold against James's lack of sympathy. "Yes and no. Oh, Effie," she said then, her voice tight with grief. "Oh, Effie, he has so changed."

Effie drew the curtain against the darkening evening, and thought of Catchpole's, and thought of the news that she herself soon hoped to give Isabella, and that would be more trouble.

"So have we all, Miss Isabella," was all she said.

Isabella said suddenly, inconsequently, "He had a doctor with him."

"A doctor, Miss Isabella. Is he sick?"

Poor girl, that would be some of it.

"He was terribly injured in the earthquake, but I think the doctor was there more as a friend."

"He was very kind to me," she said then as they moved toward the stairs.

"Your father?"

So he should be, thought Effie.

"No," said Isabella. "The doctor."

chapter

11

She and her father got over their initial shock, tumbling over themselves, then, and interrupting each other to tell their stories. His was simple to understand, except that he kept mentioning somebody called Liam, and it was his story that got told first.

"Who, Father, who is this Liam?"

Her eyes still roved over him in disbelief that even an earthquake could do so much to change him from the man he had been. But he was there and a new abrupt cantankerousness gave way every so often to a flash of the old warm charm, lifting her heart to hope that in time he might be himself again.

"Liam? Without Liam I would not be here." He laid his hands on his knees and looked at her. "Such as these are, he gave them to me. And my memory. He is the doctor who cared for me. Irish."

"An Irish doctor? But, Father, I don't understand. You said you were in a mountain pueblo: mud huts and shanties. What was a doctor doing there?"

"I have never asked him," her father said simply, "but perhaps someday he will tell me."

He held her hand in his and could not take his eyes off her, although what he saw displeased him.

"You look terrible, child. That dress. Your poor hair. Thank God your mother cannot see you."

They spoke of her then, and wept again together, and he told her of the grave in the overgrown garden of the hacienda.

"I would like to see it, someday," Isabella said wistfully.

"But of course. We will go back to Chile together."

Oh, God, she thought. He has already forgotten that I have a husband and a home of my own. And a child. All these things she had told him when she wrote.

Angus Frost's brain was not so damaged that it could not be selective about what it remembered, and what it preferred to forget. All he wanted was Isabella exactly as she had been, and he allowed the easy cloud to obliterate the rest, carrying on about her appearance.

"We will get you up to Town and get you some proper clothes; and have your hair cut decently. All the girls here seem to have it short, so I suppose it's the fashion. And you can have your own old room at Enderby."

"Father!"

She felt helpless. Was he really so damaged that he had forgotten all that was in a letter of a few days ago?

"Father, you must listen to me. None of that is possible."

Even the clothes, she thought. Imagine Schoolmaster of Brackenham's wife dressed as Isabella Frost. They'd all walk on the other side of the road!

She saw her father's face darken.

"What do you mean, not possible?"

To Angus Frost, nothing was not possible. If money could buy it, everything was possible.

"I had better begin at the beginning," Isabella said, but even before she had finished telling him about Miss Catchpole, she was frightened at the effect. His pale face suffused with fury, and the skeleton hands on the arms of his chair were shaking.

"What a diabolical woman! My poor Isabella. As soon as I am settled in Enderby we will go and visit Miss Catchpole and I promise you she will not like it."

He was hoarse with anger and his eyes blazed with the desire for retribution. Isabella looked at him, fearing for him.

"Father," she said. "What use is the money? You don't need it. It will only distress you to go and see her."

"Every penny," said Angus Frost fiercely. "Every penny."

Sadly, Isabella realized the change in him. Her father as he had been would not have stooped to chasing Catchpole.

So she was more careful as she went on with her story. Having anticipated rushing into his arms and telling him everything, she now skirted carefully around Beech and around Lance, lest her poor damaged father be racing there also for personal revenge.

He listened in silence until she told about her marriage.

"Unbelievable," he said then. "Unbelievable. No matter what state you were in, Isabella, I cannot see that it justified marrying a village schoolmaster." -

The blue day had gone gray outside the windows, and Isabella looked at it and felt in it the echo of all her hopes and plans. Gone gray with this sad, terrible change in her father. This stranger would never buy James a school. Perhaps, she thought hopefully, when he is over the shock of seeing me, he will be different.

"Father," she said carefully. "I married him because I loved him," and here a squeeze of cold misery touched her heart in the understanding of how she had failed him. "And he is not really a village schoolmaster." Carefully she explained James's ambitions, and her father listened barely with patience.

"He is saving every penny for his new school," she said, thinking to impress him with James's thrift, but he only snorted.

"I would imagine so, from the way he dresses you," he said. "We will get you a divorce."

As easy as if it were a pound of apples. But then to Angus Frost everything that cost money came as easily as a pound of apples.

"Father," she said patiently. "I don't want a divorce. What about Clara?"

"Clara? Your mother is dead."

"My little daughter. I told you in the letter."

He had forgotten. Liam could have told her that, while he remembered far back now, he could easily forget what happened yesterday.

But his eyes kindled at the idea of the child.

"She is like you, I hope," he said, anxious to be rid of all trace of this intruding husband.

"Yes," said Isabella sadly, "but she is crippled."

"Crippled!"

Angus Frost's grandchild could not be crippled any more than James Bennett's daughter who was not a son. Once again Isabella feared for him under the strain of his anger and distress, as she explained that the baby was not permanently damaged: merely that it cost more than James could afford to put her into hospital for that long.

"He wouldn't spend the money on his own child!"

"Father, he says he hasn't got it." But did she believe this in her own heart, anymore?

Her father was unmoved. Money, no matter who you were, could always be obtained for essentials.

"He could have got it somewhere," he said tartly, and Isabella thought of the Norton, bright and glittering at the side of the schoolhouse. Bleakly she knew that her hopeful picture of them all amiably together was no more than a dream.

"She can be cured?" her father was asking.

"Oh, yes," and now Isabella's face brightened with hope. Her father surely could not refuse money to mend Clara. "So the doctor said. It is just too costly for James. The price too high."

Her father snorted in disgust.

"Isabella. Be so good as to pull the bell for the maid. By the fireplace."

Mystified, she moved over and pulled the old-fashioned red-tasseled bellpull that hung beside the stone hearth.

With the attention Angus Frost had always commanded, it was only a matter of minutes before a neat, respectful maid appeared in the doorway.

"Tea, please. You'd like tea, Isabella? Tea for three, and find Doctor Power and tell him I want to see him."

Tea for three? Doctor Power?

"Who is Doctor Power, father?"

Her father looked at her as though it were she who had lost her memory.

"I told you. He looked after me in that pueblo."

"Yes. But you didn't tell me he was here now."

A curious expression crossed her father's face. Furiously independent, how could he explain to her that without Liam he would be lost? As though he was compensation for the useless legs, the cloudy brain. He was life itself.

"He traveled with me" was all he said.

Isabella was baffled and distressed almost to the point of fresh tears.

All through the sad time of waiting and hoping, she had been buoyed up by the picture of her father as he had been, coming like a rescuing knight to put everything right for herself and James and Clara. Now she was confronted by hostility to everything she cared about, not knowing enough yet about this new strange father to even guess whether she could win him round.

The shock and the anticlimax were heartbreaking: and the difficulty in believing that this wasted, suffering creature was the fine loving father who had left her. His damaged body she could understand. But as he had been, he would have been reasonable: would have tried at least to understand that time had changed things: even if they didn't please him.

And now some stranger, who had come all the way from Chile with him? Was this man in some way responsible for the changes in him? People who went up into the mountains to live with the Indians were often strange themselves. Missionary types who wanted to bring everyone to their way of thinking.

She waited, hostile, for some fanatic with burning eyes: probably a beard: and terrible old clothes. Or an Indian blanket. More Indian than the Indians.

Liam came in quietly. He had intended to keep out of the way completely today, but if Angus wanted him, that was different. He was anxious anyway about the terrible strain on him of this reunion, hoping the young woman would have the sense to go gently.

They stared at each other, each ready for antagonism, but silence took them in some shock, little less than Isabella's on seeing her father. But different. It is not clinically possible, Liam told himself in the long moment that they looked at each other, for the heart to sever itself from the great arteries, and do a small dance around the chest, and then go back again.

But that was how it felt as he looked at the exquisite girl who was for some reason glaring at him from the chair beside her father. Pale and far too thin, and tears bright along the lashes of the most marvelous blue eyes that he had ever seen. He felt at once in her a sense of strain and bewilderment, and knew it was as he had feared. She found her father sadly and impossibly changed.

Isabella herself was thrown into further confusion by the tall, well-dressed man who could not be called handsome but whose bony face held immense individuality, a lock of dark-red hair adrift across his forehead. When the introductions were over he disposed his long loose-jointed frame in another chair and regarded her with an endearing lopsided grin that changed the character of his whole face.

"Well," he said. "Isabella at last, and everything her father said she was."

As he intended, she began to relax under the calm voice and the smile.

"And what did my father say?"

For the first moment since she had come in, tears still bright on her lashes, she smiled herself.

"He said," said Liam, "and b'God he was right, that you were the most beautiful girl in the world."

She looked at her father tenderly, and he at her, and they knew their first moment also of real peace and pleasure.

The girl had arrived with the tea and was setting out the Coalport cups, and plates with delicate serviettes: plates of wafer-thin sandwiches: covered silver dishes of crumpets and hot toast to be spread with anchovy or Gentleman's Relish.

Liam saw the expression on Isabella's face, and knew that like himself when he left the pueblo, she had been some time away from such meals. He went on easily with his light talk to ease the tension.

"If some people," he said, "had known the difference between Norfolk and Suffolk, we'd have found you sooner."

"Norfolk?"

"There was this house in, was it Rottingdean? Where a parlor maid with a face like a coffin told us you had gone to a village school in Norfolk. So I went looking."

The description of Brick was so perfect that she burst out laughing, and his thin face warmed with pleasure to have brought it about. Even Angus smiled, seeing her more his own Isabella.

"The tea, Isabella," he said, and with the light tale of all Liam's experiences of all the Norfolk schools still keeping her smiling, she dealt with all the heavy silver and the teacups with a deftness she thought she had forgotten. Good old Catchpole.

"Take off that hat," said her father suddenly, and Liam saw the strain come back to her face.

"My hair," she said as she took it off reluctantly, shaking out the shiny bob that was uneven at the edges. "Effie cuts it, you see, and she's not very good."

"And who's Effie?" said Liam quickly, before her father could undermine her any more.

"Effie for a long time," said Isabella, "was my only friend." She told the whole story of Effie and how happy she was to have her with her now.

Liam was watching her with compassion, and she found herself telling the story to him, as though he would understand things that her father would not, his strange gray-green eyes fixed on her blue ones.

"You were lucky," said Liam, "to have had her."

"I don't quite know," said Isabella, "what would have happened without her."

Still they looked at each other, some secret voyage of discovery going on behind their conversation.

Tiger's eyes, thought Isabella. Like the tigers I saw in the zoo when I was a child.

Angus Frost stirred restlessly in his chair.

"She has a sick child," he said.

"Who? Effie?"

"No," irritably. "Isabella."

Now Liam looked at Isabella and saw the light die from her face.

"How sick?" he asked her. How much else trouble could she have, poor love?

"Not sick at all," said Isabella, and her smile came back as she thought of the small Clara's bubbling happiness in the world about her. "She is perfectly well, and they tell us her hip can be cured."

Liam's eyes were quiet now, professional, aware of the time he had been away from the practice of anything except the simplest medicine, and the strange special diseases of the Indians.

"What is the matter with her hip?"

As clearly as she could, Isabella told him, and Liam's lips tightened. Some clumsy fool of a midwife. Already he found himself full of antagonism for all those who had caused Isabella sorrow.

"Can you cure the child?" Angus Frost broke in.

But Liam's eyes stayed on Isabella.

"If they told you at Guy's that it could be cured, why did you not have it done?"

Painfully Isabella flushed. Always before she had managed to find excuses for James: to try to understand and forgive him. But with two pairs of accusing eyes on her, she could do no more than blurt out the truth. Dear God, but what was the visit to her home tomorrow going to be like?

"James said there was no money," she said, and Liam added James to the midwife on the list of those to whom he felt hostile.

"Can you cure her, Liam?" demanded Angus again.

Liam spread his long bony hands.

"If it is as you say, a dislocated hip, then any half-decent doctor could cure the child." He grinned at Angus. "I've done more than that with people's legs."

But Angus was not to be amused.

"But you could do it?"

"Indeed. It is largely a matter of the nursing." He smiled now at Isabella, happy to find it something well within his capabilities. "We'll have her galloping about with the best of them."

Isabella for the first time smiled her full radiant, candid smile and it took Liam like a fist in the solar plexus.

"Will we do it, Father? You can arrange it with Doctor Power?"

"Liam," said Liam, not yet entirely sure of the identity of Doctor Power, with whom he had so long lost touch.

Her father smiled, too, happy to see a flash of his old lovely Isabella. She got up and came over and kissed him.

"Oh, Father, thank you, thank you."

Here was the most important thing she had hoped for his return.

"Well, if I can't walk, at least we will see that your baby can."

"Oh, Father. Poor Father."

She kissed him again and realized that Liam was making signs toward the door. Her father did indeed look gray and exhausted.

"I have to go now," she said, "to be in time for supper with James."

But at James Bennett's name her father only snarled, and once again she looked with apprehension toward tomorrow.

"Sorry to put you out," Liam said outside the door. He looked at her as though judging what was enough for today. "We have to be careful with him. There wasn't a great deal of him when he got the pneumonia. There's less now."

She didn't speak as she preceded him down the stairs, choked with all the mixed emotions of the hour she had waited for so long; seeing no clear and happy path, except with Clara. And James was so obstinate he might even refuse to let her father do it.

Liam came abreast of her in the hall.

"Take it gently," he said to her, and longed to stroke the bent brown head as he would comfort a child. "Take it gently. It must all resolve itself. Too much has happened for everyone to take up just where they left off."

They stood together in the old cobbled courtyard, where her bicycle stood against a rusted pump.

"I realize that," she said. "I thought as soon as he came back, everything would be perfect. Oh, Doctor Power, he is so changed."

"Liam," he said, "Liam. It's a long time since people called me Doctor Power."

Why, she wondered. Why?

"You must understand," he was saying. "He was terribly damaged. He has to face the fact that he will never walk again properly and for a man of his temperament that's terrible. And a blow on the head and amnesia like that, can change a man's whole character."

"He really didn't know who he was?"

They had said all this upstairs, but she was reluctant to leave: to go back to James's cool disapproval.

Liam was equally reluctant to let her go.

"He had no idea. El Perdido, they called him. The Lost One."

"I know," Isabella smiled then. "Spanish was my first language."

It was the first thing they had said about themselves, and Liam wondered what this well-bred, beautiful girl would say if he told her what they had called him. She would, he thought with a lurch of release, understand. Accept it. He felt an urgent wish to be with her longer.

"Look," he said, "it's going to rain. Let me take you home in the car. We can tie the bicycle on the back."

Now she laughed and he looked at her changed face with pleasure.

"Tie a bicycle on the back of my father's Humber! Oh, Liam, that could finish him."

He smiled back but pitied her. It could take even less than that to snatch away the father she had just found.

"No," she said. "I'd rather ride. And think about it all."

She didn't add that she would not pile up James's disapproval by arriving with a strange man who had not yet come into the story; in a glittering great Humber.

The village would have been interested, too.

He wheeled her bicycle through the archway for her, both of them bound by this reluctance to leave the other, and when she was away, he stood a long time watching her, until even the poor old straw hat was lost to his sight in the rising ground at the end of the village.

Angus Frost was asleep when Liam went back up to him, worn out with the day, and in the dim light he looked so collapsed that as Liam came into the room he thought for a moment that Isabella's next sorrow had already come. Although he did not think it consciously, he knew it as another reason to stay. He wanted to be with her when that happened.

Slowly she rode home, oblivious of the rain, and although she had said to Liam that she wanted to think about it all, she found that she was thinking most of him.

But she did not even tell Effie about Clara, hugging that to herself until she was quite sure that it would happen.

Yes, she said, the doctor was very kind.

The meeting the next day was as disastrous as any of them might have feared.

As soon as the big car arrived outside the schoolhouse, every woman in the village suddenly found need to be in the street; discovering urgent business across the Green, so that they might sheer past with curious eyes, trying to decipher the goings-on at the Schoolmaster's house, where never had such things been seen before. Panton, the chauffeur, fiercely fended off the circle of children, all determined to lay hands on his gleaming bodywork and glittering brass.

Inside, the atmosphere was difficult and strained, only Liam keeping up a stream of easy talk to try and help Isabella do the same.

James was determined not to be pleased, offering no hand to Angus to help him down the step into the tiny parlor. I have to have the man in my house, his expression said, but further than that I will not go, and matters were not helped by Liam's carefully settling Angus into the red plush armchair that was normally sacred to James alone.

As for Angus, he gave little help, either, glaring round him in a disapproval so obvious and so intense that it could not have been greater had he been confronted with Mrs. Quickly and the sodden sheets.

"Father," said Isabella nervously, and Liam was touched that even in the impossibly hostile situation, she held herself with a firm determined grace. "Father, this is my husband, James."

Neither man wanted to acknowledge the existence of the other. Angus Frost thought James had ruined Isabella's life. James was certain that Angus was about to ruin all his plans for his own. They glowered at each other and barely acknowledged the introduction, and Liam babbled on inanely about all the trouble they had had in finding Isabella, knowing the situation so ridiculous that he knew if he caught Isabella's eye they might even begin to laugh.

James sat on his straight chair and thought morosely about the trouble he had taken to bury the letter in the snowdrift, only to have it all defeated by a damned bunch of rhubarb.

Isabella thought desperately of all that her father could do for James if only he would look at him as a benefactor and not an enemy, and her father stared in disgust around the little room that was not much bigger than his car outside the door, and his strained mind could do nothing other than scheme to get her away from the man who had brought her to it.

From the furious silence that was even bringing Liam to a halt, Isabella rushed to the kitchen, where Effie was patiently trying to keep Clara in the state of starched freshness suitable to her first meeting with her grandfather.

"How's it going, Miss Isabella?" Effie asked, but knew the answer from Isabella's face.

"Terrible. Terrible! They won't even speak to each other. Ghastly!"

Effie clicked irritable teeth. The one seemed no better than the other. This father was supposed to end all Miss Isabella's troubles.

"Here," she said. "Take Clara. Babies is good at softening people up."

"That's what I hoped."

Clara was her bubbling happy self, plucking at her mother's hair and beaming at Effie, whom she loved, but it was summer now, and she could no longer be wrapped in shawls, and the poor little leg dangled in its white sock. Isabella tried to arrange it not to show too much. At first, anyway.

She need not have concerned herself. At the very sight of the baby Angus Frost tried instinctively to rise, and swiftly Isabella put her in his lap. Tears stood in the sunken eyes.

"Isabella," he said. "My little Isabella. All over again."

All the present strains and disappointments wiped out and a fresh start for all his generous affection. As for Clara, she at least seemed to know that you must not antagonize your rich relations. Nor had she ever met a hostile human being, except her father, whom she seemed to regard as no more than part of the furniture around which her mother and Effie revolved. So she beamed at this new man and pulled his waistcoat buttons and dragged at his tie and Angus was enchanted, James completely forgotten.

Tenderly he fingered the little awkward leg.

"You can help her," he said then to Liam, and now his voice was as urgent as Isabella's might be.

"I would think so," said Liam. "Can we," he asked Isabella, "take her somewhere to let me have a look at her?"

Isabella gathered up Clara, and she tried to take with her a fistful of the white hair above the scar. Isabella saw her father wince and eased off the small hand gently.

In the tiny hall Liam saw the kitchen.

"Here," he said, "here. We'll put her on the kitchen table."

Effie had the tea tray laid on it.

"Hallo," said Liam.

"This is Effie, Liam. I told you about her yesterday."

He gave Effie the warm grin that made her at once his slave.

"Take the tea in, Effie," he said, as though he and she and Isabella were in league. "It'll give them something to throw at each other at least."

Effie's face lit. This was the kind of talk Miss Isabella needed.

"Effie," said Isabella, as she took the loaded tray. "Put on the lace cloth."

"Yes, Miss Isabella."

Miss Isabella, thought Liam. That'll go down well with Mr. Pomposity in there.

While Isabella undressed the baby, he went in to wash his hands under the scullery tap, walking in and out of the simple rooms as though he had known them all his life.

Effie came back while he was examining Clara, keeping his eyes from the terrible waiting anguish of Isabella's face.

"What are they talking about?" he asked her.

"The weather," said Effie tartly. "You'd think neither of them had ever seen it before." She searched, clattering for a knife.

"Well, they'll come to no harm with that."

He tried to make Isabella smile, but she couldn't, great eyes fixed on him. Giving the gurgling Clara, who was trying to kick herself off the table with her good leg, a last pat, he pulled down her dress and turned to Isabella.

"No difficulty," he said gently. "No difficulty at all. Only time. Your father can give her that."

Abruptly she burst into tears, a cataract of pent-up sorrow pouring down her cheeks, and Effie came back to find the doctor mopping the tears with his own handkerchief, holding her hand and talking to her softly. She gathered the forgotten baby from the table and took her upstairs. Well, there would be a thing, wouldn't it? Miss Isabella and that nice doctor. She didn't know about divorces. How'd she get rid of the other one? Never been any use, that one.

"It's all over, Isabella," Liam was saying, and even in her upset state she knew a small shiver of pleasure to hear him speak her name. "It's all over. We'll get her all right. It's only time now. It's all over. Here, have a blow." He gave her his handkerchief. "It's all over."

Isabella looked at him with drowned eyes, still dark with some resignation that tore at his heart and filled him with anger. She inclined her head toward the parlor and clearly they could hear James's measured tones telling her father all about mining in Chile.

"No," she said sadly, "it's not all over."

He must, thought Liam, at least get her to laugh at the man. It was all he was worth.

As Isabella realized, it was not all over.

"No," said James, as soon as they were gone. "No. I will not have it. It is quite impossible."

He had said nothing while her father had stated his terms for having Clara cured, and Isabella, listening to him, had felt sadly that there was little to choose between them. Would her father, she wondered, have been so intransigent had he not been sick and damaged?

"Clara will come to Enderby," he had said firmly, and Isabella was close to tears to see the soft pleasure at having the child, that lay behind his words. If only it could all have been different. Clara was going to be well, but there would be a price. She remembered telling James that there would be no price too high.

"Clara will come to Enderby," her father said. "And you, Isabella, will come with her."

She saw James's lips tighten, but he said nothing. Across the room Liam watched her with careful eyes, and tried not to show his pleasure. Or his hope that she would have the courage to stand out against James, for it was clear the mean devil was going to object.

"Of course, Father," said Isabella. "I would not let her go alone. And, dear Father, thank you, thank you."

She came and laid her face against his, and slow tears again crept down her cheeks. Her father patted her hand.

"She is mine," he said, "is she not?"

And Isabella drew away, ready in the nervous, blissful moment now to laugh. Her poor father did not make things easier. James had little use for Clara, but like Isabella herself, she was a possession, and no one else might lay claim to her.

But her father was running on happily with his arrangements, and already there was a new light in his face. Perhaps after all, thought Liam, he might in a while be able to leave him.

"You'll get a day and a night nurse, Liam. Only the best. How soon can you do that?"

Liam had no idea.

"Give me a week," he said firmly, and for a week's time they arranged it all. In a week Liam would come and collect Isabella and Clara. Effie, collecting the teacups, set her mouth in a small obstinate button. Miss Isabella'd be gone for months, and she had no intention of being left alone with James Bennett.

And James himself said nothing, and implied consent.

Until they were all gone: until they had eased and pushed her father painfully into his seat, and the open Humber was fading into its own dust cloud down the early summer road between the hedges.

Isabella knew instinctively what was coming, but turned to James with great unusual calm.

"Stick out for it, Isabella," Liam had said to her quietly before the car drove away, looking at her gravely. "She's your child, too." He also was aware that the matter was not over.

"Isn't it marvelous, James?" she said carefully, and kept the smile pinned to her face, determined not to let it fall away. "Only a week, and she will be on the way to being better. She will be well for Christmas. Perhaps walking. Isn't it wonderful?"

"No," said James.

Isabella looked at him, and above the smile, for the first time, the huge blue eyes were dark with anger.

"What do you mean?"

"Just what I say. The whole charade," he said pompously, "is quite unnecessary. We have arranged for the child to go to hospital when she is two." He snorted. "A private doctor and two nurses."

"It is that that you object to?" she said quietly. "Not to Clara being cured?"

"Not at the proper time and place."

And for you, she thought, and had never even in her mind admitted it before, for you, that time might never come if it costs money. But your pompous pride will not accept my father's doing it.

"I think," she said, "this is the proper time and place."

He changed his tack.

"What is the matter with that doctor?" he said. "Has he no work to do? Or has he been struck off?"

"He saved my father's life." Sheer cold fury filled her, fueled by her own speculations as to who and what Liam was. But if her father trusted him, so did she. And also she just—she just trusted him. "And my father needs him now," she added.

"Nice," sneered James, "to have the money to buy a man out of his practice."

His practice? In a remote Indian village in the Andes? Again she thrust down questions. One day she would know it all. Nor was she going to allow the present moment to slide down into a bicker about Liam.

"I am going, James," she said. "As we said. In a week."

"I forbid it." ·

Once if he had said that, she would have crumbled instantly. But the old Isabella was emerging. The strong, candid girl of Catchpole's: Isabella Frost, with all the assurance of her father's money behind her. The blue eyes were sad but cool.

"I am still going, James. I wish you could have done it kindly. It is for Clara, remember. I will come back constantly and see you."

"You will not," roared James suddenly, and out in the kitchen Effie heard him. Poor Miss Isabella, she thought, carefully pouring water into the geraniums on the windowsill. Hope she can stand up for herself.

"If you go," James was yelling. He saw a curious face passing the open window with deliberate slowness. In five minutes it would be all over the village that Schoolmaster was shouting at his wife.

With an immense effort he lowered his voice. "If you go, I do not want you back here until you come back properly and for good. I'm having no wife visiting me!"

Isabella stood very still, grown pale.

"And Clara? Will you not come and see her?"

He would not look at her, glaring at the floor.

"The choice is yours. You go to your father and you go alone and stay alone."

His bitter, hostile jealousy was as clear in the room as the golden bar of sunlight that danced with dust motes along the top of the polished table.

"Well, then, I go, James," she said after a long, sad silence. "I hope it will all be happier when I come back."

Now he lifted his head.

"You are not the same girl I married," he said bitterly.

She thought of herself then, ground into subservience by all that had happened. But she would have loved him if he had let her.

"No, James," she said. "I don't think I am. But if we never change, then surely we remain as children."

Like you, she thought. Like you. An obstinate child who wants everything his own way. Dominating real children because they are the easiest, and give him a spurious authority. A thread of her old love for him touched her, and with it, pity.

"You are making it very hard for yourself, James," she said softly. "Never mind for me."

"If it is hard for you, you have chosen it and must pay the price. I have to suffer it against my wishes."

"I told you before, James, there is no price too high for curing Clara."

"In your eyes," said James, and at that she turned and left him and went out to Effie.

In the kitchen Effie was peeling potatoes in an enamel bowl as though every potato were James Bennett, and she was stripping him of his skin.

Isabella was trembling as she sat down opposite her, torn to shreds by the decision she had had to make, while never doubting that she must make it. If only, she thought, she could really hate

James, because he deserved it: but a nagging residual love left her sore with guilt that she could not please everyone. There was no doubt her father could have made it easier, too, but she did not need Liam to tell her that there was no arguing with her father at the present time.

If there ever would be.

Hot, sad tears came to her eyes. With everything to decide about Clara there had been little time to come to terms with the tragedy that was her father.

Effie ground the knife with particular venom around the eye of a potato and through the open window came the evening sound of the children playing on the Green. Isabella remembered how in her first summer she had loved to listen to them, and looked forward to her own child running in the shadows of the great trees, and the tears flowed fast and bitter, confused happiness over her father and Clara, and an aching sadness that James could not allow her the happiness.

"Not my place to say so, Miss Isabella, but he ain't worth it."

She had seen the same expression of baffled grief in her mother's eyes over her stepfather. Men. They were all the same. Then her face took on a look of almost apologetic softness.

P'raps not all of them. There was one seemed different. Isabella had looked up, drowned blue eyes determined now.

"Clara is. Worth it."

"Oh, my Lord, yes. You got to do it. But Miss Isabella"—she laid down the knife almost as though she could not be trusted with it—"I ain't staying here alone with him. We'd not pass a day before there'd be trouble."

"I—I really hadn't thought it all out, Effie."

Effie had, with her usual sharp speed.

"There's Minnie Plum," she said. "Just along the street. Lost her man three weeks ago. She'd come in and clean and cook for Mr. Bennett."

She had recovered her temper enough to speak about him properly, but could not resist a mean pleasure that Minnie Plum would do nothing for him without being paid for it.

"I'll get meself something in one of the houses round."

"You will not, Effie." Isabella wiped her eyes firmly with the back of her hand, herself again. "You will not indeed. You will come to Enderby with me. I am sure they have a full staff there, but my father would think it only to be expected that I have my own personal maid."

"Like I used to be."

Sheer bliss lit Effie's pale face that never gained color even in the country sun.

"Like you used to be, Effie." Now Isabella smiled ruefully. "My father only wants to make everything as it used to be. He doesn't understand yet that he cannot. You must come, Effie. I wouldn't leave you behind, and as well, you'll be someone familiar for Clara."

"I'd 'ave found it 'ard to leave her," Effie said. "And you, Miss Isabella. Done a lot for me, you 'ave."

"It's been mutual, Effie," said Isabella, and Effie did not understand her. Knew only that she was going to stay with the two people that she loved best in the world. And going to be closer to the new, different love that was almost beginning to alarm her, as it would inevitably take her away from them.

But happiness suffused her small staid body. Her Frank's father and mother had their farm over Enderby way. Be that much closer. Much closer.

James refused to say good-bye to her on the day she left.

Through the week she had made all the arrangements with the willing and avidly curious Minnie Plum, who could not wait to take her narrow face the length and breadth of the village, speculating on the strange behavior of Schoolmaster and his foreign wife. All those visitors in that great car with a chawfoore and rugs in the back seat, had surely boded something strange. And here it was. Her narrow jaw stretched in a civil smile, her yellow teeth protruding amiably, but all the time her bright dark eyes were whipping round the house, trying to understand what was going on.

Isabella was cool and pleasant to her and told her nothing except that she was going to stay with her father for a few months, but Effie looked at her with mean secret pleasure, knowing she would well be a match for Mr. Bennett.

"And why does Effie have to go?" James asked coldly.

"I want her with me and Clara."

"This woman will cost me money. Why do I have to pay for you to go frivoling off like this?"

Isabella looked at him, and her distaste was untouched by love.

"My father will pay her," she said, and silenced him.

On the golden June morning when the Humber came to take them to Enderby, it was Liam who drove it, and Isabella was startled by the jolt of pleasure that it gave her to see the red head in the car drawing up outside the garden fence.

Within seconds half the village had found their ever-ready business in the village street or on the Green.

Even the Vicar had come in the evening before, trying hard to conceal his urbane curiosity.

"I understand you are leaving us, Mrs. Bennett."

"Only for a while." Isabella called on all her long-gone social training and smiled at him guilelessly, explaining all about Clara and her father's desire to have her in his house.

"Ah, well," said the Vicar, relieved. Marriages in Brackenham tended to be forever, even with perhaps a little sideslipping, and although his sense of duty had brought him, he had little idea in his gentle head of how to deal with a separating couple.

"You will be coming over to visit us all, no doubt."

By which, of course he meant the cold-faced, silent James, who took no part in the conversation.

"Enderby," said Isabella smoothly, "is not far away."

And with that he had to be content, but left with the unhappy certainty that he had only half the story.

They were ready to leave, Isabella in her cotton dress and faded hat not quite suitable as a passenger in the shining motorcar, where, as Minnie Plum had noticed, vicuña rugs lay folded on the back seat against the soft breezes of the day.

Effie was holding Clara, who beamed as she always did at any change or adventure, blue eyes bright under her ruffled sunbonnet.

"Liam, we are taking Effie with us. I am sure my father will not object."

Liam smiled his warm crooked smile at Effie, and touched the baby's cheek.

"What would we all do without her?" he said. "Especially Clara."

Effie was established in the open car, one of the incredibly soft rugs round Clara, the luggage, such as it was, strapped on the tonneau, and Liam waited to see Isabella into the front seat beside him. He was as aware as she was that James was not there to say good-bye.

Isabella came halfway down the path, her eyes dark with hurt and anger. Then she paused and suddenly turned back. It had always been a law that she was never allowed in the school, cold chalky kingdom belonging to James, alone.

Now she went with her head high, out the scullery door and across the backyard, through the green wooden door into the playground. The door into the school stood ajar and she went through it from the warm sun into the cold tiled hall. Beyond in the schoolroom itself she could hear the singing chant of multiplication tables, and when she went in, James stood at the blackboard, leading them, his long pointer in his hand.

The chanting of the table faltered to a halt. Never before had Schoolteacher's wife appeared like this, and expectation of some drama went like a wind across the children's faces. One in disgrace in the far corner turned his head, unrebuked, at the sudden silence.

There was no drama.

Schoolteacher's wife stood quietly in the door.

"James," she said. "I'm going."

"And I," said James, "am teaching."

Even before she had closed the door, the chant had started again, the chalk dancing in the still beams of sunlight, as though nothing had occurred. In the corner the child turned his face hastily back to the wall before he was discovered.

Isabella's face was bright with tears and anger as she came back again down the little brick path between the marigolds.

Liam pretended not to notice, and settled her into the front seat beside himself, moving off steadily, without saying anything, into the green lanes, the sun splintering in the brass frame of the windshield.

The morning was all green and gold, with the broken shadows of great trees across the road. The ditches were tall with summer grass, foaming with Queen Anne's lace and yellow loosestrife: tangled with vetch and ragged robin, and in the darker places, the tall pink spikes of foxglove.

As the sun-spattered lanes rolled on between the trees, Isabella was unable to understand herself. Liam was as silent as the chauffeur, allowing her to collect her feelings. In the careful quiet, suddenly, the tears of her husband's cruelty drying on her face, she knew a wild illogical premonition of happiness to come.

It is Enderby, she told herself. I am driving to Enderby in the Humber. To my father. It is only that I am turning the clock back. That is all. For a little while.

chapter
12

For some time after she arrived, her father made no reference to his vengeful plans for a visit to Miss Catchpole, and she hoped he had forgotten it.

The first days at Enderby were difficult, the house filled night and day with Clara's furious screams. She resented bitterly the restrictions of the splint, having found nothing wrong herself with her little dangling leg, and even through the solid walls of Enderby they were all dominated by her misery.

Isabella found it hard to stand it when her cheerful baby rejected even her efforts to comfort her, glaring at her with sodden blue eyes as though she alone were to blame for her terrible discomfort.

"Oh, Liam," she said, wan and distressed at the end of a long sleepless night. "Liam, have I done right? Will it be worth it?"

Liam grinned amiably across the polished breakfast table set for the two of them in the deep bay window of the dining room. A low bowl of fresh-picked rambler roses was between them, and the windows at their side open to the green morning freshness of the park, cattle browsing beyond the ha-ha in the shadows of the elms.

"Of course it will," he said cheerfully. "Small children are great fatalists. In a day or two she will have adjusted and forgotten she was ever any other way."

"I do hope so. I find it very difficult, and she won't even look at me."

Liam pushed aside his empty plate, from which he had scraped with relish the last fragments of scrambled egg and bacon. He helped himself to toast and the rich yellow butter from the farm behind the house.

"But you, my dear Isabella," he said, "will soon be fit only to climb in beside her."

"What do you mean?"

"Look at you. You're in shreds. You've eaten no breakfast. You haven't slept all night."

"I can't help it."

"Yes, you can. You can leave her to the nurses. They know exactly what to do, and it is no help to Clara for you to keep rushing in at all hours of the day and night. She only thinks you have come to rescue her, and it makes it all worse. In a few days it won't matter."

"She *is* my baby."

"Ah, come on there, don't be sloppy. You're far too intelligent for that."

Tears came helpless to her eyes, and across the table Liam grinned at her again above another piece of toast.

"Jesus," he said. "Now we have you bawling as well."

He got up from the table and went over to the sideboard to where three silver chafing dishes stood upon a hot plate.

"Bacon. Kidneys. Scrambled eggs. Mushrooms. I'd say a little bit of everything and a fresh cup of good hot tea."

In spite of her weak protests he put a plateful down before her and filled her teacup from the heavy silver pot.

"There, now. And when you've finished, we'll take a couple of those fine horses out of the stables and you'll show me the country-side. You *can* ride?"

Indignation distracted her.

"Of *course*. At least I used to. There weren't many horses about for the last couple of years. But Clara—"

"Doctor's orders. For Clara. A couple of visits a day from her mother when she is tranquil. No more. Eat your breakfast. That's doctor's orders, too."

She could not help smiling; and beginning to eat, suddenly found it was delicious.

"Did you bully my father like this when you were looking after him in that village?"

Liam had a memory of another world: the long sweating nights when hope was almost gone: the only sound in the sweltering darkness the click of the nun's beads and the whir and sizzle of the moths around the candle. His own hopeless mind.

"I did," he said lightly. "If I hadn't he'd have been running down the mountain the first day he got out of bed."

He could see questions in her face, but not even to distract her from her anxiety would he answer them yet.

"Have you noticed that there is one person who can keep her quiet?" he said, referring to Clara.

She looked up quickly.

"Oh, yes, my father. Isn't it strange."

Angus Frost had swept about the house in his wheelchair, organizing a room for Clara on the ground floor so that he would be able to be with her: determined not to miss even one crippled hour of this little child who with one beam from her small bright face seemed to give him back all that he had lost.

And curiously, for him and him alone would the baby's furious face grow calm and even consent to smile. He had sent Liam shopping for as many toys as would make Christmas for an orphanage, and never came to her without some fresh diversion, his own ravaged face growing more peaceful every day.

"Very strange," said Isabella again. "She hardly knows him."

The sun moved and a bar of it struck Liam's hair like fire. He wiped his mouth with his napkin and shook his head.

"No. Not strange. The old and the very young often have some strange communion that we in the middle do not understand."

Aghast, she looked at him.

"But, Liam, my father is not *old.*"

And he did not know what to say, not wanting to tell her that her father was close to death, and that amounted to the same.

"Just because he's crippled doesn't make him old," she said, forgetting her own withering shock when she first saw him.

"No, no, you're quite right. Are you done? That's better. Now come on and we'll get the horses."

They had reached the door when she stopped, flushed and embarrassed.

"What's the matter?"

She was torn between two loyalties. Two worlds. The maid

came quietly through the service door to clear the breakfast, and she had the clearest vision of Effie turning from the range with James's three rashers of bacon and two eggs. She did not know whom she was betraying, her obstinate husband or her child and her equally obstinate but damaged father. Or herself, who could not decide where she belonged.

"I have no clothes," she said, "to go riding in."

It had been automatic to stand up from the breakfast table and say yes, we will go and get the horses. But she could not go riding in a cotton dress or in one of the silk ones carefully preserved for special occasions. Nor did she know what she expected from Liam. Sympathy or contempt? He was such an enigma himself that she could gauge his reaction to nothing.

All he did was shrug and smile, he himself ready, dressed in beautiful jodhpurs and a soft white shirt, the sleeves rolled to the elbows of his freckled arms.

"So," he said. "We will go for a walk. Just as good."

The square paneled hall was quiet, the polished floor flooded with color from the stained-glass window above the door, but instinctively she turned toward the corridor that held Clara's room.

Liam laid a hand gently on her arm.

"No," he said.

"But I haven't said good morning to her."

Liam grinned his crooked grin.

"If you do, she will probably be saying good morning to you at the top of her lungs for the next hour. Have pity on the nurses, love."

An Irishman, to whom words came easy, and even the gentle look that underlay the grin. An endearment that meant nothing. Just a word. And yet deep inside her she felt some sudden vulnerable softness.

"Take it easy on yourself," Liam was saying as they went out from the cool hall, through the outer door onto the terrace, where the steps led down to the graveled drive and geraniums and lobelia blazed scarlet in great stone urns along the balustrade.

"Tell me," said Liam. "Tell me about it as you remember it. Tell me about it all when you were a child."

Trying for himself to recreate the wrecked man they had

dragged from the rubble of the mountain. Trying to get to know about Angus Frost, who had lived nearly a year as nobody. El Perdido. In Chile he had learned much about the man of business, who had commanded such loyalty that in his empire no man had moved until he came back: all his interests intact.

This was different. Another man, he must have been, in this peaceful place, and unless Liam was a useless doctor, he had come back here to die.

Isabella was only too willing to talk: touched to excitement by being at last in her beloved Enderby again. All the nightmares of the lonely years sliding away. She forgot her mortification that she could not even ride a horse because she had no clothes, and in her eager memories became again Isabella Frost, speaking with warmth and love of life with her parents in their summers in the beautiful house.

"And here we did this and here we did that, and Panton would carry a picnic lunch down here to the gazebo beside the lake. And always if it was fine we would have tea under the big cedar tree near the terrace. Sometimes at night, if they had guests, I would slip off across the park to look back at the house with all its lights on, and the people on the terrace after dinner. And know that they were there, among them."

Her eyes were brilliant with tears she would not shed, looking at him with a desperate need to be understood.

"It could never happen again, Liam."

He did not know how to answer. Of course it couldn't, with the mother dead and the father on the edge of it.

"I don't mean because of them," she said urgently. "I mean because of me."

"You?"

Once again she looked across the park, rich with summer.

"I could never again be so—so—carefree," she said.

"We all grow older," said Liam carefully.

Poor love, poor love. She had forgotten that she was not yet long past being a child.

"It is not older," said Isabella. She stopped and picked a loose piece of bark from a tree beside her, examining it as though it were precious. Then she looked up at him. "It is Cubbington's and

Beech and Quickly and what Miss Catchpole did and these ghastly people in Newstead, and learning that my only real friend was Effie."

Liam tried to ease the moment.

"You don't want to give it all away?" he asked her.

Then she smiled.

"No. No. I am not so silly. But I think I would like my father to buy James a lovely school somewhere. Where I could feel *useful.*"

Liam looked at her and his long mouth was gentle. But for the accident to her father she would be in Chile now, adored, probably useless, except as the exquisitely trained chatelaine of some splendid hacienda. Washed in carefree gold. Nor did it yet seem to occur to her that her father had disliked and distrusted James Bennett on sight, and would probably refuse to buy him as much as a pair of shoes. His one idea, fed by the obstinate self-will of his damaged state, was to get her away from him.

They had come to an elegant arched bridge where the lake narrowed, small red-legged moorhens scuttling along its banks among the water lilies and the reeds. She stopped suddenly and laid her hands on the stone of the parapet, and looked back at the house, giving the lie to all she had said by gasping to hold back a torrent of tears.

"But it's not ours, you know, Liam. We only rent it."

"And it does matter, really?" he said gently.

"Yes, yes it matters. I never thought I would see it again. I could have come, you know, it was no distance. But I couldn't bear it. And now here we are again and my mother dead and my father as he is—and my poor little Clara. And this time it will be forever, for I must go back to James and he will have nothing to do with my father and everything will be horrible and I have been waiting for him to come back for so long so that everything would be perfect."

Poor Isabella. Trapped between two worlds and trying desperately to tell herself the old one was unsuitable, lest it be gone forever.

She was crying now, great gulping sobs, and rubbing the back of her hand across her face like a child.

"Here," said Liam, and from the pocket of his breeches, gave her his handkerchief. His smile was as tender as if he were dealing with Clara.

"Have a mop and a blow," he said. "I've lots of handkerchiefs."

She did. And then drew a long, shuddering breath.

"Liam," she said, and there was almost a note of panic in her voice. "Liam, at the moment, I hardly know who I am. Do you understand? And I don't usually blubber like this."

Did he understand? He, who for over two years had lost sight of who he was. Nothing more than a sponge for *agua ardiente*.

"Poor Isabella," he said carefully, to stop himself in a rage of compassion for both her and for himself, from taking the shining brown head and laying it on his shoulder. From kissing her, and maybe himself also, back into some feeling of permanence and security. "Poor Isabella. Too much has happened in too short a time. Take it bit by bit. One piece at a time. For the moment we are curing Clara? Yes? One thing at a time. Take each thing as it comes."

So he had said to himself on the day when, almost mindless with panic he had kept entirely secret, he had set off with Groucho and the mules to the railway: to launch Angus Frost, and himself, back into the world.

He did not say to her what he thought of the jealous and possessive husband who had made it all so much more difficult than it need be. A mean bastard too, obviously.

A strand of brown hair had fallen from her barrette and mixed itself with the tears, and with a long, careful finger he pushed it back.

"Bit damp," he said, and his eyes urged her to smile.

"I'm sorry," she said then. "It's all a bit of a mess."

"Not at all," he said. "Very nice hair. There's just that wet bit that you blew your nose in."

She giggled then, knowing it to be feeble, and he sauntered on across the stones of the narrow bridge, leaving her to collect herself: infinitely comforted even though he had said almost nothing. He was quite right. Everything would sort itself out.

He turned back then and started on a tale of her father and some old Indian in the village called Groucho, each as self-willed as the other. By the time they had reached Angus, where Panton had settled him in his canvas wheelchair underneath the great shady spread of the cedar, she was laughing.

She sat down in one of the high-backed cane chairs with blue cushions, and looked at the table at her father's hand, with two kinds of sherry, and biscuits, and told herself how foolish she was just for this little time, not to give herself up happily to the pleasures of Enderby.

Not a really large house. Or a grand one. Just so perfect. The sunlit stretches of the park and the dark cool shadows of the cedar. Her father smiling as if with some especial pleasure to see them come, and Liam spreading his long length in the chair opposite, running his fingers through his red hair.

She might as well enjoy it. James and all the other problems would be there when she must go back.

"What was funny?" asked Angus.

"I was telling her about Groucho always managing to get you to do his work."

"Idle rogue," said Angus, and Isabella, her mind cleared, looked from one to the other.

Groucho had lived there. All his life, no doubt.

The earthquake had brought her father, but what had this lanky and elegant doctor been doing in the mountain village? They had never even given it a name. And why did he seem to have nowhere to go back to?

Her father distracted her.

"Now, Isabella, Clara is settled. We have to think about you."

"Me?"

"My darling, look at you. Your clothes are terrible and your hair looks as if a dog had chewed it. We have to get you put right."

Liam had never seen Isabella angry, and looked with a sudden surge of warm approval at the tightening of the lovely, generous mouth, the quick tilt of the head, and the warm flush that crept slowly up her face.

He approved even more that she did not let the anger get control of her.

"You have been gone, Father," she said carefully. "How would

I get the money for these things? My husband does not feel he can afford them. And I have to go back to him."

Funny, she thought. Even in Newstead, never mind Quickly's, they thought I was toffee-nosed. Now my father thinks I look like a pauper.

For a moment Liam thought Angus was going to blunder even further, and then, gladly, he saw the man he must once have been.

"My darling," he said. From the wheelchair, he held out his hands. "Please, come to me, I can't come to you. Sweetheart, I am sorry."

He took her hands in his and Liam could see the softening of her face.

Do whatever he wants, he wanted to cry. Do whatever he wants. There might never be a chance again. Whatever he wants. And knew from the expression in Angus Frost's eyes that he was crucified by his own clumsiness.

"Love," said Angus carefully. "Love. My Isabella. You will not be here for long. Please, please let me for this little time see you as my daughter. I'm sorry if I was clumsy. Please."

There were tears on her cheeks. She bent and kissed him.

"Darling Father. Yes. Yes. Whatever you want me to do."

He was brisk almost at once, recovered; and Liam smiled into his sherry.

"I've arranged an account at Harrods for you, pet. Take that little funny girl of yours—what's her name?"

"Effie. Clara likes her."

That was enough to set the seal of approval on Effie for him, and now Isabella and Liam smiled across his head as they might across the head of a willful child, but Isabella's heart was sore with grief that they should both feel so about her splendid father. There had been so much to settle about James and Clara that her shocked anguish over his destruction had barely been allowed to surface.

She pulled her chair up next to his and held his hands in hers.

"Anything," she said. "Anything. A tiara and a red velvet robe? Make me look like Lady Somebody? Ermine?"

It was too close to his own foolish dreams for her, and he would not smile. He had wanted ermine for her.

"No, my pet. But have your hair cut. And get clothes like you used to wear. Like your mother would have bought for you. Take Miffy."

"Effie," she said, smiling, but her tears were hot on his hands. How could you turn back the clock?

When they set out for London a few days later it was raining, the straight, cool relentless rain of English summer, the grass flattened and the bees gone from the plastered flowers in the borders. Only the sparrows on the terrace chirped and twittered as if they had secret knowledge that soon it was going to stop.

Isabella looked out at it.

"Had we better wait for another day?" she said, and her father looked at her surprised. He normally breakfasted in his own room, but today he had come down to see her off, as though it was important to him. He was in his wheelchair, only Liam realizing that since the pneumonia he had rarely had the strength to use his crutches.

"What matter?" he said to Isabella now. "Panton will put you down at the door. It will be quite correct for you to lunch there with your maid."

Correct. All the old words of the old pattern. Her maid. Words that could no longer belong to her, except for this period of make-believe that had to end for her as soon as Clara was better.

But her father was looking at her as if it was of immense importance to him, and she smiled.

"Of course, Father," she said. "I had forgotten how easy it was."

As easy as flinging a coat over your head against the rain, and racing out from the School House to see if the Meat Man might have any cheap cuts that her meager housekeeping would allow her to afford. She looked at the beautifully laid breakfast table, the choice of silver dishes on the sideboard, and the honey, the marmalade, and the strawberry jam all in their crystal jars. Abruptly she stood up, and Liam carefully did not look at her, aware of the loyalties that were tearing her.

"I'll go and say good-bye to Clara," she said.

"She's a good girl now and doing well," Liam said, and as he had intended, that made her smile and leave more happily.

"Bless her," she said. "Take care of her."

The calm mood stayed with her, Clara having let her go with smiles, and she was content going off with Effie, self-important under Panton's big umbrella down to the closed car, the side screens up against the rain. Effie had carefully sponged and pressed the dress of slate-blue silk, and she had tied a scarf in the fashionable bandeau manner round her hair to take the place of the faded straw.

From the wheelchair on the portico on the terrace Angus Frost watched her go, his blue eyes absorbed, and Liam in turn watched him and realized exactly what he was up to. And hoped it would not all result in heartbreak for them both. It had not taken him long to realize that Isabella, under all her beauty, had the same cast-iron character as Angus himself. Indeed, God knew, that was why they had both survived the earthquake.

The sparrows had been right. They had started early and by the time they reached the outskirts of London the puddles were drying on the shining streets, and they had no need of the umbrella from the vast obsequious and bewhiskered doorman outside Harrods.

Effie had never been in London before, had indeed never been anywhere until Isabella took her to Brackenham, and even her great adaptability, which had taken Enderby in its stride, was strained. She was silent, her small, slightly fishlike mouth hanging open, staring with astonished eyes at the great city.

But she knew exactly what to do when they got inside the red-carpeted treasure cave of the shop, looking at nothing, falling half a pace behind Isabella and composing her pale small face as though she had spent all her life following her mistress round such places.

Isabella could not help but smile at her. Incomparable little Effie, who could be at her side through everything that came, from port in a Brighton pub, through all the anguish of Clara's birth, and now looking as coolly professional as any lady's maid in the gilded confines of Mayfair.

Dear Effie. Whatever would she do without her.

She had come to Harrods to please her father, but firmly determined to buy only the minimum to keep herself suitable to his life-style for the months she would be at Enderby. Apart from anything else, life would be impossible with James if she was wearing clothes her father had paid for.

She sighed. It was all very difficult, and somehow or other James would have to be talked into accepting her father, who goodness knew was not being helpful, but he was after all her father and it was only chance he hadn't been there always. It was no good brooding on the fact that if he had been there always, never in her life would she have met James Bennett.

First she had her hair cut and the beautiful shining line of it swinging round her face was the first step back to Isabella Frost.

"Such thick hair, Madam, and such a lovely texture."

The blond, gentle-fingered girl tried to persuade her to let her make up her face, but with memories of the blackened eyes and scarlet lips at Newstead, Isabella firmly shook her head. Her father hated what he called paint.

She was smiling when she came back out to Effie, sitting patiently on her spindle-legged chair outside the door.

She forgot about being the perfect ladies' maid.

"Lawks, Miss Isabella," she said. "Done it a bit better than I did, hasn't she!"

And both of them beaming with satisfaction, they embarked on the main business of the day.

Isabella remembered what her mother used to do in such circumstances and asked for a private fitting room, where they sent her a refined elderly lady with protruding teeth and the overcompetent air of a spinster who has kept herself all her life: and an anxious junior, clearly terrified of her.

"And what exactly does Madam want?" asked Miss Teeth, swaying a little in front of Isabella, clearly unable quite to place her in her long experience of customers.

By the time Isabella was halfway down her careful and modest list, she had placed her. Money was no object, and if there was any difficulty in choosing between two attractive dresses, or hats, or shoes, then she would take them both. This was Effie's fault. When Miss Teeth was away happily collecting fresh armfuls of the best, Effie confronted Isabella's indecision with hissed urgings and instructions.

"Take 'em all, Miss Isabella, if you like 'em. Take 'em all. It's what your father'd want. You know it is. He don't want you home with two dresses and a hat and back here next week. Take 'em all!"

"Well, not *all*, Effie. I mean, I won't be going anywhere. Just enough to keep my father happy."

But the change from Isabella Bennett back to Isabella Frost was taking place, exactly as her father had planned, and gradually she was caught by the excitement of all the lovely things around her, the room piled with silk and ninon and georgette and plain exquisite day dresses in pale cotton lawns.

It was as if Angus had sent Effie with instructions.

"You'll be there till Christmas, Miss Isabella. Want something warmer, too."

Miss Teeth purred with pleasure, thinking of her commission, and they started again, the little junior arriving with piled arms and astonished eyes: adding velvet to the piles and fine cashmere sweaters: soft knitted suits and small close-fitting hats.

Isabella looked at her watch, and by now guilt had left her. She was only doing what she had always expected to do once her father had come back. Return to Brackenham was months away, and since James didn't want to see her, then even visiting was no difficulty. She and Effie met each other's eyes like delighted and successful conspirators.

"We'll go and have lunch now, Effie. Come back afterward to decide on the shoes and hats."

"And lingerry," said Effie firmly. "You must have lingerry, Miss Isabella."

"Lingerry? Ah, lingerie."

She grinned. Miss Teeth would be certain she was buying a trousseau, but Effie was right. Her underwear, mended and remended like cobwebs by Effie, was what she had brought from Catchpole's, and she didn't fancy getting some cotton drawers from the Thread Man. Brackenham would never know what she had underneath. What a pity James would only disapprove of it.

"Yes, Effie. You're quite right."

By the time they came out into the gray and doubtful afternoon, it took the young assistant and another, two journeys to bring all the boxes to the car, where Panton helped the doorman to pack

them into the tonneau and the back seat beside Isabella. Miss
Teeth had practically crawled along the passage from the fitting
room on her black silk knees.

Panton was seeing Effie into the front seat beside him, watching her from the Knightsbridge traffic. With a spurt of affection
Isabella reflected that everyone was fond of little competent, patient Effie. Except James, of course. She leaned forward from
among her boxes as Effie sat down.

"All that day of shopping, Effie, and we never bought anything for you!"

Effie turned.

"Thank you, Miss Isabella, but it weren't to be expected."

Then her whole plain pale little face lit up with a mixture of
happiness and regret. But the happiness could not help winning,
and she beamed at Isabella.

"But I'll tell you what, Miss Isabella. If things goes as I think,
very soon you can buy me a wedding dress."

There was no more to be said. Panton was moving out into the
traffic and the front seat was far away. Isabella was left with her jaw
dropped, trying to collect herself in the pile of boxes. She knew
Effie had been courting this young farmhand called Frank. Knew
that logically something could have come of it. But she had been so
occupied with her father and Clara, and James being so difficult,
that she had never thought of it: brought Effie to Enderby as an
essential part of her life without ever thinking any further.

She reproached herself for her selfishness and then she
thought of going back to Brackenham, and in the warm muggy day
she knew the chill touch of something that was almost fear.

She would have to live alone with James: without Effie.

Liam came out to help unload the parcels when they reached
Enderby in a clearing evening with all the flowers lifting their heads
to the last of the sun and the birds singing as madly as if they had
no permission to do it again in the morning.

At the sight of all the green boxes he whistled and grinned and
asked had they been good enough to leave anything in the shop for
any other poor souls. Isabella laughed and her eyes were dark with
happiness and excitement. He had never seen her so alive, and so

beautiful. This, he thought, must be the girl from before the earth-quake.

"You had a good day?" he asked her, his eyes warm on her over his pile of boxes.

"Lovely," she said, "lovely." And in the bustle of getting it all in, she got no chance to speak to Effie.

Liam followed her as she raced down to the sun room where they had put Clara, to find her father, as he was so often, in his wheelchair beside her bed. She even ignored Clara's clamor, to rush to him and kiss him, her arms around his shoulders.

"Oh, Father, thank you, thank you. I have got such lovely things. Gorgeous!"

He patted her cheek, but his own blue eyes were more thoughtful than indulgent.

"Really nice things?" he said. "You'll feel more like yourself now?"

"Oh, yes, oh yes! Much more myself!"

Not realizing that she was admitting to having felt otherwise.

Liam, watching, knew that with deliberate intent, knowing exactly what he was doing, her father had carefully driven the first wedge between her and James Bennett.

He did not know that in the car in the busy street outside Harrods, Effie had got there first.

She only reached her later, when she had seen Clara and played with her awhile. Effie was unpacking all the day's trium-phant shopping, laying it all in drawers and putting the dresses on hangers, the shoes and hats on shelves in the cupboards of the dressing room to Isabella's bedroom, something close to an ecstatic smile on her pale face.

This was something more like it for Miss Isabella.

"Effie!" Isabella cried from the door, nothing more than an-other girl as excited as Effie herself.

"Miss Isabella?"

Effie came from the dressing room.

"Miss Isabella? I'm just putting it all away."

"Effie, what's all this about you getting married?"

Effie looked stricken.

"Oh, Miss Isabella, I'm sorry I blurted it out like that, but I've been trying to get up my courage to tell you."

"Courage, Effie? Why courage?"

"Well, Miss Isabella, I shall be leaving you, shan't I? But I feel better about it now you're all settled here with your father and plenty of money to look after yourself. You'll be all right now, so I can go happy."

Isabella did not point out that she would be going back to Brackenham and knew again seconds of cold apprehension about being there without Effie.

But she smiled warmly, delighted over everything for Effie.

"Frank?" she said.

"Oh, yes, Miss Isabella. Who else? He's findin' out if his Dad'll let him do up a cottage on the farm. Do it mostly himself, he could. Don't want to live with his Mum much. Not far from here, Miss Isabella. I can come and see you and Clara."

Isabella was infinitely touched by the radiance of Effie's plain little face.

"Oh, Effie, I'm *so* glad for you. You love him?"

Effie nodded, and Isabella came across the room and kissed her. There was something about Effie that always looked as if she would be cold to the touch, but her colorless cheek was firm and warm. Isabella felt a surge of pure love and gratitude for her staunch little friend. Lucky, lucky Frank.

"So happy for you, Effie."

"Thanks, Miss Isabella. I did feel bad about it, but not now."

Isabella gave up. Effie must *know* she had to go back to Brackenham and James.

"Which dress shall I wear this evening, Effie?"

They chose a pale-yellow pleated georgette, the pleats all the way down the long straight dress gathered into a deep band of gold sequins at the hips. There were gold sequins, too, around the square neck, and Effie got out the new gold sandals with their one thin strap across the instep.

Effie looked almost awed.

"You should 'ave a fevver in yer 'air, Miss Isabella."

But Isabella didn't like aigrettes.

"Just that plain gold slide, Effie, the one that somehow got away from Catchpole's. You remember it."

"You're quite right, Miss. It's more like you."

She came down the wide stairs with the evening sun taking a soft glitter from all the gold on her dress, the fine pleated skirt whispering about her knees, and Liam was waiting for her at the bottom, his eyes and face full of all he was thinking. Like Effie, he looked almost awed.

"You didn't waste the day" was all he said, and took her hand. "I have a glass of sherry poured for you to help you recover from your labors."

Isabella smiled at him, delighted with herself, and unable to help responding to the stunned admiration in his eyes.

"You're teasing me."

"Yes," said Liam, and led her by the hand in to show her to her father, sitting by the long open windows of the drawing room.

Even dinner that night seemed different. More formal. The servants more deferential. As though the new mistress of Enderby was at last come home.

The days passed in elegant and drowsy leisure, through the languid heat of June and July, blasted by occasional thunderstorms that to Isabella and her father were no more than the popping of children's firecrackers.

Every week Isabella wrote conscientiously to James, reporting to him on Clara's progress, and every week it grew more difficult, looking out at the sprinklers keeping the wide lawns of Enderby green, and biting her pen trying to find words of unity and affection that were never answered.

Conscious always of Liam waiting for her downstairs, for tennis, or a swim in the cool dark waters of the lake, or with two horses ready in the stables. Or simply for a stroll around the quiet parkland, the trees growing heavy with the weight of their summer leaves. Or a spin in the shade-striped lanes with a picnic basket lovingly packed by Panton's wife, that they would open in some quiet field or by some riverbank with heavy willows growing down toward the water.

Still they talked only of Clara and her father and the things that lay about them, but they found it increasingly hard sometimes now to meet each other's eyes, fearing what they might see there, knowing that the time was already here when against their very wills they would blurt out truth, and could not stop themselves. Then all the idyll of their summer would turn into dust and discussion and the tearing apart of lives.

So they were careful, and talked and laughed lightly in the browning countryside, and sang old songs together in the open Humber and threw bread to ducks along the quiet rivers. And did not dare so much as to touch each other's hands lest they should both be engulfed in something neither of them could stop.

Wherever they had been they would come back to Angus Frost waiting for them in his wheelchair under the shade of the cedar, or by the window of the garden room with Clara.

Watching for them, and searching their faces to see how their day had gone. Engineering it all, thought Liam, and could not be angry, for who could blame him for wanting to see his daughter safe and happy before he died? Not, God knew, that it needed any engineering as far as he was concerned. All the bitter sorrow, the blind screaming sense of loss was gone: the will to death that had taken him up to that village.

Now there was only the will to a new life, and that would be as barren as the sorrow if it could not hold this lovely perfect girl with her long legs and her wide candid smile and her sense of fun: and her ability for loving as clear as her own blue eyes.

But some umbilical cord of duty still held her to that pompous and unkind fool over there in Brackenham, who cared indeed neither for her nor for the child, and he would not move until she gave him some sign that she was breaking free.

Isabella herself felt as if she were walking in a ring of light, but all around her shadows waited.

It was heaven to have her father back: to be with him every day, talking away the lost time. Even damaged as he was, he was there. And that, she had thought, would never come again.

Clara was slowly but certainly improving, and Liam promised her that she would walk, and normally.

Liam. There was the center of her circle of light, from where the journey back into the shadows would be most terrible. Liam. Whose tender, hilarious eyes she no longer dared to meet lest she drown in them and never find herself again. Whose every angular, loose-jointed movement caught her own eyes and pinned them like a captive butterfly.

Her last waking thought at night, and God forgive her, her first in the morning, even before Clara.

But then Clara would be all right. For her the shadows must close in. Liam must in time go back to Chile and to his profession. Already he was speaking of it. She would have to leave her sick father at a distance and pack up all the lovely clothes that would so displease James: take her little walking Clara by the hand and go back where duty lay in Brackenham. Without Effie.

She would leap out of bed these summer mornings and race down to visit Clara. More often than not Liam would be there: his quiet official visit of the day to the chuckling baby who had learned to accept all her difficulties.

As I must, Isabella would think as she kissed and played with her, the heavy splint now part of her daily existence. As I must.

She would resolve to spend the day alone: see only her father and Clara while Liam was not there. Be more by herself, lest she lose perspective and find everything impossible.

Then Liam would stand up from Clara's bed: another person. "Ten minutes to the stables!" he would say.

Or, "Last one in the lake's a sissy."

And she would be unable to resist the challenge of the gray eyes that held so much more than the mere invitation to a horse ride or a swim.

Laughing, she would kiss Clara and promise to see her again soon, and race out after him, her slippers slapping on the polished floors, thrusting away the shadows and slipping happily again into her circle of light.

Her father, getting up slowly into his painful morning, would see them, racing for the lake, their colored bathrobes billowing behind them: or neat on their beautiful horses cantering toward the woods. Smiling, he would go on slowly with the painful business of getting dressed, more patient now with his infirmity than he had ever been: looking forward to breakfast when two of the three last people he loved in this world would be beside him at the table.

Already in his mind he was designing a chair to have made specially for the day Clara could join them.

In the middle of July he asked Panton to call Isabella to his study, where he sat at his desk between the windows with his customary mountains of mail before him. Despite his legs he still vigorously conducted all his business affairs in every corner of the world.

He was folding a document as she came in, his eyes full of some bright conspiracy.

"Ah, Isabella darling." She bent to kiss him.

"You wanted me, Father?"

"Only to tell you best clothes on Wednesday. I have some business I want to do in Newmarket, and as it's the July Meeting we might as well go on there. All on the flat. Panton can manage the chair."

"Oh, how nice. It will be spiffing to go to the Races. But Newmarket, father? What a strange place to do business? What is it?"

Her father smiled broadly.

"You'll see. And has my typing girl come yet? Send her in when she does. I hope she's not sweating too much."

The girl who came on her bicycle through the hot lanes from Long Melford to type his letters was pink and plump and always mopping frantically at her face and the palms of her hands by the time she arrived. Apologizing as profusely as she sweated.

"We'll fan her a bit," said Isabella.

"Tell Liam about Wednesday."

"The business or the races?"

"Both. And Isabella—my broker's coming down on Thursday. Lunch, dinner, and stay the night."

"Right, Father. I'm going to play tennis now with Liam."

He smiled at her as though it pleased him.

"See you at lunch."

As she closed the door she could hear the typist panting and apologizing in the hall, but she was delighted with her father. Liam, she knew, was astonished at the way his mental faculties had improved since she had come back. And when she went away again, it would not be far. She and Clara could see him constantly. Clara had a lot to do with his getting so much better, she realized that. Given him a future.

Going back to Brackenham was something she thought of and spoke of often, as if to remind herself that it must happen. But the thought had no reality or dimension, and she made no plans for it.

Reality had become confined to now, when she was back effortlessly in the life of Isabella Frost, only her weekly letter to James, in difficult and stilted words, holding her to the duty that she knew must claim her, in the end.

She took her racquet from the sofa in the hall.

"Liam," she called in through into the drawing room. She smiled at him as he came out, lanky and loose-jointed, suited in his white flannels with his soft shirt open at the neck. His face and throat were browning from the summer days. So, she thought, he must have looked up there in that village, angular inside his cotton poncho. She realized her father had told her very little. Very little.

"I'm going to beat you today, Liam."

"You," said Liam, and looked at her with the delight that never failed him. Almost austere today with all her thick brown hair tucked away inside a white bandeau. For some reason he thought suddenly of the little green-eyed nun who had looked after Angus.

"You," he said, "and what army?"

He took her racquet from her, and smiling, they went out into the lethargic sun.

They came into Newmarket down the Cambridge road, still early so that the vast expanses of grass beyond the roadside rails were drifting in an opal-colored mist, the orderly trees like dark slabs against the skyline: and the few horses were vanishing phantoms on the gallops.

Beautiful, thought Isabella, and strange. Like a Chinese picture. She was touched by an air of mystery, as though they were entering some other world, and knew herself vulnerable and unstable, intolerably aware of Liam facing her on the folding seat, and that the world at whose threshold she stood was not one of the mind.

Her father, she knew, was in no opalescent dream. Merely driving past the gallops at Newmarket on a misty morning that made him draw the soft rug closer over his aching legs, his mind on the business ahead. And now that they were approaching the solid red brick buildings of the town, she was filled with curiosity.

They stopped at an old Georgian house whose shallow door-steps projected like a foot into the street and provided an obstacle it was difficult for Angus to negotiate. He shook his head at the elegant curve of the stairs, and told the girl who let him in that he would do his business in the waiting room downstairs. The slow struggle to get in had allowed Isabella to read from the engraved brass plate that they were in the office of solicitors, and in due course a thin elderly man came down the stairs and into the small room where they sat. He looked at them benignly through rimless glasses and was dressed in an old-fashioned frock coat, so much the conventional solicitor of legend that Isabella could not resist a small smile. But her father had solicitors in London. Why this?

He introduced himself and Angus apologized for bringing him downstairs.

"My pleasure, Mr. Frost. My pleasure. And I have everything ready for your signature, as you asked. There were no complications. Old Lady McRoss was willing and anxious to sell."

Isabella and Liam sat politely while he opened up a folder and spread two copies of a long document on the small table. He set aside a pile of letters and Isabella could see her father's new shaky signature on one of them.

Angus smiled: the wide happy smile of the contented conspirator.

"The final possession is not for me. It's for my daughter."

Mr. Proudfoot turned his mild eyes on her.

"Of course, Mr. Frost. It is all in her name. Isabella Maria Bennett. It is only necessary for you to sign here, Mrs. Bennett. Your father has done everything else."

She looked at her father: blue eyes to blue eyes.

"What, Father? What do I sign? What is it?"

It was clearly an emotional moment for him, his face full of his love for her.

"Enderby, my darling. I have bought Enderby for you."

She gaped at him.

Enderby! Dear God, how happy that would once have made her. To give her the house of all her happy childhood memories: the house where now, however hard she fought against it, every shadow held Liam's voice and face. What was the use of it when she must at the year's end go back to Brackenham? She looked at Liam and her distress and uncertainty filled her face, but he could not help her, understanding that the wily Angus was driving yet another wedge between her and that blank-faced husband of hers. He would offer no hand in helping to prevent that.

Isabella knew she could not refuse: could not upset this poor haggard father of hers who sat there, precarious on his straight chair with all the pleasure of his gift in his face. She went over and kissed him, and there were tears in her eyes.

"Dear Father, thank you, thank you. You know I have always loved it. But for as long as you shall live it will be yours. That's the only condition on which I'll take it. You promise me?"

"Oh, indeed, my darling," he said, "I promise you that."

Liam did not know if his throat tightened for himself or for Isabella. Angus for so bravely knowing that in Enderby or anywhere else, as long as he should live would not encompass much.

Or Isabella, smiling now delightedly as she put her signature where the solicitor's long dry finger showed her: thinking she had her father settled, no doubt, and that she could come and go for years from Brackenham, as she wished.

Isabella had no such illusions. All she cared was that her father was happy to be in the house he loved for as long as he wished to stay there. What would happen otherwise she did not know, and thrust it from her mind as she was learning to do through most of the hours of the dreamlike summer; that she knew must end as surely as that the leaves must fall and the frosts of winter come.

She kissed him again in the car, the long brown envelope in her hand.

"Oh, thank you, Father. You know how I love Enderby."

He smiled and nodded and pulled his thin gold hunter from his waistcoat pocket.

"Splendid," he said. "Two birds with one stroke. We'll have an early lunch and some champagne to celebrate that you're a young lady of property, and we'll be in plenty of time for the first race. Panton's going to make his fortune today, aren't you, Panton?"

Panton turned round and grinned his neat, controlled grin, and Isabella hoped desperately that he and his wife went with the house. A retired Army Corporal, there was nothing he could not do, and her father would be lost without him.

And Liam. But surely Liam must go one day. The very thought clouded the soft sun, and touched her with the uncertainty of the future. She thrust it aside.

"Liam, isn't it absolutely *charming*. Have you been here before?"

"I've never been to England before," he said, and she realized how little she knew about him.

They had lunched in the dark ancient dining room of a hotel in Newmarket presided over by a thin dragon of an old lady wearing a black dress down to her ankles in the style of twenty years before, and her thin hair scraped into a knot on the top of her head.

"I would think," said Isabella as she fixed them with a gimlet eye, "if she didn't like the look of us, she wouldn't let us in."

"Exactly," said her father, and Isabella realized that even three months ago she would not have got past the door. Or next year.

Now as they strolled around the paddock on the July course, all her broodings were forgotten, brought by the champagne and her father's pleasure to the happy state where she thought nothing of the future. Only that she owned Enderby and was with Liam: under a gentle sun in this utterly delightful place of thatched roofs and white wrought iron: long curly-legged seats and masses of scarlet geraniums and blue lobelia against the green of the perfect grass: lampposts with white globes, all in the gay and charming mood of *belle époque*.

They did well in the first two races, and were walking hand in hand and smiling as they came back to where Panton had settled Angus by the rail of the Enclosure. They were both beaming, too.

"Mr. Frost knows a thing or two, sir," said Panton, and Liam tried to pump him for the next race, but Angus would have none of it.

"Go off and find your own horses," he said. "Leave Panton and me to make our fortunes."

Laughing, they went off and placed their bets and decided to watch that one from the rails themselves: farther along, where the crowd was thinner. Shoulder to shoulder they leaned against the rail, looking down the long green channel of the course, and in a few moments fell silent, both of them touched by the beautiful perfection of the day, and by the knowledge that their enchanted world could not stand still. Both of them fearful of where it would progress.

Isabella knew suddenly that it was the moment to ask what not even her father seemed to know.

"Liam," she said, and lifted her eyes to his as if to ask only for truth. "Liam, what were you doing in that mountain village before my father came?"

Under the brim of his Panama hat his face was in shadow, but his eyes didn't falter. He looked down at her.

"Drinking myself to death."

She gasped.

"No!"

"Indeed. I had almost succeeded when your father came. That's why I say he owes me nothing. I may have saved his life, but he saved mine. Now I'm ready to use it again."

She searched his face as if looking for some clue.

"But why, Liam, why?"

And never taking his eyes from her, Liam spoke the words he had not managed to speak to anyone for four years, burying his grief and guilt as the nameless *borracho*, slowly killing himself in the high village, watched in grief by Father Ignacio, who sometimes wondered if he had killed.

Liam, in his own mind, thought he had.

"I had a wife," he said, and they might have been alone on the planet instead of in the middle of a fashionable crowd with the bookies yelling and the horses cantering down before them to the post, and the hum of expectation rising in the stands. "I had a wife and three little children. Two sons and a baby daughter. There was a cholera epidemic in Valparaiso. Not much of a one, but I managed to catch it and bring it home. I got better." He paused a moment but his voice was still calm as he went on, rolling his race card between his hands. "But by the time I got better they were all dead and buried. Every one."

"Oh, Liam." She could hardly speak for the weight of his sorrow in her mind. "Oh, Liam."

"I never even saw the grave. I walked to the edge of the city and took a lift in the first mule cart I got going off into the desert. It was my intention just to get off and wander into the desert to die. But some impulse made me walk up to that village, and I was making a very good job of the dying part of it when they dug your father out of the mountain."

"You felt you had killed them yourself," said Isabella sadly, her heart sick with pity for him.

"I did."

"You don't now."

He looked down at her.

"I couldn't have told you, if I did. I went more than a little mad. Now I can tell myself that these things happen. And remember them—and look to the future."

They stood in silence a long moment, very close, and never heard the massed yell of "They're off" from the stands beyond them. Both knew that the moment was not yet over. That there was more to be said, and that it would bring the harsh difficulties of reality into the closed world of their summer dream, where everything was possible because nothing had been acknowledged.

"And the future, Liam?"

She was a little breathless.

"I'm ready to go back. I have been in touch with the hospital and they want me back whenever I'm willing to come."

"And my father—he'll miss you."

He paused.

"I'll stay until your father is ready to let me go."

He took her white-gloved hand in his.

"But you, my darling. You know I am in love with you, Isabella."

She nodded mutely.

"And I with you," she said then. Lifting those incomparable blue eyes with all her heart in them; and he loved her for it: incapable of dissembling.

They only paused, surprised as the roar and thunder of the race came past them, the monstrous seconds of the surge of animal bodies, silks merging into one blaze of color above them: the frenzied bellow from the stands as the winner belted past the post.

"Isabella." Liam was looking at her with desperate urgency in his eyes, barely aware that the race was over. "Isabella. I want you to come back with me. To marry me."

"Marry you?" Oh, dearest God, the stuff that hopeless dreams were made of. "Oh, my darling Liam, how foolish. How *can* I?"

Liam shrugged.

"There is divorce, my love. For people with your father's money, it is not difficult." He grinned. "And he would not want you clinging to that husband."

But Isabella could not smile. She knew James Bennett. Never never would he consent to a divorce no matter what she did. Nor ever give her cause to divorce him. Sadly she shook her head.

"I know you think James is a joke," she said. "He is mean and pompous and all the things you think. And much worse than most of it." Her lovely face under the wide white hat was somber. "But I married him. He is my duty. I must go back."

"Not as easily as that, my dearest love, if I can help it." But this was no time to talk. In a moment of sudden closeness it had all come out. "I couldn't help it. I had to say it. Wrong time to choose."

Isabella thought so, too, the lovely dream day clouded back into reality.

"Oh, Liam, I wish we hadn't mentioned it today." She gave a rueful smile. Enderby was enough for today. There would be in time enough complications with James over Enderby.

"I don't want to go alone," Liam said. "How could I survive, now I've met you?"

"No Farewells," said a voice behind them, and they both whipped round, astonished. "No Farewells."

At something in their faces Panton's neat smile slipped a little.

"The winner, Doctor Power, Mrs. Bennett. The winner. No Farewells. Mr. Frost and I have done very well. He asks if you would care to join him for tea."

They held on to each other then, they laughed so much, and Panton stood civil but confused, looking from one to the other.

"Ah, yes, Panton," said Liam in the end. "No Farewells. I have backed that horse, too, and assured Mrs. Bennett it would be a winner."

"Yessir," said Panton, and still laughing, they followed him through the tiring crowd to where Angus sat waiting for them and for his tea.

"Ah, Liam. A very successful day so far, dear boy. Very successful."

Liam looked at Isabella and smiled gently.

"I hope so," he said. "I hope so."

chapter
13

She looked now at Enderby with new eyes and could not be sure how she felt about it. Once she would have been totally enchanted, taking the house and everything that went with it for granted. After her brush with the bitter world of Beech and Quickly she would never again be so thoughtlessly content with her wealth, and was faintly embarrassed by it. But not, she knew, so embarrassed as to want to go back to Brackenham and the tiny house.

And James.

Patiently and dutifully she set herself down each week to write to him and found that she had nothing to say, aware all the time that she was waiting to hear Liam come whistling in with good reports of Clara that she thrilled to hear: but were a death knell to happiness. She was aware, too, that the moment Liam did appear, full of warm vitality and plans for the day, she would forget James and forget Brackenham and all the difficulties of the future, and give herself utterly to the pleasure of being with him.

She was in love. In a manner that made her understand with hopelessness that her feeling for James had been no more than gratitude. It would have been easy to fall in love with the devil himself at that time, if he had offered her security as James did, and she was still filled with this sense of hopeless and determined duty toward him.

Until the sun shone and Liam came breezing in to ask if they would put the hood down and take the car on some errand into Cambridge, where they could stand like the forlorn criminals of old Venice on the Bridge of Sighs, and walk the gracious courts of John's and King's and in the end take a punt down the green fringed river to Grantchester for tea. Where for them, like Rupert

Brooke, time stood still, the hands of the church clock forever at half past three.

Nothing mattered then. No Brackenham, no James, no sense of duty, only a terrible sadness fringing everything, like a black cloud encroaching on the sun, sharpening all her desperate awareness of love and beauty, and the shape and colors of her world.

It must all end. Liam would go.

She was congratulating herself that in his newfound happiness in Clara, with whom he spent hours every day, her father had forgotten his vengeful designs on Catchpole.

But Panton wheeled him in one morning toward the end of July, just as they were finishing breakfast. The day was gray and overcast, the lake as sullen as the sky, among reeds and grass glowing a vivid green in the colorless day.

He smiled as he always did when he found them together.

"Brighton on Friday, Isabella," he said. "Early start. We're going to see that woman Catchpole."

"Oh, Father, do we have to?"

They had everything they wanted, and it seemed an unnecessary unpleasantness: raking it all up now.

But nobody was going to rob Angus Frost and remain unscathed. And above all, maltreat his daughter.

"Nonsense," he said. "I am not having her get away with it. Very lucky I haven't set the police on her long ago. Frighten her out of doing it to anybody else."

Isabella looked at him, the chilly light unkind to the parchment planes of his face, the white hair above the scar beginning to lose itself among the grizzling of all the rest. In spite of the flare of vitality that kept him at his desk and on the telephone to half the world, he looked almost twice his age and very ill.

Liam could have told her that he was watching this very flare of vitality with concern and sorrow. Common, sadly common, before collapse and death.

And Isabella, looking at him, could refuse him nothing.

"Very well, Father," she said. "I'll come with you."

The sun was out again the day they went, the hood down on the Humber, folded into its linen cover along the back, the celluloid side-screens up against the wind. Liam found it hard to keep his eyes off Isabella in a dress of pale pink silk, a small stitched hat of the same material, its rolled brim pulled down to her well-defined eyebrows. She looked cool and exquisite, her long legs in stockings exactly the color of her dress.

"B'God," said Liam as he handed her into the car, "every one you pull out of the bag suits you better than the last."

She grinned at him.

"I don't keep them in a bag, Liam. That was at Quickly's."

He kissed her hand rapidly behind Panton's back, and she settled herself under the vicuña rug in a state of great content. It was lovely to be going anywhere with Liam, and her father's bark was probably worse than his bite would be. And Clara that morning had been particularly blithe and happy, resigned now to her captivity as the norm of her little life. What Heaven it would be when they could take the splint off.

But Isabella's happiness left her as they reached Brighton, the familiar streets full only of memories that dragged her backward, like a relapse into a sickness from which she thought she had recovered. She wished she had not had to come. Brighton was enough, even without Catchpole.

They came down the long hill and past the Pavilion and then the open space at the Aquarium, and Isabella looked somberly at the place where she had met James. Her father was back now, and she was riding in the Humber again, in beautiful clothes, but she knew that the Isabella of that morning was gone forever, lost in all that had happened to her.

She looked then at the back of Liam's head, the Panama hat always a little raffishly to one side, and knew that although it could never come to pass, with him she could be another Isabella yet.

They were turning at Queen's Park into the square and in a moment drawing up outside the school. Isabella noticed that all the blinds were down and thought that Catchpole must be having one of her ferocious wars against the goings-on in the Park. They couldn't have all gone away, as her father had written for an appointment. .

It was a long slow business for Panton and Liam to get her father out of the car and onto his crutches. He was damned if he was going to see the Catchpole woman in a wheelchair. Isabella got out of the other side of the car, and as she stood in the quiet road, like a remembered dream she saw a small figure trudging along, pushing a handcart loaded up with laundry.

Mrs. Quickly recognized her with unnatural cheerfulness. She hadn't, Isabella noticed, got her teeth in. She could see them in a jam jar in the corner of the handcart.

"Well, bless me—Miss Frost, ain't it?"

She looked her up and down.

"You done well fer yerself, ain't you?" Then she became aware of Angus heaving himself to his feet on the other side of the car. "Oh—got yer dad back, eh? Hurt hisself, poor man."

Isabella could only gape at her. The friendly chat, the toothless smile, the actual sympathy for someone other than herself was not the Quickly she had known.

Mrs. Quickly rattled on, seeming to feel answers unnecessary.

"Best thing you ever did fer me, Miss Frost, comin' to be my lodger like that. Made me get another. Did out my laddie's old room. Lovely gentleman. We got married last month. Quickly's bin dead years."

Her little wizened face beamed, and unlike Isabella's father, she looked years younger.

"Well, Mrs. Quickly, I *am* pleased. I hope you'll be very happy."

"That's right," agreed Mrs. Quickly. "Bet I will. Well, I got to be going. Nice seeing you."

She lumbered off the handcart, and Isabella, staring after her, hopefully thought that, well, perhaps Catchpole might be different, too.

She caught up with Liam and her father, painfully negotiating the two steps to the front door: opened by a maid who stood and gawked at Isabella as if she had seen a ghost.

"Good morning, Miriam," she said. With a muttered answer the girl, who seemed thoroughly uncomfortable, showed them into the small parlor beside the front door, where parents were kept waiting for the proper intimidating interval by Miss Catchpole.

"Tell Miss Catchpole I don't want to be kept waiting," said

Angus, who had been there before, kicking his heels, and the girl gave a sort of yelp, and scurried out.

Liam eased Angus into the highest chair and they prepared themselves to wait, but it was only a few minutes before the door opened to admit Miss Rumbold, gauche and awkward as always, but red about the eyes and dabbing at her nose with a handkerchief.

She shook hands with Isabella and her father, conveying the impression of being terribly brave about something, but Angus had not come all that way to see Rumbold.

"Where," he said without preamble, "is Miss Catchpole?"

Rumbold drew in a great shuddering sigh and faced them with this air of bravery.

"I am in charge of the school," she said. "Miss Catchpole fell dead two days ago."

They all stood and stared at her, and Isabella felt like a murderer. She knew from her father's face that he, too, thought he had frightened her to death. Liam's mobile face had taken on the impassive look behind which he could hide anything.

Miss Catchpole, as might have been expected from her high color and her thin, overstuffed skin, had crashed like a felled tree at morning prayers with all the trunks stacked in the passages and the girls about to leave on their summer holidays.

"Such a responsibility," Rumbold almost wailed, pressing the damp handkerchief again to her face, and she would have gone on, bleating all the details of the disaster, but with a curt, conventional expression of sympathy, Angus cut her short and prepared to leave.

It was only when the slow, appalled procession reached the glass front doors that she said suddenly: "Did you have an appointment?"

"Yes, I wrote to Miss Catchpole."

"Well, I'm very sorry, but there are a lot of letters I haven't opened yet and yours is probably one of them. There was nothing in the book or I'd have tried to telephone you."

The lifting of appalled guilt was as palpable as a released breath. They hadn't frightened her to death after all. So the goodbyes were much more cordial, but Isabella was still glad to get away from the school and all the sorrow it had held for her.

Liam turned round from the front street and grinned at them.

"That gave you a few bad moments, didn't it?"

"I thought we'd killed her," said Isabella, still shattered by it.

"She had every reason to be frightened," Angus said severely, recovering himself.

"Exactly," said Liam. "The woman obviously died of a cerebral hemorrhage, and I'd say she was well on the way to it the last time I saw her. But the knowledge that you were back would have preyed on her and helped it on. Her own guilt killed her."

"Yes," said Isabella with relief. "If she didn't know we were coming, then it wasn't that."

"She got away with it all," said Angus bitterly.

"No," said Liam, "I don't imagine so."

And there they left it, and after a while drew into a gateway that looked over soft fields where the corn was turning to the harvest and the country taking on the golden look of end of summer. Panton got the basket from the tonneau and there they picnicked, as it was too difficult to get her father in and out of a restaurant: smoked salmon sandwiches and Mrs. Panton's delicious sausage rolls and a bottle of Liebfraumilch packed in a bucket of ice, cold and green-white in the sun. And the first of the peaches from the sheltered south wall of the kitchen garden at Enderby.

Her father had his lunch in the car and they lazed with their cool glasses on the rugs beside it, looking down over the ripening valley and listening to the silence. Isabella was quiet until Liam reached over to the bucket and took a piece of ice and laid it quietly on the back of her neck.

Her shriek could have been heard fields away.

"They will think," said her father testily, "that someone is being murdered. Why don't you two go for a walk and I'll have a nap while Panton clears up."

Isabella glared at the grinning Liam and sadly let go the idea of an ice fight. Her father would not have approved, especially if he wanted to go to sleep. He was, she suddenly realized, sleeping a great deal lately: slipping off even in the middle of a conversation.

He looked drowsy now, so she got up amiably, and went off with Liam along the narrow path between the hedgerow and the corn. They could walk only in Indian file, so there was no talk, and threading their way along the hedge they came in the end to a stile. Liam went over first to give her a hand.

"No change," he said. "Another path. Another hedge."

Isabella went no farther than the top rail of the stile and sat on it, and Liam leaned beside her. He had left his hat in the car and the sun was rich in his red hair. Like a farmhand he chewed on a long stem of corn.

"No more?" he said, and didn't seem to care.

So Isabella sat, and took her hat off, to let the soft breeze cool her head.

"Liam," she said.

"I'm here," he told her, squinting up at her past the straw.

"I felt quite sick about Catchpole this morning. I thought we'd killed her."

"I know. And if she'd had the letter it might well be true." He threw away the straw and spoke more briskly. "So forget it, sweetheart. It was nothing to do with you."

"I felt so guilty."

"But Isabella, my darling, guilt is your middle name."

"I know." Now she was somber, looking down at him with her matchless blue eyes. "I feel terribly guilty about James."

Liam looked exasperated.

"*You* feel guilty. Over a pigheaded character that will not meet you even halfway to help Clara. He is the one who is guilty."

"Words never help me, Liam. I feel guilty any day I don't spend enough time with Clara."

"Clara's all right. At the moment she doesn't miss you. Later, yes, but not now. Next one?"

She laughed in spite of herself.

"Oh, you know me. I think my father so hammered home all the virtues of discipline and duty."

"He'd never have survived up there without them in himself. You have no idea what he forced himself to do."

"I know. He's so different now. I think he's forgotten James even exists. Doesn't go on about my duty to him."

"No. He doesn't want him to exist," he said, "so he's wiped him from his mind. And we're all different now. A lot has happened."

She put her arm on his shoulder where he leaned beside her, coming close to him, and he could smell the sweet flower perfume of her hair. He knew what he would like to do with James.

"Liam. Has it occurred to you how *very* different it all is? Just how many people's lives were changed by the fact that that mountain fell on my father?"

He turned and looked at her, their faces close.

"Yours and mine," he said. "Totally."

"And Effie. She'd still be in Brighton if I hadn't married James, and now she's going to marry a farmer."

"And indeed, James himself," said Liam. "I can't see your father letting him near you."

"No indeed. James, too. And Mrs. Quickly. Imagine her getting married."

"And the Catchpole woman. She might have lived longer if she hadn't been frightened out of her wits at what she'd done."

He paused.

"And the whole village, Isabella."

"The whole village?"

"Has your father never told you about what he's done?"

"Nothing about the village particularly. There's been so much to tell."

"Well, the last thing he did before leaving the mines was to have a team sent up to the village. An engineer, a builder, and a nursing sister. To arrange to rebuild the convent roof, and make a properly fitted little hospital there. To make them a complete and proper irrigation system and put some water in the village. And to build them proper houses. His thanks for his life. Oh, and to restore the church."

Isabella was silent, her strong brows drawn close in doubt.

"But, Liam. Will these people want that?"

Liam shrugged, unconsciously echoing the thoughts of Father Ignacio.

"They will smile and smile, for they are very courteous, and they will live in the houses for a while until they stop being watched, and then they will put the pigs in them and go back to building cardboard shanties. And in due course, unless engineers keep coming, the irrigation pipes will rust and break and they'll go back to digging channels in the ground. Not even a mountain falling on your father will change their lives so easily."

He paused.

"But there was the little nun with the green eyes," he said. "He changed her life."

"Nun with the green eyes?"

He told her of Sister Jesús María and the long devoted hours spent trying to talk her father back into his mind, and of how in the end she suddenly left the convent, after he took Angus up the mountain.

"I think," he said, "she must have fallen in love with him. She left when I took him away."

Isabella's mouth curved in a tender smile, her eyes amused.

"And when you took him to the village, you went less to the convent?"

"Much less."

Gently she framed his face in her hands.

"And you are quite sure, my handsome Liam, that it was my poor battered father she fell in love with?"

He had a sudden memory of the poor forlorn girl, staring at him from the back of the wagon, clutching his old serape to her heart.

Understanding dawned in his eyes.

"Me?" he said. "Ah, sure, I was no more than a scarecrow. But indeed, the poor creature, I suppose you could be right. Still, I had no time for rehabilitating nuns just then. I was too busy rehabilitating myself."

"Poor girl," said Isabella. "We must try and find her, Liam, and do something for her. She seems to have done more for my father than anybody else. But all those people, Liam. All different because an earthquake hit my father."

Liam took one of the hands from his face.

"I hope," he said, "that ours will be different yet. And stay so. I want you for my wife, Isabella. One last change. Forever."

She would not accept the seriousness, tracing the bones of his face with a finger.

"You have beautiful bones, Liam," she said dreamily. "No

flesh on them. Like an Arab. Or those Persian princes in old pictures."

"You mean the fellow that wanted a jug of wine and a hunk of bread and thou beside me in a good lonely spot."

"Omar Khayyam. More or less."

"Now, I always thought myself"—Liam warmed to his subject and threw away his straw—"that there was a poor and sorry scene for a seduction. A jug of wine and a hunk of bread! Couldn't he add a bit of butter and a nice piece of Stilton: a good cold leg of lamb? They've lots of sheep in those places."

"And strawberries and cream," said Isabella, blue eyes alight. "All the best seductions should have strawberries and cream."

"Ah—a handful of dates more probably and a couple of pomegranates."

"And I'd be very nervous about how I was to get back from the wilderness."

"Then there should be a camel."

Isabella was grave now.

"Wouldn't do, Liam." She shook her head.

"Why not?"

"It would spoil the poem. You can't have 'A loaf of bread and a bit of butter and a nice piece of Stilton and a leg of lamb and maybe strawberries and cream but better a handful of dates and a few pomegranates and a camel and a flask of wine and thou beside me in the wilderness.' It would be different from all the rest."

Now they laughed, delighted at their own nonsense, leaning against each other in the quiet sunlight, no sound anywhere but the wind in the corn behind them, and some small thing rustling in the green darkness of the hedge.

"Gentians," said Liam, "are the color of your eyes."

"You mean my eyes are the color of gentians."

"Oh, no—God made that perfect blue and decided to keep it for Isabella Frost. But there was quite a long time to wait, so he decided to let the gentians use it meanwhile."

Gently she kissed the tip of his nose.

"You do talk lovely nonsense, Liam."

"With God's help," said Liam piously.

"But," said Isabella, "talking about Frosty blue eyes, we'd bet-

ter be getting back or my father won't be pleased if he has to wait
for us when he wakes up."

Liam sighed.

"True. There is never a good moment but it ends too soon."

"That's probably what the chappie thought in the wilderness."

He helped her down from the stile, and hand holding to hand
they threaded their way back along the edges of the rustling corn.

Halfway back Isabella stopped and laughed, pulling on his
hand.

"What is it?"

"Guilt," she said with no trace of it on her smiling face. "Can
you believe it. I have forgotten to write to James this week.
Can you believe it!"

"Easily," said Liam. "Easily. Anyone would forget to write to
him. But there's hope for you yet."

"And for me," he thought desperately and silently. "And for
me."

When they got back to the car her father was still asleep,
looking ashen and collapsed, his Panama fallen from his head. Liam
gave him one quick professional glance, and woke Panton, who was
dozing bolt upright in the front seat, the alert expression of the old
soldier still pinned to his round face.

When they got back, after her visit to Clara, Isabella went up
to her room to get ready for dinner, faintly surprised that her father
had not been with Clara—he had apologized when they got out of
the car, saying he felt he needed a rest.

But Clara was playing happily with something he had de-
signed for her: his Clara, normally the center of his life.

He had had one of the gardeners make two posts to stand on
each side of Clara's bed, and with Effie's help he had stretched a
length of thick elastic between them, and from it, within reach of
Clara's eager little hands, he had hung every toy he could buy that
bounced or dangled or rattled.

"Can you wonder that we decided he must be an engineer?"
said Liam when he saw it, and it did much to bring happiness to
Clara's captive life. She was playing with it this evening, and Isa-

bella bounced and jangled all the toys along the ends that the small hands couldn't reach.

It troubled her that her father was not there, and her face was anxious when she met Liam in the hall on her way upstairs.

"He is all right, Liam? My father?"

Liam kissed her gently on the forehead.

"Just tired," he said. "See you at dinner."

Effie was there when she got upstairs in the big pretty bedroom, still warm and gold with the day's sun. She thought of their walk in the cornfield, and of Omar Khayyam and the blissful sweetness of being able to laugh together.

Effie looked at her. It was all in her face.

"You've had a happy day, Miss Isabella."

"Yes—oh, partly, Effie, partly. Miss Catchpole's dead."

"Gawd bless me, how?"

"She just fell dead, apparently. Three days ago."

"So your father never got nothing out of her."

"No, Effie. I'm just as pleased. It was no use dragging it all up."

Effie's tiny mouth snapped into a hard line.

"You're too easy, Miss Isabella. I know we should never speak ill of the dead, but it's good riddance to bad rubbish to me where Catchpole's concerned. Never mind you. She was horrid to us girls."

"Oh, I saw Miriam."

Effie's tight little face conveyed her disinterest in Miriam.

"Oh—and, Effie, you'll *never* guess. I saw Mrs. Quickly and she's married to the lodger she took when I left."

"Quickly! Married! Well, Miss Isabella, I never. I never did."

"She looks much nicer. Happy, and cheerful."

Effie snorted.

"Well, I s'pose miracles can happen."

"I'm glad, Effie." Isabella took up her hairbrush and began dreamily to brush her hair, her eyes on the evening garden outside where the pale flowers took color in the dusk. "I'm glad to see anybody happy."

Effie was threading ribbon through the gossamer lace on one

of Isabella's new nightdresses. She gave Isabella a sharp look and then held it up.

"I'm goin' to miss all these pretty things once I've got married, Miss Isabella."

Isabella turned, distracted as Effie had intended.

"Oh, Effie, we'll have to get you some pretty things of your own for your wedding."

Effie put down the nightdress and laughed: a clear bubble of total amusement.

"Oh, lawks, no, Miss Isabella," she said. "Wouldn't do at all for my Frank. 'E'd be afraid of catching his fingers in the holes!"

Isabella laughed, too, and looked at Effie with affection touched with sudden cold dismay.

"Oh, Effie," she said. "How am I going to get on back at Brackenham without you?"

The laughter left Effie's face.

"Enderby's yours now, Miss Isabella. You stay here where you belong."

Isabella looked again, helplessly, down the green lawns to the lake, where the last light was turning the water almost white.

Why was it that everyone, *everyone*, down even to Effie, behaved as though James Bennett didn't exist? She seemed the only one who could never for a moment forget it.

They drifted through a wet and sultry August almost as if there had been a truce to forget him. To everybody else Liam and Isabella were incandescent with their love, but they themselves handled it delicately, as though it were something that one false movement could destroy: Isabella thrusting away from her the certainty that it could only have one ending: Liam tenderly unwilling to harass her, waiting for circumstances to force all the issues.

Isabella thought it was the weather that was causing an obvious decline in her father's health, and Liam carefully agreed with her. The upsurge of vitality and activity was over, the letters piling on his desk while he sat, his hands idle, and stared out at the damp green of the garden outside his windows at the side of the house. Was he, Isabella wondered, in these moist and muggy days, thinking of the high clear heat of Chile, and the white-hot sun?

He never said so. Only when he was with Clara, telling her endless stories and talking to her by the hour, her small hand in his, did he show anything of the old vitality. Clara was talking now, bubbling with it as though it made up for the active life she couldn't have.

"She's so pale, poor pet," he said one day. "As soon as she can walk, we'll take her to Chile and get her some sunshine."

Isabella was silent. If her father was well enough to travel, then Liam would be in Chile. But James would be in Brackenham.

"Father," she said, and knew she risked an explosion, "would you like me to answer some of these letters? Just to say that you will answer them properly when the weather makes it easier for you. I know this damp gives you a lot of pain."

No one told Angus Frost that there was something he couldn't do, and she waited for the roar of anger.

To her astonishment he agreed at once.

"Do that, Isabella. I'd be grateful. Get Liam to help you if he will. And I want Staines down from London. Will you arrange that?"

That, thought Isabella, will be about his will. But she didn't feel alarm. It must be changed. Her mother was dead, and there was Clara now to be provided for. Had she known it, her father's main concern was to see it all tied up so that fellow Bennett could never get at it, unless Isabella was foolish enough to put money into his hands.

She got the flustered typing girl, and got Liam, and together through that month they learned something of the size and complexity of her father's empire.

"You're going to be an indecently rich young woman," said Liam thoughtlessly one day, as details emerged of more and more properties, factories, investments, assets.

She looked at him, alarmed.

"Not for a long time, Liam. My father is no age at all."

And what has age to do with it, my poor love? Liam thought. You will know all too soon that it means nothing.

Isabella's mind was full of all the monstrous figures they had found. How, even with her father alive, was all this to be reconciled with James and Brackenham?

She joined the game of forgetting he existed.

"That's enough for today, Liam. Let's go for a walk in the rain."

In September they saw Effie married, on a golden day, in the little parish church of Clare, which was the nearest one to Enderby.

Isabella had taken her shopping into Cambridge, where they had bought all the plain and suitable clothes that Effie wanted. And a dress for the wedding.

"I don't want no wreaths and veils and things, Miss Isabella. I want a good dress I can wear after for me best."

Effie was soft with happiness, her pale eyes glowing, and Isabella looked at her and tried not to feel envy. For where was her love to lead her except to sorrow and separation? Liam was speaking often of Valparaiso now, and of getting back to his hospital.

She thrust it from her mind.

"Let's go and look, Effie."

They found her a dress in blue silk that gave color to her eyes and whose straight lines added height even to Effie's dumpy little figure.

"You had a dress like this color, Miss Isabella."

"You sneaked it away from Catchpole's for me, remember?"

In the mirrored, carpeted salon, they looked at each other, all differences forgotten: no more than two girls who had been through a lot together, and realized the coming pain of separation. There were tears in Effie's eyes.

"Dear Effie," said Isabella, and turned briskly to the saleswoman, knowing they were both of them close to foolish weeping in her lofty presence.

"We want a hat to match it," said Isabella, swallowing her own tears.

"Hets downstares," said the superior lady, looking with distaste at the sniffing Effie.

"Bring them here," said Isabella, and sat down, and there was something in her face that made the woman go.

"Nearly made right fools of ourselves there, Miss Isabella."

Effie blew her nose and composed herself, but Isabella did not want it to start again.

"We'll go to Mansfield's now for shoes, Effie, and they'll do stockings, too. And that'll about be it."

"You've been very good to me, Miss Isabella. Given me a proper start."

"We've been through all that, Effie."

She thought of Liam and her father also, and their interdependence, and marveled again at the results of the earthquake half the world away.

Frank's parents had given the empty cottage to him and Effie. No bigger than Brackenham, the crude stairs going straight up from the kitchen, and Isabella's father had made it his wedding gift to have it restored to being fit to live in: until the last couple of weeks going constantly to supervise the work; driving the workmen crazy; but presenting Frank and Effie in the end with something they thought to be a palace: even making Frank nervous of his big boots and his big body, lest he spoil it.

Isabella furnished it for them, she and Effie giggling their way round country sales to find old furniture to suit it, and with Isabella's help, Liam gave all the bed linen and plain heavy local china and their knives and forks and spoons.

"No call for you to do this, Doctor Liam," Effie said. "Grateful I am. Grateful. No one ain't ever been set up like this before. But I've never done nothing for you."

Liam looked down at her, and even with her mind and heart full of her Frank, Effie knew a moment of total flutter at the warm charm of those strange-colored eyes. No wonder Miss Isabella was mad about him.

"You looked after Miss Isabella, Effie," he said, "until I got a chance to meet her."

Effie looked back up at him, her head tilted and her small mouth severe. There was a moment of complete understanding between them.

"Well, you try and keep her now you've got her, Doctor Liam."

"I am, Effie. I am."

It was Liam who drove over to Brighton the day before the wedding, to collect Effie's mother and her smallest sister, who was going to be a bridesmaid. No mention had been made of her step-father, and Frank's warmhearted family were squeezing Effie's two relatives into the farmhouse along with all their own for the night before the wedding. Frank was to sleep in the new cottage.

"Warmin' the bed, gel," he said hoarsely, digging a giggling Effie in the ribs.

Effie was to come in state from Enderby in the white-ribboned Humber, escorted by Angus and driven by Panton. Liam was bringing Isabella and Mrs. Panton in the shooting brake. Rumor had spread as far as Brackenham as to the grandeur of the wedding, and crowds were preparing to come as eagerly as for the autumn fairs.

James, who had been invited but had not answered, brushed off all inquiries, saying that it was only his wife's maid and he would know nothing about that. The village, knowing a thing or two now about Schoolmaster and his respectability, guffawed behind their hands and said there were maids and maids and at least this one was getting herself wed. And swarmed to Clare on the serene Saturday morning, prepared to wish well to Effie, whom all of them had liked.

On the Friday evening Liam came home from dropping Effie's mother and sister at the farmhouse. Isabella met him in the hall, aware at once of a flushed face and an air of uncontrollable hilarity.

"Liam." His condition was infectious and she grinned at him. "What's been going on? Did you get them all right?"

Liam put his arms across her shoulders and leaned on her, beaming amiably.

"Be full of ale, I be," he said in a thick Suffolk accent. "God bless us, Isabella, let me sit down. I tell you, if there's one member of that family capable of standing up tomorrow, we'll be lucky."

"The wedding's begun already?"

"Begun? It's roaring."

She sat down beside him on the hall sofa. This bright-eyed hilarious Liam was new to her, and she was charmed and indulgent.

"And how did Effie's mother fit in?"

"Fit in? They never realized they didn't know her. She was just another hand to put a glass into. They'll find out sometime who she is. She's quite happy. I had to run for it before I put the

Humber in the ditch on the way home. I swear they were chasing me with the cider flagon."

"Bless them," said Isabella. "He's their only son and they're terribly pleased about Effie."

"Sho they should be," said Liam valiantly, and Isabella laughed and kissed him.

"But, oh, God, Isabella, now you must promise me not to laugh."

"At what?"

"I'm warning you so that you won't." But he began to laugh helplessly himself, running his hands through his hair until it stood up in spikes all over his head, and fleetingly she thought that this was how it must have looked up in that village when he took no care of himself. She knew a moment's fear and then dismissed it. A couple of glasses too much at a wedding party was not two years on raw spirits: alone and desperate. She couldn't bear now to think of that time.

"What is it, Liam?"

"It's Effie's mother and her little sister."

"What about them?"

Easily, as always, she reflected the smile on his face, loving the way it transformed him.

"They're all Effie," he said. "You can't believe it. They're all Effie."

She shook his hand in hers.

"What d'you mean, all Effie?"

"They're all absolutely identical. There's a middle-aged Effie and a twelve-year-old Effie, both exactly the same as the one we've got. When they all stand together tomorrow they'll look exactly like figures on a mantelpiece. The other two are a bit pinker than our Effie, that's all."

"Gosh, Liam, I'm glad you told me. I probably would have laughed."

"Wait till you see them. I spotted them at the Pier gates in Brighton and I had to go round in a circle to get the grin off my face before I picked them up."

He sobered suddenly.

"Be a good thing for that mother to have Effie to come to down here: and that nice young man."

"Why, Liam?"

The glance he shot her was full of sad pity.

"She doesn't have the look of having had an easy life."

"Well, there's another one whose life will change," she said quietly.

They sat a moment and their own brief periods of difficult times lay heavy between them.

Isabella laid down his hand and got up.

"I have to go and help Effie pack. Isn't that lovely? *I* am helping Effie pack."

Liam eased his long length from the sofa, too.

"The whole house is full of wedding," he said. "I came in through the kitchen. The gardener has the flowers for her in buckets in the back kitchen. There's rolls of white ribbon for Panton to do the car and Mrs. Panton is still dabbing and dibbing at the cake. It looked perfect to me. Big as a house."

Isabella looked past him out the open front door to the golden light on the evening grass. Her eyes were tender and a little distant.

"That is exactly," she said, "how I wanted it all for her."

The next day Effie rode, as planned, to the church with Angus Frost beside her in the back seat, a Holland cloth over it to preserve her dress, exactly as if she were some kind of grand bride in the pictures in these magazines Miss Isabella got. White ribbons fluttered from the brilliance of the brass lamps, and carefully in her lap Effie held the round bouquet of marguerites and roses and the last sweet peas.

"Oh, Mr. Frost, I feel like a queen."

Effie was not nervous, the pale eyes glowing with happiness, blissfully sure of her Frank and the life he had to offer.

Angus smiled at her.

"For today, Effie, my dear, you are one."

Liam and Isabella followed, Mrs. Panton in the back, holding firmly to the cake with a hand already hot and sticky in its white glove.

At the church when she met Effie's mother and her small

sister, blushing and beaming in pink satin, she dared not look at
Liam, remembering the three little figures on the mantelpiece. But
once the flushed and restless congregation was grown quiet, and
Effie beside her Frank at the altar in the dusky sunlight from the
narrow windows, she no longer looked the same. Separated from
her mother and sister by the calm luminous aura of the happy
bride.

When they came out of the vestry, her small hand clamped in
Frank's huge red one, pride bursting on his country face, tightly
buttoned into his best blue suit, which had grown too small for
him, Effie's mother stared expressionless, accepting everything that
had happened to her eldest child. It was Isabella, looking at them,
who choked on tears, and the knowledge of Liam's eyes on her did
little to make it easier. Dear God, if only he and she—James Bennett stood there between them, as palpable as if he had accepted
his invitation to the wedding, but Isabella forced herself to smile.
Today was Effie's day, not to be touched by her fears and griefs.

"*Dear* Effie," she said, and kissed her and meant it, and Effie
gave her a long moment's look that held her awareness of all that
had happened between them, and her gratitude for all she had been
given today. No mistress and maid. Two girls, close-tied, relinquishing the past. "Dear Effie. Be very happy."

They did not stay long at the reception to which everyone
trooped hilariously, released from the brief constriction of the
church, through the mossy tombstones of the ancient graveyard to
the parish hall, where all of Clare and half of Brackenham had
crammed themselves to watch the wedding.

"Don't want to spoil their fun," said Angus, and it was arranged that once they had admired Mrs. Panton's cake, standing
delicate above the welter of delicious country cooking, the toasts
should be drunk first on the excuse that Mr. Frost got too tired.

Liam began by toasting Effie, and then Frank beamed and
rumbled through a toast to Angus Frost: then somebody remembered Effie's mother and she gave one back for Frank's parents: the
best man toasted Frank and Frank toasted the best man and in no
time at all everyone was warmly drinking to their next door neigh-
bor, and the hot sun-drenched hall began reeking under its corru-

gated roof with the rich smell of good Sussex ale. Faces growing red and jokes carefully choked back lest they give offense.

They slipped off as the guests clattered to sit down at the long tables for the wedding breakfast, and few saw them go. Only Isabella turned back at the door, and caught Effie watching her from where she was already settled at the top table, her eyes bright and her hat a little askew from Frank's arm around her shoulders.

One small smile and a lift of the hand from her, and Isabella went.

Cool dusk was darkening the parkland, leaving the sun as always lingering in the lake, when Angus Frost looked up from his book, slamming it shut.

Liam and Isabella were sitting in the open window, the wedding talked out and little more to say. Isabella knew herself depressed by the uncomplicated ease of Effie's happiness, and the air of loss and anticlimax hung over them all in the darkening room.

"What is it, Father?"

"For God's sake, go down, and if Mrs. Panton's back, tell her to put her feet up. You go and get the car, Liam. We'll go over and take our dinner at the Bull. This house is like a morgue."

Liam looked at him reflectively.

Funny, he thought, Effie was like Sister Jesús María. Never really noticed her until she was gone away, and then you miss her.

chapter
14

Mrs. Panton's niece came in daily to be Isabella's maid, her father horrified when she tried to protest that life had taught her she could do without one.

"It is all that, my dear Isabella, that we are trying to forget."

And where, my dear father, she wanted to ask him, am I going to put a lady's maid when I go back to Brackenham? Or all these clothes? She had seen the people from Brackenham gawking at her behind their polite smiles at Effie's wedding. She and James must be giving them more to talk about than they had ever had since the days of burning witches.

She sighed. Her father just did not want her to go back to Brackenham and that was that. And nor did Liam. One of them she might fight, but it was very difficult, hopeless, with them both. Each of them for his own reasons.

There was a sort of truce between her and Liam at the moment. A waiting game, with limits set. Either that Liam must go back to Chile or that Clara would be recovered and she must go back to Brackenham. At either of those moments they must face the truth, and how could she face it when her answer must be no and Liam would not take no for an answer? There were even days when she felt that her life with the cool and condescending James and her little crippled baby had been easier.

And Effie. God, how she missed Effie at the moment.

The leaves grew dank and heavy and along the roadside ditches the flowers died in the drying grass, on the edges of fields now golden with the stubble of the harvested corn: and the huge waxing moon of September swung into the sky above the lake, the nights cool with the first hint of inevitable winter.

It was not that Liam and Isabella clung to every day that

passed, holding it as long as possible. They were incandescent with their love, holding themselves apart in their fragile truce, as though one touch of the hand, one glance too intimate, might light a fire they could not quench. More sorrow to be remembered in the bleak and dutiful life that she felt she must insist on.

Angus seemed unaware of the brittle tension lying between them, still urging them to go together here and there, although he himself left the house less and less, spending all his time either with his darling Clara, or sitting in the declining summer in his favorite place under the spreading shadows of the cedar below the terrace steps.

From their summers at Le Touquet and Antibes and their Septembers banging at the grouse across the Scottish moors, the local people from the country houses were beginning to come back, and cards appeared in the silver tray on the table in the upper hall, and engraved invitations were coming in the post.

Angus, who had loved and cultivated every social activity the county of Suffolk could offer him, tossed them all aside.

"Write and say," he said to Isabella, "that I am not able for it."

Content now, apparently, to keep his life to the ground floor of Enderby in the level rooms behind the terrace steps, no longer even having Liam and Panton manhandle his chair up the stairs for dinner in the dining room with Liam and Isabella. They came down now to dine with him, in his big room looking to the gardens at the side of the house, where the autumn sunsets turned the trees to gold and the doves sang mournfully of summer's end.

Often he would be in bed when they came.

"Liam. Is he all right?"

Isabella watched with anxiety his thinning face; his neglected desk.

Liam was quiet, reassuring.

"He has a lot of pain, love. He gets tired."

One day he sent them in to Long Melford to get him some carefully measured pieces of wood and some screws. He wanted, he said, to make a dancing man for Clara, to hang on her frame.

Isabella was delighted to see him interested in doing something, and they drove into the town in a clear lovely day still warm enough to have the Humber open. While the carpenter cut the wood her father wanted, and sent his boy out for the screws, they sat and drank sherry in the dark-paneled parlor of the Bull, marked forever in Isabella's mind as the place where life had given her back her father.

Marked forever in Liam's as the place where he had first met Isabella.

Their truce was tranquil that day, torn by none of the emotions that so easily leaped out to destroy them both. Idle talk and the quick laughter they sparked from each other: their smallest words important as though they had never before been spoken. Timeless and tranquil in the cool dimness of the little parlor.

In the end Liam held out his hand.

"Come on. We'll be late for lunch and Mrs. Panton won't speak to us for a week."

He paid the waitress in the hall and they collected her father's parcel and turned off the long, straight road that gave the town its name, into the narrow country lanes, to take them back to Enderby.

It was lucky, said Liam afterward, that they didn't come round a corner onto it.

"We'd have heard it," said Isabella, and indeed the first thing they knew of it was the belching roar around a distant bend. Then the sun glittering on brass and green enamel and the tall chimney pouring dark smoke against the sky. The huge wheels, up against the sides of the ditches, churning the dust of the narrow road.

"Liam, Liam! It's John Peter Burgess!"

"It's all the same to me," said Liam, "if it's the Pope of Rome. I have to get off the road because he won't get off for me."

Neatly and expertly he whipped the Humber into a fortunate farm gateway, and almost before he was stopped Isabella was out, her face as excited as Clara's at a new toy, standing by the roadside to watch the traction engine come, the two trailers behind it with all the sections of the carousel, and the stacked horses waiting patiently for their hours of splendid mechanical freedom.

Liam watched her face and smiled at her, not understanding her excitement, but charmed by it, as he was charmed by everything she did.

"A merry-go-round," he said. "We had them in Ireland when I was a child."

"Yes! John Peter Burgess."

The huge lumbering traction engine was coming level now, and she shouted up at the overalled figure at the small wheel.

"Where?" she shouted. "Where are you going?"

"Long Melford," he called back, against the hissing steam. "Tithe Fair."

"When?"

" 'Morrow night."

And he was gone. She didn't move while the two painted wagons passed her, blue and yellow and scarlet, and huge white painted daisies and gold whirls and scrolls.

She drew a long happy breath, blue eyes bright with pleasure.

"Oh, Liam. Will you take me?"

"My darling, I'd take you to hell and back if you asked me." She took his arm.

"Not that far, Liam. Just to Long Melford to the Fair."

It was Panton who told them what a tithe fair was, as he polished every last speck of dust off the Humber before he handed it over to Liam the following evening.

"Old days," he said, "on a certain day, all the farmers used to come into the town to give one tenth of their harvest to the land-owners. Rent, see. Fairs grew up around that. Huge, they were: close the town for a week."

"Oh, what fun, Liam. Much bigger than the fête."

"The fête?"

But she was already climbing into the car, elegant against the cool evening in a straight dress of soft white wool, with a loose jacket and a small close cap in the same white wool.

"You look like something off a Christmas card."

Suddenly grave, she looked at him.

"I've never seen Enderby at Christmas."

"This year?"

She shook her head, shaking off trouble as a dog shakes off water. Who would have won the tug of war for her by Christmas? She would not spoil tonight by thinking of it.

"What a heavenly evening," she said. "Remember, I've never even seen autumn here."

Almost greedily she sniffed at the cool breeze of dusk, touched with the first hint of dampness and decay, and the smell of bonfires from the roadside gardens. The first stars out in a purple sky and the round moon of harvest a golden disc behind the trees. She felt like the evening, knowing herself fresh and beautiful, her beauty clear in the admiration in Liam's eyes, but touched, like the year, with an intolerable sadness that must be resolved as surely as the frost must seal these fields, and the gales of winter whip the barren trees. All her emotions were drawn tight, touched intolerably by the beauty of the evening and the sense of loss for summer gone.

"Oh, Liam," she said as they turned out of the back drive of Enderby, and into the narrow road where dark was already gathered. "I'm so happy. Yet I'm not: I'm so sad."

Liam looked down at the white-capped head against his shoulder.

"Would you be good enough," he said, "to make up your mind, and I'll know how to compose my face."

"Fool," she said, and gave herself over to the happiness.

They could see the glow in the sky above Long Melford long before they came to it, and as soon as they turned into the long street, the fair was before them in all its blaze of light and noise, the whole wide center of the town blocked with stalls and swing-boats and a helter-skelter and in the center the blaring music of the carousel: coconut shies and shooting galleries and the dark night lost in the hissing light of the naphtha flares above the stalls.

"Can I do everything, everything, Liam?"

"If your strength holds out."

He was puzzled by her, something almost feverish in her intense determination to enjoy the fair: to lay hands on everything it offered.

They went first on the swings, opposite each other in the shallow painted boat, heaving on the scarlet woollen handholds on the end of the ropes: higher, higher, with every pull, her excited face daring him to be the highest, up to the blue-and-gold bar.

"That was marvelous, Liam. Spiffing."

"I think," said Liam cautiously, almost a little afraid of her by now, "you have a better stomach for it than I have."

"Don't be such a drip. Oh, look, can I have a toffee apple?"

Then it was the coconuts, and he had to hold her toffee apple, licking them both alternately, and cheering, with all the people watching, as she knocked off a coconut, jumping for joy as Clara, please God, would soon be jumping. Her pleasure and triumph when he failed to get one was immoderate, but he beat her on the shooting gallery and presented her with a pink teddy bear with a stylish bow-tie in purple check.

"Clara will adore him."

"Your father no doubt will hang him by the neck on that contraption."

"She adores that, too. Oh, look, Liam. Toffee!"

" 'Peggy's Leg' we called it at home when I was a child," he said, watching the vast shouting gypsy woman whipping and pulling the striped ropes of toffee over a hook on the wall.

"I suppose you want some of that, too."

"Everything, everything. I don't care if her hands are dirty."

The gypsy gave her a bag, because, she said, she was a beautiful lady. Everybody else got theirs in their hot hands. But Liam agreed with the gypsy. Never so beautiful as on this night of unfathomable excitement, the dark-blue eyes brilliant, cheeks flushed under the little white cap in the flare of naphtha, touched by some slight air of wildness he did not understand.

They bought a little colored ball on a piece of elastic, that she said was for Clara's contraption, but she teased him through the fair with it, flinging it at his head and snatching it back just before it hit him.

"Was it for Clara or for you?" he said, grabbing it.

"Me first and then Clara."

Then she wanted to throw rings over pegs, six rings a penny, charmed when she won a little black celluloid doll with eyes like saucers and arms that went up and down.

By the time they reached the merry-go-round and the spotless painted horses rising and falling in their blaze of light and music, they had so much that they had to ask a child to look after it all on the promise that he could have a ride when they came off.

"Will we have a horse each?" he said.

"Of course!"

And one ride was not enough, sweeping there beside Liam, who, on a dark-brown horse, watched her indulgently and wondered what it was possessed her. Up and down and round and round, sliding on the golden poles, her lovely smile enchanted, her long silk-stockinged legs as neatly crossed as if she wore her black habit and rode her father's finest horse. Even John Peter Burgess, lifetime purveyor of enchantment, watched her with some special gentleness.

"Daisy Daisy" and the "Blue Danube" and round and round again, and when they finally got off she looked back at her piebald horse waiting for his next rider.

"I had Dasher, Liam," she said, "Dasher."

And to his astonishment her eyes were full of tears.

"I had Caroline," he said. "A great lady."

He retrieved their prizes from the child and put into his grateful, grimy fingers enough for half a dozen rides.

"I think, pet, you're tired," he said to Isabella. "Will we go home now?"

"Please."

Their prizes in their arms, close together, they walked out of the maelstrom of light and noise and color, leaving it behind them as they might leave a door open onto a warm and lighted room: into the thick country darkness where they had left the car, the moon gone and the stars pale in a misty night. Liam took her arm to keep her steady on the road they could barely see. He felt her shaking.

"Isabella. Isabella, my darling! You're crying. What's the matter? What is it tonight?"

She was crying as Clara might cry, great gulping sobs, and no heed of the hot tears on her cheeks.

"It was—was so lovely, Liam. So gorgeous. Such fun."

"Well." Liam laid his burden of teddy bear and two bottles of beer and the bag of Peggy's Leg down in the dark road, aware of the cool smell of damp from the ditches close beside him. He took her gently in his arms, the big-eyed doll between them, torn by her distress but trying to ease her out of it. "Well, my dear sweetheart, if it was so gorgeous, you have a peculiar way of showing it. Will I bawl my head off, too?" He shook her gently. "My love, what is it?"

"You see, last year," she said, "I couldn't go on anything."

She knew she wasn't making sense, and gathered herself together, taking the handkerchief he gave her to wipe her face, and then it all came out, slowly and painfully, as if she could live with it no longer. To begin with only the lonely story of the village fête and her longing to ride on the beautiful painted horses and throw balls at coconuts and all the things that even Lady Lyndly had felt free to do. And all she had was James's cold uninterest and her little crippled baby, but even that—

"Even that was tolerable then, because I knew no better. Now everything is changed," she whispered. "There is Enderby and my father and, dear God, oh, my Liam, there is you. How am I ever going to go back?" She gave a small shaky laugh. "How am I going to leave the lights of the fair?"

He held her very close, his hand on the small white cap, and found it hard to answer, for to him there was only one answer and he knew she wouldn't accept that one. Or would she? It was the first time she had ever complained or doubted, her frail balance tottered by the carefree, childish pleasure of their evening.

She felt him sigh against her.

"I'm sorry to be so soppy, Liam."

"My pleasure," he said, and felt her smile. "But, Isabella, *mi corazón, mi alma.*" In the depth of his desire to convince her he fell into the Spanish terms of love. "My heart, my soul. You do *not have* to go back. In the way he has behaved over Clara, he deserves nothing. He wouldn't even come to poor little Effie's wedding."

"He always disliked Effie."

She sounded weary, as though it was these small things that had been too much.

"She saw him for what he was," said Liam, "but, Isabella, let's not talk about him. Come with me, my darling. Come with me." He tried to make her smile. "We can deal with James long distance."

"What about my father?"

There was a perceptible pause.

"An English winter would be no good to him," Liam said then. "And you know he doesn't want you to go back."

"Oh, it's all so *difficult.*"

Isabella moved from his arms and began to walk along the dark road.

"Even the sort of practical part of it. Enderby, all my lovely clothes, the money my father has settled on me. He'll be expecting me to put it all in a box somewhere and come back to Brackenham exactly as I left it. And of course he'll never really have any use for me, because I can't have his son. Or any other child."

She sounded bitter and despairing.

"Who," said Liam sharply, "said you could never have another child?"

"The doctor from Lavenham. When Clara was born."

He took her arm and looked into the pale shadow of her face.

"Do one thing for me, if nothing else. Village doctors can be very good, but they don't know everything. Go up to London and see a proper man. Promise?"

"I promise. It might help."

It seemed little to promise, when all the rest of life she longed for was falling away.

"I cannot go with you, Liam. Oh, dear love, you know how much I want to go. But I am James's property and he will never, never let me go. And you know, my sweet," she added sadly, "I would not be very good at living in sin."

He knew it to be true, and was silent. They had reached the car, the hood still down and the seats damp under their hands.

"Here, get the rugs from the back. Panton'll flay me."

They sat a moment before he engaged the ignition to start the car.

"I won't ask you again, my love," he said. "If you change your mind, then we'll ride forever on the painted horses. But I don't want to distress you by pestering you."

Sighing, she said that she supposed it would all work out somehow when he was gone. "But when, Liam," she added, "will that be? It could, my love, even be a little easier for me when you are not here, although I could well die of it. How, Liam, how will I manage without you?"

The big brass lamps on the side of the windscreen shot their beams along the narrow road, black night becoming the tangle of hedgerow pale in the white light.

"It will be soon, I am afraid, my Isabella. Soon, I will have to go."

As they moved off she looked back at the glow of the fair, diffused pink against the misty sky. Faintly the music still reached them. Like my life, she thought. Going from the light back into darkness.

Halfway home Liam suddenly chuckled.

"What is it?"

"In the middle of the road outside Long Melford," he said, "we have left one teddy bear, two bottles of beer, and a bag of Peggy's Leg."

And happiness, thought Isabella. And happiness.

That huge golden moon swung down on Liam's bitter disappointment, and the next night there was another and another, each one smaller than the last, as though they shrank like the circle of his own hopes.

It seemed to Isabella that the same moon watched her, as she watched it from her window, sleepless. Watched her as if it waited to know what she would do.

She did nothing: hopeless, trapped. Often she thought of the nun he had spoken of, who had looked after her father. A little nun with emerald eyes. So must she have felt, thought Isabella: torn with the pain of love, half the world away, for the same man. As conscious as she was now in every nerve of her being of the red hair falling over the high-boned face, the long, almost gawky body: the gorgeous lopsided grin that so transformed his face.

So must that little nun have suffered, tied exactly as she was, by vows she could not break.

But Sister—what was it?—Jesús María had broken them, Liam said: going off back into a world she had promised God she would leave forever. Only, the wrath of God was far more distant and unimaginable than the wrath and vengeance of James Bennett, a few miles across the moon-blanched fields in Brackenham. God, too, might forgive the little Sister with the emerald eyes, but James Bennett, she knew, would never forgive her.

Nor did the nun have any hostages. Who knew what the law might allow James if his wife had gone off with another man? And would her love for Liam ever in this world be able to comfort her if she lost Clara?

She wanted, she realized sadly, everything or nothing. She wanted everything, and could have nothing.

I'm sorry, Liam, she said night after night to the waning moon. Sorry, sorry, sorry. Her face in the lonely night leaning against the cold glass of the window, thinking of all the things she had said to him on the white magic night of the fair when the moon was full. And could not unsay.

Why, she wondered, sick with sorrow, did he not go away? He spoke of it so often, and surely to God it would be easier without him there around the house, the bubble of all their summer pretenses broken. Nothing between them now but naked pain.

Still he did not go, and almost in her desperate unhappiness she could have turned him from the house to give her peace.

"It is mine," she told herself. "Enderby is mine. I do not have to have him here unless I want to."

Then she would meet the sad tenderness of his eyes, and be torn with sorrow that he should have to go at all.

It was only the crescent moon of the new month climbing the night sky that provided her with a diversion. Her father was planning, as though it were every celebration in the world rolled into one, for Clara's birthday.

It gave her great pleasure to see her father rouse himself to all the organization of the great day. Isabella was not even allowed to arrange the cake, her father summoning Mrs. Panton and going solemnly into all the details of pink or white and the decorations on it, and the candles. Isabella found it hard to listen. Last year she and Effie had been the only ones to remember that Clara had a birthday, scrimping to buy her a small stuffed doll from the Thread Man.

But she noticed that Angus did not summon Panton and go racing up to London, as he would once have done. All his shopping was done by telephone, but he was happily successful, Isabella coming home from a walk with Liam two days before the birthday, to find him in the hall in his wheelchair, beaming with pleasure as Panton cleared away all the paper and string that had covered a beautiful rocking horse: dapple-gray with a fine bright eye and silky mane, his red leather harness hung with little golden bells.

He was certainly as fine, and almost as big, as any that swam around on the gilded poles of John Peter Burgess.

He was like a symbol, and Liam was careful not to look at her.

"That's a fine piece of bloodstock you have there, Angus," he said. "Will you be racing him at Newmarket?"

Angus grinned and Isabella put out a finger and set the horse rocking.

"He's gorgeous, Father, but Clara can't use him!"

"She will, she will. And until then she can look at him. She'll love him."

"I don't doubt that."

Isabella felt almost hysterical. Where, for heaven's sake, was she supposed to put *that* at Brackenham? It wearied her the way her father behaved as though nothing would ever change, and there was no tomorrow.

On Clara's birthday, gray with the mist of an early autumn, sun and summer gone, the horse stood in the shadows of the hall outside her room, and Isabella, all her emotions tight as strung wire, felt unreasonably that he was watching her with his white rolling eye with a certain look of triumph. Trapped her forever on the painted carousel.

She laid a hand on the white silky mane.

"But you can't," she said sadly. "You can't. If I say no to him, do you think I'd say yes to you?"

She rearranged all the other brightly wrapped parcels on a tea trolley, ready to be wheeled into the room, and the cake stood waiting on a side table. She smiled. What would Clara, who didn't understand the word "birthday," make of it all?" She couldn't wait to see the beaming little face. Next birthday she would come running to her presents.

Next birthday. She must not think of it. Without Liam.

He came down the stairs then and along the hall, long legs

taking the steps two at a time, smiling, the dark-red hair falling over his forehead.

She smiled back. He was here today.

"All ready?"

"Yes. And Clara's awake. Nurse tried to put a birthday bow in her hair but she just shrieks with laughter and pulls it out. I'll go and get Father. I expect he's sitting facing the door in his best suit!"

Liam laughed and went in to Clara, and she went over the big square hall to her father's room on the other side.

Silence seemed to come with her when she came back, standing alone in the door, her face white with shock: silence that spread immediately to the nurse and Liam, halting their laughter with Clara.

"What is it?"

"Liam," was all she said, whispering. She did not have to tell him more, and as they crossed the hall, his arm around her, the silence spread around them to the whole house.

"You knew," she said to Liam later in the evening when the undertaker's men had come and gone and Angus Frost lay peacefully in his bed, all the agonies of his broken body smoothed from his face. More now like the father Isabella had waited for.

"You knew, Liam."

She was carefully in control of herself, the wet ball of her handkerchief wadded into her hand, the blue eyes dry now but dark with shock and sorrow. Liam took her limp hand in his, his own eyes full of pity, so much more agonized for being filled with love as well. He would have spared her anything, but he had known right from the beginning he could not spare her this.

"Yes, I knew. I was only glad he had you back even for so short a time. After the pneumonia on top of everything else, I knew he had very little time."

"He never came back really, you know," she said sadly. "The person who came back was not really my father."

"He was, inside himself. And you gave him months of happiness."

"I suppose so."

Only, he thought, in the vivid blue eyes and the quick lovely movements and the open candid smile of his daughter, did the real Angus Frost live on.

"Why did you not tell me?"

"Because it would have spoiled happiness for both of you. You would have been watching for it every hour of every day, and it would have communicated itself to him."

"You are very good."

There was a long silence, and absently she played with the long strong fingers twined into hers. In the end she lifted her head and looked at him, the sad blue eyes searching his.

"This," she said, "was what you were waiting for. This was why you didn't go away."

"Yes."

" 'Soon,' you kept saying. And you knew it would be soon."

"Yes," he said again. "I wouldn't leave him as long as he had need of me."

"Oh, Liam." Tears welled again into her eyes. If only she had been able to find him anything but good. If only she had been able to find one breath of meanness or selfishness, then it might have been easier. She untangled her fingers.

"I must go and say good-night to Clara," she said. "She may be fretting for him."

She went down through the darkened house, where Mrs. Panton had gone round solemnly lowering all the blinds. Outside the dull October day was growing dark itself, and in the lower hall the only light was from Clara's open door. It shone on the shining flanks of the dapple-gray, and caught the white of his fine rolling eye, where he stood there, like all the others, a symbol of lost happiness.

She had him buried in Brackenham.

"No," she said. "I don't want to take him back to Chile. By the time we got there it would all have stopped meaning anything. He loved Enderby and I am sure it would please him to die here. And I was very fond of the little church at Brackenham. And the Vicar. He was very kind to me when I saw the advertisement about my father. No. I'd like Brackenham."

"As you wish," said Liam, who was doing everything for her. "Only you, my love, have to be pleased."

So they buried him in the pocket-handkerchief graveyard of the tiny church at Brackenham, on a gray day when the first bitter wind of winter plastered the Vicar's cassock against his thin body.

Strange, thought Isabella, for a man who had lived all his life in the sun: and Liam stood very close to her, knowing that beautiful composure was as fragile as the petals of a blown rose. One hostile wind, and it would break.

James honored them with his presence, no doubt concerned as to what the village would say if he didn't: erect and indifferent, but correct, buttoned tightly into his black coat, his hard hat down across his eyebrows.

Many of the local people whom Angus had refused to see came out of courtesy, understanding that he had been ill, and speculating on a rumor that had got about that he had, in fact, bought Enderby. Only had that one daughter, they whispered to each other, so now presumably she got it all. Mines, they understood, in Chile.

Among them was Lady Lyndly, elegant and sophisticated in unrelieved black, which she always thought to suit her: only a diamond aigrette that was going a little out of fashion, in her velvet turban. For all her social training her thin jaw dropped when she saw Isabella coming in behind the flower-heavy coffin, her plain black tailored clothes making poor Caroline Lyndly feel unwillingly provincial.

Discreetly she dug her husband in the ribs.

"Who on earth?"

"Daughter," he said succinctly.

"But—" she hissed.

"I know."

Angus Frost's daughter, in the exquisite clothes of the very, very rich, came up the cold flagged aisle of the little church and settled herself into the ancient front pew beside the other person who had walked behind the coffin. A tall thin man with dark-red hair and an interesting face, gentle and concerned toward Isabella: followed by a small, dumpy young woman in homemade clothes, her pale eyes red with weeping.

Minutes after came James Bennett, husband to Isabella, and sat down in the pew behind them. Isabella turned as if to ask him to join them, but he gazed stonily ahead.

"Well, I *never*," whispered Caroline Lyndly. "Well, I *never*."

After the chilly burial in the windy graveyard, where Isabella promised herself a plain flat slab of marble, exactly the same as the photographs he had had taken of her mother's grave, Isabella, looking uncomfortably around for James, stood in the old moss-grown lych-gate with Liam and thanked them all for coming.

The good people of the village who did not quite understand what was happening, but Schoolmaster's wife had always been a nice lady, and no one liked to lose their dead.

Effie's Frank, with all his family, crimson with shyness and wringing her black-gloved hand in his great red one until she almost cried out loud.

A posse of civil and correct men in dark clothes: lawyers who would not leave for days.

And Lady Lyndly and all the people like her, murmuring their confused condolences, and being invited back to Enderby for drinks and buffet lunch. Accepting mostly out of curiosity, and a feeling for the future, for Angus Frost's only daughter must now be a very, very rich young woman.

But where did it all fit in with the village schoolmaster?

He came last of all, stiff and chilly, and Liam had a primitive longing to put his fist through the pompous face.

"You will come to the house, James?" she asked him, when he had recited the empty words of his condolences.

He replaced his hard hat.

"No, thank you, Isabella," he said. "I will see you when you bring the child back to me."

Liam did not wait for him to move away, almost pushing her into the big black Daimler.

"Savage," he said viciously. "Damned savage."

"Did you expect," said Isabella, "that a mere death would change James?"

The village gawked and stared and dug each other in the ribs as they watched Schoolmaster's wife drive off in the black limousine with the red-haired man and Vicar and his wife, while School-master tramped back alone across the windy green.

Liam stayed with her through three weeks of lawyers and end-less telephone calls to and from Chile. Isabella found herself the possessor of wealth beyond anything that she thought sense.

"What am I going to do with it?" she asked Liam. "I can't use all that."

"Found a couple of hospitals in Chile," he said.

"Yes," she answered, and meant it. "But I am surprised," she added, "that he left you nothing."

He looked at her, his eyes grave.

"He left me everything. Everything. He wanted to leave me money, too, but I refused it. I have no need of it. I was," he went on by way of explanation, "the son of a Limerick doctor with a long, long family and a short purse. As they do in Ireland, they farmed me off to an uncle and aunt with no children and pots of money. God save them, they were both lost when their yacht foun-dered one ghastly day off Skibbereen. They left me everything." He smiled now, gently. "So you see, I was never after you for your money."

She couldn't smile.

"I never thought of it."

"You still will not come, Isabella? You will have to go to Chile anyway, you know. You have a village on your hands."

"Among a few other things," she said, appalled by the magni-tude of it all. She shook her head. "Before I can do all that, I have to get my life straight here."

"Duty is a cold bedfellow."

She looked at him.

"James is a cold bedfellow."

He did not ask her again, and left for New York on the White Star *Olympic* at the beginning of November.

She went to Southampton with him, and on a raw gray day, spiked with miserable rain, well suited to the death of life and love, she watched him walk away up the covered gangway of the first-class section of the liner. There was a terrible conviction that if she should put a hand in underneath her furs, she would find it wet with blood: so deep the cold loss that she felt to be bleeding her very heart away.

He did not look back, nor did she wait to try and find his face among the eager people waving from the decks. She turned abruptly and left the dark cliff of the ship, unable even to look at the compassionate face of Panton as he put the rugs around her, lest she begin to weep: and never stop.

In the empty house that had held so much happiness, every day was a week and every week was a year. Waking early every morning to walk the house and watch the red sun rise through the cold winter sky. Watching sleepless as the moon of the new month hung above the lake, a pale poor thing against those splendid moons of autumn, like a last golden consolation before the death of the year.

The death of everything she felt, and she knew almost anger that in all her sorrow she must collect herself together and decide what way to approach her husband.

It took her a long time, unwilling to face back into what seemed a hopeless situation: unwilling to see him. Not very willing herself to live at all. Only for Clara, who would soon be free of her splint, Liam having left her in the quiet care of the young doctor from Lavenham, was she still her smiling self, parrying carefully all the demands for Ganpar. Clara was still very small. She would soon forget.

Every time she left the baby's room, she laid a hand a moment on the shining paint of the dapple-gray. Like a talisman that she touched for strength. And duty.

She got herself first up to London, to a specialist recommended by the doctor from Lavenham, and after the examination she faced him over the vast expanse of his mahogany desk, pale winter sun coming through the spotless white net curtains, and beyond that the hum and clatter of the traffic along Welbeck Street.

A kind-looking man with a narrow face, nose and chin so long that he reminded her of Clara's picture books about the man in the moon. He smiled at her, a deep sweet smile, and she thought of course he must be compassionate who spent so much of his time promising rich future life: or nothing.

"I'm pleased to tell you, Mrs. Bennett, that there is nothing amiss now. You should be able to have all the children you please. And more easily than the first one."

She stared at him. Dear God, if it could only be Liam's sons he was promising her.

He misunderstood her expression.

"Don't blame your doctor," he said. "After a very difficult birth, things are often a bit—disorganized."

He was a little puzzled. Women who came to him to find if they could have more children were usually delighted when he said yes. This lovely creature looked as if he had given her a death sentence. Not for him to pry. He stood and held out his hand, his mind already on the next case.

She got herself out into the pale sun and the traffic, and Panton waiting a little way along the road. Now she had this to offer, too. Surely it would be enough to make James content. The life he wanted. The school he wanted. And, please God, sons. Enough to make him forgive her all her failings and inadequacies, and allow them to start life again.

Forsaking all others, as the marriage service said.

It was impossible to bring herself to hurry to it, and she knew that James would never come to her, but it was not long before Christmas that she finally forced herself to go to Brackenham. Even then she took the pony and trap rather than the Humber, as if she could not bear the faster speed of the car.

She was past dressing herself to suit him. James must make some concessions, too, and she wore a sleek straight coat and a little cap of rich Canadian squirrel, the vicuña rug wrapped tight around her feet against the cold. The pony made no effort to bestir himself, nor did she press him, clopping gently under the barren hedges beside the winter fields, his hooves ringing on the hard road that would by night be white again with frost.

He could have Enderby for his school, it seemed to her the perfect solution, and she could go on living there and Clara could grow up there as her grandfather had wished. And James's sons that she could now bear. The house was not entirely suitable. They would have to build, but it could be done at the back where it wouldn't show. Exactly the kind of setting he had always wanted. And all the money necessary to keep it going.

There was no warmth in her. Only determined resignation as cold as the frozen fields. But she was doing what was right and surely even James could not refuse what she offered. Somehow they should carve a life together from it.

The pony clopped round the last bend in the narrow road, and she was coming to the schoolhouse and the village beyond it, silent in the winter afternoon, straight smoke from all the cottage chimneys telling of the warm fires within. The sky had the pinky-purplish look of snow to come.

It was as she was looping the reins around the garden fence that she became aware of the sudden stir along the curving village street: voices and doors crashing open, and across the green the Vicar with a man: running, holding his cassock up to run the faster.

Only then did she see the cart, coming in from the far end of the village, a man leading the horse and the crowd around it growing as the curious rushed out from their houses.

Only she stood still frozen by the terrible certainty as to what was in the cart, crabbed even on the instant with guilt and horror. Then she too began to run.

"He should 'a knowed, Mrs. Bennett," one of the men said to her afterward, when they had laid James on the kitchen table in the schoolmaster's house to await the doctor, who could only tell them what they all knew. "He should 'a knowed to break his gun before he crossed a stile. 'E bin out shooting often enough with us now."

Isabella looked down at the unchanged face on the kitchen table. James had blown most of his middle out, but even that had not altered his expression. Only his color showed that he was dead. Even his own death had not changed James.

Outside, the restless pony whinnied in the cold.

"Bin out shooting often enough with us," the man had said. But he had never been out shooting when she was with him. Only when he was left alone.

She buried him beside her father, Effie expressionless at her side, and in the weeks to follow she could find little grief, because all honesty told her that except at the beginning, James had given her small happiness. Grief was for what she had thought him to be: sad foolish girl who had indeed bartered her life for what she thought to be love and security. But she was appalled, submerged in guilt so thick and terrible that it was like a sickness, convinced in some devious fashion that it was her illicit love for Liam that had caused James to die. There was no sense of release: no feeling that she was now free to live her own life. That was like a novel, she thought, where the writer could think of no better ending, pulling it all together to get the thing finished. Happy ever after. Everybody paired off properly.

This was no happy ending. The misery of guilt would never leave her.

It took weeks, and Effie, to shake her out of it.

Effie came to see her, riding the flat nine miles to Enderby through the frost-white fields on her old bicycle, even her pale cheeks reddened by the bitter cold of a hard January. It was too high for her and she lurched from side to side to reach the pedals. For the first time since the funeral, Isabella smiled at someone besides Clara as she watched her swaying up the drive.

"Effie! You must be exhausted. That's too high for you! Can't you lower the saddle?"

"My Frank's bin using it. Nut's rusted. I just give it to Panton fer a drop of oil."

"We'll have some tea, Effie. I am so pleased to see you."

Effie wasn't so pleased to see Miss Isabella looking thin and haunted and unhappy. That James Bennett was able to make her miserable beyond the grave. Deceitful monster.

Thirstily she drank her hot tea, grateful for the warmth of it, and set down the beautiful cup with the care that it deserved. Her small mouth pursed and she folded her hands determinedly.

"Miss Isabella," she said. "I've left you awhile because it was a shock like. But there's something you should know."

Isabella looked at her. A new Effie, bless her, deep happiness lambent in the pale eyes, but an increased sharpness: a contented authority.

"First, Miss Isabella, Mr. Bennett didn't die because of anything that you did. He died because he didn't hold his gun right. My Frank said 'e was a right blooming fool."

Isabella began to speak but Effie got there first.

"Remember we got that widow to look after Mr. Bennett when you brought Clara here?"

"Yes. Mrs. Plum."

"Well, it took him only a couple of weeks to get rid of her. Then 'e gets in that Peggy Jones from along beyond the Green. Remember her?"

"Not really, Effie. No."

Effie didn't describe her.

"Fifteen" was all she said. "And in no time, Miss Isabella, with you all guilty about Mr. Bennett and only trying to do the best for poor little Clara, she was there all hours of the evening and often even forgot to come home at nights."

"Effie, are you sure this is true?"

"Whole village knows it," Effie said bluntly. "Ask them. Right pig they thought he was."

She paused and looked Isabella in the eyes.

"Had a baby three weeks ago, she did. Full term."

There was a long, long silence in the firelit room.

"But, Effie—" She couldn't put it into words.

Effie could.

"Yes, Miss Isabella, before you ever left. Out round the fields and in Sam Grubb's hay barn. Out of the way, that was, until he caught 'em at it."

And he wouldn't, was all Isabella could think, he wouldn't sleep with me at nights.

"What was the baby, Effie?"

"Girl."

And Isabella smiled.

"She's in a great taking, it seems, because 'e'd promised to provide for the baby and now he's dead. Her mum'd gladly kill her. He'd lost his job anyway, it seems, with all the scandal."

"I'll provide for the baby, Effie. As long as I'm sure it's Mr. Bennett's."

"Says she's never bin with anybody else, and she ain't never been seen."

Effie took a long, deep breath, all the difficult business over.
But someone had to set Miss Isabella straight.

"Goin' to have one meself, Miss Isabella."

"Oh, Effie! Then, for goodness sake get off that bicycle!"

Effie gave her cackle of laughter.

"Take more than that to shift my Frank's baby!"

Clara came in then in the arms of her new young nursemaid,
pink-cheeked from her afternoon walk, shrieking with delight to see
Effie: standing for precarious seconds holding on to the furniture.

There were tears in Effie's eyes.

"Yes, Effie," said Isabella, "it was all worth it, wasn't it?"

"Yes. But just get you going, too, Miss Isabella."

"I'll get going, Effie. Probably on a painted horse."

And Effie patted Clara and began buttoning her coat, not
understanding, but knowing from the look on Isabella's face that
her time had not been wasted.

Isabella gave it very little thought. It was just something that
had to be cleared up and put right, like Clara's room when she
stopped being an invalid and became a little girl who wanted a
bright, happy nursery.

The very next morning she drove the pony and trap into Long
Melford and sent a cable to Valparaiso.

So sure was she of the answer that she had Panton drive her to
Brackenham in the afternoon.

She saw the Vicar and asked him to care for the two graves in
her absence, bringing tears to his eyes with the size of the check she
gave him to restore his beautiful rotting roof and the crumbling
stonework of his beloved little church.

"Oh, Mrs. Bennett! We'll never need to have another fête."

She looked appalled.

"Oh, Vicar, no. You must never do that. Promise me you will
always have a fête. With a merry-go-round."

"Of course."

He knew all the secrets of the village and had felt deeply sorry
for this lovely and charming young woman. There was something
in her face that told him now that his concern was no longer
necessary.

"I will pray for you," he said nevertheless.

"Please," she said, and smiled at him and went away.

She had a difficult interview with a truculent and unwilling grandmother in the Jones's small overcrowded cottage until it became clear that she had come to offer to arrange provision for the child. Then the furious woman became all smiles and would have kept her, but Isabella only wanted to get away from all reminder of her husband's mean deceit.

It could never be denied. The only time she smiled was when she looked down at the red-faced baby and pitied it as she would pity any girl who had to grow up with James Bennett's pompous face, that she had once found handsome.

She went from the village as quickly as she could, through the ironbound fields under a snow-filled purple sky, and knew that her one and only winter in Enderby was almost at an end.

But there would be others, happier ones. She would keep the house and come to it as her parents had come, as a haven, where she and Liam could stay as they pleased: and Clara: and all the children that she and Liam would have.

She sat in the warm kitchen with a cup of tea and told the Pantons what she wanted, which was only that they close the house and care for it as they had always done. But they were pleased, and said so, to be doing it now for her.

Doors seemed to have opened onto sunlight, and she felt warmed with affection she had neglected for weeks as she went down to say good-night to Clara. The dapple-gray stood now in pride of place in the bright nursery, and as she passed she bent and kissed him on his shining nose.

The next morning she wrote to the London lawyers to say where she would be, and wrote to the Cunard Steamship Company for two first-class cabins on the *Mauretania;* then tore it up and wrote for two staterooms instead. As she moved about, occupying the patient hours until in the late evening, the lamp of the postman's bicycle threaded its way up the drive and he stood on the doorstep in the flood of light, with the first snowflakes white on his dark coat, and the answer to Isabella's cable in his hand.

She sat by the fire with it, her burst of activity ended; only wondering how she could possibly pass the days, the hours, the minutes, until he met her, as the cable promised, in New York. Ever since Charles Lindbergh had flown the Atlantic the previous year, she had read of planes beginning to fly mail and even passengers all over North America. If only she could get one of them to New York.

But she knew that time would pass: just as it had passed in the terrible times, as when her father was first missing, and Quickly's. She thought of the day she and Liam had talked of all the changes in people's lives because of the earthquake overtaking her father. This was the last, the final change, for this would be forever.

Ride forever, he had said, on the painted horses. Forever.

She would never have to leave the lights of the fair. There was no price to pay.

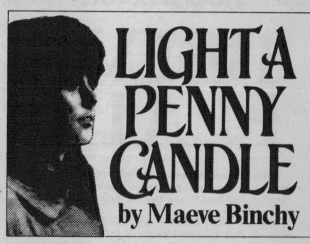

**She was born with a woman's
passion, a warrior's destiny,
and a beauty no man could resist.**

Firebrand's Woman

Vanessa Royall

Author of *Wild Wind Westward* and
Come Faith, Come Fire

Gyva—a beautiful half-breed cruelly banished
from her tribe, she lived as an exile in the white
man's alien world.
Firebrand—the legendary Chickasaw chief,
he swore to defend his people against the
hungry settlers. He also swore to win back
Gyva. Together in the face of defeat, they will
forge a brave and victorious new dream.

A Dell Book   **$2.95   (12597-9)**

At your local bookstore or use this handy coupon for ordering:

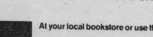